I KILLED THE KING

I KILLED THE KING

REBECCA MIX
ANDREA HANNAH

MAGPIE

Magpie Books
An imprint of HarperCollins*Publishers* Ltd
1 London Bridge Street
London SE1 9GF

www.harpercollins.co.uk

HarperCollins*Publishers*
Macken House,
39/40 Mayor Street Upper,
Dublin 1, D01 C9W8
Ireland

First published by HarperCollins*Publishers* Ltd 2025

1

Copyright © Andrea Hannah and Rebecca Mix 2025

Typography by Corina Lupp

Rebecca Mix and Andrea Hannah assert the moral right to
be identified as the authors of this work.

A catalogue record for this book is available from the British Library.

ISBN: 978-0-00-878213-9 (HB)
ISBN: 978-0-00-878214-6 (TPB)

This novel is entirely a work of fiction.
The names, characters and incidents portrayed in it are
the work of the author's imagination. Any resemblance to
actual persons, living or dead, events or localities is
entirely coincidental.

Printed and bound in the UK using 100% Renewable Electricity by CPI Group (UK) Ltd

All rights reserved. No part of this publication may be
reproduced, stored in a retrieval system, or transmitted,
in any form or by any means, electronic, mechanical,
photocopying, recording or otherwise, without the prior
written permission of the publishers.

Without limiting the exclusive rights of any author, contributor or the publisher of
this publication, any unauthorised use of this publication to train generative artificial
intelligence (AI) technologies is expressly prohibited. HarperCollins also exercise
their rights under Article 4(3) of the Digital Single Market Directive 2019/790 and
expressly reserve this publication from the text and data mining exception.

This book contains FSC™ certified paper and other controlled sources
to ensure responsible forest management.

For more information visit: www.harpercollins.co.uk/green

For Sam and Violet. You can read this one.

*And for Aunt Diane and Uncle Dusty,
because you've read every book I've written,
even the terrible ones.*

PANTHEON OF THE DIVINE TWELVE

The Builder and the Lover
The Huntress, the Dreamer, the Gardener
The Historian, the Sage, the Arbiter
The Mystic, the Shifter, the Courier
The Weaver and—
Removed from record.

1

THE KING

KING Costis has miscalculated.

Voices rumble from below as Costis strides through the modest stone halls of Castle Avendell. It's an old building, older than the Vernevau lineage itself. As a boy, he dreamed of replacing the floors with shining marble, like that mad fool to the south did before he declared war and brought all of Costis' plans to ruin. Had he more time, Costis would have redone the grounds next: ripped up his mother's gardens, replaced them with saplings of oak, cedar, and elm. Something to withstand the approaching chaos. Something to last.

But that was before, when Costis had assumed his reign would span decades. Now he'll be lucky to see dawn.

In his mind's eye, he sees the cause of his dread, curled on his pillow, petals damp: a single winter lily.

Costis shudders and hurries around a corner. Gaudy silk banners wave overhead. Green and red, representing Avendell and Istellia's patron gods, twine together in a unity braid, celebrating an end to their devastating ten-year war. The treaty signing is scheduled for dawn, and it's the whole point of this ball Costis can't afford. Invite merchants, noblemen, and diplomats to witness before every dead and sleeping god that Avendell and Istellia have finally, impossibly, agreed to *peace*.

It will all be for nothing now.

At the castle gate, guests arrive: nobles, performers, and scholars in their finest livery, pouring in like hungry ants. Costis ought to greet the new arrivals, but any one of them could be the enemy. He cannot risk it. When the pastry chef approaches, Costis flinches and stumbles back, but she only wants to know if he'd like raspberries or blueberries placed on the lemon tarts. Behind her, two servants rush to the windows, breath fogging the glass.

"Look," one says. "Snow! This late in spring?"

Costis walks faster.

Two guards are posted outside his private chambers. They snap to attention, and Costis hesitates, comparing their faces to the scrawny orphans he plucked from poverty ten years back. He can't help but notice the swords at their hips and the muscle cording their forearms. They look as Costis remembers. He thinks.

Costis clears his throat. "You're dismissed."

The guards frown. They glance at each other, at their king, then back to the door.

Costis forces himself to smile. "They've just finished the lemon tarts. Get some before the prince pinches them all for himself."

After another moment's hesitation, they bow and murmur gratitude. Costis steps aside, turning so they cannot access his unprotected back. He waits as the thuds of their boots fade. No danger from the guards, then.

Costis places his palm on the gold-wrought handle. He knew

this day would come. His job now is to buy what time he can—for his country, and for his son.

He opens the door.

Five young faces turn toward him.

Costis examines them. There's the Evercraft healer, with his tired face, haunting eyes, and single black bead gleaming on the golden chain hanging from his neck. Next to him is the Istellian princess, her dark hair braided into a crown and studded with rubies, hiding her displeasure with a polite bow of her head. It's not the princess he wanted, but she'll have to do.

The third guest, though—that's not the beast tamer he sent for. Her scar is familiar: a sinuous, twisting white cord that winds down her neck. Irritation pricks him. Why didn't Gaspar warn him the Beauforte girl came in her father's stead?

The creak of a leather sword belt comes to his left. Oak, Costis' personal guard, stands straighter than his namesake, eyeing the strangers with mistrust. A tiny gold stag glints on his lapel. Costis relaxes.

That leaves only—

"Father," a petulant voice demands. "What is the meaning of this? And *why* did you insist I wear these hideous clothes?"

Kellam.

Costis bites back a sigh. His only child and sole heir to the throne lounges comfortably in the corner, antlered circlet tipped sideways, legs sprawled in a manner Costis can only describe as *indecent*. He has a point—Costis believes his instructions to Gaspar for Kellam's livery were to make him look ridiculous, and the grand chamberlain certainly delivered. Costis needed to be sure it was him. Even the gods could not replicate that awful overcoat on a whim.

At the sight of his son, Costis nearly loses his resolve. He wants to apologize. He has not prepared Kellam for what's coming. But something stronger than love holds his words hostage.

Costis locks the door behind him. The princess and the beast tamer's daughter stiffen.

"Thank you all for joining me," Costis says, swallowing the lump in his throat. "I apologize for the lack of transparency, but I've summoned you all for a . . . delicate task."

He eyes them again: heir, guard, tamer, healer, foreign princess. What do they make of each other? What will they make of him once this is all over?

Perhaps he's made a mistake. But it's too late to turn back.

Snow patters against the window. The lights dim. In the stunned silence, just beyond the door, comes a single featherlight footstep.

Panic shoots ice up Costis' spine.

"I've received word from the Istellians." The wind begins to howl. "Kellam and Melarie are to marry and sign the treaty. *Now*."

"What?" cries the princess, Melarie, spots of color rising on her pretty cheeks. "King Costis, I don't understand. I was sent here to represent *my sister's* engagement. Elodie—"

"Has decided you will be a better fit for Kellam." The storm swells, casting long, ghastly shadows across the five panicked faces staring back at him. Did the door handle just creak? "Think of how thrilled our guests will be. A ball to celebrate a marriage, instead of a mere engagement. If the treaty was strong before, now it will be ironclad." He hopes.

"Father." Kellam leaps up. "Can we discuss this first?" His eyes fly not to the strangers but to Oak. "Alone?"

"No." From his robes, Costis pulls a thick bundle of cream papers. The treaty was meant to be signed at dawn, with the entire court and all their guests as witnesses. A drunken healer and a beast tamer's daughter will have to do.

"Now, the two of you"—Costis nods at Kellam and Melarie—"come stand together, please."

Kellam and Melarie throw each other panicked looks. They move slowly, painfully, as though they're approaching a morgue rather than marriage. Kellam reaches out to take Melarie's shaking fingers in his; she whirls to Costis.

"King Costis," Melarie begs, her lilting accent made sharp by desperation. Her eyes dart frantically about like a trapped bird, seeking some kind of escape. In the light of Costis' chambers, the rubies glued around her eyes look like flecks of blood. "This is ridiculous. I've only just arrived, there is no one here from my court to witness, I do not even have a *bouquet*—"

From his pocket, Costis withdraws the winter lily. It's only been an hour since he found it, but bruises already mottle the edges. With trembling fingers, he places it in her hair.

"Forgive me," he says quietly. "But I must do this before the bargain comes due. Take each other's hands, please. And repeat after me. By the grace of the Twelve, under witness of the king, I bind my soul to yours—"

Thunder cracks. There is something sweet in the air; something familiar.

"Father," Kellam protests.

I Killed the King

"Your Grace," Oak whispers.

"Why," the healer slurs, "are we here?"

"Shhh," scolds the beast tamer's daughter.

The lights go out, and Costis' heart stops when he smells it: the cloying, mountain-sweet scent of winter lilies, with that familiar wet-earth edge.

In the cool darkness of his chambers, wrapped in shadow and the hum of a storm building, Costis is a young king again, kneeling in frigid waters and bargaining not for glory, country, or legacy, but for his son. Always his son.

The wind screams. Lightning flashes, painting the five of them in deathly white. They plunge back into darkness.

And a knife meets Costis' ribs.

It's expert placement, slicing under his lower rib and angling up, piercing his heart, cutting straight through the still-mending flesh of the archery wound he suffered two moons prior. They've even done him the kindness of lacing the blade. Costis is pleasantly numb by the time his head strikes the carpet.

He only regrets he was not fast enough. He should have called them the moment he found the flower.

It's too late now. What comes next is in the Weaver's hands.

"What was that?" someone whimpers.

"Who touched me?" a second demands.

"Gods," a third whispers. "What have I done?"

Below, the castle doors fling open. Partygoers rush in with a gust of snow, relieved to be out of the cold, chattering about the oddness of the storm and pointing to the blackening sky.

With a pathetic flicker, the mage-lights wink back on. The

first thing Costis' private guests see is blood, spreading in a deep crimson pool, staining the carpet beyond repair. Someone screams.

And six pairs of eyes stare in horror at the king lying dead at their feet.

ONE HOUR EARLIER

2

KELLAM

KELLAM cannot get the acorn to grow.

The crown prince of Avendell kneels before the library window, a tiny pot cradled in his palms. Heat leaches from his skin into the worn clay. In the center, pressed into the soil up to the cap, is a single, sad acorn.

"Grow," Kellam whispers. "Please?"

He'd thought himself clever when he'd found the acorn gleaming like some distant summer jewel on a rare patch of snow. It's meant to be a funny gesture. Oak's been giving Kellam that *look* again—the disappointed one, the tired one, the one he always gives any time he catches Kellam kissing someone in a dark corner.

With Kellam's future closing around them like a noose, the tree will be a peace offering. And a promise, ahead of tonight's terrible change. An oak, for his Oak.

Except the acorn will not grow.

Kellam clutches the pot. This is his birthright. His father, and his father's father, and every king before them were blessed by the Gardener herself to call life from the earth and make roses dance.

Surely Kellam can grow a single *tree*.

He remembers his father's lessons and pictures the acorn swelling, cracking, visualizes the pale tendril that will worm free and reach for the sky. He can see it in his mind's eye: a great green tide, swirling from Kellam into the pot. It coils around the acorn, testing the limits of the outer shell, and sinks in.

And does nothing.

"Useless!" Kellam flings the pot over his shoulder, wincing when it shatters. He's nearly eighteen now, and still the magic resists him. Years of lessons, all those healers and their strange experiments, and for what? He cannot even grow a measly dandelion, let alone the rows of steady conifers King Costis can raise with a single twist of his hand.

Kellam listens as footsteps thud down the hall beyond. There's a nervous hum to the castle today; after a decade of war, Avendell and Istellia have agreed to peace, and not a moment too soon. Avendell barely made it through the winter, and Istellia is just as bad off. Their countries are too small and intertwined to endure further conflict.

Kellam ought to be elated that tonight will bring an end to it all. With the stroke of a pen and a promise of nuptials, King Costis will marry their countries together, just as their patron gods, the Builder and the Lover, once did. There will be peace at last.

So why does Kellam feel only dread?

Memory stirs—of that fateful day all those years ago, back when Costis had been quick to laugh, a man full of life, a stark contrast from the haunted, paranoid shell he is now. They'd been in the kitchens the morning the war began. For reasons no one understood, Istellia had crossed the border in the night and burned an Avendellian village, Magnivelle, to the ground. There were no survivors.

That evening, when Costis called Kellam to the garden, he seemed to have aged several years. The antlered crown of Avendell had looked heavier on him than usual, as though its weight threatened to crush Costis where he stood. The king knelt before a rosebush and beckoned his son closer.

"Kellam," he'd called. "What do you see?"

The rosebush had been swarming with insects—mostly ants and aphids, with a few stray lacewings flitting nearby, their delicate wings turned translucent by the midsummer sun.

"Bugs," Kellam had said, annoyed. Their closest ally had sent a declaration of war, written in Avendellian blood, and his father wanted to talk about *insects*? "Father, shouldn't we—"

"Look," interrupted Costis.

One of the lacewings landed, and the ants reacted as one— swarming the larger creature, biting into its carapace and delicate wings. The aphids carried on, oblivious to how close they'd come to death, harvesting sap to create sweet honeydew for the ants to carry away. Costis reached forward, swiped away the line of ants, and watched as the lacewings began to feast.

Costis glanced up at his son. "Avendell and Istellia are part of the same ecosystem. When one side is wiped away, we're all vulnerable."

Dread had turned every part of Kellam cold. Mountain-locked Avendell and farm-rich Istellia. Two halves of the same whole. The little nations shared everything, from customs and crops to their very gods. Many in Avendell had family scattered across the border, and many Istellians had made a life here. The countries had stitched themselves together to survive. War had torn them apart.

"Are we the ants or the aphids?" Kellam had asked, his skin prickling.

"I don't know," admitted Costis, and that scared Kellam more than anything. "Let us pray to the Twelve we never find out."

A knock sounds on the library door, jolting Kellam from memory.

"Prince Kellam," whispers one of his guards, clutching a paper-wrapped bundle against his chest. "King Costis has summoned you."

Kellam deflates. The first carriages are arriving after days of struggling up Avendell's muddy mountain roads. Kellam's father has spared no expense—diplomats from any nation with even a half interest in the Avendell-Istellian conflict were invited, alongside nobles, musicians, trade workers, and apparently, even a beast tamer. Whatever that means.

"Prince Kellam?"

Kellam closes his eyes. "Can it wait?"

"He said now, sir. And he, um, he has sent . . . clothes for you."

Kellam unwraps the package Reed brought and gapes. It's one of the ugliest overcoats he's ever seen: pale, pea-soup green, rough-stitched with Istellian red in the most haphazard pattern imaginable, as though the seamstress got drunk and changed her mind several times halfway through.

Kellam blinks. For all his faults, Costis has always been a man who believes in the power of smart dress. The color of the coat combined with the golden, antlered circlet Kellam wears is going to make him look less like a prince and more like a frantic baby deer that fell into a swamp and emerged covered in algae.

"Is this . . . some kind of joke?"

The color drains from Reed's face. "The king wishes for you to put this on and come immediately. That's—that's what Grand Chamberlain Weatherington said before he, uh, sent me away."

Ah. So the grand chamberlain is behind this.

Kellam isn't certain if Gaspar Weatherington is a real person or a joyless bundle of wasps that have aligned to make his life miserable—but if Gaspar (or the wasps) are good for anything, it's holding a grudge. Avendell's second most powerful man decided long ago to make Kellam his enemy. He'd jump at any chance he could to humiliate the prince—including, clearly, putting the fear of the Twelve into Reed to ensure the crown prince attends the ball dressed like a bowl of soup.

It's not Reed's fault the coat is hideous. As much as Kellam hates to lose to Gaspar, if he refuses to wear the coat, it will be Reed who suffers.

"Very well," Kellam sighs. "Tell the grand chamberlain to sleep with one eye open. I'm ordering Oak to put a snake in his bed."

Reed flees in obvious relief. The noises of the impending ball slip through with the first unsteady threads of music as the entertainers for the evening warm up. The scent of lemon tarts wafts up from the kitchen. Kellam takes one last look at the pot, changes into the most hideous coat he's ever seen, and leaves the library behind.

The halls are a flurry of activity. Kellam walks quickly and avoids eye contact with everyone who passes. At dawn, Costis will sign the treaty, Kellam will be engaged, and the last scraps of hope he's been clinging to will vanish. But this is his duty, is it not? Surely this is a small price to pay, to marry a girl he's never met, if it means his people will be safe? If it means *Oak* will be safe?

This is for the best. This peace, this treaty, is a gift from Costis to Kellam, an end to a decade of war.

So why is Kellam so miserable?

He heads toward his father's chambers, then turns down a different hallway, trying not to catch his own pea-green reflection in the windowpanes as he strides past. If Costis wants him, he likely wants Oak, too. Kellam will steal what little time he can.

Costis didn't even bother to make eye contact with Kellam when he told him that he'd be married off to Istellia's crown princess, Elodie. He kept his eyes on the papers on his desk and muttered something about *country over heart* and *duty before desire*, as though Kellam had used up the last reserves of Costis' patience.

As he approaches a familiar door, all Kellam can dream of is some way of ensuring tonight never happens.

Get me out of this, he thinks, tossing a prayer to whatever gods may be listening. *Make something happen. Anything. Just make tonight stop.*

He doesn't care how. Perhaps the princesses' ship will be lost at sea, or the kitchens will catch fire. Perhaps the guests won't show, the food will spoil, or the treaty will be stolen and tossed to flame.

Or maybe Kellam will get lucky, and his father will simply drop dead.

3

OAK

OAK will need a smaller bag.

The first time he stuffed the satchel with his few personal belongings—his undergarments, an extra tunic, a bar of sage-scented soap—he'd almost laughed. The satchel had looked and felt empty, the tan leather hanging against his hip like loose skin. Oak hadn't minded. All he needed was a bag and an opportunity. He was not picky about either.

But the king had called Oak into his chambers for the third time that day, whispering about enemies plotting against him, and Oak had sighed before returning to his own stuffy chambers to unpack his bag. Costis had given him a home when he had none, had sponsored his entry into the kingsguard and entrusted Oak with his life as soon as he had turned eighteen, despite Captain Laurent's protests that Oak was not ready. He owed too much to the king. He couldn't leave Costis lost in the maze of his mind.

The second time Oak had pulled the satchel out from under his cot had been only a fortnight ago. Again he dropped his belongings into the bag. Slid the buckle closed with a definitive click.

He'd gotten halfway down the hall before he was stopped by Kellam.

"And where are you off to?" The prince's voice had echoed off the stone walls. The doorway to the stables was *right there*. The scent of early spring grass and manure hovered just beyond the threshold, coaxing him to a new world.

Oak turned. Kellam stalked toward him with the air of someone on a mission to ruin a good mood, so intent on Oak that he accidentally crashed into a hanging vase containing a freshly potted maidenhair fern. It shattered on the floor.

Oak sucked in his stomach as if he'd been punched. The fern was sacred to the Gardener, the goddess of growth who blessed Avendell's heirs. Though Oak was not a believer himself, the Vernevau family was. Well, *Costis* was. The king had chosen the Gardener as his patron goddess, and that was enough for Oak to choose her, too.

Kellam blinked at the soil-stained fern and then whirled, spying a staff member who'd just stepped from the servants' quarters in a sleep tunic and slippers.

"Mason!" Kellam cried, as if they were the dearest of friends. "Blessed be the Gardener, just the young man I was looking for. Be a saint and clean this up, would you?"

Mason paused, the protest clear on his face, and then softened. Oak didn't have to look at Kellam to know the smile he was flashing at the boy. With only a show of teeth, Kellam could beguile a merchant into giving him their coin—or in this case, a servant into cleaning on their day off. He always complained that his charm never worked on Oak, and Oak allowed him to believe that lie.

"Of course, Your Grace," Mason said with a quick bow. Twelve help them, he seemed genuinely pleased to clean up Kellam's mess. "I will find a broom."

"A true saint, you are," Kellam said with a wink. "What would I do without you?"

Mason turned pink and began to back away.

"No," Oak said.

Mason froze. He looked between Oak and Kellam, torn between obeying Oak's command and pleasing his prince, whose expression had gone stony.

Oak cleared his throat. "Mason is not on duty today. But if you'd like help cleaning up your mess, I'd be happy to assist."

The air stilled between them, and Kellam actually had the audacity to wilt. He rolled his eyes and gave Mason a conspiratorial look. "All he does is torture me. Very well, then. Point me in the direction of a broom. I couldn't live if I disappointed the noble Kingsguard Ducasse."

Oak turned, refusing to reward the prince with his smile.

They worked in silence, the sounds of glass scraping over stone echoing around them. Kellam pushed the last of the fronds into a pile before cupping his slender hands around Oak's knotty ones to lift the debris into the canister. A spark caught beneath Oak's ribs. Kellam flicked the last lingering sliver of green off his palm, his eyes twinkling, and said something about Oak being a relentless taskmaster before flouncing away.

Oak sighed heavily. He bent down to pick up the frond, carrying it like a precious jewel back to his chamber before unpacking the bag once more.

But that was then. A lot had happened since that moment between them.

This time, Oak will not return to this room.

He shifts the satchel over his shoulder, the almost-empty bag hanging limp at his side. Oak glimpses his reflection in the small mirror above his wardrobe and winces. He is the king of Avendell's personal guard, Costis' most loyal staff member, and tonight he looks every bit the part. His forest-green uniform is pressed to perfection. The sash fits snugly over his broad chest, and the gold antlers pinned over his heart gleam. Even his dark blond hair has been shorn so short that the damp coolness of the castle has settled against his scalp.

The small pot of lemon balm beside his cot catches his eye in the mirror. A gift from Costis, something green to brighten the drab, windowless room. It was a miracle the thing had lived, but the king always said Oak had a way with plants. Costis had said it so often that when Oak was little, he'd pretend that the peonies bloomed and ivy unspooled as he trailed behind the king. Oak has always been one to fall prey to dreams.

In fact, he should already be on his way to the king's chambers to guard the door, staring at nothing while dreaming of everything.

Which is exactly the problem. As his king's condition has grown worse, so has Oak's. He should be at his most diligent now, yet each time he settles into his post, his mind wanders. It is only a matter of time before Oak makes a mistake that will ruin them all.

He won't wait. Instead, he'll pluck the dreams from his head and take them out into the bitter cold to see what they're made of. To see what *he's* made of.

Oak runs his hand over his scalp, examining his reflection. There are bags under his eyes the color of ripe plums—a parting gift he'll take with him tonight. The king's behavior has gotten even worse in the days leading up to the ball. Most nights, instead of sleeping, Costis paces the hall, rambling about vengeful gods or whispering to his long-dead wife. It is all Oak can do to trail behind him like a watchful ghost.

Oak blows out a long, low breath and fiddles with the satchel again. He leans into the mirror. "You can do this."

Yes, Costis gave him a home, a job, a purpose. And, yes, Oak loves his king, though Costis' mind is clearly rotting. But Oak is eighteen now.

How can he possibly know what he wants if he's never left?

Oak's stomach hitches. No, that isn't quite right.

He knows what he wants. He also knows he can never have it.

A sharp knock at the door jolts him from his thoughts. He quickly rubs his face, adjusts the sash so it lies neatly atop his left shoulder.

A second knock.

Oak grows still. *It can't be—*

A third knock, just as sharp as the first two.

One, two, three. No more, no less. Impatient and dramatic. Just like Kellam.

His pulse quickens. Oak looks down at the bag. The crown prince of Avendell waits for no one. Oak has only seconds. He drops to his knees and slides the bag back under the bed, careful not to crush the fourth item he packed this time.

The door swings open. Oak sits on his heels, his palms slick with sweat as they rest atop his thighs. He glances up at the figure in the archway.

Kellam stands before him, arms crossed over his chest, his expression almost as foul as the overcoat he's wearing. The corners of Oak's mouth hitch.

"Don't," Kellam warns.

"I wasn't going to say anything," Oak answers, lifting his hands in surrender.

"Gaspar had it made."

"Ah." That explains it. While the grand chamberlain and Costis' second-in-command seems to hate everyone, he's always been particularly dedicated to making Kellam's life miserable—not that Kellam doesn't entirely deserve it. And, quite honestly, Gaspar is so busy torturing Kellam that most days he barely tosses a glance in Oak's direction. Oak prefers to keep it that way.

"Come," says Kellam. He reaches up and adjusts his circlet—a nervous tic Oak has come to know well. "We've been summoned by my father. If the Istellian princess sees me in this, I'll need you to mercy-kill me."

Oak lets out a breathy laugh. "It's not that bad, Your Grace."

"You will put a poisonous snake in Gaspar's bed for this," says Kellam. "A big one."

"I will not, Your Grace."

Kellam mutters something under his breath and stalks out the door. Oak watches the sleek lines of the prince's overcoat as he leaves. For a moment, he considers crawling beneath the cot and retrieving the satchel. He won't leave the most important possession inside to be forgotten.

A single dried fern leaf, soft and fragile.

4

VESRYN

VESRYN arrives at the castle to kill a king she's never met.

The invitation to the ball had shown up without fanfare: a cream-colored envelope, remarkable only for its golden stag seal. The king's royal emblem.

Ms. Gisele LaRue, it had read. *You are cordially invited . . .*

Vesryn had accepted the invitation, with a caveat. She'd scrawled her response along the bottom: *Gisele does the job. It's Everly Bardot who will attend.*

And then she'd gone shopping for a dress.

She'd chosen a satin gown the color of a storm—dark enough to move through rooms undetected, no heavy velvet to weigh her down or puffy tulle to catch on a closing door. It was the right choice. The necessary choice.

But as she approaches the guard at the entryway, she can't help but think she's made a terrible mistake.

"Name." It's not a question. The towering man before her is dressed in a forest-green uniform, the sash across his chest featuring a constellation of gold pins.

Amazing, she thinks. *Even the guards are better dressed than I am.*

"Everly Bardot," she answers smoothly. Of all her aliases, this is Vesryn's favorite. It glides off the tongue, and its mellifluous cadence feels like traveling over rolling hills. Her mercenary alias, Gisele LaRue, may carry an air of mystery, but Everly Bardot is the name of someone who gets invited to lavish balls—a girl who knows her worth. It's the kind of name that feels like a promise.

Time slows. The guard's eyes flit down, down, down the list.

Vesryn swallows. She drops her gaze. He had promised to include this alias on the list. Certainly he wouldn't have summoned her here and not followed through . . . right?

The guard's brows knit together. "What did you say your name was again?"

"Everly," she says with a confidence she doesn't possess. "Everly—"

"Bardot," a new voice finishes. "I'm so pleased you could make it."

Vesryn's head snaps up. A tall, lanky man hovers behind the door guard, his face puckered as if he'd bitten into a lemon. His hair is gray and clipped short in the military style, but he wears the resplendent green robes of a higher-ranking member of the Avendellian court. He shifts before she can glimpse the gold pin on his chest. "Miss Bardot was a late addition. See to it that the records are updated. I won't have any of our guests made to feel unwelcome."

"Yes, m'lord. Apologies, m'lord." The guard makes a hurried note on his list and mumbles, "Enjoy the ball, miss."

Vesryn doesn't need to be told twice. She lifts her chin and struts past as if she's a duchess of some far-off province.

"Miss Bardot?"

Vesryn turns, the hem of her dress swishing over her ankles. *Act like you belong here*, she tells herself. The stranger in green is watching her with the cool calculation of a hawk eyeing a rabbit. A chill skips down Vesryn's spine.

"It is a masquerade ball." The corner of his mouth lifts. "Masks are required."

"Ah." Before he can catch the slight quiver of her fingers, Vesryn shoves her hand into the hidden pocket of her dress. There are two items tucked within the folds. She's extra careful to reach for the feathers instead of the metal.

The mask slides from her pocket, ocean-blue feathers shimmering beneath the mage-lights. She hurries through Castle Avendell's ornate doors, fastening the mask before the nobleman—or anyone else—can notice the gaps in the fabric where some of the fake gems have already come unglued. Buying a new dress was a big enough stretch; Vesryn was forced to make the accessories herself.

A wall of heat slams into her, a welcome break from the cold. Despite the spring season supposedly being well underway, Vesryn awoke this morning at the inn down the road to snow freckling her window. The flurries have not stopped since, and as the hours crept on, Vesryn thought it best to walk the short distance to the castle before the snow was up to her knees.

"What is the holdup?" she murmurs, standing on her tiptoes in a meager attempt to see over a drunk woman's bouffant. The woman stumbles, and Vesryn finally glimpses what the guests are crowded around.

It's the most dazzling mural she has ever seen.

Vesryn has seen an authentic trompe l'oeil only once before, and it wasn't nearly as massive or impressive. The rich, glittery murals are so lifelike that they've been known to induce vertigo in the admirer. There are only a handful of artists throughout

Avendell and Istellia capable of such sacred work, as their talent has been blessed by the Dreamer herself.

The entire pantheon of the Divine Twelve sprawls before Vesryn. In the center of it all are Avendell and Istellia's patron gods, the Builder and the Lover. Vesryn can't help but smile at the depiction of the Builder—a man just as somber and burly as the bear who represents him—while the Lover's lithe frame is reminiscent of her spotted genet cat. Their two eldest children take their places in their domains: the Sage atop her mountain and the Mystic beneath the sea. The rest of the pantheon orbit around them: Courier, Huntress and Dreamer, Gardener and Historian, Arbiter and Shifter.

Vesryn's gaze drifts to the solitary island off the Istellian coast. A goddess composed of sharp angles stands alone, draped in a tunic the color of nightshades. *The Weaver*, she thinks. Though the goddess is the youngest child born to the Builder and the Lover, and a part of the original pantheon, it's rare for her to be depicted in pottery or paintings. While most gods and goddesses tend to stick to one human form, the Weaver has been known to take on multiple identities—even emulating the bodies of humans who already exist.

The goddess' right hand clutches the spindle of destiny. Her left hand is open by her side, the center of her palm stained with the blood of her lost child. Her eyes bore into Vesryn with such sorrow that her own throat knots with the threat of tears.

The Weaver's surviving child, the Courier, hovers at the coastline, his back turned from his mother and the island that serves as the site of her banishment. The goddess of fate, in all her power, reduced to a warning: There are consequences for every action. Even mistakes.

"Pardon!" A woman jams her elbow into Vesryn's shoulder blade. Guests slide into the sliver of space between Vesryn and the mural, dragging her back to reality. "I suppose it is quite stunning," the woman drones without missing a beat. "As a piece of art, of course. Though I am hardly one of those quaint little peasants from the villages who believe the gods are simply asleep."

"Don't be too harsh on them," says a portly man beside her. "Without proper education, they couldn't possibly understand it was our own human-born brilliance that figured out how to use magic efficiently without the gods. Death knocks on the door of a deity with no worshippers."

A woman raises a half-empty bottle of mead. "The gods are dead. Long live the king!"

Something Vesryn hasn't felt in a long time stirs within her. It isn't quite anger, and it isn't embarrassment—no, she will never be ashamed of her faith. It's a more skittish thing, something that nips at her, urging her to do something, to show these pompous heathens how wrong they are.

Oh, how convenient it is for the highborn to dismiss the gods in favor of a king who has kept them wealthy, despite the war. It must be nice to have always lived in a place that radiates with magic from the Builder or the Gardener or the Historian—so much so that their lineage has never known what it's like to live without it.

She gazes up at her chosen goddess, the Arbiter, and without warning, tears prick the corners of her eyes. "I'm sorry about them," she whispers. "But I believe in you."

She quickly blinks and turns to enter the ornate ballroom. Vesryn has barely begun to take in the opulence when a man twice her size slams into her and she stumbles. Her arm juts out before her face meets the wall, palm just dodging the hanging planter and slapping against stone. "Excuse me, mademoiselle!" the man drawls, giving Vesryn a limp pat on her shoulder while his eyes search the crowd. "Oh, there he is. Magistrate Crowley! So good to see you again. . . ." The rest of his words drop away as he marches toward an older man in Avendellian green, his sash speckled with glittering pins.

Vesryn gingerly pushes off the wall and flexes her wrist. This is getting deeply annoying.

She takes a moment to smooth out the lines of her dress, straighten the mask, *reset*. Hanging low on the wall, a riot of verdant green spills from the planter box. She leans forward and breathes in its loamy aroma. Even in this dreary northern castle, King Costis' greenmage power remains unparalleled. The man can grow anything, though his signature tends to include all the dark and feathery plants found deep in the woods—of which there are plenty here tonight. She can't help but wonder if the king has left any room for his son's signature green magic to blossom among this lavish abundance.

The entire ballroom is packed with fresh greenery, pots and planters overflowing with ivies and maidenhair ferns, wintergreen and wood sorrel. Even *flowers*. The king has somehow managed to ensure they are synced in full bloom, the blue asters and mountain laurel and—

Vesryn snaps her head back. There's no way.

She blinks. They're *real*. Hidden among the laurel are a scattering of cream-colored blooms, as delicate as a kiss and as toxic as a lie.

People should not be able to get this close to them, especially not *these* people—the drunk and important ones. If there was one thing Vesryn had learned during her short stint at the Academy of Healing Arts, it was that most wounds were the result of dumb mistakes. Sometimes they're even the kind that can't be healed.

She spins back toward the crowd, her gaze flitting from planter to planter. From here, it's impossible to tell the difference between the blossoms. There could be poison everywhere.

But what does she care? It's not like these people have ever expressed empathy for her kind—the kind without a title or proper upbringing or pile of coin. And yet the urge to help has never left her. To leech disease from a child's blood with ancient ritual magic or swipe a salve over a dying woman's lips, if only to relieve the pain long enough to kiss her lover one last time. The urge to right a wrong nestles in the very marrow of Vesryn's bones.

In that way, being a mercenary isn't all that different from being a healer.

All Vesryn's previous marks were terrible people, people who pilfered and pillaged, who took more than they ever gave. Their deaths were a blessing, their strangled last words a benediction to set their families free. If that isn't restoring some kind of right-wrong order to the universe, Vesryn isn't sure what is.

Yet she has always, always been merciful. She is extremely precise with the knife—a narrow slit between the third and fourth rib, a clean puncture through the left ventricle of the heart. And before the blow, Vesryn is sure to lace her blade with a potent nerve-blocking elixir. She feels good knowing the victim experiences no pain as the light leaves their eyes.

Well, maybe not *good*. But at least the small touch of compassion allows her to sleep a bit more easily at night.

As she weaves through the ballroom, her hand creeps to the knife hidden in her pocket. She'd already done the work of sterilizing the blade, then smoothing the nerve-blocking elixir over every inch of it before leaving the inn. There's nothing left to do now but make the kill.

No more stalling.

This is the last one, she tells herself. *This is it.*

Vesryn slips into the shadowy hallway on the other side of the ballroom. She pauses, pretending to examine a holly bush that's exploding with ripe berries as dense and deadly as blood clots. Her mind is elsewhere.

She studied the map of Castle Avendell until her eyes burned with exhaustion. She just has to orient herself. Then she'll know exactly where the hidden staircase is, where the king's private chambers are.

It takes only a moment for her eyes to adjust to the dimly lit hallway. The alcove to the kitchen, the private wine cellar, and—

Yes.

At the end of the hallway sits an unkempt statue of the Gardener, her face slick with mold caused by time and neglect. And beyond it, Vesryn knows she will find the staircase.

She smooths down the fine hairs of her bob and turns to leave.

A horn blares through the ballroom, its tinny sound amplified by the cavernous space. Vesryn jerks to a stop.

A wildfire of nobles surges into the party. Most are wearing Istellia's scorching red, though their waistcoats are speckled with metallic pins denoting rank, status, and honor. These are not humble servants—these are war veterans. Along the edges, Avendellian guards, their sashes adorned with gilded antlers as a symbol of their pledge to the Crown, scan the guests with careful, unmasked eyes.

And standing in the center of them is the Istellian princess.

Despite herself, Vesryn feels her lip curl. She's never much cared what anyone else does—especially what they wear—but the princess' attire is a bit much. Her dress is a strapless ball gown beaded with such an egregious blend of red and orange jewels that they have the effect of making the princess look wreathed in flame. Red satin gloves cover her arms; a red mask, depicting a bird in flight, dangles uselessly from her fingertips. But it's her hair that gives Vesryn pause. Half the princess' hair flows down her back in a black sheet, but the top half has been woven away from her face to form a braided circlet studded with rubies. The effect is impossible to miss. The princess has arrived in enemy territory wearing a crown.

Vesryn's gaze falls on the only other guest who seems as uninterested as she is in this whole spectacle: a girl about her age in a white feathered mask, wearing a ballet-pink dress with so much tulle, it looks as if she's wearing a soufflé. Her honey-blond hair hangs in loose, messy curls—clearly she styled it herself. She pretends to pick at her nails, fiddles with her puffy dress, wraps a curl around her finger. Like Vesryn, she looks as though she doesn't belong here.

Vesryn shakes away the thought. What does it matter?

Get on with it already.

She takes the gift of diverted attention and slips into the hallway, past the darkened rooms, the decrepit statue, and up the staircase just beyond it. When she reaches the second floor, Vesryn pokes her head out and listens.

Nothing. Not even the creak of a floorboard.

Again, she orients herself. Library to the right, private chambers to the left. She counts the doors—*one, two, three, four*—and stops before the last one.

There's no guard.

How could there possibly be no guard?

It's almost too easy.

Vesryn creaks open the door, just enough so she can peek inside. It's instantly clear that this is, in fact, the king's private chambers, just as the map had indicated. She decides to consider the lack of on-duty guard a gift instead of a trap, and pulls the door open wide enough to slip inside.

The entry chamber is even more opulent than anything Vesryn could have dreamed up. The entire ceiling is painted gold, so even though thick storm clouds press in against the windows, the room still feels like stepping inside a sunset. And everything is so *pristine*. Each piece of fine mahogany furniture is covered in so much lacquer, casting light in every direction, that it's almost hard to look at it all without squinting.

From somewhere in the chamber, a door bangs.

Her pulse stutters. She scans the room, the pieces of her plan clicking into place. It's Costis—it has to be. When the next slam, and the next, seem to be getting closer, Vesryn hurls herself toward the tallest piece of furniture in the place: a wardrobe.

The chamber door swings open. Two sets of footfalls sweep into the room, one light and nimble, the other heavy and methodic. There's a pause, and then a loud sigh.

"He's not even here," a voice complains. Then, brightening: "Do you think he's still got some of that Istellian wine hidden somewhere?"

"Kellam," a second, deeper voice sighs.

"It's under the bed, isn't it? Thank the gods. Remember when he used to hide the flasks in his shoes? What a waste. Never could get past the smell."

There's a rustle, a thump, and the popping of a cork. Vesryn holds carefully, painfully still, keeping her weight away from the wardrobe door lest it swing open.

A soft knock interrupts them. There's a flurry of footsteps, and a third voice wafts through the room like a fine perfume. "Your Majesty, I am Princess Melarie Atilelet of Istellia, fourth daughter of the king." She clears her throat. "Of the . . . deceased king. Thank you kindly for this private invitation. I'm honored to represent my country in the treaty this evening, and I . . ." Her voice trails away, and when she speaks again, it carries a sharper edge. "Where is King Costis?"

"Don't know. Where's your sister?" Prince Kellam retorts. There's the audible glug of the wine bottle, and the thump of someone flopping into one of the ornate chairs. "Istellia can't even be bothered to send the heir to sign a war-ending treaty? This bodes well."

Vesryn swears she can almost hear Melarie's jaw clench from here. "Sir, I assure you, I—"

What is going on?

Another light knock. A second later, the door slams open. A new guest saunters into the room, a *shh, shh, shh* sound following each step. "King Costis," a voice says. Vesryn leans in so close that the edge of the door digs into her cheekbone. A mountain of pink tulle floods her vision as the honey-blond girl bows. "Thank you for your invitation this evening, though I am quite confused, I must admit. I . . ."

"Father's not here yet," chirps the prince. "Wine?"

What in the name of every sleeping god is going on?

"*Oof!*" A loud *thump* reverberates through the room as yet another guest stumbles in. "How'd that table get there?" a voice slurs.

Vesryn freezes. *No. It can't be.*

"I heard someone requested my"—the boy hiccups—"presence?"

Ice floods Vesryn's veins at the sound of that voice. Her heartbeat crashes in her ears, muffling the growing unrest in the chambers. There's a strange quiet, and a new voice speaks.

"Thank you all for joining me."

King Costis. Vesryn holds her breath. She listens as Costis begins to ramble about marriage, but that slurred voice has sent her pulse racing, and now Vesryn cannot think straight. The voices grow louder, tenser, but she can't make out what they're saying. She tries to calm herself. *What in the Arbiter's name is he doing here?*

Thunder growls. The mage-lights flicker.

And then everything goes black.

Someone screams. There's a frenetic shuffling of bodies. Someone slams into the wardrobe with a groan. The door swings open, and Vesryn tumbles to the floor.

The darkness is so cloying that she can't even see her hands in front of her. Someone's heeled shoe jams into the fleshy part of her thumb and Vesryn yelps. More movement, more panic, all of them scrambling like rats in a trap.

Vesryn slides her hands over the floor. Her fingers graze something solid, and the lights snap back on.

King Costis is dead.

And five people who should not know she's here are staring back at her.

The princess lets out a bloodcurdling scream. The pink-dress girl claps her hands over her mouth and the guard stares silently at the floor, his face a sickly shade of gray. The prince extends a shaking hand to the king but does not touch him, the corpse's eyes wide and unblinking.

"Vesryn?" the healer whispers.

Her eyes lift to meet his. *Ellion.*

They stare at each other from across the dead king, an entire lifetime of lost memories and unspoken words sprawling between them. When Vesryn looks at the long gold chain hanging from Ellion's neck, her blood runs cold. A single black bead gleams on the loop.

Help me, Ellion's eyes plead.

Vesryn will not be helping him out of this one.

TWELVE HOURS
TO DAWN

5

ELLION

ELLION is fucked.

From where he stands, Ellion Evercraft has exactly four problems.

One: His past has come back to haunt him. That can be the only explanation for the girl who burst from the king's wardrobe with blood flecking her gown. She looks entirely different and painfully the same, an older, sharper rendition of the violet-eyed girl of his youth, her horror a mirror image of the day Ellion lost everything.

Two: His harmless exaggeration of his nonexistent healing abilities has—to put it lightly—taken a turn for the worse. The stuffy palace man who offered Ellion tonight's job had failed to mention he'd be acting as personal healer to the famously paranoid king of Avendell.

Three: That same king has just been *murdered*. And though Ellion was expelled from the Academy of Healing Arts before completing his course on the ramifications of medical negligence, he wagers that letting the *gods-damned king die* does not bode well for his passionate interest in remaining alive.

Which brings him to problem four: Ellion is hopelessly, terribly drunk.

Blood seeps across the floor. The snowstorm howls, the mage-lights flicker, and all Ellion can do is sway. King Costis is dead, Vesryn is here, and that Avendell elm brandy hit far too hard.

What is she doing here?

It's been four, five years since he's seen her last. Surely he's dreaming. Surely this is a nightmare come to haunt him.

Or maybe Ellion's had a rare stroke of luck and he's already dead.

"Help him," the prince begs, snapping Ellion from his daze. There are tears in his eyes. "Please."

There's no helping Costis, but Ellion ought to at least put on a good show. He fumbles for his pockets, hands trembling as he tries to keep his eyes from Vesryn's face. Weight hits his palm, followed by a slosh of liquid, and his shoulders drop.

"Is that a healing elixir?" the princess asks, her pretty face the very picture of hope.

"Yes," Ellion says slowly. "This is . . . a most precious draught, blessed by healing acolytes of the Courier for channeling only the most potent of magical cures."

It's vodka.

Ellion drains the flask and drops to his knees beside Costis. The moment he reaches for the king, cold shoots up his arm, bringing with it the scent of old earth and the pull of a power Ellion has spent the last decade running from. He flinches and snatches his fingers away. It's been so long, he'd forgotten the cold, the draw, the *temptation*.

The guard checks his king's pulse. The prince sinks to his knees.

Ellion has a terrible idea.

It's dangerous. It's forbidden.

It might just work.

He looks at the dead king again. Costis entered the room in such a state that even Ellion's drunken haze was pierced by icy spears of panic. Long before Ellion was expelled from the Academy, in the hope-bright days when he'd believed he, too, would honor the Evercraft name and become an accomplished healer, Ellion's father had made it clear that serving the royal family should be his greatest—and only—dream.

The burning of Magnivelle was the beginning of the end of it. Ellion still remembers where he was the day the news reached the Evercraft estate. He's never shaken the dread that it's at least a little bit his fault.

Ellion may not understand much about the day his necromancy rose, but he understands this: the day his magic changed, the world warped with it.

Maybe that's why he's here tonight, a king bleeding at his feet and Vesryn standing before him. It seems the Twelve have finally come to collect.

Ellion ought to flee. But that whisper of power beckons him closer.

It's been years.

What if it's better now? What if *he's* better?

He's never been anything but a failure. Disowned by his patron god, numbing himself to keep his power at bay, running from the ghosts of the ones he's let down. Everything he touches turns to ruin. His golden healer's chain and its single black bead, the weight of its failure heavy around his neck, reminds him of that every day.

But what if he can help?

A strange thrill rises in him. In a split second, Ellion makes a choice.

He's already lost everything that matters beside his life. Maybe this last-ditch effort will be enough to save it.

Beside him, the prince is a frozen statue of horror. The guard has a white-knuckled hand clamped onto his shoulder, the enormity of his grief etched in every line of his stoic face. The blond in pink shrinks into herself, and the princess paces, picking uneasily at the jewels glued to her face. Only Vesryn is stiller than death, staring at the king with something verging on guilt.

Ellion moves so he's kneeling directly over the body and raises his hands. When he speaks, his voice comes out harder than before, sharper. An echo of the boy he'd once been, the man he might have grown into, before everything went so horribly wrong. "Everyone get back."

"He's dead," the guard croaks. Is that a hint of blame in his voice? "You're too late, healer."

"I am no healer," Ellion whispers. "Move aside. I wasn't banned from the Academy for disgracing the sanctity of human life for nothing."

"Ellion," Vesryn warns, her eyes widening as she realizes what he's about to do. "*Don't.*"

Ellion rips open the front of Costis' shirt—and slams his hands to the king's chest.

And this time, when death reaches for him, Ellion reaches back.

Everything snaps to black.

It always begins the same.

A plunge into darkness, a crush of cold. The first time it happened was an accident. Ellion had just found a baby robin on his doorstep, neck twisted at a terrible angle, when he'd felt it—a stir, and a call.

He'd touched the corpse—and it had moved.

In the beginning, it felt like a miracle. Ellion couldn't heal, but what was a necromancer if not a healer who was just a tad late? Maybe the Courier hadn't abandoned him. Perhaps the pantheon's strangest god had simply gifted Ellion a different kind of healing.

He began his self-directed training with bugs. Insects were easy to kill, easier to revive, and when they inevitably began to pull their own wings from their bodies and bite off their legs to put an end to their agony, their tiny, disfigured carcasses were a breeze to hide. He moved on to lizards, and then birds, and once, the groundskeeper's cat. He still feels bad about the cat.

But the magic always demanded more.

Ellion feels it now, the presence that's haunted him since the day he and Vesryn tumbled into the gorge and something deeper than Ellion's bones was broken beyond repair. It answered when he resurrected the bird, the farmer, *Luma*—and Ellion paid the price.

He swore he'd never heed that call of power again. But when was the last time Ellion kept a promise?

Beyond the sinking dark, he sees it: a tangle of threads, quickly fading, glowing a gentle, new spring green.

Costis.

People never get it right when it comes to dying. In his years at the Academy, Ellion had heard all the theories—lights at the ends of tunnels, bodies floating in rooms, lives flashing before eyes like some kind of twisted personal-theater performance. They were good theories. But Ellion knows better.

When people die, it's not their own lives that keep them lingering.

It's the ones they're leaving behind.

Ellion touches the threads, and the world shifts.

Snow falls in thick flakes from a velvet black sky, suspending the world in the kind of precious, muffled silence that always comes with a winter storm. Costis kneels before a violent split in red rock, a decade younger and a lifetime healthier. He's beautiful, in a gilded, eerie way—the very picture of a man who has never known hunger, the shining, golden king who promised to bring Avendell glory.

In his arms, frail and barely breathing, is a boy.

Ellion moves closer. Costis trembles; the child sags limply in his arms like an old doll whose stitching has come loose.

"Anything," the king rasps. "I will give anything. Please, just save him."

The air is a swirl of love and grief, all of it linking back to the boy in Costis' arms. The boy's eyes flutter weakly, but he doesn't stir when Costis sets him on the rock. Something about this has the feeling of a nightmare Ellion's just awoken from—familiar, already fading, leaving only vague scraps of dread behind.

Still, that red rock, the scent of cool water and old earth.

Ellion almost swears he's been here before.

Costis is still speaking. He stiffens as something answers. The young king trembles, his face etched with agony, looking from the child in the water to the snow falling overhead, and bows his head. "Very well. You have your bargain. Ten years."

The hair on Ellion's arms stands on end. It's just a coincidence, surely.

Ellion seizes the king's arm.

Costis jerks, and the image shatters. The boy vanishes, and with it the gorge, the snow on the rocks, the final echo of love plaguing a dead man.

But Costis grows more solid. His eyes bulge. "Let me go."

"I'm sorry," says Ellion. He means it.

Ellion says a prayer for forgiveness to whatever god is listening and drags King Costis back from the dead.

The world crashes in, and something is terribly wrong.

It takes a moment for Ellion to return to his body. When he does, the world is bright, too sharp, too *alive*. Ellion's hands are braced against Costis' chest; his fingernails have pierced the man's skin. Everyone stares at him, stunned by the sight of a healer disgracing the body of their king. The storm howls; the lights flicker.

And Costis gasps.

Someone screams. Unearthly cold cuts through the haze of alcohol Ellion has come to rely on to numb himself. Something familiar lingers in the air—the sense that something is watching, and the cold-sweet scent of a winter lily. He should not have done this.

Ever since that day in the gorge, when people come back, they come back wrong.

On the floor, Costis writhes. He gasps, a horrible, wet sucking noise leaving him as he fights the blood pooling in his lungs. His face grays.

"King Costis," Ellion demands. "Who killed you?"

Costis jolts. Outside, the wind howls.

"Father?" the prince whispers.

Costis turns to look at Kellam, his eyes glassy. There's a brief spark of recognition, and Ellion wonders if perhaps he got it right this time; maybe there is a way to fix this and save them yet.

Maybe, for once, Ellion can help instead of hurt.

Then Costis lunges for his son.

The princess screams. The king grabs a fistful of Kellam's ugly green lapel, yanking so hard it tears. Blood trickles from his nose. His gaze is wild, fixed only on the prince.

"Chaos comes for you," whispers Costis, his face the very picture of a man haunted.

The king keels sideways, fingers still gripping Kellam's coat, as his head hits the floor with a gentle thump.

And this time, when King Costis dies, he dies for good.

6

MELARIE

MELARIE is fairly certain she's cursed.

That can be the only explanation for the constant upheaval that haunts her like some kind of poisoned cloud. Take, for example, her kingdom: a tiny farming nation cradling the sapphire-bright Starless Sea, pitched into chaos on the cruel whims of a mad king the day he decided to burn Magnivelle to ash and drag her country into war. Or the ill fates of her late father's wives—dying one after another, until Melarie's mother, the fourth and final queen, decided it was better to abandon her daughter and disappear before she, too, ended up in a royal grave.

When King Costis dies a second time, Melarie's suspicion turns to certainty.

"What . . . ," wheezes Prince Kellam, "what have you *done*?"

Costis' eyes are wide and unseeing, his face a frozen mask of terror, his fingers still curled around the prince's hideous lapel.

The "healer" sways on his knees, looking for all the world like he's only a few minutes away from joining Costis in the afterlife. His gaze slides to Costis. "Well. Pretty sure it's permanent this time."

Prince Kellam lurches backward, bringing the dead king with him, and the noise that leaves the prince's throat can only be described as something between a scream and a mewl. "Get him off me," Kellam gasps. "*Gethimoffmegethimoffme—*"

"Your coat," blurts Melarie. "Prince Kellam, remove your coat!"

There's an audible *rip* as the lapel finally tears away. Finally, Costis' hand thuds to the floor, still clutching the fabric. Kellam rockets backward and plasters himself against the wall. Melarie's heart rises in her throat. She steps forward.

Kellam cringes away. "Stay away from me. All of you—stay back!"

The realization seems to finally hit the room at once. Costis is dead—and his murderer stands among them. Melarie backpedals so quickly she knocks a picture frame off the wall. She grasps hopelessly for something—anything—she can defend herself with.

"Guards," Kellam says. "We need to call the guards."

"No," cries the girl from the wardrobe.

"Yes," gasps Melarie.

Some of the color returns to the kingsguard's face. He blinks as if waking from a long sleep and bellows, "*Guards!*"

Melarie's fingers close around something hard and smooth. A vase. It's beautiful—cream porcelain painted by hand, depicting the Lover and the Builder entwined in an eternal embrace in sweeping gold. It's no weapon, but if one of the killers comes for her, she can at least get a good strike at their head. Melarie clutches it in front of her chest.

"Hold on," the healer protests, raising his hands. He starts to rise, and everyone flinches. "Let's all be reasonable here—"

"Don't move," Kellam sputters. "Don't come near me."

"What, you think I killed him?" the healer demands. When Kellam doesn't answer, his eyes bulge. "I tried to *save* him!"

"Did you?" snaps the guard. "That was no healing magic we just witnessed. Was that all an act designed to cover your tracks?"

Panic flutters through Melarie. This reminds her too much of the castle she came from; the accusations, the tension, the finger-pointing. Too much is at stake. And Kellam looks like he's one sharp movement away from summoning a bunch of thorned vines to spear them all where they stand.

"Come now," Melarie protests. "There's no need for us to accuse each other."

Without thinking, Melarie steps forward—and the *hiss* of a sword being drawn fills the chamber.

Her blood chills. The guard stares at her, his gaze flinty and cold. "Remain where you are."

Hysterical laughter threatens her. He thinks *she's* a threat? Melarie, the useless princess? The forgotten fourth daughter in her ridiculous red dress and this gods-awful ruby mask? It's so absurd that were there not a dead king at their feet, Melarie might think he was mocking her. But there's no humor in the guard's face.

She stumbles back, away from the point of the sword. The vase trembles in her hands. Where is her attendant and chaperone, Antoine? Where are the Avendellian guards? Where are *her* guards?

She should have never come here.

When Melarie's father died, the first thing his daughters did was broker for peace. Well, technically the first thing they did was celebrate, but that could hardly go into the official record. It was Solene, the second eldest, who'd written the treaty and marriage proposal in her neat hand while their father's body still cooled, calmly fielding Delphine's sly suggestions of marriage and Elodie's stiff requests for an end to the suffering. They'd wept with their arms around each other when Avendell's acceptance arrived sealed in gold.

It was decided almost immediately: Melarie would travel to Avendell as Elodie's emissary, sign the treaty, and secure their future for good.

"You are the youngest," Solene had said with a careless lift of her shoulder, the invitation pinched between her fingers like a dirty rag. "We will be too busy here to waste our time at a ball."

Secure the treaty, Antoine had whispered. *And I'll look the other way if you wish to board a ship headed anywhere but home.*

It had been a beautiful dream. Her chance to escape; her first and only window to truly live. Melarie had dared to picture a new life for herself, free of Istellia, of the weight of her name and her father's dark legacy. She saw herself traveling, meeting people and seeing places she'd never known, dedicating her life to leaving the world a little better than she'd found it. Melarie had been stupid enough to hope.

And now everything is ruined.

The howl of the storm fills Costis' chambers. Even the healer is sobering, but instead of watching them, he stares only at the gray-gowned girl, who is doing her best to look everywhere but at him. Melarie's attention darts around the room, cataloging the faces before her for the first time. Guard, prince, healer, tamer, and . . . the newcomer, the girl who appeared as if from nothing.

The killer could be any one of them.

Kellam's distress could be real or an act; the guard is the only one with a weapon. The "healer" is dressed as a Courier acolyte, but his magic is nothing Melarie has seen before. And the beast tamer? There's murder in that girl's eyes. Melarie's skin crawls.

Oh, what was she thinking, telling Antoine she didn't want an escort for her audience with the king? She should have at least brought her guards—Kaylie or Pierre. Someone good in a crisis. *Anyone.* Even Antoine would make her feel safer. He always knows exactly what to say.

"How long," the beast tamer inquires coolly, "are we meant to wait?"

Panic flashes across the guard's face, so brief that had Melarie not been staring at him, she might have missed it. He gestures at them with his sword. "Remove your weapons. Set them in the middle of the room."

They stiffen. Melarie opens her mouth to protest—but Kellam steps forward, his smile snapping back into place.

"Just a precaution," he says smoothly, looking at them each in turn. His face is so open, so warm, Melarie might think him genuine had she not spent a lifetime at court being lied to and manipulated by vipers who wore that same smile. "We're all in the same predicament, are we not? So let's make a show of good faith and disarm. Look, I'll start!" The prince makes a great show of removing a tiny golden knife from his left sleeve and tossing it to the floor with a magnanimous sweep of his arm. It's almost quick enough to hide the way his hand shakes. Almost.

Melarie's fingers tremble as she reaches for Elodie's knife.

When she stepped into Castle Avendell, armored in Solene's finest overcoat and blazing in Delphine's favorite bloody red gown, Melarie had sworn that, for a moment, she could taste freedom, as bright and sharp as sea salt on the wind. And when she saw the lilies blooming high on Avendell's walls, she'd dreamed, foolishly, of Gabriel.

Her only friend. Her favorite confidant. Gabriel had been Melarie's only bright spot of hope in those long, dark years when her father was at his worst—until, of course, King Raphaël dismissed Gabriel in one of his typical fits of paranoia and rage. Melarie never saw him again. She'd waited for Gabriel to reappear after her father's death, and when Antoine offered Melarie her freedom, Melarie's plans changed.

If Gabriel wouldn't come to her, Melarie would find him herself.

Now she may not live to see dawn.

With her free hand, Melarie undoes the knife sheath on her hip. She slips her fingers in—and her blood turns to ice.

It's empty.

Melarie cannot help herself.

Her eyes slide to Costis' wound.

Buried between the king's ribs, the ruby genet cat handle of Elodie's knife gives a single taunting wink.

Melarie doesn't know which god has cursed her so thoroughly— but it's clear they intend to have their fun tonight before Istellia's fourth and least-essential princess joins her father in the grave.

7

CLOVE

CLOVE has never met a beast she could not handle. Humans, however, are a different matter, a species she has much less experience with, but even she can tell that the ones trapped in this room with her are one crisis away from showing their fangs.

Heavy clots of snow pummel the glass—again, and again, and again—allowing the mage-lights only seconds to recover before snapping back off. Each time the chamber is flooded with darkness, Clove's breath catches. Gooseflesh prickles her skin as she listens for any shift in stance, brush of fabric, or whispered threat that she is about to be attacked.

Why did she have to accept her father's invitation? Clove had read the note tucked into the invitation herself—a promise written in the king's own hand. It had felt like a dream as her eyes traced over every gilded swoop and swirl. She'd forced herself to put down the letter, splash cold water onto her face, and read it again just to be sure it was real.

There was no way she could have turned it down. But now, the likelihood of the king's promise coming to fruition is . . .

Her lower lip begins to tremble. She clamps it between her

teeth before any of the others take notice. The facts. Go back to the facts. There is absolutely no reason to panic.

Yes, there is a dead body at her feet, and fresh blood the color of mountain poppies has begun to seep into the soles of her sparkly heels. But in truth, the violence is more familiar to her than anything else in this entire castle. This she can handle.

Besides, she's innocent.

The mage-light snaps back on with a half-hearted flicker, and this time, it stays on. Five ghostly faces stare back at her. The resplendent prince, his dark hair matted with sweat. The guard with his sword at the ready. The willowy princess, who has abandoned her ridiculous mask and now clutches . . . a vase? The skulking stranger in gray from the wardrobe. And the healer—Ellion?—who strutted into the room as if they all were ever so lucky to be graced with his presence.

If only she had her bow. She wouldn't even need her quiver—a single arrow would be enough to get her out of this mess.

Her gaze shifts past them to the door. She was a fool to expend so much energy wrangling that baby unicorn this morning before she left for the ball. She always forgets how vicious they are.

If she runs, will she still be fast enough?

"The rest of you," the guard says, drawing Clove back to the present, "disarm."

Clove's pulse stutters as the guard moves in closer. *I am innocent. I've done nothing wrong here*, she chants to herself. She lifts her arms, palms to the ceiling, and shrugs. "I'm a beast tamer. Why would I bring a weapon to a ball full of humans?"

His eyes sweep over her. Clove bats her lashes and tips her head to one side. "You can search me if you'd like." She pretends not to notice the pink in his cheeks as he nods curtly.

She lets her shoulders drop. The illusion of flirting evaporates. Playing the pretty blond in pink has always served her well enough, especially around men in power. Better for them to think of her as an empty-headed, rosy-cheeked plaything than as the capable young woman she is, so she can do as she pleases. Really, is there any need for the guard to know about the tranquilizer pill secretly tucked between layers of tulle?

"And what of your magic?"

Clove blinks. The guard is still standing before her, refusing to budge. She clears her throat. "Excuse me?"

"Your *magic*," he snaps. "Swords and daggers are not the only danger to the Crown."

Oh, so it's come to this. Yet another moment in her life where Clove will lay bare her station and all her misfortune with a single sentence: *I have no magic.*

There are points of concentration scattered throughout Avendell and Istellia where believers insist the gods slumber far beneath the earth, put to rest by an unknown force long ago. People who live near one of these points tend to express some sort of magic related to the closest god—like the Vernevaus. The Gardener's magic emanates from the lush, rolling hills west of the castle, and both Costis and Kellam are greenmages.

But the land around these so-called magic points was long ago bought up by the wealthy and noble, of which Clove is neither. She is a poor girl from the mountains, well out of range of the Builder and the Gardener. Even the closest goddess, the Arbiter, is perched too high up the craggy cliffside for any of her magic to reach the Beauforte property.

If you believe in all that.

Which Clove never has. Her family isn't religious; it was her mother, Yvette, who dragged them all to the Arbiter's scales every equinox to drop a coin on each plate, and neither Clove nor her brothers have been back since. There has never been anything but dirt-caked fingernails and calloused palms in the Beauforte lineage. Usually, Clove is proud of that.

But the way these strangers eye her now makes her think twice about speaking that pride aloud. She tries to read the guard's face. Will it help or hurt her to possess magic in this situation? Her eyes cut to the healer wobbling unsteadily beside her. Well, *he* definitely has some kind of magic, and all it's done for him is raise more suspicion.

Clove meets the guard's gaze. "There is no magic in the Beauforte line."

To her absolute humiliation, no one seems surprised. The guard simply nods and moves down the row, while Clove prays to any god, real or imagined, to put her out of her misery.

He stops in front of the healer. "If this is a weapon, then I'm the next king of Avendell," Ellion says, clutching his flask to his chest. "Bad joke. You know the Evercraft reputation, but as far as my magic, I'm as much in the dark as you are. For all I know, I'm just a byproduct of one of the Courier's twisted jokes. I can talk to dead things. My understanding begins and ends there." His nose wrinkles. "You can call me a necromancer, if it makes you feel better about the whole thing."

"It doesn't," Oak says. His eyes drop to the bead. "And that?"

Ellion's expression grows cold. "A mistake. And one that has nothing to do with the king."

Interest pricks at Clove. All those sworn to the Courier wear a necklace of gold once they've earned their robes. Most healers proudly sport a line of gleaming white beads, each symbolizing a life saved.

But black beads mean the opposite. Each one represents someone the healer failed to save. Clove has seen plenty of healers whose necks have hung heavy with the beads of life and death in tandem, but never anything like this.

Oak moves on.

Before the guard can turn to her, Melarie sinks to her heels in a blur of red and sets the vase on the floor. "That's it, that's all I have. The Atilelets are disciples of the Shifter, but he's not bestowed gifts onto anyone since . . . since my father came of age. But Elodie will be next, for certain." She lifts her chin, as if daring someone to challenge her.

Every eye in the room slides to the girl who burst from the wardrobe. Oak looms over her with new resolve and opens his hand. "Your weapon."

It almost isn't fair; he's at least a foot taller than this wiry girl with the severe bob and hollow eyes that look as though they've seen death a hundred times over, and he has more strength in his pinkie finger than the rest of them combined. He could take down all of them with his body weight alone.

But Oak doesn't need to; he has another weapon at his hip, and unlike the rest of them, he gets to keep it. When the girl doesn't immediately respond, his free hand wraps around an ornate hilt and slides a glittering sword from its sheath with a *thwick*.

"Fine," the girl grumbles, lowering her gaze. She retrieves a tiny throwing star from a hidden breast pocket and drops it into the guard's hand.

Oak waggles his fingers. "And?"

The girl rolls her eyes and huffs, but she hikes up the skirt of her silky gray gown, unstraps a small, secret dagger from her inner thigh, and drops it into Oak's palm. "There," she says, baring her teeth. "There are no more. Would you like to pat me down to be sure?"

"Your magic?"

The question is more of a courtesy than anything. Even Clove knows the answer just from looking at the cagey girl, who is trying much too hard.

"None," she says softly. "But I do still worship. I can tell you my patron goddess."

"That's not necessary," Oak says with a flick of his hand. "But what I would like to know is who in the name of Twelve *are you*?"

The necromancer reanimates as if climbing out of his own grave. His face is still too pale and slick with sweat, but the color is slowly coming back into his cheeks. "Ah, this is Vesryn Novelle. An . . . old friend of mine." His eyes narrow. "The wardrobe? Really, Ves?"

Vesryn wrinkles her nose. "It's not like you knew I was there."

Oak jabs his sword in the necromancer's direction. "You knew this intruder would be here? Are you conspiring together? Was this all a plot to—"

"—kill the king," Clove finishes.

All eyes turn to her. Clove makes a half-hearted attempt to smooth down her tulle skirt and clears her throat. Can they truly not see it? The cheap dress, self-imposed haircut—kept short and out of the way—the haunted look in her eyes. The *throwing star*.

When no one utters a word, Clove blurts, "This girl is clearly a mercenary."

The air in the room grows heavy as they continue staring at her, stock-still and silent. Clove's throat tightens. Maybe her instincts were off this time and—

"It's true," Vesryn says quickly, her face blotchy. "But you misunderstand my mission. King Costis hired me as his guard for the evening. He suspected that someone close to him was trying to kill him."

Oak stiffens. "That doesn't make sense. *I'm* his personal guard."

"Perhaps the king had his suspicions about you, too."

Though Oak stands a full head taller than her, Vesryn holds his stare with a gaze that would make grass wither. She adds, "Look, when someone hires me, the only question I ask is when I'll get my coin. I don't know why the king thought my services were necessary; I merely did my duty and answered his call. Perhaps duty is something you're unfamiliar with."

The words hang in the air. Red creeps up Oak's neck. He opens his mouth to retort, but before he can get a word out, Prince Kellam steps between them.

"Oh-*kay*! None of that." Kellam glances down at his father, pales, and snaps his head back up. "We're all in a terrible situation. I'm sure there is a very reasonable explanation for all this. Why don't we start over? I'm Kellam. The handsome angry man with the very big sword is Oak. Ellion, meet Melarie. Melarie, meet Ellion. And now we're acquainted with Vesryn, too. Lovely!" He forces a smile and looks at Clove. "And you are . . . ?"

Clove clears her throat. "I'm Knox Beauforte's daughter. Clove."

"Like garlic?" asks the necromancer, Ellion.

"What?" She scowls. "No, like the spice."

Ellion nods sagely and whispers, seemingly to himself, "And garlic."

Twelve help her. Clove's going to die here surrounded by idiots.

"Great." Kellam claps his hands together. The lights flicker off and back on again. He's smiling at them as if they're all old friends, but his collar is black with sweat, and he's edged back behind his guard. When the prince speaks again, it's in the same dulcet tone Clove used with that ornery unicorn. "Now that we're all acquainted, I'd ask you all not to panic. I'm sure Oak has a plan for how we're going to get help. Don't you, Oak?"

The guard has been staring at the body of his king with empty, soulless eyes. At the sound of his own name, he quickly blinks. He pulls in a shuddering breath, so subtle that Clove wonders if she's the only one who notices. "We are not going to call for help again."

"Right," Kellam repeats brightly. "We are not going to ca—pardon?"

"The guards will already be at their stations throughout the castle by now, safeguarding the entryways and court members. I am the only guard on this floor tonight," Oak says softly. "But this is a problem far outside the jurisdiction of the kingsguard anyway. We need to go higher." His eyes lift to meet the prince's. "Seek out Magistrate Crowley and bring him back here. The castle is crawling with Avendellian military; you will be protected. But be quick about it. Tell no one what has happened. I will remain here with the suspects."

"Suspects?" Melarie demands. She draws herself up with a

shudder. "You have no right to treat us like this." Her eyes narrow; a cat about to pounce. "Nor the authority."

It's an odd accusation—but at her words, Oak and Kellam freeze.

Melarie speaks before either of them can. "You are not king until the treaty is signed and legitimized. Who is your regent? You must have one since you are not yet eighteen. Who would rule in Costis' stead should news of his death get out?"

Kellam turns greener than his hideous overcoat. "We do not want the regent involved."

A wave of nausea sweeps through Clove. Did he know? Does the prince know what Costis offered to restore to her family with a swoop of his quill at dawn? She assumes that the person Costis chose as his second-in-command would certainly follow the king's edicts to the letter, but his flighty, spoiled son? Perhaps King Kellam has no plans to make good on his father's promises.

"That does not answer my question," says Melarie. She's getting bolder now, even as Costis' body cools before them. "Your mother is dead, your father too. You have no siblings. Who did Costis appoint? Perhaps I will seek them out myself."

"You do not want the regent involved," Kellam warns again. All the color has drained from his face, along with the pomp and charm. The prince stands as stoic as the stone Gardener on the floor beneath them as his eyes bore into Melarie's.

What is going on here? Clove searches the faces of the others, but the mercenary looks just as confused as she feels, and the necromancer has become absorbed in tracing his finger around and around the lip of his flask. She has to get out of here. Again, she looks to the door. If she pretends to examine that vase Melarie placed on the floor, then maybe she can smash it to cause a diversion and—

"However terrible you think this situation is," Kellam continues, "I can assure you, it will become a nightmare if Grand Chamberlain Weatherington is allowed to seize power."

Every thought drops away. Every sound in the room sputters out and dies. Clove's pulse pounds in her ears.

That name.

Clove was a young girl when Gaspar Weatherington first came to her father's estate, wearing robes the same color as the lush forest around them. She was so young then, she can remember it only in flashes. The king's seal pressed into the scroll. The grand chamberlain's chapped lips as he read the decree. The parade of guards leaving their land, arms full of unhatched basilisk eggs, as they seized all their assets and partitioned off their land. The whole of the Beauforte legacy was erased in a single afternoon, and with it, Clove's future.

She cannot have her fate tied to that man. Perhaps her father's hateful musings were true—that the order came from Costis, and Costis alone—but it no longer matters. Costis is dead, and Clove will never forget the glint in Gaspar's eyes the day he came and ruined everything. The grand chamberlain was a man who enjoyed causing pain. He would not hesitate to obliterate the only dream Clove has ever had: to reclaim the Beaufortes' land and safeguard the beasts that are rightfully theirs.

"The king is dead," Melarie says. "And if Kellam cannot yet ascend the throne—"

"Gaspar Weatherington was once lord of Magnivelle," Kellam says softly. "Well, technically he still is, for whatever a village reduced to a pile of ash is worth. You will find no favor with him. Of that, I can assure you."

Melarie goes still. The name of the village rolls through the air like a storm. Even Clove, sheltered in the far north, has heard of the day the Istellians burned Magnivelle to the ground. She was too young then to understand what, exactly, had happened to that little village on the border, but even she knew what it meant when Avendell turned on their former ally and declared war.

"Even still," Melarie protests, her voice wavering, weaker in the revelation that the man who stands to seize power would punish her for her father's crimes. "He will have a duty to the realm . . . the king has died. . . ."

She starts forward, as if to flee, and Clove's mouth opens before she can think better of it.

"He is a cruel man."

They freeze. Every eye in the room turns to Clove. She cannot panic. She has done nothing wrong. Her family deserves the reparations the Crown has promised them, and she is not leaving this godsforsaken castle without it. "I do not know much of royal politics, but my instinct has never led me astray. I crossed paths with the grand chamberlain as a girl, and even then, I knew his heart was full of rot. If you want to leave here alive with your treaty signed, I think it's best we start with the magistrate."

"She's right," Ellion adds uncertainly. "I . . . I would trust Crowley over most people at court. He was fair to me when I didn't deserve it. And at least he doesn't have a penchant for executing people for minor crimes." His eyes slide to Vesryn at this, who seems to understand, for the first time, just how much danger she's in.

Costis lies in the middle of them, his eyes dull and unseeing, his face a mask of frozen horror, an echo of his final words.

Chaos comes for you.

Oak steps in to take command once more. "Kellam will fetch Magistrate Crowley. He will be discreet and quick. The magistrate will come; he will treat everyone fairly. He will protect those of us who are innocent."

No one speaks. The final word lingers in the air, and with it, the sting of the implication.

"Very well," Prince Kellam says finally. He looks at Oak for a beat too long, worry heavy in the crease of his brows. "Try not to kill each other while I'm gone." And in a flash of pea green, the prince vanishes.

The wind lets out a low, deranged howl as snow slams the windows. The mage-lights flicker but, this time, mercifully stay on. Whispers swell as Vesryn drags a stumbling Ellion to the chaise. Oak's gaze follows the pair. His shoulders only soften when they sit down instead of making a break for the door.

The guard mumbles something about checking the locks before stalking into the sitting chamber.

It's only Melarie and Clove.

But the princess seems to have forgotten all about Clove. Melarie's eyes are wide, unblinking, as she stares at the knife still jutting out from Costis' gut. Her delicate fingers twitch, as if she is itching to reach for the hilt.

Interesting. Clove inches closer, eyeing the ruby-crested knife. There's a small image pressed into the metal. It looks like the spotted genet cat, the wild form of Istellia's patron goddess, the Lover—

Her heart stops.

The wound is *frothing*.

Clove leans in, careful to keep her heels from soaking up more blood. She squeezes her eyes closed, clearing her vision, and looks again. In a matter of seconds, the froth has expanded, bubbling up from the wound and onto the knife. The familiar scent of curdled milk and wood sorrel slaps her in the face.

This can't be real. It simply can't be. Clove forces her shaking hand into the imperceivable sewn-in pocket amid the layers of puffy tulle, feeling for the single tranquilizer pill. *Still there.* She hadn't swallowed it and somehow forgotten. Clove isn't hallucinating.

She'd feel a lot better right now if she was.

She'd know that stench anywhere.

A lifetime of training returns. Of her father, and his father's father, and all the Beaufortes who came before them and carved out their now-tarnished legacy in blood, sweat, and venom. Before Clove could read, before she had her first blood, she knew everything there was to know about the basilisks that made her family famous.

It's basilisk venom that leaks from Costis' wound.

Clove sways. It's impossible. The venom is incredibly difficult to harvest, and harder still to preserve. The process has to be done just so, and then either stored or used within an hour of extraction. The only people in the whole country who know how to do that are the Beaufortes.

The only person who knows how to do that in this castle is Clove.

She presses the back of her hand to her forehead. Her skin is cold and clammy. And her mouth is unbearably dry. She wishes Ellion hadn't drained that flask.

Someone here must know about the nerve-blocking agent in basilisk venom and decided to use it to quell Costis' pain in his final moments. It's possible they extracted it from the snake outside the castle and never brought the deadly beast inside. But knowing what she knows about Gaspar Weatherington, it seems unlikely that the grand chamberlain would go through the trouble of seizing every basilisk in Avendell only to allow one to roam freely in the cold. Not when he knows what he can do with them.

The other option is that the beast was brought into the castle. And it's still here.

Someone knows the real reason Clove came to the ball tonight, and this is a message meant just for her.

8

KELLAM

KELLAM barely makes it to the potted mint at the end of the hall before he vomits.

Back in his father's chambers, it had been essential to keep up a front. But here, in the hallway, he comes apart. Kellam's hands shake as they clutch the ceramic edge of the planter; sweat drips from his nose. He stares miserably at the mint. It'll surely die now—and he doesn't even have the magic to fix it. Some king he'll be.

The thought sends a new wave of panic crashing over him.

His father is dead. *Murdered.*

If Kellam isn't careful, Gaspar Weatherington will take his place. Once Gaspar ascends, the grand chamberlain will not give up the throne to Kellam when he turns eighteen. Not without another war.

The prince presses his knuckles into his eyes. There is a murderer in his father's chambers. Someone has killed Costis and orphaned Kellam on the eve of his kingdom finally having peace. But who? *Why?*

And was the knife meant for Costis—or Kellam? If someone had wanted to stop the treaty, either of their deaths would have done the job.

Kellam can dither later. He must find Magistrate Crowley.

Oak's reasoning was only a half-truth. Certainly, Crowley will be fair and discreet. But the magistrate's powers extend beyond murder investigation.

Crowley also has the power to legitimize Kellam as king.

Kellam just needs to find him before Gaspar discovers the truth.

He forces himself to straighten. Every moment Kellam wastes is a moment Oak is trapped alone with a killer. And every second lost is another chance for Gaspar to steal everything Kellam holds dear. Kellam checks his clothes for bloodstains, dons his mask, and steps into the ballroom.

In a blink, his world is chaos; a riot of sound and smiling faces, of clammy hands clasping his fingers, his sleeves, his shoulders. Hot mouths press kisses to his skin and whisper wishes with dulcet, hungry undertones against his ear.

"Prince Kellam," breathes some sweating, power-hungry dignitary whose name he can never remember. "You look striking."

Kellam forces himself to smile and wink at the dignitary's sour-faced wife. "And yet I don't hold a candle to your guest!"

Kellam circles the ballroom, scanning for Crowley. He tells hungry-eyed nobles how pretty their ugly daughters are and sickly diplomats they've never looked sharper. He flatters, preens, and deflects. He is spoiled but not whiny, bombastic but not grating. He glitters and laughs, wearing the mantle of the shining, careless prince like a shield.

Sometimes, Kellam isn't certain what parts of his role are a performance, and what parts are all he's ever been. By the second turn, Kellam has greeted anyone of note; by the third, he's even entertained the bootlickers who aren't. Now the truth is impossible to deny.

The magistrate isn't here.

It's just like Crowley to hope his absence wouldn't be noticed. He's a shy man, more prone to holing up in his office and poring over legal requests than placating preening nobles. Very well. Kellam will just have to go to him.

Hang in there, Oak. Please.

If something happens to him—if one of those treacherous snakes *dares*—

Kellam can't think about that. It's going to be fine. It will. It must.

Except his father is dead.

"Prince Kellam!" Councilman Aubert wheezes. "Have you met my daughter Serena—"

"Pleasure," Kellam says numbly, brushing past.

Avendell's grand main doors stand before him, thrown open to allow a river of guests to pour through. Kellam keeps his head down. The magistrate's home is only a short ride away. All Kellam needs is a horse and a quarter hour, and soon he'll put this nightmare behind him.

He steps through the door. Cold blasts his face.

Though it's late spring, it might as well be high winter. Snow comes down in whirling gusts, already piled past Kellam's hips. Kellam can't see the castle's outer gates, let alone the road. Guests hurry past, shivering as they shake ice from their hair and stamp feeling back into their frozen feet.

When was the last time it snowed like this? Five years ago? Ten?

Memory stirs—of snow piled over his head, and his father's face grim as he learned their latest shipment of food to the soldiers posted at the border had been stalled by the storm. By the time the roads cleared, the soldiers had starved.

"Prince Kellam?"

Kellam whirls. A figure fights their way toward him through the drifts. One of the stable hands?

"I need a horse," Kellam calls. "And quickly."

"And where," says Grand Chamberlain Gaspar Weatherington, "might you be going?"

Kellam freezes. For a brief, ludicrous beat, he wonders if Gaspar will hurt him. The grand chamberlain has made it clear to anyone who will listen that Kellam is unfit for the throne. And what a wonderful opportunity this would be—for Gaspar to wound Kellam here and leave him to freeze in the snow. The prince's death could be blamed on anyone. Gaspar's status as regent would suddenly be permanent.

Behind Gaspar, the main doors to Castle Avendell hang ajar, spilling light and laughter into the dark whirl of cold beyond.

Gaspar squints at Kellam. "What in the name of the Twelve are you doing out here?"

His mouth goes dry. Kellam forces himself to sound flippant. "Crowley has not arrived. Father is furious. He sent me to fetch him."

Gaspar's face twitches. It's no secret he lobbied against the treaty from the moment Costis proposed it. He's only ever advocated for Costis to wipe Istellia off the map—a debt repaid, for everything he'd lost. The peace they achieve tonight will be a public humiliation, a legally binding reminder of every way Gaspar has failed to avenge Magnivelle.

"Crowley arrived moments ago. You must have missed him." He squeezes Kellam's shoulder too tightly for the gesture to be affectionate. "Where *is* your father?"

Kellam's certain he didn't see Magistrate Crowley arrive. But already the thoughts soften and slip away. It's a busy crowd; it's likely he's just wrong. Still, where hope ought to stir, only dread curdles.

If the roads are closed, they'll have to wait until morning for the city guard. Somehow, Kellam is going to have to catch a murderer, survive the night, and keep the treaty from falling apart.

They're trapped.

"In his chambers, of course," Kellam answers truthfully. "He'll appear when he sees fit."

He lurches past Gaspar, surging back toward the castle. He needs to tell Oak. He needs to ensure they're safe before anything else goes awry—and before Gaspar can get a sense of why, exactly, Kellam's father has not been seen. The grand chamberlain follows him soundlessly and shuts the grand doors with a resounding thud.

"Best stay inside, Your Grace." On his tongue, Gaspar manages to make the title sound denigrating. "It seems the Twelve are truly in a foul mood tonight."

The crowd surges between them. Kellam turns, shivering and dripping from the snow in his hair, but the grand chamberlain is gone.

Something sharp pricks against his ribs.

"Don't panic," Vesryn murmurs. "Don't draw any attention at all. I mean you no harm. I come as a friend."

He freezes.

"Do friends often hold knives to each other's ribs?" Kellam asks. "I thought Oak confiscated your weapons."

"So did he." She gives him a gentle prod. "I swear in the name of the Arbiter, I just want to talk."

Kellam doesn't believe her for a second. But what choice does he have? If he shouts, she'll have the blade in his heart in a blink. And if Vesryn was wily enough to slip out from under Oak's nose, she can almost certainly find somewhere in the palace to hide until the storm is over. Plus, the Arbiter is the goddess of justice and judgment, and has a way of punishing those who use her name in vain.

For all her faults, the little assassin doesn't seem stupid.

"Down the hall," he grates out. "There's a linen closet with a soundproofing spell. I don't suppose you're also hoping for a private tryst? You're a little scrawny for me, but you're pretty enough. Shall I find us somewhere more comfortable?"

Vesryn makes a horrified noise and shoves him forward a little harder than needed. Even as his hands shake, Kellam can't help but smirk.

His smugness dies as they turn the corner.

Here, absent of guests twirling in gauze, velvet, and silk, the marble sconces carved in the likenesses of the Divine Twelve seem garish in their opulence. Gold-limned wood paneling sweeps up the wall, and lilacs kept in permanent bloom by his father's magic fill the air with their heady fragrance. Every bit of the palace screams old wealth, and Kellam has never felt smaller, propelled down the hallway with a knife to his ribs.

What had his father always said?

Be wary of those with nothing to lose.

"Where?" Vesryn demands, the slightest shake to her voice.

"There," Kellam says, nodding toward the closet.

Vesryn yanks the door open, shoves him inside, and then they're alone.

The moment the door clicks, they're plunged into silence. A tiny mage-light flickers on in the back of the linen closet, illuminating stacks of neatly folded rags. Vesryn eyes the closet with a curled lip and shudders. She keeps her knife raised.

"Well," Kellam says, "now that you've threatened me with bodily harm and kidnapped me, what exactly do you want, Vesryn?"

Vesryn starts, as if alarmed Kellam remembered her name, and Kellam can't help but feel the smallest prick of pride. For all his faults, he's nothing if not an excellent host.

"You hired me to do a job," she says slowly. "It's done. I want my coin."

For a moment, Kellam can't make sense of her words. He blinks, once, twice, wondering if he tipped into a strange new reality.

Finally, all he manages is a baffled, "I beg your pardon?"

Vesryn holds his gaze, her violet eyes glittering like twin amethysts, and then her other hand flies toward his chest. Kellam flinches, but instead of the bite of a blade, there's a crumple of paper. Irritation flares in him. He's growing tired of the little peasant's theatrics, and if she doesn't get to the point soon, he might as well call the guards and—

His blood turns to ice. It's a letter, plain and unremarkable were it not for the familiar wax seal that's been broken in half.

Vesryn opens the envelope and slides the message clean.

"*Miss LaRue,*" she reads slowly. "*I require the use of your services. I fear my father is no longer fit to serve the country, and I believe it best he be removed from his duties. Permanently.*"

The walls close in; the room spins. Suddenly, Kellam flashes back to his study, where he holed up to avoid his father's paranoid ranting and Oak's strained expression. His hand cramps as he writes the words that could either damn his country or save it.

But, no. This is impossible. His signet ring remained on his finger that night. He melted the wax for the seal but never had the stomach to finish the work.

"Where," Kellam rasps, "did you get that?"

"You sent it to me."

The floor threatens to tip out from under him. "This would be treason."

Her gaze is steady. "I know."

"You must believe me," Kellam rasps. "I never sent that letter. It was a mistake. A moment of panic, one I regretted as soon as I inked the words. I discarded it right after."

"And yet it arrived at my door." Her face gives away nothing. "You hired me to do a job. It's done. Now give me my coin and get me out of here—unless you want me to make a mess of your ball."

Horror chokes Kellam as the implication of Vesryn's words hits him in full.

Of course she would have more than one alias; it's not like she could show up to kill her mark with the same name she was hired under. And she certainly wouldn't use her *real* identity.

Vesryn is the infamous assassin Gisele LaRue. She's *here*.

And Kellam's father is dead.

As Vesryn stares at him, the events that will surely follow play out before him. The treaty will be canceled. Gaspar will seize power. The magistrate may try to protect Kellam at first, but that letter seals his fate. Kellam's going to lose everything. His title, the crown, *Oak*. Oh gods, what will Oak say? If this gets out, it won't matter whether Kellam hangs. He'd be as good as dead to Oak. And without Oak, his life might as well be over before it begins.

If Kellam tackles her, can he get the letter? He could try. But something tells Kellam that if he picks a fight with Vesryn, he'll lose.

"You lied," Kellam rasps finally. "My father never hired you to protect him."

"Careful, prince. With deduction skills like that, you might have a future in crime investigation." Vesryn squirms. "I'll have my coin now. Unless you'd like me to announce to the entire ball that the king is dead and his son was the one who sealed his fate."

Kellam forces himself to breathe. He looks at Vesryn—really looks at her. Though her eyes are hard and her chin raised, sweat gathers at her temples. Her throat pulses as she swallows her discomfort.

She's desperate. And if she's desperate, there might be a way out of this yet.

What does he know about Gisele LaRue? Only whispers. That she moves in the shadows, targeting the wicked and the wealthy, and leaves no trace behind. Why else would he have written that blasted letter to begin with? An assassin of Gisele's caliber never would have been so sloppy. After years of existing only in myth, she never would have let them see her face.

What if it wasn't her?

He could ask, of course. He could accuse her of lying. But she'd just counter with another untruth. Here is a girl with nothing to lose and everything to gain.

Beyond the closet door, the ball builds to a steady roar, nearly loud enough to drown out the storm raging beyond the castle walls. Nearly.

I Killed the King

A terrible idea gnaws at Kellam.

He stares at Vesryn, casts a prayer to the Twelve, and gambles with his life.

"I'm not going to pay you," he says. "Not yet. I hired you to do a job discreetly, and you failed. You have put me at risk, killing my father before I was crowned. Even if I wanted to pay you, I can't. Only the king can draw the amount of coin I offered from the coffers."

A lie. But Vesryn doesn't know that. He hopes.

Kellam leans in. "You want your coin, *Gisele?* Very well. I have a new job for you. Resolve the problem you've created for me and I'll pay you twice what was offered."

Vesryn rolls her eyes. "Let me guess. You want me to fetch your magistrate or find your father's killer?"

"No," Kellam says softly. "I wouldn't dream of wasting your skills on something so trivial."

His words linger in the air, coiling around them, blooming to their full implication. Even as Kellam says them, he wants to snatch them back.

But it's too late. Understanding brightens her gaze. "You want me to kill someone else."

It's not a question.

Kellam's stomach turns. If this gets out . . . if *Oak* finds out . . .

No. He's come too far to lose everything tonight. His country is relying on him. If he is to be king, he must learn to balance choices like weights on a scale. Kellam has too many problems whirling before him—the treaty, his father, the presence of a killer back in the chambers, the magistrate, Gaspar.

If Vesryn is here and willing, why not put her to use?

"Yes," Kellam rasps. "I need a problem eliminated before the night's end."

Vesryn seems to harden before Kellam's eyes. She grows stiller, colder, transforming from the girl who looked at Ellion with soft, stricken eyes to an assassin even the Divine Twelve might fear.

Vesryn tucks the letter back into her dress. "I hope you understand why I need to hold on to this. No offense. And I will need some kind of insurance from you—a token that the guards will understand, to allow me to move through the castle without question."

Kellam slides his signet ring from his finger, unable to ignore the irony of how the very thing that might damn him will now be entrusted to an assassin.

"If you are caught, I will deny all of this. You will be on your own." He swallows the bile rising in his throat. "But if you succeed, I'll give you and your goddess more than you could ever want for."

Vesryn gives him a small, sad smile. "The gods will always want more than we can give."

Before Kellam can respond, she extends her hand, fingers forming the rigid shape of an ax about to fall. A chill creeps through him. It's the Arbiter's bond—one that promises that betrayal from either party will meet a swift and terrible end.

"Now," Vesryn says. "Give me the name."

Kellam hesitates. But what choice does he have? When he's king, his fingers will inevitably become stained with blood. He may as well wet them early.

Kellam forms an ax with his own hand and lowers it to Vesryn's.

And he swears—though it's ridiculous, though he's not a believer and it's likely just a trick of shadows and a desperate mind—that the moment they touch, some winged creature in the corner stirs.

"Gaspar Weatherington," Kellam rasps, and he drops his ring into Vesryn's waiting palm.

9

VESRYN

VESRYN has never held so much power in the palm of her hand.

The weight of it makes her breath catch. It takes everything in her not to hold the signet ring up to the flickering mage-light and examine the gold, the emerald, the crest designed just for the prince of Avendell. She could get a lot of coin for this. More than enough for her to escape into an entirely different life.

But the prince has promised to give her even more.

Vesryn adjusts her mask, careful not to touch the precariously placed jewels by her temples. She slinks through the crowd, staying close enough to the verdant foliage that she doesn't give off the impression that she'd like to dance, yet far enough away that she doesn't accidentally graze the toxic blooms hidden in plain sight. She sidles up to a limestone fountain in the shape of a massive mosswillow bear—the kind found only this far north. It is customary to have a tribute to the Builder in every dwelling throughout Avendell, even if the family has chosen a different patron deity. Though the Vernevaus worshipped the Gardener, they, too, were not beyond honoring the founding god of their country. Vesryn eyes the polished stone. A tribute of this magnitude certainly must have pleased the gods.

She turns her attention to the ball. The scene before her swirls together like melted glace. She squeezes her eyes shut behind her mask before a renegade tear can roll down her cheek. It surprises her, this flood of emotion over the king's death. Vesryn learned long ago to separate the human from his deeds in this line of work, and Costis Vernevau had his fair share of blood on his hands. He deserved his fate.

Didn't he?

Kellam's panicked face flits through her mind—how his hand trembled as it lowered to cross hers, how his skin was damp with sweat despite the biting cold. The prince is much smarter than she gave him credit for, and quick to pivot as necessary. He'll make a good leader. If he gets the chance.

Get it together. Vesryn's eyes snap open, and the ballroom sharpens into focus. She reminds herself of her mission. *Look for the men in green.*

She scans the crowd, her gaze skipping over the women dressed in macaron-colored pastels and glittering metallics, past the guards and attendants donning fiery Istellian red. Each time her eyes land on a guest in forest green, she looks not at their face but at the gilded brooch pinned to their lapel.

Antlers, antlers, antlers again, Vesryn chants in her head. She knows from her research that Costis' guards wear golden antlers as a symbol of protection for their king, whose signet is a stag—the symbol of the Gardener. But each of the king's most important advisors wears their own unique pin according to their station. Avendellian advisors wear forest-dwelling creatures, except for two. The grand chamberlain wears a gold lily, and Samson Crowley, the magistrate, wears the Sage's wide-eyed owl.

The mage-light catches on a man near the back of the room, and Vesryn swears, for a moment, that she can just make out the pointed tip of a wing. She holds her breath as she rises onto her tiptoes for a better look.

"May I have this dance?"

A man with peppery gray hair and an upturned nose positions himself directly in her line of sight, eclipsing her view of the dance floor. Vesryn pulls her bottom lip between her teeth to keep from screaming or swearing, or maybe both.

"You're much too pretty to stand among the wallflowers," the man says. Vesryn instantly recognizes the nasally, drawn-out vowels as the accent of Istellian nobility. One glance at his scarlet uniform and sparkling brooch confirms it.

Before she can blink, his hand is reaching for her. She freezes, unsure of what to do here. It's no secret that men of a certain station think they can take and touch whatever they want. Maybe she can grit her teeth and deal with whatever unsanctioned caress or hair tousling is about to befall her so as not to make a scene.

Or maybe she can shove her knuckles into his eye sockets until they bleed.

With the lightest touch, his hand brushes past her cheek to the greenery hanging on the wall behind her, retrieving a delicate bellflower. He cups the blossom in his palm. "Ah, la campanule. These are quite rare on the southern coast."

The coast. Of course. If this man traveled all this way to tend to the princess, then he must reside in Castle Istellia—a sun-bleached château tucked up against the Starless Sea. Her gaze drifts to the pin on his lapel: an octopus.

He's one of Melarie's personal attendants, then. Someone close enough to the princess to pry information from, perhaps even a connection that Vesryn could use to get aboard the next ship out of port, even if she doesn't get her coin from Kellam.

"La campanule est très belle, non?" Vesryn purrs, making sure to overarticulate the vowels, her mouth contorting into the same shape it made when she used to blow dandelion seeds into the wind. She plucks the blossom from the Istellian's palm and twirls the stem; violet petals brush against her parted lips.

"Antoine," the man says, his voice low and husky. "My name is Antoine. Et vous?"

"Everly Bardot," she says, tucking the flower behind her ear and hooking her arm through his. "Shall we?"

He wastes no time. The moment the first baleful notes of the violin announce the next waltz, Antoine carefully guides Vesryn's hand to his, palm to palm. His touch at her hip is so light that it takes her a moment to realize he's staring at her, waiting to begin their dance. Beneath the buttery chandelier light, Antoine's face looks more timeworn, but softer, too. There's a kindness in his eyes she didn't see before.

She sets her left hand on his shoulder, and they begin. The dance is up-tempo, and Vesryn's cheeks burn with heat by the time they reach the chorus. "I must say, Monsieur Antoine," she says, breathless, "it's quite a surprise that you've let our princess out of your sight on a night as important as this one."

He spins her before she can glimpse his face. She knows

her Istellian accent is good . . . but good enough to fool a royal attendant into believing that she's a native? Her pulse hitches as Antoine pulls her to his broad chest. "I could tell you were Istellian from across the room, even with the mask. These northerners are a bit uncouth, are they not? The kitchen staff couldn't even be bothered with setting out utensils with the desserts. What do they expect, for us to pick up the tea cakes with our fingers, for goddess' sake?"

"Heathens," Vesryn says, her voice raspy. *Thank the Twelve. It worked.*

"To answer your question, Princess Melarie has shimmied off to the powder room, though I suspect she found herself some entertainment along the way—perhaps even that pompous Avendellian heir." Antoine shrugs. "He is quite nice to look at."

The violin's mournful melody reaches its crescendo, and Antoine spins her again, faster this time. A blur of green and red swirls around her as Vesryn tries to collect her thoughts. But the music is so frenzied, and the artificial rose perfume of the woman dancing beside her makes her jaw ache, and there are just *too many people*. She's losing focus.

Broad hands reel her back in. Spots still float across Antoine's face as they begin to dance again. "No one cares much what happens to our littlest princess, c'est vrai, non? Melarie will never inherit the throne. Attending this ball will probably be the most important thing she does for Istellia in her small, senseless life."

Vesryn winces. The attendant's words are harsher than she'd expected. "Ah, that isn't true. Though she may never take the throne, the princess is certainly capable of great things."

This time when Antoine tries to spin her, Vesryn wriggles

free from his grip. She stumbles backward and bumps into a woman in a saffron-colored dress. The woman hisses something Vesryn is certain is not nice in a thick Istellian accent before flicking her train behind her and marching off. When she looks up, Antoine is wearing an expression that makes her breath catch in her throat.

The Istellian seems to have forgotten about finishing his dance with her. He stands stock-still among the swirl of dancers, chin lifted, dark eyes skipping over the crowd. Worry knits a crease in his brow. Whoever he's searching for, they're not here.

Something else gnaws at her. The way he described Melarie . . . from the brief interaction Vesryn had with the princess, she didn't seem like the type to be content with a senseless existence.

Something isn't right.

"May I cut in?"

Vesryn and Antoine turn in unison toward the voice. It's the man from before—the one who ensured Vesryn's entrance to the ball. His gaze is fixed on her, arm outstretched and palm open expectantly. Instinctively, her eyes slide to his lapel, but she can't make out his brooch from this angle.

Antoine lets out a mean little laugh. "Are you not too busy to dance this evening? Shouldn't you be off investigating shadows?"

The man's face remains blank at the insult, his eyes on Vesryn as he says, "Perhaps you should speak for yourself, old friend. Istellian royalty is riddled with its own brand of madness, is it not?" He shifts, and the glint of gold catches Vesryn's eye: a lily. The man tilts his head in her direction. "I am Gaspar Weatherington, grand chamberlain to the king. May I?"

Everything in Vesryn goes cold.

In that moment, Kellam's ring is an impossible weight in her pocket. Gaspar offers her his hand. Everything in Vesryn is screaming to run the other way.

Instead, she takes her target's hand and lets him pull her into a dance.

For a moment, Vesryn allows herself to sink into the rhythmic pulse of the movement—though she has to take two steps for every effortless glide of her partner's. They're dancing in the long, loping motions of a traditional quadrille as the woodwinds rush in to accompany the solo violinist. It's so warm in this part of the castle, and everything and everyone emanates a hazy, otherworldly glow. Even this strange man smells faintly of woodsmoke and powdered sugar, like a suitor from a fairy tale.

"Forgive my intrusion. You looked even more miserable in Antoine's company than I typically am—a feat I thought impossible." He spins her, but not with the same dramatic flair as Antoine, and for that, Vesryn is grateful. "I don't believe we've officially met."

She bites the inside of her cheek. How best to play this? This may be the closest she gets to Gaspar Weatherington tonight. She needs to keep him this close until she can stick her knife in his side.

She can't blow this.

"My name is Everly Bardot. Istellia is ma résidence principale," Vesryn coos in her poshest accent, "but I have many relatives in Avendell as well."

It takes everything in her to hold Gaspar's gaze as they sweep across the dance floor, and to seem like she's *enjoying* it, though she wants to crawl out of her skin. Honestly, the flirting is more difficult than the murdering part of this job.

She needn't worry. Gaspar seems almost bored by her presence. Vesryn has the feeling that his interruption had nothing to do with her and everything to do with insulting Antoine.

The grand chamberlain's eyes stray. "Well, it was a pleasure, Miss Bardot."

Before she can talk herself out of it, Vesryn opens her eyes even wider and glances up at the much older guard from beneath her dark lashes. "I must say, Avendell has many . . . assets I hadn't considered before. I've been searching for property to purchase near Lyonne, where my uncle is an earl, for a potential move. It's just all so abysmal down south. Ever since the eldest Atilelet daughter inherited the throne, the country has been in shambles. It's only a matter of time before all of Istellia crashes and burns under these four sisters, and gods help us if the youngest ever comes into power."

"I'm afraid we are not much better off in the north. Surely you've heard rumors of Prince Kellam's weakness," Gaspar says. "Some believe the Vernevaus to be cursed."

She pulls away, just enough to witness the pensive expression staining the grand chamberlain's face. "And what do you believe?"

"I believe Prince Kellam doesn't need the intervention of the divine to prove he's unfit to rule," Gaspar snorts. "He's a foolhardy, selfish joke of a boy—and certainly not worthy of the throne. But I take comfort in knowing the gods have a way of dealing with those unfit to rule."

Little do you realize, she thinks.

"They might want to hurry," Vesryn says lightly. "The treaty will be signed at dawn, will it not? I welcome the peace it brings, no matter who wears the crown."

"If it even happens," Gaspar mutters.

The last reedy notes fill the air before falling silent, bringing their dance to a close. Vesryn's pulse quickens. She's running out of time. "What do you mean?" she says, her hand still clamped onto Gaspar's shoulder.

"Certainly you've heard about our king's affliction—not unlike your own king's before his passing. I can assure you that whatever you've heard, it's much worse." He lets his hand drop from her waist. "It would not surprise me in the least if Costis did not manage to carry out his duty at dawn, if he just simply . . . fell asleep."

Vesryn's heartbeat crashes in her ears. She drops her hand from the grand chamberlain's shoulder. "But surely Prince Kellam would sign the treaty."

"Would he?" Gaspar scoffs. "Even the Evercrafts couldn't fix what rots within that boy." He sinks into a deep bow. "Thank you for the dance. I must be going."

"Wait!" Vesryn reaches for him, but pulls back at the last moment. She straightens, pushing back her shoulders to collect herself. "I mean, excusez-moi, but I—I believe I've heard the name Evercraft. They're quite distinguished healers, are they not?"

His eyes narrow ever so slightly. Though the highest court members never don masks during a ball, Gaspar might as well be wearing one. His face is infuriatingly unreadable as he says,

"Perhaps at one time, but whatever healing talent lies in their bloodline stops with Alistair's son. As soon as I discovered the boy was a fraud, I told Costis immediately. Something had to be done."

Had. Something *had* to be done . . . as in, it already was.

Vesryn can't breathe. Her lungs feel like they're filled with ice water. She presses her hand to her heart. "P-perhaps Ellion just needs a bit more time to get acclimated to the role," she says, trying to force the shakiness from her voice.

The grand chamberlain goes rigid as he stares down his nose at her. "I don't believe I ever mentioned his name."

Every curse word she can think of streaks through her mind. It's suddenly too warm in here—is she sweating? Her hand slides to the back of her neck to find the skin moist and clammy.

"What did you say your surname was again?"

"Bardot," she says weakly. A wave of misery crashes over her.

Gaspar's gaze lifts to some other point of interest behind her. "Ah, I believe that's Master Crowley over by the fountain. I must go, Miss . . . Bardot."

Vesryn blinks, and Gaspar disappears into the crowd. She closes her eyes again and forces air back into her lungs. She wipes the sweat from the back of her neck.

And then she follows him.

It's only a matter of time before Gaspar takes his suspicions about her identity to the guards, or even the magistrate himself. Perhaps that's what he's doing at this very moment. She has to get to him first, tell him that the prince has an urgent matter and—

He's not there.

Vesryn stares up at the enormous stone bear, crystalline water trickling from its mouth. Gaspar said Master Crowley was by the fountain, didn't he? She scans the knot of people chattering nearby. No one is wearing Avendellian green.

She turns just in time to see a flash of dark green disappearing down a hallway.

Gaspar lied about seeing the magistrate, she thinks, putting all her manners aside to shove a squat man out of her way as she exits the ballroom. But why? What is he hiding?

It takes her a moment to realize that she's in this hallway alone.

Vesryn's pace slows to a stop. She glances around the shadowy space, but there aren't many places to hide. It's more of an alcove than a hallway, really, and the only door has been sealed off with chains. She turns. *"Where did he . . ."*

Hushed voices echo through the darkness. She presses her back against the stone wall and holds her breath.

"It must be done before first light." *Gaspar.* The grand chamberlain frames the entryway to another wing of the castle, blocking the source of the second voice. Vesryn creeps closer.

"Of course it will be. I'm no fool."

Time grinds to a standstill. *That voice.* She's heard it before; she's certain of it.

But where?

She inches even closer, just enough to peer down the hallway with the slight angling of her head. But there's no one there.

Not Gaspar. And not the source of that voice. Hadn't they been there seconds ago?

Something makes a fluttering sound, like dried-out parchment caught in a breeze. Vesryn squints into the dark, and her heart stops.

I Killed the King

There, pressed against the stone archway, is a moth so pale it almost glows. The Arbiter—her goddess.

The hair on the back of Vesryn's neck stands on end. It's oppressively quiet—much too quiet. She squeezes her eyes shut and forces herself to breathe.

Vesryn barely has time to open them before the first blow.

10

OAK

OAK has trained his entire life to protect the king with weaponry and blunt force. But this is a moment that calls for a different sort of strength.

He marches toward the limp figure draped across the chaise. "Healer!" Oak barks.

"Necromancer," Ellion corrects.

"Whatever. You're familiar with corpses?"

At this, Ellion shrugs. "Unfortunately."

Oak points. "You and the beast tamer will help us take the king's body into his sleeping chamber and place him in bed as if he were napping."

"Why do I have to do that job?" Clove says, pouting. "I'm wearing a dress!"

Oak groans. "*Because*, tamer, I assume you've dealt with your fair share of death as well, between beast attacks and extracting scales and bones from corpses before rigor mortis sets in." He lifts his eyebrows, daring her to deny it.

Clove rolls her eyes, confirming his suspicions. She stomps toward Costis' body as the healer lurches unsteadily after her. When he uselessly extends a hand toward her, she swats him away, muttering something about this being the worst day of her life.

"What about me?"

Oak turns to find the princess still standing in the middle of the room, her face flushed. He nods to the chaise. "Sit and wait."

Melarie scoffs. "I'm more than just a lady-in-waiting. I could examine the paperwork for the treaty, perhaps read over the language—"

Oak huffs. This girl is not just going to sit down and be quiet. What does he care if she wants to flip through some papers she's already read? The king was smart enough to keep important documents far from his desk anyway. "Fine," he says with a wave of his hand. "Go do whatever it is you think you need to do, then. And where is the little one?"

"I believe she mentioned needing the washroom," Melarie says, already halfway across the room to Costis' hulking mahogany desk.

He frowns, his gaze sliding to the darkened hallway leading to the washroom. The servants' entrance is there, the door camouflaged with the same hideous floral wallpaper that patterns the entire room. It also serves as an emergency exit should the king find himself in danger. Most castles have such a door in the king's chambers, though not all are found in the washroom. Certainly the peasant mercenary couldn't know that?

Even if she did manage to slip from the chambers, Vesryn's weapons still sit in a pile on the floor beside Melarie's abandoned vase. He should absolutely hide those before one of the others gets the idea to use them. He scoops up the knife, dagger, and throwing star and—

"Aarrgggh!" Ellion yelps. There's a loud *thump*, followed by a squeal and a second *thump*.

Clove's voice carries from the sleeping chamber. "You weak, gutless little—"

"He's heavy!" Ellion whines.

Oak shoves the weapons into his pockets and rushes into the chamber with the princess close on his heels. When he sees the scene splayed out before him, he jerks to a stop, and Melarie crashes into him.

Somehow, Costis' corpse has ended up back on the floor—this time at the foot of his sprawling four-poster bed. The whites of his eyes have begun to yellow. His limbs are bent at painfully awkward angles, and the side of his gut is oozing a putrid, frothing liquid.

Clove, for all her grumbling over her dress, sits on the floor, cradling the dead king's head in her lap. When she glances up at Oak, her cheeks are wet with tears. "We dropped him," she says, her chin quivering. "What are we even doing? *How did I even get into this mess?*" A shaky little laugh escapes her lips, and it dawns on Oak that the beast tamer is losing it.

"It was my fault," Ellion says. The sincerity of his tone takes Oak by surprise. "I, um, I think I need to sit down. Right now, and also forever." Before Oak can give him anything else to do, the healer sinks to the floor and stretches out face down on the carpet with a groan.

He is glad that Kellam isn't here to witness this disgrace. And whether the mercenary is simply taking longer than usual in the washroom or she has escaped, Oak is suddenly glad that she is absent, too. He can almost feel the remnants of the feral girl's energy pressing in, and he does not care for it.

Her beady little eyes sear into his mind. *Perhaps the king had his suspicions of you, too.*

I Killed the King

Oak grits his teeth. Costis—his king, the good and noble man who raised him—trusted Oak with his life. He knows that for certain, without hesitation. The king would not have hired a secret guard. Not when he had Oak.

The girl is lying. Oak also knows *that* for certain. Without hesitation.

But he does not have time to figure out the truth—not yet, anyway. Right now, his king's corpse is quickly growing gray and rigid at his feet. He takes over cradling Costis' skull from Clove, careful not to look at his face. The healer looks over and begins to shift, but it's the beast tamer who circles back to the king's feet.

She glances up at him. "Ready?"

Oak's pulse pounds in his ears. He is not ready. He will never be ready for this.

"Ready when you are."

Together they lift the deadweight; the body is surprisingly heavy. Oak's muscles strain with the effort of lifting Costis' upper half. There's a flurry of movement as the healer and, astonishingly, the princess join him, each wrapping one of the corpse's arms over their shoulders.

The four of them make quick and quiet work of it. Oak gently lays Costis' head on his pillow, while Clove removes the king's boots. Ellion drapes a light blanket over him, tucking it beneath his chin. Melarie touches each of the king's eyelids and tenderly draws them closed for good. The four of them stand at his bedside in the dark for a long moment, as if they were waiting by his sickbed for him to die, instead of already having watched it happen. Twice.

Oak runs his hand over his face. He has never felt more tired in his life. "Go," he rasps, and thank the Gardener, they actually follow his order. Though the princess hesitates at the door before disappearing into the foyer.

When he's certain she's gone, he turns his attention to the knife still jutting from Costis' side. The Istellian crest—a spotted genet cat, sacred to the Lover, surrounded by fleur-de-lis—is barely visible amid the froth and blood.

He knew who the knife belonged to as soon as the mage-lights snapped back on. As soon as he saw the genet's tail taunting him from the wound, it took everything in him not to blow it all right then and there.

Captain Laurent always told Oak that rage is the deadliest weapon; it will obliterate everything in its orbit—including potential allies and evidence. *Our job is protection*, Laurent said during training. *We only attack when we know with certainty that we will not bring the whole castle to ruin.*

So he bit his tongue, pretending not to notice the Istellian rubies winking beneath the mage-lights. Instead, he watched the princess—watched all of them, actually—and listened carefully to the spaces between their words. One of them was a danger to his charge and he would find out who. And when Kellam got back—gods willing—he would tell the prince about all this. Certainly Kellam could not marry someone who might be plotting to overthrow the Avendellian crown.

He should not make it so easy for her to do so.

Oak wraps his fingers around the hilt and pulls until the blade slides free with a *thwick*. He bites the inside of his cheek to keep himself from screaming. He makes quick work of balling up the once-pristine sheets and pressing them to the wound to stanch some of the bleeding, even though it no longer matters.

I Killed the King

He can't bear to look at Costis' face while he holds the sheets to the corpse. Only hours ago, his king was ruddy-cheeked and ranting about the Vernevau family curse yet again. The topic had come up frequently in the past weeks as Costis' sanity dwindled. Oak would often enter the chambers to find the king mid-rant, waxing on about how he had *fixed this curse issue already* and how his *child will not succumb to rot*. What he wouldn't give to bear witness to those mad soliloquies again.

He abandons the balled-up sheets. Then he drops the knife, along with the confiscated weapons, behind the armoire.

Clink.

Oak freezes. Did the knife hit something? He shoves his fingers into the sliver of space between the armoire and the wall and slowly pulls. Each of the weapons falls to the floor and lands on the carpet with a series of soft thuds.

And something else.

He picks up a small glass vial and holds it in his palm. A yellow-tinged liquid glints in the light.

Basilisk venom.

Oh gods. Saliva pools under his tongue. He's going to vomit.

There is a highly deadly—highly *illegal*—substance in the king's sleeping chambers and Oak is holding it in the palm of his hand. If any of the others see him with this, his career—his life—is over.

The right thing to do would be to give it to the grand chamberlain. Gaspar took up basilisk lore as a part-time hobby years ago . . . although by the sheer existence of this venom in the castle, it could probably be classified as more than a hobby. But Kellam's words echo through his mind: *It will become a nightmare if Grand Chamberlain Weatherington is allowed to seize power.*

What is more powerful than the world's deadliest poison?

Outside the room, the others chatter. The princess paces past the door, her skirts blazing behind her.

Oak turns back to the armoire and opens the bottom drawer. Costis' undergarments are still neatly folded and white as snow. He tucks the vial in a pair of braies, smooths out the fabric, and shuts the drawer with a final click.

11

MELARIE

THE sight has not left Melarie's mind: Elodie's knife, buried in Costis' ribs. A tense quiet blankets the king's chambers, broken only by the miserable whimper from the—what did he call himself again? A *necromancer?* Whatever Ellion is, he curled into a ball shortly after helping with Costis' body, and no one seems entirely certain what to do with him.

Melarie's hands won't stop shaking.

Even if she denied it, the blade's ruby-crusted handle is unmistakably Istellian. The room narrows to a single, panicked focal point.

Think, Melarie, Solene's voice whispers. *What do you know? What do you need? What do you see?*

In the days before their father died, when his violent spells grew particularly erratic and it was only the girls and a few spare servants locked in that great, terrible castle with its king, Melarie and her sisters developed their own game of survival. It hadn't mattered that they'd all come from different mothers, or that Elodie would inherit the crown, and with it, the power to leave them with nothing.

They were sisters. They would protect each other no matter what came.

Ask the gods for a sign, Elodie's voice whispers. *And they will answer.*

Melarie once resented Elodie for the way she floated through life with devoted detachment, one foot planted in reality, the other firmly lodged in the realm of the divine. Prophetic dreams, whispers around corners, and visions of the Lover's genet cat had begun when Elodie was only a child. Melarie can't fault Elodie for insisting they're a part of some greater godly edict. She's just never been able to bring herself to believe it. If the Twelve have some kind of plan for Melarie's life, they've certainly never bothered to send her a sign.

Melarie is on her own.

What do you know? What do you need? What do you see?

Here is what she knows: That is absolutely her knife. But if Melarie can destroy the evidence, make it through the ball, and see that treaty inked, her bargain with Antoine will still stand. Melarie can board a ship and never return. And her sisters will be safe.

As for what Melarie sees . . .

"On the count of three, whoever murdered Costis should raise their hand," the necromancer slurs. "One . . . two . . . three. Tag, not it."

What Melarie sees is a disaster.

The beast tamer, Clove, has drifted toward the king's desk and is eyeing it as if she doesn't know whether to rifle through it or set it on fire. The necromancer trembles on the floor, his beaked mask askew. The guard marched back into the room after placing the dead king in bed and now stands at the door, staring at nothing. The girl who claimed to be hired protection—Melarie thinks the necromancer called her Vesryn, but she can't be sure—seems to have locked herself in the washroom.

Melarie forces herself to breathe. So it's back to this. Imprisoned once more in a castle with a murderer.

She needs an ally. She needs information. Her gaze darts to the vase, still on the floor, and then to Oak. Now that the light has evened out, Melarie can see that despite his size, he's just a boy—hardly much older than her. His eyes are swollen and red. He's either genuinely heartbroken or the best actor on the continent.

Gods help her, she sounds as paranoid as Delphine.

The necromancer, Ellion, has somehow found more wine, but his hands are shaking too badly to uncork it. He cradles it to his chest, twitching occasionally, his eyes half-lidded. Melarie can't help but stare. For all the books on mythology she's read, she's never heard of anyone whose magic dabbles in resurrection. She runs through a mental list of the Divine Twelve. All healers pray to the Courier, the god of life and death, but *this*? Raising something from the dead? Melarie can make no sense of it.

Clove turns from the desk and shoots Ellion a withering look. "Are you hoping to drink yourself to oblivion before they can take you to the gallows? You're doing a great job, if so."

"It's for your benefit," Ellion mutters. "Not mine."

Melarie peers at him, morbid interest pricking her. Could his magic be a punishment from the Courier? A warning to other healers of what will happen if they stray too far? Melarie has met very few acolytes of the mysterious god, but it always seemed like their patron was a punishing one.

If only Gabriel were here. Her father's temple advisor used to sneak Melarie dozens of books about the Twelve and their descendants. In those dark, lonely days, trapped high in the castle, the sea a distant glimmer, it had been easy to lose herself in stories of mages bound to the Courier and his hell-bound heron, of seers driven mad, mediums possessed by vengeful spirits, and tricksters getting the best of greater gods. She has always prided herself on being able to place which temple a practitioner belongs to. But for Ellion, she has nothing.

A different memory stirs. Of a myth Gabriel told her only once about the Weaver. As the heads of the pantheon, the Lover and Builder allowed themselves to create two extra children each to serve them—the Huntress and Dreamer for the Lover; the Gardener and Historian for the Builder. But that privilege did not extend to the three children they bore together, the ones who were just as powerful as their parents. Those three were each allowed only one child. The Sage created the Arbiter, the Mystic created the Shifter, and the Weaver created the Courier. All was well—until the Weaver made a mistake. While working the threads of fate at her loom, she pricked her finger on the spindle's end, and from her drop of blood, a second child sprang, slain before they could even learn their name.

Melarie can't help herself. "What happens if you don't drink?"

"I start seeing dead people," Ellion groans. "And they start seeing you, too. Very bad for everyone involved. Ask me how I know." Ellion shivers, pulls his legs to his chest, and closes his eyes.

Melarie watches him through narrowed eyes. His misery seems genuine.

But is he truly suffering from his magic—or his guilt?

Clove pokes Ellion with her foot. He groans but doesn't move.

From the sea of tulle, she fishes out a small sachet and retrieves a rather large pink pill. "Swallow this."

Oak scowls. "Where did that come from?"

Clove ignores him. With an incredible degree of patience, she angles Ellion's face to the ceiling, places the pill on his tongue, and pinches his nose. The necromancer coughs and thrashes; Clove's face remains calm, as though he's little more than a dog being given a flea charm for his own good. Ellion gasps, and Clove seizes his jaw in a funny way that makes his mouth pop open. She peers at his tongue to make sure the pill is gone.

"Good boy," she says dryly. At their stares, her shoulders draw up defensively. "It's only a tranquilizer. What? It works on unicorns."

Melarie needs to get out of here.

Once, after a particularly bad morning, Gabriel found Melarie cowering in one of the castle's lower alcoves. There had been no breeze that day; even the sea was still. He had arrived bearing a plate of olives, shining with oil under the summer sun—but his mischievous smile had frozen when he saw the bruises on Melarie's arms and the blood crusting her jaw.

"He usually hurts Elodie instead," Melarie whispered.

Gabriel had turned away, his voice oddly level as he said, "Make me a promise, little princess. One day, when you have a chance to escape—you will take it."

"Papa keeps the doors locked," Melarie had whispered dully. "There is no leaving this place."

The advisor's fingers curled into a fist, but when he looked at her again, mischief had returned to his eyes. "When the Weaver's threads close a door, find a window. And if it's locked? That's what rocks are for."

Melarie eyes the room. If only Gabriel were here now. She always felt safer in his presence. At least *someone* cared what happened to her.

Or maybe he hadn't cared as much as she'd thought, given that he'd never come looking for her once her father died.

No matter. Melarie learned a long time ago that all the stories about dashing men rescuing trapped princesses were nothing but nonsense.

Melarie will have to save herself.

Footsteps sound from somewhere behind her. Prince Kellam bursts through the washroom door like a bat from a cave, his face ashen. "Oak. I must speak with you. *Now.*"

Melarie straightens. "Anything you say to him, you say to us. Where is the magistrate?"

Kellam gives her a look of pure loathing. The prince thins his lips and turns toward his guard, ignoring her. "If we could speak privately? The roads have snowed over, so I'm afraid we may need to revisit our . . . strategy."

"We're *trapped* here?" Melarie demands. Her heart picks up speed.

She needs to get out of this room and find Antoine. If Kellam refuses to listen, she'll get his attention another way.

"In the foyer, Oak," says Kellam. "Now."

Melarie grips the vase—and hurls it against the wall.

The shatter is earsplitting. Porcelain bursts in all directions, littering the floor with delicate fragments of white and gold, and for a precious, beautiful moment, the room falls into stricken silence as they gape at her.

"You," Melarie gasps, pinching her thigh until tears spring to her eyes, "will not *treat* me like this!"

Melarie rips a painting from the wall and flings it across the room with a satisfying *crack*. She whirls and seizes a second one. She locks eyes with Kellam, her heart thudding, her fingernails sinking into the wood. Everyone gapes, except for Ellion, who lies on his back with his mouth open, drool trailing down his cheek.

"I may be a guest, but I am still royalty," Melarie spits. "I will not be held like some common prisoner because you've failed in your duty to keep proper tabs on the whereabouts of your court."

"My father is *dead*," protests Kellam. "I am doing my best while—"

"Your best has kept me trapped in a room with *murderers*!" Before Kellam can stop her, Melarie hurls the painting to the floor and sends her foot through the canvas.

The prince makes a pained noise, but he's not nearly as distraught as Melarie wants him to be.

There must be *something* in this room a person as vain as Kellam cannot stand to lose. Something precious. Something—

There.

Near the foyer, so small it's barely noticeable, hangs a different piece of art. It lacks the professional hand of a Dreamer disciple, so stark compared to those rich oil paintings blazing in golden frames throughout Costis' chambers. It's a simple sketch, framed in plain, polished beech. The image is of two little boys, one blond and one dark haired, beaming as they sit with their legs sprawled in the grass, their palms full of pale pink clusters of catkins. There is no flair to it; no ego.

It's perfect.

Melarie lunges for it—and a hand locks around her wrist.

"Not," Oak warns, "that one."

Though he's young, Oak is as immovable as his namesake. Melarie pushes against him, but the boy doesn't budge. He's strong; frighteningly so.

Oak's fingers still gripping her wrist, Melarie turns and locks eyes with Kellam.

"You cannot keep me here forever," she breathes. "My attendant, Antoine, has surely taken note of my absence. Do you truly want to add the abduction of a princess to your looming political nightmare?"

Prince Kellam looks back at her with an expression of pure misery. He reminds her, faintly, of Elodie—too beautiful for his own good, trapped in a role he never asked for. Melarie can only hope he's easier to manipulate than her eldest sister is.

"The foyer," Kellam says finally. He turns on his heel and disappears without seeing if Melarie follows, Oak trailing behind him like an obedient hound.

Melarie expects Clove to protest, but the beast tamer seems shocked into silence. Melarie steels herself and pushes her way into the foyer after Kellam. He and Oak are in the middle of a hurried conference, but when they see Melarie, they grow quiet. For a beat, she hesitates, her mind spinning. The castle is snowed in. There is a killer loose. Her plans have crumbled.

She needs to get to Antoine.

"Prince Kellam," Melarie begins. "I am your ally."

"Here we go," says Kellam. "This ought to be good."

"Let us work together," Melarie wheedles. "Let me attend the ball while you continue your search for the magistrate. I will breathe word of this to no one. I need the treaty as badly as you do. You and I can take turns visiting with guests—when one of us is out there, the other will be back here. And together, we may just survive the night with the treaty intact."

Kellam's brow furrows. Melarie gives him her softest smile, blinking up at him through her lashes, the picture of a woman tamed by a greater man.

"It would be ideal to have an ally," Kellam admits.

Melarie suppresses the urge to laugh. Delphine would eat this boy alive.

"You ought to attend the ball first." Kellam beams. "Oak shall go with you."

"Kellam," Oak barks, so startled he forgets his place. "No—"

Melarie's heart trips. "Oh, that's very kind, but unnecessary—"

"I *insist*." Now it's Kellam who reaches for her, eyes colder than the winter storm raging outside. "Oak will search for the magistrate while you make an appearance. I wouldn't want anything to happen to you. Nor would I want any more of your knives to end up in odd places."

The world spins. Melarie cannot breathe; she cannot think. Her lips move, but no sound comes out.

Her knife.

"I found it on the body," Oak says quietly. "Don't lie, princess. I know it's yours."

Cold horror creeps over Melarie.

"I'm sure there's an explanation," Kellam says with a tight smile. "It's like you said. We're allies, right?"

"Right," Melarie breathes. "Allies."

"Splendid!" Kellam releases her. He gives Melarie a bow that's far too deep for their shared status, and when he stands, the twinkle in his eye is so infuriating she wants to slap him. "Enjoy your dance, princess."

The door clicks shut behind him, and then it's just Melarie and Oak. She inches back, suddenly aware of how small she is compared to the guard. How much weaker. If he's the killer, Kellam might have just sealed her fate.

Oak's face reveals nothing. "Shall we?"

Melarie nods. She tries to breathe evenly, but as they slip into the hallway, she can't help but feel like she has escaped one trap for a second. She needs to find Antoine.

One way or another, Melarie is going to leave Castle Avendell and her foul luck behind tonight—or she'll die trying.

ELEVEN HOURS TO DAWN

12

CLOVE

CLOVE watches the chamber door close with a click. A sense of hopelessness settles into her bones. If this is what her beasts feel each time she locks the corral gate behind her, even though she means them no malice, she is truly sorry.

She has seen how much of a fight a literal princess had to put up for Kellam to allow her to leave this room—and with a guard, at that. The chances of Clove, a lowly tamer from a disgraced family, getting out of this room anytime soon? Approximately zero.

Clove shivers and clamps her arms over her chest. The prince has sequestered himself at his father's desk, his brow furrowed as he rifles through piles of parchment. She looks over to the freshly medicated healer, who has dragged himself onto the velvet chaise. He stares back at her with a vacant, heavy-lidded gaze before giving her a thumbs-up.

Basilisk roaming the castle or not, she has to get out of here.

Clove scans the room. When the princess and the guard left, Kellam made sure to lock the door behind them and shove the key into his breast pocket. But the mercenary . . . where is she? Vesryn said she was going to the washroom ages ago, yet no one seems concerned that she hasn't shown herself since. What if there's a way out in there?

"Excuse me, I need to use the washroom."

"Vesryn is still in there," Kellam says without so much as a glance in her direction.

"Oh! I had forgotten," Clove coos, a sweet smile playing on her lips. "It's been quite a while. Should I check on her?"

The prince stops rifling through the piles. He stares at Clove, his face unreadable. "No."

What little hope Clove had managed to muster sinks like a stone in her stomach. She bites her lip to quell her rising panic. "It is very important that I use the washroom," she says slowly, articulating every word. She stares at Kellam, willing him to understand.

She needs to go to the washroom.

She needs to get out of here.

If not for her own freedom, then to search for that basilisk before it has a chance to find anyone else. The more Clove has mulled over the venom-laced blade in Costis' side, the more certain she is that the beast is somewhere in this castle. She feels the truth of it in her bones.

Kellam drops the scroll he was holding with an irritated *thump*. He presses his knuckles into the desk and leans, his eyes boring into hers. "You need to stay in this room," he says, imitating her tone, "or else I will tell the magistrate that you have suspiciously tried to flee."

Clove huffs. "Fine." She marches back into the room with a wave of tulle cascading behind her. When she plops onto a velvet chair, her skirts puff out around her like a petal-pink macaron. Satisfied, Kellam goes back to the mess of parchment before him.

She eyes the prince from behind a layer of gauzy tulle. His face is smooth except for the crease between his eyebrows, but he appears more focused than fearful. The rest of his body is relaxed—shoulders low, muscles unwound, the sweat staining his collar evaporating by the second.

He must not know.

How could Kellam possibly know that a deadly snake lingers among his nation's most important courtiers tasting the sweat in the air with its forked tongue, and not be racked with worry?

That said, Clove does not know the prince very well—or at all, even. His talent for lying could be just as potent as his charm. There's only one way to find out.

She pushes down the tulle so she has a clear view. "Prince Kellam," she says lightly, "what is your opinion on Avendell's law that owning or housing any breed of basilisk is illegal?"

Kellam pauses to scratch his head, his eyes still skimming the parchment in front of him. "Huh? Oh, um. I believe Father's stance is—well, *was*—that basilisk keeping must be highly regulated, but it isn't illegal by any means."

Clove's mouth drops open. *This* is certainly news to her. And it's certainly not what Gaspar Weatherington proclaimed when he knocked on the Beaufortes' cabin door all those years ago. She jumps to her feet in a flurry of pink. "And what is the grand chamberlain's stance on it?"

Finally, the prince stops what he's doing and lifts his gaze. "Why are you so interested in knowing? If you're looking for someone to blame for your family's misfortune, perhaps you should look inside your own home."

That does it. Rage burns through Clove with so much force that she wouldn't be surprised if Kellam felt the heat radiating off her skin. No one knows better than Clove and her three brothers that Knox Beauforte prefers the woods and whiskey to his own kin. After their mother died, he was never the same. But it was the grand chamberlain's visit that permanently broke him.

She reaches into the pocket hidden among her skirts and slams the envelope down on the desk. "Then what do you make of *this*?"

For a moment, neither of them moves. The only sounds in the room are the healer's garbled sleep talk punctuated by the snap of the wind outside. Kellam's mouth works. He slides his hand to the cream-colored envelope and runs his thumb over the broken wax seal: a stag surrounded by mountain laurels.

It's then that Clove notices Kellam's own signet ring is missing from his hand. She heard once that the prince bore a fawn and laurel buds—the juvenile versions of his father's emblem. In that way, Clove pitied Kellam; as the youngest, and the only girl, her family had deemed her weak and useless straight from the womb. She suspected that, like Clove, Kellam hadn't been given the chance to prove himself, either.

The prince slides the invitation from the envelope, and a separate note flutters out with it. He picks it up from the desk and reads. "Father said he wanted to 'give back what was taken,'" Kellam says slowly. "What did he . . ."

The rest of the question falls away as Kellam begins sorting through the parchments again. Clove taps her nails on the desk.

They don't have time for bookkeeping. "Prince Kellam, I—"

"Here!" he says, unrolling a bound scroll on top of the pile. "The final copy of the treaty. If my father had intended to restore something of value to the Beaufortes, and invited your father to this ball to present it to him, then it will be written among the decrees that will go into law when this document is legitimized." The prince slides his finger down the page as he reads. "There are twenty-seven decrees—most are things having to do with the aftermath of the war, like restoring temples and reparations—but maybe there is . . . wait."

Clove's pulse hitches. "What is it?"

Kellam frowns. He starts again at the top. "I know there are twenty-seven decrees. Father made me memorize the number. But there are only twenty-six on this copy." Before Clove can say anything, the prince is on his feet and rifling through the drawer. He pulls out a second, smaller scroll and unrolls it. "This is the draft," he murmurs, already reading.

"There," Clove breathes. She points to the last and final decree: the twenty-seventh. "*All property and assets previously seized from Knox Beauforte are to be returned to his estate, effective immediately upon signing.*"

Kellam looks at her, his bottle-green eyes laced with panic. "Why would my father take this out at the last moment?"

Spots appear in the corners of Clove's vision. She grips the desk to steady herself. "I don't think he did," she says softly. "Gaspar Weatherington was the one who seized those assets in the first place. And I think he intends to keep them."

Kellam pulls in a breath. "And what were those assets, exactly?"

"Basilisk eggs."

Clove closes her eyes and tries to force air into her lungs. She must look deranged to Kellam, and in truth, she kind of is. Clove is certain that every stitch holding her together is about to pop. She swallows. "Prince Kellam, does anyone in this castle know anything about basilisks?"

When the prince doesn't answer, Clove opens her eyes. Now *Kellam's* eyes are pinched shut, and the sweat dotting his collarbone has reappeared. "Prince Kellam?"

"Gaspar," he croaks.

Clove lets out a long breath. She knew it. That manipulative, power-hungry maniac hadn't taken the Beaufortes' basilisk eggs and killed all their living snakes on the directive of the king. Or if Costis had told Gaspar to do it, it was only because Gaspar had whispered lies about the threat the Beaufortes and their beasts posed to the Crown. Until then, her father had worked diligently for the Vernevaus, tending to their menagerie when called and providing any talons or tufts of fur for elixirs with honor.

"Grand Chamberlain Weatherington has a bit of an obsession with them," Kellam continues, rubbing his hand over his face. "My father has allowed him to retain a pair on the grounds for years, so long as no one knows where they're kept." Kellam drops his hand and looks at her with baleful eyes. "I'm sure you already know why as few people as possible must know of their presence."

"One basilisk could produce enough venom to kill the entire Istellian high court by sunup," says Clove. The words taste like acid on her tongue.

She has to tell him. Now. "Your father's wound . . . that strange froth to it? That's what happens when blood interacts with basilisk venom."

The prince's head snaps in her direction. "What? How—"

Clove lifts her palms. "I don't know. I don't know how, or who, but I do know this: The venom has to be used within an hour of being harvested for it to be effective."

The heaviness of the implication hangs between them. After a moment, Kellam nods. "There's one in the castle, then. There has to be. Right?"

She opens her mouth to confirm it, but the words catch in her throat. This is something that she has never spoken aloud. Something she was certainly never planning on telling the prince or any of the others.

But that was before they were trapped here with no escape, before Clove knew the depths of Gaspar Weatherington's depravity. People could die—no, they *will* die if she doesn't tell Kellam the truth.

She takes a breath. "Sometimes I can . . . feel them. Basilisks mostly, but other creatures, too. My skin will prickle with cold as a nearby snake slithers through a snowdrift, or the scent of raw meat will come out of nowhere and I'll know that the wilderwolves are hungry. I can see their shadows, if they're close enough." She bites her lip. "There is a basilisk in the bowels of this castle."

Kellam says nothing. He stares at her for so long that Clove is tempted to reach out and shake him. Finally, he says, "Who is your patron?"

Clove blinks. "Of all the things I thought you might say, that was not one of them."

"Well, you've never considered that maybe this *skill* of yours is a bit more than natural instinct? Perhaps there's a god or goddess who believes in you, whether or not you believe in them."

The prince's words flicker in her mind like a freshly born star. Is it even possible? Could someone—a god, even—have chosen her? The only deities Clove has any experience with are the ones who are rumored to be dormant in the mountains: the Sage and her daughter, the Arbiter. But both of those goddesses are associated with reason and logic, not with . . . with whatever this is. The other Avendellian gods—the Builder, the Gardener, and the Historian—don't seem to fit, either. And Clove knows nothing of the gods buried on Istellian land.

So who could it be?

"I had a tutor once who insisted that everyone has some kind of magic," says Kellam. He stares into his open palm. "It just doesn't come as easily for some of us."

An expression Clove can't interpret settles onto the prince's face as his eyes lift to a potted fern on the corner of the desk, its ruffled fronds cascading to the floor. A thought blooms in her mind. For all that Clove has heard about King Costis' unparalleled green magic, she's never heard a word of Kellam's. Wouldn't the Crown want to make it known that Avendell's heir is just as deft with his magic as his predecessor, especially as Costis' health waned? Clove shakes away the thought. What does she know of royal politics? Plus, it's not like she's exactly been paying attention while hunting for beasts in the woods.

"I just really believe," Kellam says, curling his fingers into his palm, "that anyone can be chosen."

Clove considers this. *Chosen.* The word is as foreign to her as

Istellian wildlife. Clove has never been chosen for anything—not by her father, or her brothers, or even a boy. She is no one special to anyone but the beasts in her makeshift sanctuary back home.

Maybe that's the point? Her eldest brother, Cypress, always joked that every sick and wounded beast eventually found their way to Clove; it was like the wild could smell the empathy on her. Only Cypress hadn't called it that. He'd said it was weakness.

Clove isn't weak—she knows that for sure. A beast would never approach someone who didn't have the heart, or the resources, to protect them. They're much too smart for that.

"How do I do it?" Clove whispers. Her cheeks burn.

"First, you need to relax." Warmth flares on her bare arms and Kellam positions her to face him. He stares at her without speaking for so long that Clove begins to sweat.

"So . . . is this what relaxed looks like for you?" Kellam says.

She glares at the prince as she lets out a long, slow breath that sounds more like a hiss. He shrugs. "Good enough. Now close your eyes."

Kellam's voice floats through her mind as he tells her to *breathe*, and *calm down*, and *listen*. Before she can consider how silly this all is, the world drops away, replaced with earsplitting silence.

There are beasts everywhere.

Clove can *feel* them. Something with wings hovers in the northern turret. Another creature, this one smaller and quicker, flits past the chamber door.

A low hiss echoes in her ears, and a gritty cold presses against Clove's stomach. The basilisk slowly slithers up, up, up a stone staircase.

A resounding *thud* ricochets through the chambers. Clove's eyes snap open and Kellam jumps. It came from down the hall. Before either of them can move, the mercenary appears in the sitting room, looking as if she'd come straight out of a nightmare.

"Vesryn," Kellam breathes. "What happened?"

Already the cut beneath the girl's eye has begun to swell. She spits blood into a potted plant and turns to them. "Where," says Vesryn, wiping her mouth, "is Ellion?"

13

ELLION

ELLION had forgotten how awful it is to meddle with the dead. He hates the way their emotions linger long after their lives have slipped away, leaving a trail of broken images and terror in their wake. Were it the elderly and the satisfied whose final moments Ellion bore witness to, perhaps they would have left him with a sense of peace, some words of comfort for their families, even a grain of wisdom from a life well lived.

But so far, the only souls Ellion has ever tried to wake have been the sick and the damned.

Pain wracks Ellion's entire body, and even with the tranquilizer numbing his magic, chills roll through him in occasional, terrible waves. In the gaps the tranquilizer cannot fill, the dead of Castle Avendell stir. He cannot get the taste of Costis' horror out of his mouth—nor the other feeling that came with it, the one Ellion doesn't understand.

Why would a king feel guilty over his own murder?

Uneasy quiet blankets Costis' chambers in Princess Melarie and Oak's absence. The beast tamer and prince stand behind the massive desk, a riot of parchment spread before them. They're as still as death, and neither is looking at him.

"Ellion."

That voice. Yet another ghost come to haunt him. Reluctantly, Ellion picks his head up and peers at the girl he has not seen since that ill-fated day back at the Academy.

"Ves," he croaks. "Hey."

A dozen emotions flit across her face, but her eyes still crinkle in that gentle way, their vivid hue softening to lavender. And suddenly, Ellion is just a boy again, hopelessly in love with his best friend. "Hey."

An awkward silence stretches. Vesryn has grown; her cheeks are sharper, and she's taller, though she still has that skinny, knobby frame that Luma once snarked was *painfully malnourished*. The memory of that name makes Ellion's necklace hang heavier.

Gods, if Ellion doesn't wish he and Vesryn had reunited anywhere else. At the very least, he would have worn a clean set of robes.

She streaks across the room and leans over him. Her face comes into sharper focus; her lip is split, and her eye is blackening. Ellion's thoughts swirl, muddy and out of reach. Was she bleeding earlier? He can't remember.

"Ellion," Vesryn says, her face guarded, careful not to look at his necklace. Blood drips from her lip. "I need to talk to you."

She's here. She's *real*.

And her left eye is definitely swelling shut.

How long has he been out? He swore it was only minutes, and hadn't Vesryn said she was just going to the washroom? The room spins on a dizzy tilt. The tranquilizer has cut off his access to his magic, but it's also made it difficult to stand or think. He's dreamed of finding Vesryn again after everything went wrong between them, playing out the self-punishing fantasy over and over in his head. He's even gone so far as to rehearse the first thing he'd say to her in his mirror.

I miss you. I'm sorry. Come home.

Instead he blurts, "What happened to your face?"

Storm clouds roll across Vesryn's face. "That's all you have to say to me? *What happened to your face?*"

"No, wait—*Ves.*" Ellion tries to reach for her but ends up lurching and falling on his face. Self-loathing burns through him. He's a mess. He knows it. What he wouldn't give for those easy, hope-bright days before this parasitic magic crept in—when he was clearheaded and sharp-tongued, and it wasn't a miracle to walk steadily instead of stumbling. What he wouldn't give to *sleep*, peacefully and deeply, without ward charms clutched to his chest to fend off hungry ghosts.

Finally, Ellion manages to pick himself up.

Whether it's the sharp edge of regret or the tranquilizer loosening its grip on his mind, his head is much clearer when he's standing. Vesryn positions herself with her back to the desk. She puts a finger to her lips and glances meaningfully in the direction of the washroom. "In there."

"Hold on," Kellam says, "no one needs to go back into that washroom."

"I need ten minutes in there with Ellion," Vesryn says, drawing out the words. She reaches into her pocket and pulls out something gold and shiny, then tosses to Kellam. The prince's eyes flash as he seems to recognize what it is just before catching it in his palm.

"Ten minutes," Vesryn says, turning on her heel. "If we're both not out by then, feel free to call the guards. Come on, Ellion."

Ellion half lurches, half walks into the washroom, and sinks to the floor. Vesryn steps around him and shuts the door. For a beat, quiet stretches between them. The washroom blurs at the edges. Ellion can barely keep his head up, let alone find the right words for Vesryn after all this time apart. He thinks he ought to start with *I miss you.* He wants to tell her to come home.

Instead, all that comes out is, "Some party, huh?"

Vesryn's face does a dizzying series of twitches. She pinches the bridge of her nose, clearly searching for patience, and when she speaks, her words come out soft, quick, and furious. "What happened to you? I've not seen you in years. I have missed you and worried about you, and finally I see you again and you're—you're—"

"An embarrassment to my family name and an absolute wreck?"

Her lips quiver. "I didn't know if you were alive, Ellion. It's been ages. And then I come here, and you're a trembling mess, and the king is dead, and I'm meant to believe your presence is a coincidence?"

Ellion's heart flips. Even in the haze, he catches the dark undertone of her words.

What is Vesryn getting at? That she thinks *he* might have killed the old bastard?

Maybe she's changed more than he feared.

Ellion hides the crushing sensation in his chest with a shrug and a flippant, "I mean, given the optics . . ."

"This isn't funny!" Vesryn hisses. She casts an uneasy glance back at the closed door. "For once in your life, can you be serious?"

"Sure. What are *you* doing here, Ves?" Ellion levels a stare at her. "Or do you prefer to be called *Gisele* these days?"

Vesryn freezes.

"I remember when I first heard about the killings," Ellion continues quietly. It's a monumental effort to make his words come out solid instead of slurred. "All these terrible men, all over Avendell and Istellia, suddenly dropping dead, each with one common thread: They died painlessly, poisoned by a healing tonic brewed too strongly."

Vesryn's face is coldly blank. "Strange."

"My father thought so, too," says Ellion. "The rumors were so bad he was forced to do a full audit of the Academy of Healing Arts' students and staff, current and former, but everyone who had passed through the Academy's halls long enough to acquire that kind of knowledge was accounted for." He stares at her. "All of them except for one."

Silence stretches between them. Ellion's heart pounds so hard it hurts. A part of him aches for her to deny it, but he can't say he's surprised when Vesryn lifts her chin and says, "You've always been straight with your words, Ellion. Ask me."

"Did you kill the king?"

The words hang between them. If Vesryn killed him—if after all these years he's finally got her back and her presence here is the very thing that could bring Ellion doom—

What would he do? Who would he choose?

His country? His life, what little he has left of it?

Or *her*? The only girl he ever truly loved. The sun his planet orbits around, even now.

Ellion knows the answer before Vesryn speaks, and it sends a chill far colder than the winter storm outside straight to his bones.

"It wasn't me," Vesryn says finally.

It takes everything in Ellion not to slump with relief.

"I was invited here to remove Costis from the picture, but someone else got there before me. And just because I got an invite, it doesn't mean I would do it."

"Ves," Ellion croaks. The cold in her face breaks him. It's one thing to hear the rumors; it's another to know. "I don't understand. You wanted to heal. You wanted to *help*."

"No, you wouldn't understand," Vesryn says flatly. She looks away. "We don't all have a famous name and a rich father to bail us out. I make ends meet in any way I can, and I try to do it in a way that still saves a shred of my soul. So, yes, I was hired to kill Costis. But I hadn't yet decided if I was going to follow through. I was still investigating when you all barged in."

"Investigating," Ellion scoffs. "What are you, some type of rogue constable?"

"I have a line." Her eyes narrow. "I may no longer wear his chain, but you'd see none of the Courier's black beads on my neck. I would never hurt an innocent."

"Like how you'd never hurt Luma?" The words pop out without him meaning them to.

All the color drains from Vesryn's face. "Luma was an accident."

"Was it?" Ellion has the sense that he's standing on the edge of the cliff and watching a dam collapse. He can't help himself. That bead around his neck has been a weight that grows worse with each passing year, and right now, Ellion's neck feels like it's going to break.

When he dreamed of finding Vesryn again, this wasn't how he wanted it to go. But he can't seem to stop himself. He can't shake the sting of the accusation she just lobbed at him, as if his life has been so perfect and easy since that day. *A famous name and a rich father.* As if after everything they've been through together, Ellion is just another spoiled noble boy who can bend the world to his will.

As if Ellion hasn't also lost everything that mattered.

The room blurs and spins. Words long buried spill out before Ellion can stop them, buoyed by a tidal wave of fresh hurt. "You know, I've never really been able to figure that out. You were better at antidotes than anyone else, but suddenly, Luma is the one you couldn't save?"

Vesryn goes deathly pale—and Ellion knows he has gone too far.

"Ves," he says. "Wait, I'm sorry. That wasn't—that came out wrong."

"Cook told me something once," Vesryn says flatly. "She told me not to get too close. To remember I was never truly one of you, but someone who served you. That it didn't matter we were friends, that I kept your secrets and you kept mine. One day she told me something I'll never forget—*to the Evercrafts, you'll always be something to own. And the thing about belongings is they're easy to discard.*"

Ellion flinches. "Come on, that's not fair. You know I didn't mean—"

"No, you never mean it," Vesryn says softly. "But you said it. And if you won't listen to me, I guess we're done here."

"Vesryn, wait, *please*—" Ellion tries to lunge for her, but he misses entirely and collides with the wall instead. Vesryn sidesteps him easily, her face carefully blank even as tears spill down her cheeks.

And before Ellion can stop her, before he can explain—she's gone, vanishing through the washroom door the way she came.

Ellion lies on the floor, moaning as crippling, blistering cold moves through him in waves. His hands have not been warm since he arrived at the snow-battered castle, but the icy dread that flows through him now knocks the breath from his lungs.

He just needs to find her and explain. Apologize, and finally tell her the whole truth.

And he'll start with Luma. It'll make him sound like an ass, but he'll tell Vesryn that while he cared about Luma, the truth was that the thing he liked most about her was that she liked *him*. There had never been any substance to her, and it wasn't entirely her fault; she was a merchant's daughter, spoiled and pretty, and when they were in a room full of people, the way she glittered made her easy to like. But it was never Luma he wanted, or any of the girls who batted their eyelashes at him—it was the girl by the hearth.

He knew Vesryn could never return his feelings. They would have only been a burden, and it had taken a decade for her to feel safe with him. He refused to ruin her trust in him over something as fickle as a childhood crush. Feelings could fade—and Ellion had truly believed it would be him and Vesryn forever, thick as thieves until the end.

But now, Ellion worries that by never telling Vesryn just how much he loved her, he let her believe she was never loved at all.

He needs to tell her he's sorry. That he's missed her terribly, and he doesn't give a damn about a dead king or his stupid, spoiled son and their frost-laden ball. He just wants her to be all right. Vesryn is the only person on this earth who ever truly felt like family. He lost her once. He can't lose her again.

But first he needs to get up.

The pain eases. Slowly, the world creeps back in; the distant heat of the king's hearth, the coolness of the tile, the clamminess of his skin. Something vile coats Ellion's front. He vomited on himself without realizing it, and the insides of his palms are lined with bloody crescent moons from where he dug his fingernails in.

Ellion stares at the door. He's only just gotten Vesryn back.

So why does it feel like he's already lost her?

14

VESRYN

VESRYN has often had nothing except the clothes on her back, yet she has always had hope. She *has* to. There is no worshipping the Arbiter without believing that despair will be tempered by something brighter one day. The scales always eventually balance out.

But in this moment, there's only devastation, bleak and brutal, with no end in sight.

As soon as she spins away from the king's chambers and Ellion's stupid face, the tears come with a fury that frightens her. Vesryn dips her head as she marches down the second-floor hallway, careful not to make eye contact with any lingering guards or servants.

As she descends the hidden stairwell, a familiar darkness envelops her like a traveling cloak. Her footsteps slow. She pauses somewhere between floors, no longer with the rotting king but not yet among the boisterous party. When she's certain she's out of sight and earshot of any drunk stragglers or sharp-eyed guards, she stops, touches her forehead to the frigid stone wall, and sobs.

How could she be so naive? For a split second in time, she allowed herself to hope that things could go back to the way they were. Vesryn had simply been yearning for the old Ellion, but this was who was left after . . .

After.

She pats her face dry with her palms and turns. There is a single window cut high into the stone, but the moon and stars are nowhere to be found. Only an eerie glow from the freshly packed snow against the glass. Farther down, two mage-lights flicker. Her eyes search for moths.

The winged creatures have presented themselves to her more frequently as of late, which has only made Vesryn double down on her nightly prayers. There's an old country belief that the more devout one is to a god or goddess, the more it feeds them—the more energy it gives that god so they can reward your devotion, no matter if you reside near the place where they slumber or not. She has never fully believed it, but she wants to. She has to believe there's a reason to continue carrying all this, or else she will crumble.

Vesryn closes her eyes and presses her chilled hand to her chest to calm her racing heart. Even though she currently hates him, Ellion still finds her in the blackness. A memory as vivid as the summer sun overpowers her, thrusting her back into the stuffy dorm room at the Academy of Healing Arts, with Luma's shaking hand reaching for hers as the light left her eyes.

It had been frigid that night, too, and Vesryn's lips were blue by the time she knocked on Ellion's door. When it swung open, a girl with copper hair to her waist stood in the frame. Her eyes darkened for only a second, but it was a second too long. Even then, Vesryn noticed everything.

"You brought the cat, yay!" Luma chirped a little too forcefully. Vesryn glanced down at the silky black cat nestled beneath her cloak, its two triangular ears poking out from under the wool.

Each student at the Academy was assigned a non-magical animal on their first day—usually a stray cat, but sometimes a weasel or fat bullfrog if they were running low on felines. The purpose of the pet was to practice minor spells and incantations on them, all with the purpose of granting them the greatest health possible, and most students didn't get attached. But Vesryn wasn't most students.

Before Vesryn could respond, the cat's head popped out from the cloak and it hissed. Luma narrowed her eyes before spinning back into the room, the door still hanging open. Vesryn pressed her lips into the soft patch of fur between its ears to stifle her grin. "Be *nice*, Rue," she whispered, slowly clicking the door shut behind her.

"We were just about to practice for our baccalauréat," Luma cooed. The slender girl sat perched atop Ellion's lap like a little bird, puffing out her chest and preening. It took everything Vesryn had not to roll her eyes. They'd met twice before, and each time Ellion's girlfriend acted as if Vesryn would snatch him out from under her the second she looked away no matter how many times both Vesryn and Ellion assured her there was not, and never had been, anything between them.

"And how are you planning to study? It's a practical exam," Vesryn said, making her way over to the clicking radiator. She rubbed her blue-tipped fingers together as the warm air caressed her skin.

In order to graduate, every secondary student in Avendell had to pass their school's version of the baccalauréat—a cumulative exam that had a reputation for being soul-crushingly difficult. Most schools required a written test. The Academy of Healing Arts required a practical exam. Each student would stand before the administration while a dying animal writhed and yowled on the marble floor at their feet. Within ten minutes, the student had to identify which poison had been used, create an antidote, and dispense it to the creature before its heart stopped. Ellion had joked that he'd rather take a fifty-page exam, even though he was garbage at taking tests. Vesryn had always been an excellent test taker, but she had agreed.

Vesryn turned to find Luma's eyes glinting in the lamplight. She hopped off Ellion's lap and reached for her bag. A series of clinks and clanks filled the room as she pawed through its contents. "Ellie got a little information on which poison they're using for this season's exam."

Vesryn's eyes narrowed at her friend. "Oh, did you, *Ellie?*"

Two splotches of pink rose high on Ellion's cheeks. He pretended to fiddle with the row of quills on his desk. "You know how my parents are. They were asking some of their old classmates, who are on the board now, and one thing led to another, and they got the inside scoop that this season's test poison is—"

"Basilisk venom!" Luma blurted. She held up a tiny glass vial of translucent liquid, a smug smile playing on her lips.

But Vesryn barely registered the poison. Her eyes slid back to Ellion. This time, his gaze lifted to meet hers, as if daring her to say the words festering beneath her tongue. Before she could think it through, the accusation flew from her mouth. "It's cheating! Your parents come from a long line of royal healers. You already have every advantage possible." Vesryn's shoulders sagged. Exhaustion swept through her and, not for the first time, she wished she had stayed in her own dorm room on the other side of the grounds. Ellion stared at her, the pink in his cheeks beginning to cool. And then Vesryn saw it: his chin trembled.

It had always been his tell, even when they were kids. Ellion may have gotten good at fooling everyone with his hypnotic eyes and sharp jokes, but he still felt things. He was feeling them now; Vesryn was certain. "You're so smart, Ellion. There's no reason to cheat. You're too good for this."

As soon as the words left her lips, Vesryn knew they were exactly the wrong ones. Ellion Evercraft may have felt things, but he didn't *like* to. And he especially didn't like it when someone noticed.

His mouth clamped shut, and any emotion that had betrayed him was quickly locked away in the recesses of his mind. He stood from his desk chair and smoothed out his tunic. "You're right. I don't need to cheat, but who's to say I wasn't trying to help out a *dear friend*?" As he said the last two words, Ellion arched his brow. *Try me, old friend.*

Luma's eyes darted between them. "Does anyone care that I have this—"

"You don't think I can pass on my own." Vesryn's voice was softer than she had wanted it to be, and it cracked at the end, but she refused to look away. "I'm an excellent test taker. I have much more practice with herbal remedies than you, and I aced my poisonous substances practicum."

A muscle twitched in Ellion's jaw. "But magic, Ves? Not so much."

Ice shot down Vesryn's spine. The cold pressed on her lungs, heavy and unforgiving, leaving her gasping. *How dare he bring that up, and in front of Luma.*

Everyone at the Academy knew that healing elixirs were only one part of the job. An effective healer had to be able to channel magic through their hands and into the patient to fully restore their health, which was why so many of them paid weekly alms to the Courier. Potions would only take them halfway; at best, they bought everyone a bit more time. Technically, healers didn't need to have magical ability, which Vesryn did not. But they had to remain open channels worthy of the Courier's power.

Which Vesryn was not.

And Ellion knew it.

"Hellooo." Luma's voice cut in, breaking the spell Ellion had over her. Vesryn glanced across the room. The copper-haired girl still stood in front of her open bag, one hand on her hip, the other still clutching the tiny vial. "The easiest solution here is to try it out."

Ellion spun around. "Excuse me?"

"Why not?" Luma shrugged. "She says she's got this exam in the bag, so why not give her a chance to prove it?" She waggled the vial in front of her face, the liquid sloshing angrily up the glass. "Let's see what Vesryn can do."

A cold sweat formed on Vesryn's brow. "And who do you suppose we poison?" she said, forcing her gaze to stay locked on Luma. She didn't want the girl to think, even for a second, that experimenting on Rue was an option.

Luma hardly even blinked before saying, "Me."

Heavy footfalls echo above her, shaking Vesryn loose from the memory. She closes her eyes, and the relentless cold of the stairwell rushes in to greet her. *Rue.* She hadn't thought about the cat in a long time; she tried not to, actually. After she'd been kicked out of the Academy, she never saw him again. She's always clung to the hope that the advisors rehomed him, but a deeper part of her knows the cat probably never made it into another student's arms.

Vesryn holds her breath and listens. Muffled voices in terse conversation join the footsteps. Vesryn can't make out the words, but just by the urgency of the movements on the floor from which she came, she already knows: People must be looking for her.

She only looks more suspicious now that she's on the run again. If they find her, she's certain Kellam won't even give her the chance to prove herself; they'll take her straight to the magistrate. There will be an investigation, if only for show, and they will dig into her past, and then they will see why she got kicked out of the Academy when she was only a fortnight away from graduating. They will see Luma's death, and perhaps all the others, on her hands. Vesryn will spend the rest of her life rotting in the dungeons, if they don't immediately send her to the gallows.

It may be a small life, but it's still hers. She spent her last coin to get here, and it looks as though she will not receive payment tonight. And Ellion . . . now that she knows for certain that whatever they once had is irreparable, this life is all Vesryn has left. She will not spend it as a prisoner. *Think.* She squeezes her eyes closed.

Think about this, please! Ellion's voice, strung out with panic, forces her back into the memory. Even then, Vesryn knew his plea held no weight. Luma had already swallowed the poison.

"I trust you," Luma had said. "You're the best healer in this place. If she can't heal me, I know you will."

The rest comes in pops and flashes, like festival fireworks, as it always does. Vesryn had read once that the Historian could restore fragmented memories, but even if the god weren't sleeping, she wouldn't ask for that. She prefers that some parts of this moment stay hidden in the darkest corners of her mind.

Like the death rattle of magic sputtering out in Vesryn's veins, while Luma's eyes rolled to the back of her head.

Her nicked-up fingers shaking as she tried to crush the scarlet poinciana flowers for the antidote.

Ellion's mournful bellows as he thrust his own hands to his girlfriend's convulsing body.

The deep-rooted knowledge that Luma was already gone, and the horror of watching a bloated, broken *thing* shaped like her rise from the dead at Ellion's desperate touch.

In the stairwell, Vesryn's mouth has gone dry. She knows what comes next in this memory, and she also knows there's no way out of it. It won't release her from its grip until she sees it through to the end, just as she has a million times before. She tries to swallow.

The Luma-shaped thing's screams of agony, begging for relief from the pain.

Ellion's baleful dark blue eyes looking up at her. *Do it*, he whispered. *Ves, please.*

The weight of her paring knife, slick with berry juice and her own blood, as it sliced through the undead thing's already graying neck.

Vesryn's eyes snap open. She presses her hands over her mouth to prevent herself from heaving.

She couldn't channel enough magic to save Luma. Vesryn had hoped beyond hope that this time would be different, that her emotions would light a match to the magic and it would spread from her veins to Luma's like wildfire. But it was the same as always: not enough.

Because no matter how talented Vesryn was with healing elixirs, there was no room for that kind of gray area in service to the

Courier. The god would never claim an acolyte who acted as an agent of death, and she had committed unforgivable acts to follow Ellion to the Academy. Small odd jobs here and there, jobs she heard about on the black market that were quick, and painless, and lucrative. Jobs that involved a little blood, if you could handle it.

Vesryn could always handle it. She had no magic of her own to claim, but she thought that if she did, it would be her ability to take a life without losing her heart. In the end, it was this gift—the very thing Ellion had shamed her for—that saved him from having to spill his dangerous secret power to the board. Though they still kicked them both out.

Later, she'd heard that Ellion's parents had made a hefty donation to the Academy, and that he'd returned to finish his studies. Vesryn never went back. She couldn't.

She could not heal when death was her calling.

And Ellion could not forgive her when healing was his.

A gust of wind slams against the window with such force that the stones quake beneath her. The mage-lights flicker once, twice, then die in quick succession. Her pulse stutters.

What is she doing, hiding away in the dark like the grimy pest Ellion and the others think she is? Vesryn knows more about how this world works than anyone else in that room; she's traveled both their countries from shore to shore, paid alms at every abandoned temple she's come across from the mountains to the sea.

That presence in the alcove—that voice whispering to Gaspar? It's familiar in the same manner of a bad dream. Vesryn knows the tone of it, the memory of something dark and power-hungry, but she can't make out the details. Whoever—or whatever—that voice belongs to, Gaspar Weatherington knows it exists, and that is enough to prove that it's dangerous.

Vesryn mumbles a curse word under her breath. And then she takes the stairs two at a time back the way she came. When she reaches the second floor, she turns in the opposite direction of the king's chambers. The old mahogany doors creak only a little when she opens them, and when she's certain no one is coming after her, Vesryn finally breathes.

If there's anywhere in Avendell that will have an answer to this mystery, it's the royal library. And, mercifully, it's completely empty. Small clusters of half-melted candles on various desks and end tables cast buttery light on the rows of cloth-bound books. Vesryn has no idea what to search for or where to start, but instinct pulls every muscle in her body taut. Her time is dwindling, and quickly. She lifts a candle from the nearest surface and starts down the first aisle.

A voice whispers, *I can give you what you long for . . . if you're willing to bargain for it.*

She pauses. The voice *sounds* like Ellion, but he's still back in the king's chambers. He can't be here . . . can he? Vesryn glances over her shoulder. Only dusty books bound to the shelves by chains wink back at her.

If you're willing, the voice says again. This time, the words shake something loose within her.

Those are the same words, spoken by a different voice at the bottom of the gorge. The voice that whispers to her in her dreams, never allowing her to forget that she will spend her life trying to right her wrongs with a knife and a prayer, and it will never be enough.

Vesryn bargained with that voice for Ellion's life once before.

Perhaps this is an omen that she has paid her penance. Maybe, finally, she will have earned her peace.

Her breath catches in her chest. She turns down another aisle, her fingers skipping over the spines, searching, searching . . . *for what?* She prays that she'll know it when she sees it.

As if the gods heard her thoughts, Vesryn's fingers snag on a midnight-blue tome with silver lettering. The book slides out from under the chains and lands on the marble floor with a *slap*. The yellowing pages flutter for a moment before settling. Vesryn sinks to her knees and begins to read. A drawing of a narrow canyon, each side piled high with cracked, heavy stones, spreads across the page. Farther down, a diagram of a soft-petaled flower.

And suddenly, her entire life snaps into focus.

"It all makes sense," she whispers. "Oh gods." *The white winter lily.* Vesryn had *known* there was something strange about it being here. And if Costis hadn't planted it, then that means—

"Vesryn? Are you in here?"

She freezes, the pads of her fingers still pressed firmly onto the pages. That voice again. Her eyes dart around the expansive library, but the candles have mostly melted in their sconces, condensing their light to tiny pools atop each table. She glances at the half-melted candle in her hand, trying to decide if its light is a favor or a threat.

Before she can decide, the hanging mage-lights sputter back to life, casting the library in a tepid glow. Standing at the end of the shelves is . . . Ellion?

"What . . . ," Vesryn starts, but the rest of the question dissolves on her tongue. Her stomach clenches. Why would he follow her here? *How did he know she was here?*

Something flickers behind Ellion's eyes as he says, voice as clear as a festival bell, "There you are."

Vesryn positions the candle sconce beside the open book and stands. She curls her hands into fists to keep them from shaking. "Ellion." Her eyes cut to the cracked doors behind him. "Did anyone follow you here?"

He takes a step closer. "No, of course not. Those two are all beauty and zero brains. They didn't even notice either of us left."

Instinct hums a warning within her. Vesryn takes a step back and says, "You're . . . different." She narrows her eyes at the lanky boy before her. Ellion is wearing the same clothes, and his chiseled cheekbones and messy hair are the same, but he's somehow sharper. As if he has been out of focus the whole night, and now his image is as crisp and clear as mountain runoff.

"Ha." Ellion grins sheepishly. He pulls out his scuffed-up flask and waggles it. "Nothing but water in here. I play an excellent drunk, don't I?" He takes another step forward, and another, and suddenly, he's close enough that Vesryn catches the subtlest hint of baking cinnamon—of *home*. She clenches her teeth to hold back tears.

Ellion dips his head low enough for his hair to graze her shoulder, making her tremble. "It's easier to observe what's really going on around here when everyone thinks you're just a pathetic drunk."

Vesryn closes her eyes, and for a moment, her memory takes her somewhere other than the claustrophobic Academy dorm or the cramped king's chambers. Vesryn is back in the Evercraft kitchen, rolling dough for spice pies with Ellion's mother while her best friend adds too much cinnamon to the batter. For all their faults, the Evercrafts had been unreasonably kind to her. Ellion was their only child—a boy of every privilege and powerful magic who was slated from birth to follow in their footsteps as the next royal healer. They had every reason to discourage his friendship with a lowly street rat, but they hadn't, not until Luma's death.

She's missed him so much.

Vesryn opens her eyes, and for a split second, she swears she sees something flit across the room. Maybe it's just the mage-lights, or the last gasp of a dying candle. But maybe, just maybe, it's a moth. A sign from her goddess that things will finally be okay.

"Ellion," she breathes. "I don't think I can live the rest of my life knowing you hate me."

An expression she can't quite read skips across the necromancer's face. He wraps his arms around her and pulls her into a hug so tight it takes Vesryn's breath away. She softens.

Vesryn has often had nothing except the clothes on her back—that part has always been true and probably will continue to be so. But when she also has Ellion, it's been more than enough to see her through.

He holds her a little tighter. Her lungs constrict. Vesryn winces, trying to unravel herself from Ellion's arms, but he's much stronger than she remembered.

"All is forgiven," the necromancer whispers, his lips grazing her ear. "But I can't let you ruin my night."

15

OAK

OAK breathes a sigh of relief when he enters the ballroom.

While he would rather eat nails than leave Kellam upstairs with those heathens, he is supposed to be here, silently searching among the drunk and sweaty guests. There had been a plan for this sort of predicament, and according to that plan, *he* was the one who was supposed to get the magistrate—Oak, not Kellam.

Costis had told Oak as much before he died. *If anything happens to me*, the king had said, his eyes boring into Oak's, *you must be the one to talk to the magistrate first. You will tell him this phrase: The stag has fallen.*

But there had been no better option at the time. The necromancer had just defiled Costis' body, the Istellian's knife was stuck in the corpse, the surprise *mercenary*, for goddess' sake—no, the right thing to do was to send Kellam *out* of that room, away from the chaos to a ball where every eye would be on him. Besides, Costis had assured Oak that the moment he whispered that phrase into Crowley's ear, the magistrate would know exactly what to do to protect the throne. What did it matter if Kellam was the one to bring him to the room?

I Killed the King

Oak shivers and blows into his hands. Has it somehow gotten colder in here? He's not usually one to catch a chill, but the castle is particularly drafty tonight, even with the crush of bodies clogging up the lower level.

He just isn't *ready*. He can't possibly face a future that doesn't involve his king, but he will have to. The idea that he will have to repeat this story, again and again, during questioning makes his stomach lurch. He will have to recall the details of Costis' bruised and bloated face at least a hundred times over.

He thinks of his satchel, still hidden beneath his cot. Oak feels a hundred years older since he last saw it.

He could do it now—he could go and grab his bag and slip out of the servants' quarters on the other side of the castle without a single soul being aware of his absence.

But he also could have done it during Kellam's seventeenth-birthday celebration.

And the summer solstice festival.

And on any given evening after the rest of the castle was well into their dreams.

And yet Oak never has. Again and again, he tucked the bag away in the shadows, another broken promise he had made to himself in order to keep the one he'd made to the king long ago. Costis' hand over his, the stag of his signet ring glinting in the light. *He is meant for other things*, the king had said, watching as Oak's tea-colored eyes followed Kellam's every movement. *Stay with me so neither of us is alone when he figures out what they are.*

Oak has never been particularly bright, or agile, or charming—he knows his own weaknesses, through and through, as any good warden should. But he has always kept his promises. Even the ones that leave his own dreams gathering dust beneath the mattress.

The princess blazes across the dance floor like a living wildfire. Several dour-looking men in Istellian red trail after her like dying embers. For her part, Melarie is doing an excellent job of making sure every last guard and guest witnesses her presence at this ball. Oak's mouth curves into a small smile, despite his best efforts. Melarie Atilelet may be a spoiled, sheltered princess who so obviously waltzed into the king's chambers with a knife at her hip, but there's a depth to her he wasn't expecting. She is a girl who has seen too much and endured much more—Oak knows this for sure. One heartsick soul can always recognize another.

The princess barely has a moment to catch her breath before someone else approaches her for a dance, and though she probably didn't intend it, her constant movement has made it easier for him to search.

Every time Melarie moves, the crowd tends to follow—duchesses crowding in close with their own partners to brush shoulders with a foreign princess or men of both countries watching intently. But Oak cannot find the magistrate.

Again, he surveys the room.

He swears he has looked over the same guards, the same nobles all dressed in familiar green more times than he can count. The ballroom is so overcrowded, and Crowley looks like any standard Avendellian courtier: average height and build with short, graying hair, dressed in the same uniform. Kellam was right; as far as Oak can tell, the magistrate is not among them.

Dread curdles in his stomach. Oak shakes out his hands, hoping to release the tension in his tightly wound muscles that press him to move, to protect, to *do something*. But Costis doesn't need him anymore.

And anyway . . . Kellam will soon be king.

A sadness, deep and ancient, bubbles to the surface like an algae bloom. It spreads so quickly that Oak can barely breathe. The tears come hot and fast, catching him off guard.

Oak must stay by Kellam's side. The thought only makes him sadder. His future plays out in his mind. Standing guard in front of Kellam's door as he brings every man and woman he can get his hands on into his chambers. Oak staring into the distance, trying to think of literally anything else to drown out the sounds wafting out from behind the door. Oak wants to scream.

For a moment, he thinks that perhaps he *has*; the ballroom is suddenly quiet as the music lulls and dancers are escorted from the floor by their partners. Melarie kindly curtsies to an Istellian noble before joining her personal attendant—Antoine, he thinks she called him—at the dessert table.

And there, standing in the archway leading to the kitchens, is Samson Crowley.

Thank the Gardener. It takes everything Oak has not to cut straight across the dance floor and plant a kiss on the man's cheek. His eyes do not stray from the top of Crowley's gray head as he makes his way to the far side of the room.

"Master Crowley, I must speak with you." The words tumble out of Oak's mouth before his manners have a chance to catch up with him.

Whatever the magistrate was relaying to his guest dies in the air as he takes in Oak. The smile fades from his lips. "Ducasse. I imagine this is important?"

Oak's throat closes up. He can't get the words out. He can barely breathe. He only manages to give Crowley a weak nod before croaking, "Can we speak privately?"

Master Crowley whispers something into his guest's ear before kissing her temple. Then he follows Oak out of the ballroom and into the alcove nestled between the staff kitchens and the long-abandoned dungeons. Crowley asks the question the moment Oak turns to face him. "Is it Costis?"

Say it, Oak thinks. *Say the words.*

He pulls in a shuddering breath. "The stag . . . has fallen."

He doesn't know what he expected to happen when he finally spoke the words aloud, but it wasn't that Crowley would simply stare at him. He *did* say it out loud, right? His pulse picks up speed. Did he do this right? Had Costis been wrong or—

"All right," Crowley says. He puts his hands on his hips and lets out a long, low breath. "This has been confirmed?"

Oak whispers, "I was there."

"All right, then." Crowley nods, as if convincing himself of something. "There are several actions that must be taken immediately, and they must be done with the utmost caution—one slipup and it could cost Kellam the throne."

Oak nods miserably. "I am loyal to the Vernevaus."

"I know that, and so did Costis," Crowley says, his tone softening. "That is why he made me agree to protect your honor at all costs. But we will need to talk specifics in a more secluded area. Meet me in the library in one hour, and please, be discreet."

The magistrate pats Oak's shoulder, then heads in the direction of the ball without a backward glance. Oak stares after him, the dread in his stomach only growing. But he did it. He followed through on his king's last order, and that thought is the only thing that spurs him to reenter the ballroom and pretend like he isn't crumbling inside.

Oak waits a beat for Crowley to enter, then follows suit. He pivots to move toward the hallway with the staircase and comes face-to-face with Gaspar Weatherington.

"Oh," Oak says dully. "Good evening, Grand Chamberlain Weatherington."

Gaspar's eyes narrow. "Ah, Ducasse, finally you've arrived. King Costis must be here as well then, yes?"

His mind is too frazzled, his heart too shattered to try to navigate this conversation. Oak stares Gaspar in the eyes and says, "Yes, of course." He weaves around the grand chamberlain and marches through the crowd before he is subjected to any more of Gaspar's wheedling.

As Oak climbs the stairs, the wind lashes the castle so ferociously that he winces. The cold rattles his bones the way the storm shakes the windows. This chill must be something more than snow clinging to the other side of the stone walls because it refuses to leave him. He pauses on the top step and rolls up the sleeve of his uniform. The hair on his arm stands straight as a pin.

Something isn't right.

He draws his dagger. Just as he begins to creep down the hallway, something crashes in the room two doors down.

The library.

A cold sweat drips down his back as he grazes the handle. The door opens with a sweeping hush. He peers inside.

This time, Oak is certain the scream he hears is coming from his own mouth. He stumbles back. He squeezes his eyes shut and forces himself to breathe. When he's regained control, Oak opens his eyes and reenters the library.

The girl lies on the old mahogany table, her arm curled beneath her head like a pillow, her eyes open and mouth agape in a nightmare that will never end. Oak's hand shakes so violently when he touches her neck that the whole desk shudders. She's cold to the touch. No pulse.

Vesryn is dead.

TEN HOURS
TO DAWN

16

ELLION

As Ellion's headache eases, the dead of Castle Avendell lean in. He can barely remember the days when his life wasn't like this. He was a bright student once. Clever and handsome, though he was never quite as smart as Vesryn. It's almost funny how far he's fallen.

In her absence, a lull fills Costis' chambers. With the princess and the guard off doing gods know what, Ellion has only Kellam and Clove for company—if one can call it that. The prince's mind is clearly elsewhere; he glances at the door every two seconds. Clove leans on her forearms, hunched over the king's desk, focused on the parchment before her. This is all fine with Ellion, given his current state of wanting to be dead.

Footsteps pad toward Ellion. He ignores them, resting his temple against the tile.

"I thought I remembered you." Kellam squats down near Ellion's head, a funny look on his face, and snaps his fingers. "You look so much more like your father now than you did as a boy."

Every part of Ellion goes still.

"I was sickly most of my childhood. My father hoped that if anyone could save me, it was Alistair Evercraft." The prince's gaze is pensive. "I don't . . . remember much. I remember being in pain on the journey to your estate; and later, when your father's magic burned me from the inside. Eventually, he gave up and left me in some dim room. I was terrified. Then some little boy wandered in, followed by a maid with ratty braids." He looked thoughtfully at Ellion. "You read me some old fable, about the Weaver and her cursed child, the little godling the Twelve ordered slain. The girl—she held my hand. And, suddenly, I wasn't so afraid."

And Ellion can see it. The manor had been in a frenzy that morning—everything scrubbed, polished, and shined before dawn. Cook had scolded Vesryn for burning the rolls. She and Ellion were ordered to stay out of sight, so they hid together on the stairs above the main foyer when the carriage arrived and a handsome, golden-haired man walked in with a too-thin boy, far too old to be carried, far too weak to walk.

"There is," Ellion's father had said, his voice carrying to the second floor, "one more thing to try."

The golden-haired man had frowned. "If you can't save him, Alistair, I don't know who can."

"Maybe it's not a who," Ellion's father had said. "Maybe it's a what."

It was Vesryn who'd insisted they look in on Alistair's mysterious patient. Ellion read from their favorite book while Vesryn held the boy's hand. When the adults returned, Ellion's father gave the golden-haired man a folded paper, and they left in a hurry. Ellion never heard of their guests again. The next time he received a visit from someone at court, it was on much darker terms.

"That was you," Ellion breathes. And then he remembers something else. "You never gave me back my book!"

"I'm sure it's here somewhere." Kellam gives a distracted wave and frowns at him. "What happened to you, anyway? I find it hard to believe the heir of Alistair Evercraft has fallen this far. I thought your entire line was blessed with healing magic by the Courier."

Ellion can't be sure what leaves his mouth in response. It could be something along the lines of: *My father thought that, too, which is why he took my magnificent failure quite personally, given it happened the year he became dean of the Academy.* But there's an equal chance all that comes out is: *Uuughhhhh.*

Ellion's mind churns sluggishly. What was wrong with the prince again? He can't entirely remember. It floated through the estate in whispers, but he recalls the scent of herbs and plants, and later, his own father's haunted face.

He is not meant to be king.

Kellam's eyes narrow, snagging on another memory. "What happened to the girl?"

"You've met," Ellion groans.

The color drains from Kellam's face. "The *assassin*?"

"She doesn't like that word." Ellion's eyes flutter. "She—"

The doors bang open.

It's Oak. He hunches over, gasping for breath. Melarie rushes in behind him, eyes blotchy and red. Kellam bolts to his feet. Time grinds to a halt. For a beat, Ellion is living in two moments. The one that exists before Oak speaks—and after. Always the terrible after.

Oak looks directly at Ellion.

"I'm sorry," he rasps. "Your friend. She's dead."

Ellion is used to corpses. After so many bodies—after Luma—they all start to look the same. He's long mastered the disinterested detachment necessary for dealing with the dead. At some point, he truly started to believe nothing could shake him.

He was wrong.

Vesryn is dead.

Ellion blinks, but the image remains—Vesryn, splayed out on the library table like a broken bird, eyes wide, face stark with fear. Dark purple bruises ring her neck. Somehow, the bruises are far more nauseating than Costis' blood spilling from the gash in his side. This strangling took time.

It feels personal.

Pinned to Vesryn's chest, petals already beginning to wilt, is a single winter lily—and a note.

Bring out the king, it reads.

"Twelve help us," Kellam breathes. "What is this?"

"I—I heard a thump," Oak stutters. "And I came in to check and . . . she was like this."

Ellion feels . . . he's not sure. He should be crying, right? Having a panic attack? Instead, every part of him is numb. He spins the bead on his necklace and stares blankly. Vesryn would likely diagnose him with shock. She was always better at field assessments than he was. She was better at everything.

Ellion looks closer at the demand the killer left pinned to her chest. There's a hole in her dress. As if the murderer pinned the note, considered the dramatic effect of its placement, undid it, and pinned it somewhere else, like Vesryn was merely an art piece up for display. *Bring out the king.* If only they knew.

And the flower . . . it's the same one Costis put in Melarie's hair. Is this intended to mock them? Or is it a threat—a warning that whoever killed Vesryn knows what happened to Costis, too?

Behind him, Kellam, Melarie, and Clove hover, all looking equally ill.

"We were in the ballroom until I followed him," Melarie says, her voice wavering. "Oak couldn't have done this."

Kellam paces. "The necromancer and beast tamer were with me. Unless this is the most creative suicide we've ever seen . . ."

"The killer isn't any of us," Oak finishes.

"Which means either someone else was in my father's chambers when he died," Kellam rasps, paler than the snow beyond the window. "Or there are two murderers within these walls."

The gravity of this settles on all of them. Even Ellion, in his numb horror, understands their situation has gone from bad to doomed. He just can't quite bring himself to care.

Vesryn is dead.

And then Oak says:

"You could bring her back."

Oak's face is calm. It's a guard's expression—blank slate, no emotion, even as his chest rises and falls. It's identical to the expression healers are trained to wear right before they inform a family there's no chance of saving their loved one.

"No," says Ellion. "Out of the question."

"She might have answers. You can ask who killed her."

"*No.*" Ellion takes a step backward, his chest rising and falling rapidly. "I can't—I won't—I *promised* her—"

"She's gone." Kellam puts a hand on Ellion's shoulder. His face is a mask of sympathy, and Ellion hates him for it. He hates them all. Who is Kellam, to act like he's sorry when Vesryn is only a means to an end? "Oak is right. We're all in danger. If Vesryn has information that can protect us, it's worth it."

"My answer is no."

They all stare at him.

Kellam's cheeks redden. "As your sovereign—"

Ellion laughs, the sound low and bitter. "Finish that sentence. I dare you."

"Prince Kellam," Melarie interjects, her dark lashes fluttering, "Ellion has just lost a dear friend. Have some grace. Give him a moment."

Ellion turns away. He doesn't want to look at them; he doesn't even want to breathe their air. The walls threaten to press in around him. Ellion promised Vesryn he would never do that to her. Not after how it went with Luma. Not after the vow she'd made him swear.

And yet.

What if he gets it right this time?

Costis hadn't wanted to come back. Once he warned Kellam, his soul was ready to move on. There was no unfinished business to keep him here.

But Vesryn was so *young*. She had an entire life ahead of her. Dreams and hopes and plans, all of them now erased with one cruel act. And Ellion can think of at least one person she has unfinished business with. It can't be an accident that they reunited tonight. Not now, not after all these years.

Clove's eyes dart uneasily between them. "Are we sure this is a good idea?"

"We need answers," Oak says, a little coldly. "Is there a reason you don't want the girl brought back?"

Clove looks at him, startled, and her shoulders hunch defensively. "*No.* But it's not like I have an endless supply of tranquilizers."

Every eye turns to Ellion.

He fumbles for his flask, but it's empty. The last bits of the tranquilizer are wearing off. His head pounds terribly, and his body aches as though he was run over by a carriage, but he's far more alert than he was when Costis died.

What if he can do it?

So what if Vesryn despises him? At least she'd be *alive.* Ellion had thought he couldn't bear to live in a world where Vesryn hated him, but he was wrong. He could bear it, so long as he knew Vesryn was still a part of the world at all.

"Okay," Ellion whispers. "Fine."

Kellam and Oak exchange quick, relieved glances. Clove's frown deepens. Melarie pulls in a shuddering breath.

Ellion approaches his friend, dread rising in his throat. His hands shake. She looks so small. An unfamiliar hatred boils up in him.

He's going to find whoever did this. And he's going to make what happened to Luma look like mercy.

"Find something to knock me out after," Ellion says flatly. "I'm going to need it."

Ellion puts his hands on Vesryn's corpse and calls for the dead.

Darkness and cold, but less than before. Either the Veil is getting warmer or Ellion is getting used to being here. The latter is a lot more concerning.

The dead of Castle Avendell reach for him. His mouth floods with the grave dirt of a hundred dead kings, the servants buried in the back wood, the mice rotting in the garden from the overachieving castle cat. A part of him wants to reach out, to see what he might do with bodies that have long stopped hosting souls. But, no. There's only one spirit he seeks.

He finds her all too easily.

A swirl of butterscotch yellow, the faint chime of the Arbiter's prayer bells, the cedarwood incense to match. Vesryn was always so stubbornly devout, insisting the long-dead goddess of justice and judgment would protect her from life's ills if only she prayed hard enough. Ellion had been less than half-hearted in his patronage to the Courier and his promises of healing. It caused several spats with Vesryn over the years. Ellion's lack of faith had only strengthened hers.

This was not how Ellion wanted to prove his skepticism right.

He reaches for her—and stops.

Every soul has an anchor moment. For Costis, it was Kellam. When Luma died, it was her mother. But when Ellion looks into the moment keeping Vesryn tethered, he sees nothing of the family she lost or the people she killed.

He sees himself.

"Screw them," a much younger Ellion says. Something wiggles in his arms.

He remembers that day. It was their first at the Academy, when every student received a uniform and an animal that would be in their care for their tenure. Vesryn had been so determined to prove she belonged there, same as Ellion and all the other students who came from families wealthy enough to carve their names above the halls they studied in. But when she'd walked up to collect her welcome packet, she found her uniform cut to pieces and the cage door for the bird she'd been assigned swinging open.

"The maid already failed the baccalauréat on her first day," one of the students had snickered. "I knew our averages would go down when we let the peasant class in, but this is truly remarkable."

Vesryn fled in tears.

Ellion should have gone after her. Instead, he'd hauled the student with the biggest smile behind the dining hall and broken his nose. Ellion's never been a fighter, but he always made exceptions for Vesryn.

When Ellion finally found her huddling in a service closet, he brought company.

He'd held out the kitten, wincing as it scratched him. "Look who I found. Not sure why they thought a birdcage was a good fit for a cat, but he didn't make it far."

In his hands had been the ugliest disgrace of a kitten Ellion had ever seen. He'd found it in a dumpster—underfed, one eye swollen shut, wobbling and hissing. It was missing several patches of fur, its tail was broken in three places, and it was plagued by a truly mortifying infestation of fleas. Ellion was fairly certain that the cat had been born with a single mission: attempt to kill anything with a heartbeat. Take no prisoners, spread hatred, and reign terror.

Vesryn loved it instantly.

The memory shifts; Ellion's younger self fades, but the cat remains, starring in a series of quick, flashing memories. Eating from Vesryn's hand for the first time. Responding to that odd little name Vesryn gave it, *Rue*. The night it stopped hiding under her bed and slept curled in her lap instead.

"You've got to be kidding me," Ellion mutters.

He's not Vesryn's anchor moment.

It's the fucking cat.

Ellion hadn't known it was possible to feel humiliation even when crossing the Veil in search of the dead, but he does. The *cat?* Really? He knew she loved that thing, but come on. They grew up together. They were best friends! They'd nearly died for each other multiple times! And the thing keeping her soul temporarily bound to the earth was her *cat?*

The memory dissolves into smoke.

Vesryn stands in front of him, staring at something in the distance.

The cat from the memory, Rue, twines around her ankles. Just what Ellion needs. Rue sees him and hisses, and Vesryn turns. Her eyes widen and she lurches back. Or she tries to. Given that she's currently a spirit trapped in the liminal space of the Veil, it's more of a . . . wobble.

"No," Vesryn cries. "No, Ellion, don't you dare."

"Ves." Ellion holds up his hands. He doesn't have long. "I'm not bringing you back. I promised, and I'm keeping that promise. I just need to know who killed you."

Vesryn hesitates. Confusion moves in where fear and anger resided a moment before. "What?"

"Kellam and Oak wanted me to resurrect you, and I refused, but something strange is happening here. Who killed you, Ves? What happened?" He pauses and glares at the cat. "What's Rue doing here?"

Rue hisses at him. He always wondered what had happened to that furry little asshole. It must have died years ago and has been waiting for Vesryn ever since. Souls tend to do that, animal and human alike—if there's someone they're waiting on, or a problem they haven't solved, they might spend months, even years, floating in the Veil and resisting the call to pass on. That was usually where trouble began.

Vesryn stares at him. "Ellion. *You* killed me."

"*What?*" Ellion demands. "I—Ves—*what?*"

She shakes her head, shoulders hunching up to her ears. "I went up to the library. It was empty when I got there. Then you came in. And you looked . . ." Her face crumples. "You looked normal, Ellion. How you used to, before all this started. And you strangled me."

Horror creeps through him. Horror—and shame. Because the light in Vesryn's eyes when she talks about the old him, the Ellion who existed before his necromancy manifested and ruined all he loved, is so wistful it makes his heart wither.

That's the problem with ruining your own life. Even when you try to contain the self-inflicted implosion, it's usually the ones you want to protect the most who end up becoming collateral damage first.

"Ves," Ellion says. "I would never—" He cuts himself off. *He'd never hurt her?* They both know that's a lie. "I was in Costis' chambers with Kellam and Clove. Oak and Melarie found your body and they came to get me."

She looks at him, small and frightened. "Please, just let me go."

This is the frustrating thing with spirits. They don't listen; Vesryn is too freshly dead, too attached to her worldly mission to hear him out. Ellion reaches out to shake her, but his fingers pass through her like smoke.

And then something stirs.

He feels it—cold, eternal, and bored. It's coming closer, and it's coming fast. He has to leave. Ellion doesn't want to find out what happens if his spirit is caught in the Veil with whatever is approaching.

"Ves," Ellion begs. "Is there anything you can tell me? Anything at all?"

Vesryn shrinks into herself, thinking. She's not moving on. She's growing more solid by the second, and this is bad, because if Vesryn gets stuck here, there's no telling how long it will take for her to cross over—if she ever does.

"You looked healthy," she says in a small voice. "And you brought me a flower."

It's getting closer. He has to leave.

"Send me through," Vesryn begs. "Ellion, please, *let me go.*"

The presence is almost here.

Spirits are always irrational, so attached to lingering worldly concerns. There has to be some way he can get something useful out of Vesryn. Some clue she doesn't realize she's leaving behind.

"Vesryn," Ellion says desperately. "What unfinished business do you have here? How can I help you move on?"

Vesryn stills. She looks at Ellion, her brows knitting together. "Do you remember that day—the voice we heard? This is all our fault, Ellion."

"In the gorge?" Ellion frowns. "You can't possibly still be worried about that. Ves, give me something to work with."

"Gaspar Weatherington," she says faintly, as if trying to recall a distant dream. "Kellam asked me to—"

Pain cracks through Ellion. Cold punches his chest, as though some invisible force is trying to physically shove him out of the Veil. Vesryn had Ellion wrong. In the beginning, he wanted to believe. For much of his early life, he prayed. First to the Courier, and when the god didn't answer, to the rest of the Divine Twelve. Frequently, fervently, desperate as he was to fill his father's shoes, and later, when it all fell apart and he had nothing else to turn to. He never received an answer.

But now, a voice splits through Ellion, cold, eternal, and alive: *Leave*, it whispers. *My game has just begun.*

"Ellion," cries Vesryn. "Send me on!"

He can't. He's failing her, again. All he's ever done is fail her.

Something small and soft twines around Ellion's ankles.

Ellion falls, flung from the Veil, forced to leave Vesryn behind as he crashes back into his body.

And something else slips through.

17

CLOVE

CLOVE does not like what's happening at all, not one bit. The necromancer groans and an aura of midnight blue curls around him. She blinks. The swirl of color is still there.

Her hands tighten into fists. She could wring Kellam's neck for suggesting she "open up" to magic. Clove has lived her entire life without a drop of magic in her veins and has done just fine for herself, hasn't she? She knows how to nurse a unicorn foal by hand and hatch an abandoned dragon egg with nothing more than her body heat and a prayer. When Clove found that eyeless owl in the woods and had no idea what to do with it, she read everything she could find on the species in her father's reference books until her eyes burned with exhaustion.

The thing that leaps from the glittering blue is not a typical beast. No amount of research would tell Clove what to do with *that*.

The scraggly thing freezes on the library floor, the triangles of its ears perked and listening. Its eyes—one amber, one an unsettlingly familiar shade of violet—survey the room with an otherworldly glow.

Its gaze settles on Clove. The thing tips its head and meows.

No one else seems to notice the ghost cat that has appeared from literally nowhere and is now pawing at the threadbare rug.

Clove's ears feel like they're stuffed with cotton. She lets out an unhinged little laugh. "Tell me I'm not the only one who can see this."

The guard clears his throat. The prince won't meet her eye and the necromancer is, fortunately, still unconscious. Only the princess responds. When she does, her voice is so tender that it makes Clove want to cry.

"What do you see?" Melarie says, her dark eyes laced with concern. *Actual, real concern.* It dawns on Clove that she has never seen that look directed toward her—not from her father or brothers or anyone in the village. What she'd taken for concern, Clove realizes, was nothing more than pity.

The princess of Istellia has no business being this kind to her, yet she is anyway—a fragile gift Clove doesn't know what to do with other than try not to break it with a lie. She pulls in a deep breath. "There is a . . ."

It's gone.

The ghost cat is gone.

Clove blinks. She turns her head just in time to see the flick of a long black tail before the creature leaps straight into—and through—the heavy stone wall.

"What is it, Clove?" Melarie's voice is too kind, her face too pretty, her worry too real when everything else in this godsforsaken castle is not. Clove groans and rubs the soft skin between her eyebrows.

Wait . . . the cat. It's still here.

Well, not exactly *here*, but just beyond the wall. Clove can practically feel the icy stone beneath its paws as it paces outside the library doors. And it isn't the only one.

Ghostly creatures crawl and coast and slither in every corner of Castle Avendell. Feathered wings flap near her ear, rustling the hair on the back of her neck. Something lithe and velvety gallops down an abandoned hall in the east wing. A slippery creature that smells like the sea descends into a basin of dishwater and vanishes.

The cacophony of hooves and heartbeats is enough to drive Clove mad. Is this what the necromancer experiences all the time? No wonder he drinks.

A low hiss slices through the noise in Clove's head. Instinctively, her own stomach clenches as the gritty sensation of scales on stone reverberates through her. *The basilisk.* What was it that Kellam told her to do in order to tap into her magic—relax? Clove forces her shoulders from her ears and unclenches her jaw. The pounding in her head dulls.

The snake is somewhere cold. An ethereal chill seeps through the layers of Clove's dress, making gooseflesh rise on her legs. But there's something else, too; a hint of melted wax and roasted meat lingers on the tip of her tongue. Without warning, a gust of hot, sticky air greets her. Then a new feeling—the gritty cold on her belly softens to something warmer, and plush. Like the carpeted staircase leading to the second floor.

Clove gasps. Her eyes snap open as she stumbles on her skirts. Melarie's arm darts out to grab Clove's wrist to keep her from falling. Before the princess can ask again, and before she can talk herself out of it, Clove blurts, "It was nothing." She rights herself and smooths out her dress. "I was mistaken. I didn't see anything."

Clove does not meet Melarie's eyes as the princess releases her wrist. Across the room, Ellion begins to stir, drawing the prince and the guard to his side.

She pulls in a shuddering breath. There is no mistaking what Clove felt just now—the beast has found its way to the main floors of the castle. She will tell them about the snake, and soon.

But the rest of it? It's too unknowable, too feral. This burgeoning thing inside her is a wild creature that must be tamed before it can be shared with the others. It's a magic she doesn't understand and a liability she isn't willing to risk her life for.

After all, Clove is simply a creature in need of protection, just like any other. She'll claw her way to safety by any means necessary or die trying.

18

KELLAM

KELLAM has only just calmed his thundering heart when Ellion careens back to the world of the living.

The necromancer crashes backward, colliding with one of the bookcases, lurching away from Vesryn's body as though touching her burned him. For a moment, he wobbles unsteadily on his feet, face gray and dripping with sweat.

"I can't . . . see anything," Ellion croaks.

Melarie's eyes widen. "He's going to faint."

She lunges. Melarie catches Ellion right as he crumples, grunting as his tall, lanky weight pulls her to the floor. The princess adjusts and angles Ellion into her lap, pressing the back of her hand to his forehead.

Snow and wind rattle against the window. The roof groans. Kellam wonders if it's occurred to anyone else yet that depending on what Ellion learned, their temporary truce may crumble as quickly as it was forged. Kellam edges toward Oak, flinches, and backs away again.

Oak was the one to find Vesryn. What if the princess was wrong about the timeline? What if he killed her before Melarie followed him?

No. He can't think like that. Kellam flexes his freezing fingers into a fist.

There are many things in this world he can accept, but Oak being a potential threat is not one of them. Kellam may not have the Arbiter's blessing of justice and foresight, but he knows in his bones that Oak Ducasse is not his enemy.

He hopes.

Ellion's eyes flutter open. They have the unfocused, glassy sheen of someone who's slept too deeply for too long, yet he's never looked more tired. "Nice catch, princess."

Melarie actually smiles. "My sister, Solene, is prone to fainting. After years of her wilting at court, I developed an eye for it."

"Lucky me," Ellion says wearily. Slowly, the necromancer sits upright, blinking several times as if to clear his gaze. His eyes narrow as he stares at something across the room. "Has anyone seen a cat?"

The room grows silent. Finally, Oak ventures an uneasy, "A what?"

Ellion pinches his eyes closed and rubs his temples. "Nothing, just a leftover memory from the Veil." His gaze fixes on the floor. "I found her. She didn't want to come back. But she did tell me something helpful. I think I know who killed her."

His words chill the air. Every part of Kellam vibrates, caught between fight or flight. Somehow, he finds his voice. This is his home. Two people have died within his walls.

Kellam is to be king. It's time he starts acting like it.

"Who?" Kellam rasps.

Now Ellion looks up at him, his gaze darker than a storm. Kellam has the strangest sense that Ellion is examining him. Finally, he says, "Weatherington."

Cold creeps through Kellam. It's one thing for him to have a personal vendetta against Gaspar. To feel like his father's respected second-in-command has always been out to get him. But to know the truth? To know they're trapped here with him as a blizzard rages, and Kellam does not have the power to stop Gaspar from seizing the throne if the truth of Costis' death slides free?

Kellam has never felt worse.

"Gaspar is grand chamberlain," Oak rasps, his face white. "He has served beside King Costis for twenty years. They were boys together, Costis *warded* in Magnivelle during his childhood."

"Gaspar Weatherington is a cold, calculating snake of a man," Kellam finishes, every part of him hollowed out. "But he's always been loyal to the Crown. I never took him for a killer."

Ellion looks at the floor, his eyes vacant and haunted; he had the expression of a man who had rediscovered the warmth of the sun only to be plunged back into eternal cold. "Vesryn said something about Gaspar. Maybe she was following him?"

Kellam's mind spins.

Could Ellion be mistaken? Or is something stranger happening here?

"Is there a chance Gaspar killed them both?" Melarie's eyes dart between them in a clear bid for a truce. Kellam regrets they didn't meet under better circumstances. In another life, he might have liked Melarie. He might even have been willing to give her his heart—were it not already taken. "The lights were out. All of us have a reason to want Costis alive. And now we know about the tunnel in the washroom."

"Gaspar would have known about it, too," Ellion murmurs.

Kellam can't help himself. He glances at Oak. Just the sight of him makes some of Kellam's resolve crumble. When he looks at Oak, he sees everything he stands to lose. It's a strange thought.

Oak has never been his in the way Kellam wants. Kellam's always been a boy living on scraps of his affection. But he will cling to those shreds with bloodied fingers.

He can lose his father. He cannot lose his friend or . . . whatever Oak is to him.

"It's possible," Kellam says. Clove's lips thin, but she says nothing. "That only makes our job harder. You must understand; Gaspar has been part of my father's council longer than I have been alive. If we are to accuse him of something as grave as this—if we intend to attempt to strip him of his rank, his title, and his power—our case must be ironclad."

It takes everything in Kellam to swallow the hysterical laughter threatening to spill out of him. This is what he wanted, is it not? To lead? To be treated as something other than the frivolous, useless prince? To be seen as a true heir to the Gardener's power, though her magic has yet to flow through his veins?

The words sound as ridiculous as he feels. Kellam's eyes slide around the room, grasping for something, anything, leaping from the puzzled faces of his companions to Vesryn's corpse, the edges of that damn flower already browning, the note curled at the edges—

The note.

Kellam unpins it from Vesryn's body, careful not to tear the paper as he reads. *"Bring out the king."*

"A strange demand," Clove muses.

"Is it?" Kellam counters. The first threads of a plan swirl before him. "Think about it. We locked the door after my father died. When I went searching for the magistrate, the first thing Gaspar inquired about was my father. Then he finds Vesryn tailing him . . ."

"Gaspar either suspects King Costis is dead and is eager to seize power," Oak says slowly, "or he's guilty of the king's death and is seeking a way to exonerate himself."

"For his regency to be secure, he can't be linked to the king's murder. It needs to be blamed on someone else." Kellam paces. "And the timeline makes sense. If he wants the regency, he knows it must happen before the treaty is signed and legitimized by Crowley. Otherwise, he loses his chance."

Hope and dread put equal weight on his chest. Can it really be that simple—and that complicated?

Oak rubs the space between his eyebrows and braces himself against the wall. Kellam's fingers twitch with the urge to reach for him, but he can't. It would only complicate things.

Country over heart, Costis always said.

Kellam is starting to understand.

"Prince Kellam." Though Oak wears his mask of calm, Kellam can see the cracks of panic in the way Oak's shoulders shake and his white-knuckled grip on the hilt of his sword. "There's another problem. If Gaspar is regent, I am sworn to him."

The words linger between them.

If Gaspar seizes power, the years of affection and friendship or . . . whatever it is that glows between Oak and Kellam will not matter. Oak will choose his duty over everything. Even Kellam. Ellion lets loose a low whistle; Melarie's and Clove's faces are blank with dread. Though their truce is temporary, things will become far more difficult if Oak is forced to hunt them.

He already knows too much.

Kellam paces in the library in one slow, painful loop. He trusts no one except Oak. He has no power and no allies. If Gaspar seizes the throne, Kellam has no doubt it will only be a matter of days before a basilisk "accidentally" ends up between his bedsheets or poison makes its way into his cup.

One of the people in this library could very well be his father's murderer. But he believes them when they say they did not kill Vesryn.

And for now, that will have to be good enough.

"Oak and I will search Gaspar's chambers," says Kellam.

Oak's eyebrows shoot up. "We will?"

Kellam holds up the note. "If we can match his handwriting, we'll have more than a dead girl's word and a decade of slights and bad blood. We'll have proof."

"He could kill you," Ellion points out. "If he catches the two of you in his office, he'll put two and two together. And if he killed Costis *and* Vesryn this efficiently, without anyone knowing..."

"If he killed Vesryn, who next? If we can match his handwriting, we can at least tie him to *her* murder." Kellam paces. "We're trapped here, at least until the storm ends. We might as well use the time we have. We'll look for evidence Gaspar was plotting against my father. If we can tie him to my father's death, even Gaspar can't escape the charge of regicide."

"And if he didn't kill Costis?" asks Melarie. "If there are two killers—will the death of an assassin be egregious enough to prosecute him?"

Kellam winces. She probably could have phrased it more kindly, but the princess has a point. "I would like to think so, but..."

"Girls die in strange circumstances every day. Vesryn is a problem they can ignore," Clove says quietly, her voice grim. "Costis is not. If we want to take the grand chamberlain down, we have to tie him to the death of the king. Or we lose."

Kellam nods. They all look at each other, strangers bound by foul luck. It takes everything in Kellam not to laugh.

So this is what the fate of his kingdom has come down to. A useless prince, his stoic guard, a flighty princess, a penniless beast tamer, and a drunk necromancer. What miserable company they make.

Melarie rises and smooths her skirts. "Ellion is right. If Weatherington finds you snooping, we're all in danger. Let me handle him. I'll have my attendant Antoine follow him, and I'll distract him while Oak and Kellam do their search."

"How?" asks Clove.

"I'm an Istellian princess and the daughter of the man who burned Magnivelle," Melarie says dryly. "I think I can find a way to rile him up."

Clove chews thoughtfully on her lip. "Prince Kellam, is there somewhere in the castle that stays cold year-round? A place few people would have access to? If there's a basilisk in this castle, that's where its nest will be. I can start there. If I can't find the beast, I might yet find evidence to prove Gaspar was the one who brought it in. Eggshells, scales, even dried blood from when they were feeding."

"Hold on," Ellion says. "Did she say *basilisk*? In the castle? As in, the deadly beast that's so poisonous we've got myths about them wounding the Divine Twelve?"

Clove rolls her eyes. "Yes, I believe you were unconscious for that part, but there was basilisk venom in Costis' wound. I suspect Weatherington may have let one loose."

"Oh," Ellion says. "Well, if that's all."

Oak straightens. "You ought to search the dungeons. They're

locked, but I can get you the key. His Grace largely discontinued their use because he thought it inhumane. And because there were . . . rumors, of prisoners hearing whispers that drove them mad." He shudders. "If Weatherington wanted somewhere to hide the beasts, he would keep them there."

"Clove," says Kellam. "If you manage to find the basilisk, I have one request."

Clove freezes. Her lips part as she holds his stare, no doubt replaying the day Kellam's father took everything from her family.

"Secure it alive if you can," Kellam says. "Otherwise, Gaspar could claim we just hauled a dead snake in here. We'll need a new menagerie, anyway, once the treaty is signed. A living basilisk would be an excellent start, don't you think?"

Clove blinks once, twice, her throat bobbing. She nods quickly and turns away, whether to conceal the wetness of her eyes or the hope that flashed dawn bright on her face, Kellam isn't sure. It's strange, the way he warms at the sight of her gratitude—and stranger still that he must hold it at arm's length.

If Clove killed his father, nothing Kellam promised her can be delivered. But if she's innocent? If she helps him *catch* whoever did it? Forget her estate. Kellam will give her the entire northern province, for all he cares.

"What about me?" asks Ellion. "How can I help?"

They look at him. To say Ellion looks the worse for wear is an understatement. It's as if every time he enters the Veil, he leaves a piece of himself behind. His skin has the pallor of a corpse, and his fists shake even in his pockets.

"Perhaps you can stay with Vesryn's body," Kellam says, not unkindly. "Bar the door until we return."

Ellion's lower lip juts out. "You don't need to treat me with kid gloves. I'm more familiar with death than the rest of you. Just because Vesryn is—was—my friend doesn't mean I can't be useful."

"Crowley was supposed to meet me at the library," Oak offers. "It would be helpful if you remained here. He likely got distracted or pulled away, but he knows we need his assistance. If he arrives, you can ensure he remains until we return."

Ellion glares at him. It's a pity job, and he knows it, but given that no one is offering anything better, the necromancer folds his arms. There's something on his face that sets Kellam's nerves on edge. Ellion is holding something back, but Kellam isn't entirely certain what. The necromancer seems . . . paranoid. His eyes dart around; he jumps at the slightest sound.

"Ellion," says Kellam. "Is there anything else you discovered? Anything you need to tell us?"

Ellion looks at him. He hesitates, jaw working, and Kellam knows then that he's lying.

Again, he has the strangest sense that Ellion is examining him. The hair on Kellam's arms stands on end.

Does Ellion think that *he* killed Vesryn?

The necromancer presses his lips into a line and looks away.

"No," says Ellion. "Nothing else. I'll stay here. But if you guys aren't back soon, I'm launching a ghost attack on Castle Avendell."

"Can you do that?" Melarie asks curiously.

"Let's not find out," Kellam says quickly. They have enough problems. The last thing he needs is Ellion meddling with the dead and accidentally stirring Castle Avendell's long-sleeping spirits.

Ellion is hiding something. Of that, Kellam is certain. But he has to focus on one problem at a time.

"It's settled, then," says Kellam. "Melarie will distract Gaspar as Oak and I snoop. Clove will look for the basilisk. And Ellion will guard the body. And for the love of the Twelve, if *any* of you see Crowley, tell him to get to the library before I have him strung up by his toes in the courtyard." His eyes stray to the clock. "One hour. We'll meet back here at eight. May the Weaver guide us. We're going to need all the help we can get."

As if in agreement, the storm howls, and the corner pane of the nearest window cracks. When Kellam shivers, he's not certain if it's because of the cold, his nerves, or something else. He wants to believe this will work. He must act like it, to preserve the confidence of those around him.

But if Kellam is being honest?

He's not convinced he'll make it through the night alive.

19

MELARIE

AS Melarie returns to the ball, her mind is haunted by Vesryn's corpse. It's not as though she *liked* the little assassin. But still. This is only the third dead body Melarie has ever seen. She's not exactly thrilled about it.

Elodie would be disappointed in her; of the four sisters, she's always the best at keeping her head. Solene often hides her temper with a smile, and Delphine with a facade, but Melarie's never been good at hiding her feelings.

Melarie pauses before she turns the corner and pinches her thigh through her dress. She will not cry. She will not panic. She will keep her promise to the others.

Find Antoine. Tell him what's happening and distract Gaspar.

Antoine will know how to fix this. He always does.

Melarie holds her head high and steps into the fray.

Immediately, a puffed-up man wearing the council's green robes asks for a dance, sweat rolling in thick beads down his greasy temple. Melarie responds with a numb smile and a nod. She detaches from her body, letting her limbs play the role while her mind wanders. She's passed to the next dancer, and then the next. Melarie scans the crowd as she dances, seeking the familiar, proud line of Antoine's back. Overhead, the hands of the clock tick down.

She cannot fail.

The music dips, signaling the dancers to switch partners. Melarie turns without looking.

"My, no wonder Antoine is obsessed with you," a dry voice says. "He always did love a lost cause."

A hawkish man in Avendellian green watches Melarie with a flat slate stare. He wears council robes; stag antlers gleaming on his right lapel signal him as a member of the court. Her heartbeat increases. On his left lapel, gleaming under the mage-lights, is a golden lily.

Gods help her. That means he must be—

"Gaspar Weatherington." He extends a pale hand toward Melarie, his eyes bright with disdain. "And you must be the prince's betrothed. How unfortunate for you."

Fear curdles in Melarie. She thinks of Vesryn, that terrible note pinned to her chest, the haunted light in Ellion's gaze. Her eyes flick to the clock. The hour hand creeps toward eight.

She must buy Kellam and Oak time.

"Pleasure," Melarie breathes, bowing just shallow enough for it to be an insult. "Shall we dance?"

Gaspar's face twitches, but he offers her his hand.

Melarie steadies her nerves and takes it.

For a beat, they dance in silence. Melarie's lessons with Antoine about the Avendellian territories and their ruling families return at a crawl. She knows little of Gaspar personally, but his ties to Magnivelle ought to be enough. She needs to set the grand chamberlain on edge, but she must be careful. If he suspects something, their plan to distract him long enough for Oak and Kellam to search his office will unravel.

"Are you enjoying the ball, my lord?" Melarie asks.

Gaspar laughs, a cruel, cold little bark that only deepens the chill in Melarie's bones. "I've had more fun at funerals."

"Ah," Melarie stammers. The hatred shining in Gaspar's eyes makes her breath hitch. She steadies herself. She can do this. She pictures Elodie's disarming kindness, Solene's unflappable calm, and Delphine's knifelike grace. Melarie swallows and forces herself to smile. "Still, it's a beautiful thing, to see Istellia and Avendell come together at last."

Gaspar's expression sours. "Is that what they told you when they shipped you off here? You ought to return home, princess. It's hard to imagine this was worth the three-week journey." His eyes stray to the crowd, already bored. The music lulls.

She's going to lose him.

His grip slackens. "It was a pleasure—"

"I cannot wait to be queen of Avendell," Melarie blurts.

Gaspar freezes.

Oh, Weaver help her. She wanted his attention. She has it now.

The music shifts, binding them to a second dance. Gaspar wants to think of her as some airy, stupid princess come to ruin his country? Very well. She could play that role.

"Everyone ignores me back in Istellia," Melarie whines. "I was never given anything to *do*. But once I am queen of this quaint little country, I can do as I please."

Gaspar's eye twitches. "I do not believe that was a condition of the treaty—"

"Oh, but Kellam *promised* me," Melarie breathes. She leans in, close enough that it's improper. Her breath fogs before her. It's as if Weatherington himself is emanating cold. "He said he doesn't want me to bother with duty, but I have always loved studying law. And I already have some changes in mind!"

Gaspar regards her with dull loathing. "You know, my parents were having dinner when your father's soldiers stormed the border and burned Magnivelle to the ground." He spins her a little too fast. "I always resented my home being a place of little note. I suppose the start of a war is one way to make it live in infamy—though it wouldn't have been my first choice."

Melarie sways, and it's only Gaspar that keeps them in time with the music.

"I am . . . very sorry for your loss," she says faintly.

"Well, then," Gaspar deadpans. "I suppose all is forgiven."

Melarie's heart pounds. He hates her, and can she blame him? It doesn't matter that Melarie was a girl when her father's soldiers attacked; nor does it matter that she's here to bring an end to it all. To Gaspar, Melarie and her country represent everything he's lost.

Gaspar leans in, his sour breath tickling Melarie's ear.

"I don't know what game you're playing at, but I can assure you, little girl, I play it better." His grip on her tightens until it's painful. "I know Kellam is hiding something. That boy wears his panic as openly as his stupidity. I know you're helping him. I know so much more than you could possibly understand."

Melarie reels back, her blood roaring. Her eyes dart to the clock and then back to him. "I'm afraid I don't know what you're talking about."

Gaspar's smile does not reach his eyes. "Very well, then. You can drown with the rest of them."

The music stops, and they halt with it. Melarie's blood sings with panic. She failed. She did not hold him for nearly long enough, and worse, she learned nothing. All she's done successfully is cast herself in a suspicious light. Melarie grasps for something, anything to say, when a familiar voice cuts in.

"Gaspar," drawls Antoine. "Why is it every time I turn a corner, you're terrorizing some pretty girl who looks like she'd sooner die than spend another second with you?"

Melarie has never been so happy to see him.

Gaspar tilts his head. Something strange passes between them, but before Melarie can place it, he turns and gives her a mocking bow.

"A pleasure," he drawls. "Enjoy your night, princess."

And then he's spinning away. Melarie whirls to Antoine, whose eyes are tight with worry.

"Don't mind him," Antoine begins. "The Weatheringtons were bitter isolationists long before we burned their sorry estate to the ground. I've been prodding the guests to dig up their opinions on the treaty, and on your presence here tonight. Everyone else has been delighted." He falters. "Princess, what's wrong?"

The music picks back up. Melarie clings to Antoine like her life depends on it. The last few hours rise up in a panicked, icy wave. Costis is dead. Vesryn is dead. Kellam and Oak are in Gaspar's office and he is likely on his way there at this very minute. They are in danger and they are trapped and—

"Your Grace," Antoine says in a low warning. "You're sweating. There are many eyes on us."

Melarie seizes Antoine's left hand and squeezes four times. They worked out the code years ago. One squeeze if she needed refreshment; two if she needed to retreat. Three squeezes if she needed him to keep a handsy noble away from her.

And four if she was in danger.

"The king will not be attending tonight," Melarie breathes.

"But the treaty—"

"Antoine," Melarie murmurs. "He is dead."

And though his eyes widen—though every last bit of color drains from his face—somehow, some way, Antoine doesn't miss a step. Goddess above, she adores him. When Melarie thinks of her father, it's not King Raphaël she sees. It's Antoine who taught her letters; Antoine who explained, calmly and kindly, what it meant for a princess to bleed. Other than her sisters, Antoine and Gabriel have been the only points of joy in Melarie's sad little life.

And unlike Gabriel—Antoine has remained.

He will help her. She knows it.

Antoine tilts his head toward her, pretending to share a private joke as he whispers, "How?"

"We do not know."

"*We?*"

"The prince and I and—others. Allies." She struggles to find a way to explain. "A second is also dead. Antoine, I—" Her breath comes in a panicked gasp, loud enough that a nearby nobleman glances over. Melarie forces her voice back to a whisper, spinning faster as she shakes like a leaf. "We think Weatherington is involved. And even if his hands are clean . . . he is the *regent*, Antoine."

She doesn't need to explain the threat this poses. Costis may have waged war against her people—but Gaspar Weatherington would seek to wipe Istellia from the map entirely.

Snow assaults the windowpanes. Here, in the ballroom, the

ferocity of the storm is on full display. Though it's not even fully evening yet, the storm has blackened the outside world to night. The endless swirl of white beyond the glass would be beautiful were it also not imprisoning her. Thunder cracks, and Melarie flinches. She didn't even know you could *have* thunder in a snowstorm. Quickly, she tells Antoine everything she can without putting the others at risk.

"I was trying to distract him, but I failed," Melarie breathes. "I need your help. I need you to keep him here, in the ballroom, at all costs. At least for the next hour."

Antoine reels. The music lulls; they will have to part soon. Melarie's heart sits in her throat. Antoine could all too easily ignore her. He loves her, but it's Elodie his loyalty is sworn to. And Melarie's role tonight is clear. In the gloom of the storm, he looks older, the lines on his face deeper, more permanent. His face twitches, and then his jaw sets.

"You must do exactly as I instruct," Antoine says.

Melarie nods furiously, too grateful to speak.

"I can keep Weatherington distracted. Of that, I can assure you. I'll have Pierre search for the magistrate. Find Kaylie. Tell her she is not to leave your side. Do not enter any rooms alone. Do not, under any circumstances, leave the ballroom. If you are in the public eye, you will be safe."

Melarie's heart trips. She promised the others she'd come back—but what does she owe them, really? Every second she's trapped here puts her in danger.

"Melarie." He squeezes her hands. "I am going to get you out of this. Promise me you'll remain here."

"I promise," Melarie rasps, but it is a lie. Though it's foolish, she feels . . . some type of infuriating obligation to Kellam, Ellion, Clove, and Oak. She trusts them.

She should not trust them.

Antoine passes her to the next dancer, and Melarie is alone.

Her eyes scan the crowd. Any one of them could be the killer. She'd thought finding Antoine would bring her a sense of peace, but with every change of song, her anxiety only mounts. What if Weatherington finds out Antoine knows? What if Weatherington is innocent and one of her own people is the killer? Her throat closes. Oh gods. It could be Pierre. It could be anyone. She likely just put Antoine in danger. She needs to go after him; she needs to *warn* him—

A hand finds the small of her back.

"You're not supposed to be here."

Melarie whirls—and the world goes quiet.

It's been years since she's seen the man who brightened those dark, dreary days in her father's castle. Years since she heard that voice, saw those eyes, that cutting smile, as though only he and Melarie shared the world's best private joke. But he's here, and he hasn't aged a day.

It doesn't matter that he wears a mask; that most of his face is concealed behind the leering visage of a carnelian-studded fox. She would know him in any place, in any life, from the tilt of his shoulders alone.

And suddenly, everything that's happened tonight feels like it might just be worth it.

When Monseigneur Gabriel smiles at Melarie, the heat that floods her erases any memory of lingering cold.

"Princess," he says, his voice featherlight. "Might I steal a dance?"

20

KELLAM

As they creep toward Gaspar's office, Kellam has never felt more exposed. Here, away from the ballroom and in the councilmembers' wing, quiet blankets the castle. In any other circumstance, it would be peaceful. A scene so familiar Kellam could replay the roles in his dreams. Just him and Oak, sneaking off to cause trouble or pry where they're not meant to be.

But there's a dead girl in the library, and a corpse in the king's chambers above them. And Kellam can't help but feel it's his fault.

He wrote that letter to Vesryn, though he still doesn't understand how it ended up in her hands. He ordered her to go after Gaspar. He put her in danger, twice, and now Vesryn is dead. And the way Ellion looked at him . . .

The necromancer knows something. Kellam just isn't certain what.

It takes everything in him not to panic as Gaspar's office door looms ahead.

It's a simple enough affair: sturdy pine, set back against the frame. A hundred grand chamberlains have worked here. A hundred more shall, Twelve willing. Yet as Oak kneels and picks the lock, hands shaking in the cold, something in Kellam stutters. What they find here could change everything.

Or it might leave them worse off than before.

"Got it." Oak blows warmth back into his hands and gives Kellam a rare, crooked smile. "Don't tell Laurent. I've done this a few times to change my schedule to a better shift. He never notices."

"You're an outright criminal," Kellam says weakly, but the joke doesn't land. They look away from each other, reminded of why they're here. Kellam curls his fingers into fists. "Oak, it's you and me, right? Always?"

Oak looks up at him, still kneeling in the hallway. There is something searching in his gaze. It makes Kellam prickle.

Does Oak . . . suspect him?

As ridiculous as it sounds, it didn't even occur to Kellam until now. Oak was the only one he assumed innocent. He figured the sentiment would go both ways.

Finally, Oak nods.

"You and me," he whispers. "Always."

Kellam swallows his dread and nods. His nerves are getting the best of him.

Oak pushes the door open, and together, they slip inside.

Shadows blanket the grand chamberlain's office. For a man of such power, it's a simple room; modest in size and understated in furnishings. A long wooden desk backed by bookshelves sits to the right, lit by the glow of the snow piled against the windows. The fireplace is cold, the armchairs empty and bare, and only a plate with a half-eaten lemon tart sweating on the corner of Gaspar's otherwise immaculate desk indicates he uses the space at all. It's almost sad. To Kellam's knowledge, Gaspar never returned to

Magnivelle after his family home was destroyed with his family inside. He's not bought a new estate or attempted to regain his lordship.

For all his loyalty and patient conniving, this is the legacy of Gaspar Weatherington: an empty little room.

"Check the bookshelves," Oak murmurs. "I'll search for a loose floorboard or a trick stone. You look for anything that we could bring to Crowley. And quickly."

Kellam nods. They need something written in Gaspar's hand, but more would be better. His words to the others return. If they cannot pin Gaspar to Costis' murder, this could all be for nothing. Kellam moves to the bookshelves, feeling along the stacks for—he's not sure. A loose book? A trapdoor?

He turns to the desk, fingers grasping for anything out of place while he keeps an ear trained on the hall beyond. But too quickly, his eyes stray to the titles. For all his lurking presence in Kellam's life, Gaspar Weatherington has always been a bit of a closed book. When Kellam pictured the types of texts the grand chamberlain might fill his shelves with, he assumed Gaspar would be collecting titles on policy, law, and how to eke out a pathetic existence as a miserable shell of a person.

But every book in Gaspar's collection is about mythology.

A History of the Disappearance of the Twelve, the first text reads. *Methods of Worship for the Sect of the Builder*, promises the second. And beside it: *Manifestations of the Divine, Third Edition*.

At first, it seems like he's in the wrong section. But the more Kellam searches, the more he finds. Book after book, text after text, all curated around a central thesis: the Divine Twelve, their disappearance from the world, and theories that the gods are not dead, merely sleeping and waiting to return. At the end of the shelf, a book hangs out farther than the rest. Kellam pulls it free.

The title simply reads: *The Thirteen*.

Odd. There are only twelve gods in the Pantheon. Maybe this book is about something else? Kellam flips it open.

Every page is blank.

"What . . ." Kellam's breath fogs before him. "Oak—"

"Kellam," Oak says at the same time. "Look at this."

Kellam turns.

Oak kneels by the fireplace. He gestures for Kellam to come closer, and suddenly, Kellam understands why it's unlit. Where old ash and logs ought to sit, instead is a tiny shrine. It's crudely made; a pathetic wooden imitation of the grander creations made to honor the Builder and the other gods of the Twelve. Half-burned prayer slips are scattered around the base.

Every part of Kellam turns to ice.

It's the same handwriting as the note.

"It's him," Kellam breathes. "It's Gaspar, Oak. He's the killer. He . . . why are you looking at me like that?"

Oak is holding something in his hands. It's a journal, the cover long battered and worn smooth, the pages filled with cramped, urgent writing. With his brow furrowed, Oak begins to read.

"There is no cure for Kellam. Costis has done the unthinkable. The unforgivable. Even my love for him cannot withstand this, and so I have resigned. He offered me the post of grand chamberlain. I declined. But tonight, the Builder spoke to me, as he did all those years ago, the night Magnivelle burned. He told me the prince is not fit to rule. I will never be king, but I can be a kingmaker. I can stand between my country and the decay that would rot it from within."

The world threatens to tilt out from beneath Kellam. Carefully, he places the book back on the shelf. Oak raises his gaze to him.

"Prince Kellam," he asks carefully. "What is this about a cure?"

"I . . ." Kellam's skin feels cold and hot. He forgets his place in Gaspar's office. He forgets the storm beyond the window, the ball, and even his feelings for the boy before him. Kellam is just a child again, plagued by a constant, aching cold.

Country over heart, Costis always said. *Some secrets must be swallowed. Even the ones that poison.*

"I don't know." Kellam licks his lips. "I don't know what any of that means."

It's a half-truth. But he cannot tell Oak what he does know. What Costis confided to him only weeks ago, on the day Istellia agreed to peace and Kellam's fate was sealed with it.

"He's clearly mad," Kellam rasps. "Oak, come look at these. They're *all* about the gods. And that entry. What does he mean, the Builder spoke to him? He can't possibly believe that, right?"

His heart thuds. Oak watches him with a pinched, suspicious look. He looks at the journal again, his fingers tightening on the edge.

And from the hallway, they hear a voice.

". . . *wasting* my time with that frivolous little princess of yours."

Oak's face turns dead white.

"Please, Gaspar," a second voice says. "Humor her. The girl's never tasted freedom before. And you know what she means to me."

They need to get out of here.

Oak tears a single page from the journal. It's not the evidence they need to tie him to Costis, but at least they can match the handwriting to the note on Vesryn's body. Kellam reaches back for the blank book, but it's gone.

He blinks. He must have dropped or mis-shelved it. But, no, all the shelves look full—

"Kellam," Oak hisses. "Let's go."

Kellam lurches out the door. He starts to head right; Oak drags him to the left and around the corner just as Gaspar and a man dressed in Istellian red appear. Oak swears and presses Kellam to the wall, flattening them both into the shadowed corner. They don't breathe. They don't dare move an inch.

"I appreciate the efforts, Antoine, but you won't convince me otherwise," Gaspar says stiffly. "Our personal history aside, I cannot forgive Istellia. And I intend to see this treaty fail."

Kellam spins. With his body flush against Oak's, his sense of the world fades at the edges. He's not sure where the thunder of his heart begins and Oak's ends. The stone wall is cold against his back, but it does nothing to quell the warmth between them. Oak's fingers burn on Kellam's wrist. It takes everything in Kellam not to lean his head forward; not to nestle it against the line of Oak's throat.

They've always fit together so perfectly. Two crooked halves making one solid whole.

Beyond them, Gaspar's and Antoine's shadows twist against the far wall.

"You did not always have so hard a heart, Gaspar," says Antoine. "I worry where this road leads you."

Gaspar's shadow reaches for the handle of his study door. Oak stiffens, every line of his body going taut against Kellam's.

The door.

They didn't lock the damn door.

"Don't worry about my path," Gaspar says coldly. "Worry about how you'll stay out of my way."

A shout comes from the other end of the hall—guards or councilmen or guests, it doesn't matter. The door creaks. Gaspar hisses in a breath—and Oak moves.

He steps away and drags Kellam down the hall. The moment they turn a second corner, they break into a sprint.

The last thing Kellam hears is the grand chamberlain's voice, cold and steeped in warning.

"I know you love that princess," Gaspar says. "You were always too kind, Antoine. So let me return that kindness and bury our history once and for all. Find a different princess to love. You cannot protect her from what's to come."

21

MELARIE

MELARIE and Gabriel dance in silence. He's real. He's *here*. They move through the ballroom in a whirl of color, and the world fades away. It's only Melarie and Monseigneur Gabriel, his hand on the small of her back, his gray eyes holding hers.

"You," she breathes.

"Me," he agrees.

She doesn't know where to begin. She drinks in the sight of him. He looks sharper, somehow; more real. His icy blond hair has grown longer, cut just above his shoulders and slicked away from his face. Unlike the nobles around her, his clothing is simple: black wool lined with floral silver thread. A single silver ring, cast in the form of a fox mid-leap, glints on his index finger. Melarie cannot quite process the sight of him. She's gawking like a peasant girl on her first day at court. She supposes that's not too far from reality. The day Gabriel first arrived for his seat at court as a temple advisor, dressed in the indigo robes of the Weaver, neck heavy with the red beads of the Lover, Melarie's first thought had been that he seemed so *young* to be among her father's officials.

Her second thought had been that Gabriel was the most beautiful man Melarie had ever seen.

"It has been *over a year*," she says. The accusation comes out petulant, like a child. "I thought perhaps my father had you killed! Where have you been?"

Surprise flashes across his face, but only briefly. "You remember me?"

Melarie blinks. "You think I would forget?"

The thought sends a pinprick of hurt through her. His impact on her was life-altering; it stings to think the feeling might not be reciprocated. That to handsome, worldly Monseigneur Gabriel, Melarie had only ever been a fleeting fascination. A lonely princess to pity and sneak stories and books to, but nothing more. Not even worth remembering the moment he walked out the door.

Alarm flashes across Gabriel's face, there and gone in only a blink.

"Your father accused me of heresy and conspiracy." Gabriel looks troubled. "I thought it safer if I left quietly. I did not think—forgive me, princess, but what are you doing here? I thought your sister would be in attendance."

"I could ask the same of you," Melarie retorts. "Elodie sent me in her place. It was meant to be a simple task but so far this night has been pure chaos."

Gabriel smiles briefly. He holds her closer than is proper, his eyes drawing down the length of her and then back up again. "You look beautiful."

"The gown is Delphine's," Melarie says. She immediately feels foolish. She's waited so long to see him again, and this is the best she has? A comment about her sister's dress? "Why didn't you return? I looked for you at my father's funeral. And after. I thought when he died you might . . ."

Her voice trails. Her father had appointed Gabriel to his council only to banish him right before his death. Something about how Gabriel had ties to the Weaver cultists in the far south. Melarie doesn't recall the details, only the pain she felt when she'd rushed into his office to tell him her thoughts on the book of myths he'd brought her and found him gone.

Gabriel spins her again. His hand is warm through the fabric of her dress. She's so close to him she can smell the incense on his skin, and something else—something sweet.

"Forgive me," he says quietly. "I thought you were safer if I stayed away. I couldn't bear for my presence to cause you pain."

Melarie's throat bobs. Her confession catches in her throat. *It's the lack of your presence that pained me.* She swallows it and looks away. "And why are you here?"

"I serve an Avendellian temple now," Gabriel says with a crooked smile. "They sent me to beg the new king's favor, in hopes of additional support and tithes. I worship the Arbiter, if you can believe it. Though between you and me, if the goddess of justice ever woke, I don't think she'd be very impressed with me."

Melarie's mood sours. Yet another thing her father has ruined. In Istellia, Gabriel was the temple advisor for the entire nation. But thanks to her father's madness, this is what he's been reduced to: a simple acolyte for a goddess he doesn't believe in, begging for scraps at the feet of a prince whose nation he was forced to flee to.

It's no wonder he didn't seek her out. To Gabriel, Melarie is merely a reminder of how far he's fallen.

Though if he feels that way, he's doing a good job at hiding it. Gabriel watches her with eyes that dance behind his mask.

"Come, no more of that dismal expression," he says finally.

He spins her quickly. "What happened to the little princess who always dreamed of grand balls and begged for stories of the Divine Twelve's ethereal revels? What was it you told me? Something about how someday your nights would be a blur of glittering gowns and every suitor in this kingdom and the next begging for your hand?"

It had been a pretty dream, once. In those days, she would have married a toad to escape her father's palace. For a breath, she wants to tell him everything—about the body, the engagement, Vesryn's corpse still cooling in the library, the grand chamberlain, who is one accident away from seizing power and plunging them all into ruin.

But though she has longed to see Gabriel again, she is leery, too.

"This evening is turning out to be quite the disappointment," Melarie says.

He gives her a small, private smile. "Then we'll have to find a way to make it memorable."

Gabriel pulls her closer, and though she's still scanning the crowd for Antoine, a part of Melarie relaxes. This was what Antoine ordered her to do, was it not? To remain in the ballroom? At least, with Gabriel, she will not be alone. The heat of his hand burns through her dress. And though it's not proper—though someone is certain to talk—Melarie cannot help herself. Melarie leans her temple against his chest, and he tucks her closer, his chin resting on the crown of her head.

"I have missed you," she whispers. An improper confession if there ever was one. "I wish—I understand why you left. But I still wish you'd stayed."

"I know, princess." Gabriel twines a lock of Melarie's hair

around his finger before tucking it behind her ear. "I know. But I am here now."

She is so tired, and so relieved to be in the arms of someone she trusts. Her thoughts turn to liquid. Her anxiety about Costis and Vesryn and returning to Istellia drift away. What she would not give, to live in this moment; to pause time itself and remain here forever.

He's here. He's solid, and he's real.

"How?" a voice croaks.

The warmth evaporates.

Ellion stands in the middle of the ballroom, beaked mask dangling from his ear, eyes blown wide and color drained from his face. He looks at Melarie and Gabriel as though he's seen a ghost.

"Ellion?" Melarie's heart leaps. "What are you doing here? Aren't you supposed to be with V—aren't you supposed to be resting?"

Ellion sways.

"How?" he slurs. "How are you dancing with *her*?"

Dread curdles in Melarie. "I beg your pardon?"

Ellion grabs Melarie's arm, too tightly, wrenching her out of the arms of the monseigneur. His hands tremble. "What kind of game is this? What are you playing at?"

"Let go of me." Melarie's voice rises. She wrenches backward. "Ellion, I said *let go*."

Ellion stumbles and goes sprawling. He's off-balance, far too drunk. Melarie's irritation collapses into smoke, replaced by a wash of concern. She doesn't want to care about the necromancer, but he's truly pathetic, like a stray dog that's been kicked one too many times. And though it would be in her best interest, Melarie's always had a hard time turning a blind eye to broken things.

"Ellion," she asks. "What's wrong?"

Ellion looks up at her with drowning eyes. He touches his necklace with shaking fingers, as if searching for a missing bead on the chain.

"I failed her," he rasps. "All I've ever done is fail her."

He lurches to his feet and crashes away, knocking into other dancers. Only his mask remains, glinting sadly in the middle of the floor.

Melarie picks it up and turns. "I'm sorry about that. I don't know who he could have possibly mistaken you for—"

She's speaking only to empty air.

Gabriel is gone.

22

ELLION

ELLION can't forget what he saw: Melarie twirling on the dance floor, her face the picture of bliss, and Vesryn in her arms. Not the Vesryn of tonight, but the Vesryn of Ellion's youth: bright-eyed, rosy-cheeked, and full of hope. She'd been so beautiful she'd practically glowed, her head tossed back as she laughed, dark hair swinging as they twirled.

Then she'd met Ellion's eyes—and the world crashed in. Vesryn's neck had purpled; her skin lost its color. Ellion had tried to rip Melarie away from her and when he'd looked up, Vesryn had loomed behind the princess like one of the Divine Twelve, woken from eternal sleep and hungry for justice.

"Your fault," Vesryn had said, unblinking as blood trickled from her nose. "All your fault."

And then she was gone.

"She's dead," Ellion whispers to himself. "She's *dead*. Looks like you earned yourself another bead, asshole."

He'd thought he was punishing himself enough with Luma. That spot of ink on gold, staring him in the face every day; the absence of any white to balance it out. It felt right to shame himself that way. To know that anyone who looked at him would see what a failure he was.

Its weight is nothing now compared to what Vesryn's will add to his neck.

Without the pleasant numbness of alcohol or tranquilizer, everything about the castle feels heightened. Death lingers all around Ellion. He hates places like this—places as old as the land itself, where so many have walked, loved, and laughed, their emotions lingering long after their bodies have crumbled and their souls have fled.

Ellion aches for a drink.

He staggers farther away from the ballroom. Ellion had no intention of actually staying in the library, not when the others were off doing something useful, but now he's begun to regret his plan. Perhaps he ought to have accepted their pity and stayed behind.

A servant passes with a tray of sparkling wine. Ellion's hand lifts—but he thinks of Vesryn. He needs to pull himself together.

Ellion ducks into a hallway, lunges for a window, and flings it open.

Cold blasts his face. In an instant, his cheeks are numb. He can see nothing of the world outside—only a wall of white, growing thicker by the minute. The road is totally gone; soon, the trees will be covered.

Why did Vesryn think he killed her?

It doesn't make sense. And then there was that—that *feeling*. The presence in the Veil, too powerful to be just another spirit. He hadn't told the others about it. What was he supposed to say? Some disembodied voice had warned him of a game currently in play?

No. He likes the others well enough, but he doesn't trust them. He needs information before he puts himself at risk.

Something else is going on. Vesryn suspected it. Ellion wasn't ready to listen then, but he's ready now.

"Help me out, Ves," whispers Ellion. "What did you figure out? What are we missing?"

Behind Ellion, something shifts.

For a moment it's Clove's face that flits across his mind. *Is there somewhere in the castle that stays cold year-round?*

Gooseflesh prickles his skin. He swallows. Right. There's a deadly venomous beast gallivanting through the halls this evening. Forgot about that.

Something mews. He turns. Snowflakes swirl through the hallway, forming a veil of twirling ice. For a moment, the image before him doesn't make sense. Ellion blinks once, twice, but it doesn't clear.

Sitting in front of Ellion, tail twitching irritably, is one of the most screwed-up cats he's ever seen. He'd know it anywhere.

"*Rue?*"

There's no mistaking it—the jagged, torn left ear, the crooked tail that never healed quite right. The cat's black fur gleams under a fresh coat of snow, and when a snowflake hits his good ear, it gives an irritated twitch.

But something is wrong with Rue's eyes. The left eye is the shining amber Ellion recalls, but his right eye gleams a familiar violet.

The hair on his arms stands on end. He feels like a complete and utter fool as he whispers, "Vesryn?"

Rue rises, stretches, and trots down the hall. Ellion remains where he is, snow gusting at his back.

And then the cat stops.

It looks back at Ellion and gives an annoyed, high-pitched meow. And perhaps Ellion really *is* losing it—because he swears the cat twitches its tail down the hall in a *this way* gesture.

"Okay," Ellion whispers miserably. "Sure. I'll follow the fucking ghost cat. Why not."

Ellion closes the window and steps into the dark.

He hasn't been to this part of the castle yet.

Rue—or Vesryn pretending to be Rue, or the hallucination that's appearing as Rue and is an indicator Ellion has fully gone mad—leads him into a wing he's never seen before. Dust blankets the carpet, and unlike the polished gleam of the rest of the castle, the door handles here are dull and untouched. The only signs of past life are tiny paintings along the baseboards; dozens of painstaking pastel strokes that form a trail of flowers and vines. They were probably beautiful once. Now the paint is chipped and faded.

No one has come this way for a long, long time.

A heavy grief hangs in the air.

And Ellion feels the dead a moment too late.

One moment, he's in an old hallway; the next, he's walking through memory. Every part of him wants to flee, but Rue is ahead of him, violet eye winking in the gloom, and Ellion has no choice but to follow. The emotions of the dead swirl around him; the acidic bile of grief, the tender, warm cinnamon of new love. And in the center of it all—a pull.

Come closer, something seems to whisper. *Come witness.*

So he does.

Rue leads him to the door and stops. Everything is coming

from the room. Ellion hesitates in front of it, casting an uneasy glance over his shoulder. But whatever lingers here, whether it's ghost or ghoul or just a memory printed into the stone, doesn't feel malevolent.

It feels desperate to be heard.

"Vesryn?" Ellion whispers.

He opens the door.

The cat has led him to a nursery.

It's a small, cozy space. Wooden toys collect dust on pale green shelves; a small beechwood crib sits in the corner, long grayed by time, waiting patiently for new life to return. Paintings of flowers spiral up the wall, done by the same hand as whoever decorated the baseboards.

When Ellion steps into the room, the air around the crib shimmers and pulses with cold. Two translucent figures materialize beside it. Ellion's shoulders relax. Of all the spirits, apparitions are his favorite. They're not trapped souls or vengeful ghouls; just echoes of intense emotion from souls long passed, caught in an eternal loop. An imprint trapped in time.

He draws closer. The images solidify—and voices bleed through.

"I don't understand."

Costis is the youngest Ellion has ever seen him, the king's face open, bright, and unlined. In the half-light of evening, the signet ring on his index finger practically glows.

The other apparition is a woman—young, dark haired, and beautiful. She shakes her head, lips thin with worry. "It could pass."

"My love," Costis says quietly. "This does not look like something that will pass."

The cat winds around Ellion's ankles and leaps onto the edge of the crib. It doesn't move. Ellion files this away. So he's definitely hallucinating, then. Which would typically be a concern, but the alternative is that Vesryn's beloved cat has returned from the dead with one of her eyes, and that seems much, much worse.

Ellion drifts closer to join them, curious what could be so important that it would keep this memory of Costis' here.

An infant lies in the crib.

It's so small. A newborn still, his little face wrinkly, red, and furious. Withered, blackened plants surround the baby in a strange ring. Gently, Queen Greer reaches for something off to the side—whatever it is, it's no longer in the room. Her hand draws back into the memory and Ellion's blood freezes.

In her palm, petals spread wide, is a winter lily.

That flower. First Costis pulled a lily from his pocket before he died; later, they found the same flower pinned to Vesryn's chest. A mirror to the lily blazing on Weatherington's family crest.

It can't be an accident. He needs to tell the others.

But first Ellion will hear what the dead of Castle Avendell are so desperate for him to know.

"I thought it was a myth," Costis says. "My uncle was born silent. Everything around him rotted. When he died in his first year, the official story was the plague, but my father always spoke of a curse on our line." Pain carves canyons in his face, a warning of the lines of misery to come. "I thought it nonsense; the paranoid whispers of old kings. A magic not meant for our world. I never thought my son . . . I never dreamed it was a problem we would face."

Horror wraps a cold vise around Ellion. What is Costis saying? That Kellam is . . . cursed? That something lived—or still lives—within him that might put them all at risk?

His mind loops back to Vesryn. To the unnatural storm, the impending chaos, and of course, Kellam himself. Kellam seems to believe Gaspar Weatherington's vendetta against him is born from personal motivation and bitterness. But if Kellam's truly meant to be king, where is his green magic?

And if he doesn't have it, what lurks within the prince instead?

Greer's lips form a bloodless line. "There is nothing to be done, then?"

Costis stares at Kellam.

"There is something," he says hesitantly, "that Alistair suggested we might try."

The world threatens to close around Ellion.

"There's a place near the border. Gaspar has been digging through old myths. And his research is backed by Alistair's claims." His eyes go to Greer. "What do you know of Godmaker's Gorge?"

Ellion staggers back.

Twelve help them. Vesryn was right.

Greer places the lily in the crib. Costis looks on from behind her, and as she does, his expression shifts from worry to fear. Before Ellion can step forward again, the memory dissolves into mist. Costis, Greer, and Kellam vanish.

Unfortunately, the cat remains. It blinks at Ellion, then leaps from the crib and slips into the hall. Ellion storms past it, his accelerating pulse having nothing to do with the alcohol leaving his system.

The flower. Kellam. Vesryn. Gaspar. And *his* father, wrapped up in this from the beginning.

Something foul is happening here—and it's tied to Kellam Vernevau.

23

KELLAM

KELLAM and Oak say nothing as they flee back to the library. With every step, Kellam's mind whirls. Gaspar Weatherington is a killer. They have evidence matching his handwriting; they might even have something near motivation. But what ought to feel like a victory or a confirmation only adds to Kellam's dread. With every step, the distance between him and Oak grows.

What is this about a cure?

Kellam has always told Oak everything. But this is one secret he cannot share.

He doesn't even realize he's having a panic attack until he's on the floor.

The terror comes in waves; ice-bright and biting, crushing his lungs, his ribs, his heart.

"Your Grace?" Hands on his shoulders, pulling him up. "Kellam." In the privacy of the library, Oak folds Kellam into his arms. The guard squeezes Kellam's hands, and even in his frenzy, Kellam thinks it a shame that the only time Oak touches him like this is when Kellam is in the midst of an absolute breakdown.

"Kellam," Oak murmurs again. Kellam loves how his name sounds on Oak's tongue. "Just breathe."

"My father," Kellam gasps. "Vesryn, the treaty, *Gaspar*—"

Oak cups Kellam's face in his hands.

"None of that," Oak says. "We'll figure it out. Breathe. Count with me, okay? Just breathe and look at me."

Kellam forces himself to meet Oak's eyes.

Gods help him. Oak is so beautiful.

People always talk about love at first sight, of lightning strikes and cold sweats, but when Kellam looks at Oak, he knows this love developed over seasons. Day after day, year after year, like a stubborn winter finally giving way to a thaw. The older they grew, the more it was impossible to deny: Kellam Vernevau was hopelessly, stupidly in love with his father's favorite guard.

Oak has always been Kellam's favorite form of torture. But Kellam can never tell Oak how he feels. Even if he wanted to, Oak has never expressed interest in, well, *anyone*. And even if there was a chance? Even if maybe, someday, Oak could feel the same way?

Kellam is a prince. A betrothed one, at that. Oak is not his to want.

"I don't suppose," Kellam says weakly, "you could punch me in the face?"

"Maybe just this once," Oak drawls.

And that's what does it. Not the corpse, not his father, not Gaspar's betrayal or Kellam's fatal secret or the doom bearing down on them all. It's Oak's hands on his skin and the dry humor in his voice that breaks the last of Kellam's resolve. This whole scene is so normal. Kellam having a meltdown; Oak comforting him.

Oak deserves better than this.

Before Kellam can stop himself, before he can think twice, the truth slips out:

"It's my fault."

And Oak freezes.

The fire in the library grate burns low.

"It's my fault Vesryn is dead," Kellam whispers. "I hired her to come here. I hired her to kill my father."

He remembers the moment like it was yesterday. Costis had grown more and more irrational over the years, his once-patient temper shortened to nothing, like a candle burned to the last of the wick. And Kellam took all of it in stride. The slights, the triple-locked doors, the paranoid meetings and inflated guard ranks they could not afford.

Until that day when, suddenly, bearing it was no longer an option.

Oak, to his credit, doesn't panic. His voice is even when he asks, "Why?"

"I saw him threaten you," Kellam whispers, throat aching with the threat of tears. "Two weeks ago, in his chambers. I was on my way to—"

The words catch. He'd been on his way to plead with Costis not to send Oak away. Costis wasn't stupid. He knew Kellam's erratic behavior was a bid for attention. Every man and woman brought to his bed, every party thrown, and even that unfortunate time he'd leaped from the balcony naked (he tried not to think about that) had been an attempt to draw Oak's weary eye.

What did it matter if Oak was looking at Kellam with disappointment, so long as he was looking?

Everything changed the moment the treaty was on the table. Suddenly, Kellam's feelings weren't some silly childhood crush; they were a liability, guaranteed destruction for Costis' plans to save his country by marrying Kellam off. As soon as Istellia sent their bid for peace, Costis reassigned Oak from Castle Avendell to the day watch at Godmaker's Gorge. And the worst part was that Kellam had understood. Oak could not remain in the palace if Costis was to keep Kellam from burning their newfound peace to the ground.

If Kellam was to become what Avendell needed, Oak could not remain here.

On paper, it was perfect. Kellam would do his duty; Oak would have a normal life without the prince distracting him. They each could build their futures and serve the kingdom as they were meant to. It was best for everyone.

Kellam had planned to get on his knees and plead with Costis to let him keep Oak anyway.

But when Kellam had entered Costis' chambers, the king was not alone.

"He had a knife to your ribs," Kellam whispers.

The scene is burned into his mind. Oak, his face drawn and pale, holding still as a statue as Costis pressed the point of a knife to Oak's side with deadly, focused calm. And Kellam had understood, then and there, how love could drive even the softest hearts to do terrible things.

"I saw him," Kellam whispers. "I heard him threaten you and I—I panicked, Oak. I wrote an invitation for the assassin and instructions, but I *swear*, I never sent the letter. I don't know how it ended up in her hands. I don't know how she got here at all, but now my father is dead, and she is, too, and—" His voice breaks. "Say something, please."

The silence that follows is the longest of Kellam's life. Oak is breathing rapidly, his nostrils flared. His hands fall from Kellam's face. He curls them into fists, but it does nothing to hide the way they shake.

"Why?" Oak croaks.

The world tilts. "What?"

Oak's face wipes clean. Kellam hates when he does that—when he retreats behind his mask. Kellam wants to break down that wall every time, brick by brick, and drag Oak back out by his ankles.

"You tried to kill your own father," Oak says evenly. "Why?"

Kellam jerks backward as though he's been struck. Did Oak miss everything he just said? "He had a *knife to your ribs*."

"I'm just a guard."

"Don't be ridiculous, that's—"

"Was it to stop the treaty?" Oak demands. "To stop the marriage?"

"No," Kellam protests.

"Did you hate him? Did you grow impatient for power?"

"No, that's not—I would never—"

"He was your father," Oak says, his voice rising. "And I am just a guard. So why, Kellam?"

"I can't—"

"Why risk everything you have? Everything you could be?"

"You're not—"

"You tried to kill the king," Oak says harshly. "Tell me *why*."

Kellam can't take it anymore.

"Because I love you," Kellam blurts.

Oak freezes.

And suddenly, Kellam has all the words in the world.

"Did you truly not know?" He breathes. "I could bear being forced to marry someone else. I could endure pining from afar. But you are the sun my world spins around. You are my best friend, Oak. You are all the better parts of me. I love you; I have *always* loved you. I think I have loved you from the moment I saw you, and I think I would love you until my end, even if I never laid eyes on you again." Kellam's voice cracks. "There is no act in this world that would be too terrible for me to commit if I thought it would keep you safe."

For once, Oak has nothing to say.

Kellam reaches for him. He cradles Oak's face in his hands.

If this is the last time he gets to touch Oak, Kellam wants to make it worth it.

"I would grind cities to dust for you. I would send men to war, set fleets aflame, and gladly damn this country and everyone in it a thousand times over if it meant I could protect you. So, *yes*, Oak, when I thought my father was going to hurt you—I planned to have him killed." Kellam's next words are breathless. "But you must believe me when I tell you: *I did not send that letter.* My greatest sin in all this is that once Vesryn was already within the castle, I asked her to kill Gaspar. Even though I wanted to, even though I would, I did not kill the king."

The silence that fills the library is deafening. In the wake of his confession, Kellam feels hollowed out. He's not sure who is trembling harder, him or Oak. Every last bit of color has left the guard's face.

Beyond the library doors, the roar of the party continues. Kellam's world spins. He has broken the only promise he ever cared about keeping—the promise he made himself, all those years ago, that he would never make his feelings Oak's problem to bear.

Kellam has ruined everything.

And Oak is just . . . staring at him.

"Say something," Kellam whispers, and it's quite a feat, really, that he manages to sound as pathetic as he feels. "Say you hate me. Say you plan to arrest me. Say you never want to see me again. Just say something, Oak, please."

Oak's eyes dart from Kellam to Vesryn's body to the door and back again.

"I—I think," Oak stammers, "I need some air."

Before Kellam can protest—before he can plead or explain or somehow make things worse than they already are—Oak is moving. He pries Kellam's fingers from his cheeks and practically flees from the library.

And then it is only Kellam, with Vesryn's corpse splayed behind him, kneeling on the library carpet and staring into nothing, drowning in the sea of everything he has surely lost.

24

CLOVE

CLOVE has told several lies tonight, and it will cost her dearly.

First, she had agreed to Kellam's conditions. Of course, in an ideal world, she would placate the beast and stow it away in a dungeon cell without harm. But basilisks are temperamental, vicious things, and Clove has been out of practice for years. She can make no promises that they'll both live through this encounter.

Then there's the issue of the cat.

When Clove followed the others out of the library, each one of them had marched right past the ghostly creature and started down the steps without so much as a glance. Clove, however, froze. The cat slinked and purred, its pink tongue darting from its mouth to lick its paws. One wild eye was the color of honey straight from the hive; the other the same shade as swollen summer plums. Both eyes watched her.

Then the cat spoke.

Its tiny porcelain-white teeth glittered as it said, *You are the one who can call them in.* And—this is the part Clove can barely stand to admit—its voice wasn't entirely unfamiliar.

It sounded like Vesryn.

"Clove?" Melarie had called from the staircase. "What's wrong?"

Though Clove had grown vaguely fond of the princess in the short time they'd known each other, she couldn't force the words from her throat. *Hey, so, you see that talking black cat, right?* Of course Melarie hadn't or couldn't see it—she'd stepped right over it without a moment's hesitation. And neither Kellam nor Oak had seemed to notice its presence as it slinked about the library, either. Which meant that only Clove and the mentally unwell necromancer could perceive it.

Oh no.

"Nothing! I'm coming," Clove had answered quickly, before lifting her chin and stepping past the cat as if it were nothing more than a stain on the carpet.

But the cat would not be ignored. The pinks of its ears glowed beneath the flickering mage-lights as it wove between them, its tail occasionally catching on Clove's tulle. *Ghost cat, please,* she begged. *Not now.*

As if the cat had heard her, it shot her a withering look before bounding the rest of the way down the stairs and disappearing. To Clove's relief, the cat wasn't waiting for her at the bottom, and it hadn't trailed after her as she wound her way across the ballroom to the opposing hallway. She'd thought she'd seen a flick of its tail as she'd tiptoed toward the dungeons, but it was gone in a blink.

When she's certain no one is watching, she slips into the alcove beside the dungeon entrance and unlocks the ancient wooden door. She descends the stone steps two at a time. As the cool and quiet press in, Clove's muscles relax. *This,* at least, is familiar. If nothing else, at least this tiny reminder of crisp mountain air is enough to carry her down, down, down.

The farther she descends, the less likely it seems that the basilisk has escaped this prison. Maybe the sensations she felt in the library were wrong—just her own panic flaring. But those marks ringing Vesryn's neck... only a pair of supernaturally strong hands or a feral basilisk could have made them. Clove shakes away the thought. One thing at a time.

First, she has to find this snake.

A chill creeps up her spine when she reaches the dungeons. It's even darker in here than she'd thought it would be; only a single emergency mage-light casts a sickly green glow throughout the room.

Clove tiptoes toward the closed-door cell, pausing every so often to listen for scales slithering over stone. She hears nothing—it's so dreadfully quiet down here that it jangles her nerves. It's not the same quiet of the mountains or woods. That kind of quiet is a balm. This kind feels more like a bomb.

She lets out a puff of air when she reaches the cell. *Thank the gods.* The iron door is shut tight. If Gaspar really did hide a basilisk down here, let's hope he was sensible enough to lock it inside this cell. A little laugh escapes her lips as she pokes the door. All this worry, for nothing.

The door creaks open and green light floods the cell.

There is no snake.

"No," Clove breathes. She rushes into the cell and kicks the loose pile of hay on the floor. "*No.*" She spins through the room, running her fingers over every stone, every crack. The snake is not here.

But it's *here*—the elongated shadow of the beast projected against stone. Whether some sort of apparition or latent magic or simple instinct, Clove's bones ache with the truth of it: The snake is somewhere in this dungeon.

She squeezes her eyes shut. In the words of Ellion Evercraft: *Fuck.*

The sound starts off impossibly soft—so soft that for a moment, Clove considers this may be another hallucination. But as it crescendos, her blood runs cold. Clove's eyes snap open.

It's a snake's hiss.

Clove runs out of the cell and stumbles. She can't tell where it's coming from. She spins, pausing to listen, but the hiss seems to have multiplied. It assaults her from every direction, the sound vibrating in her ears as if it were coming from a hundred beasts instead of one.

"W-what is this?" she whispers. Every muscle in her body coils in preparation to *run*. Clove may not trust magic, but she never second-guesses her instincts.

She runs.

Clove can hardly hear the hissing over her heartbeat roaring in her ears. Her useless heels pound against stone as she traces the path she came back to the stairs. The gaping maw of the stairwell appears and her heart hitches. *Almost there—*

"Oof!" Clove yelps as her foot slams into something solid and heavy, sending her flying. Her knees slam into the stone floor, and even through the layers of tulle, the blow reverberates through her bones. Whatever she tripped over skids away and lands in a pool of green light.

A book. Vesryn was in the library.

She bites back a whimper as she crawls toward it. It's a compact tome bound in leather. Clove picks it up and tips it to the murky light, but the title is too worn to discern.

What is it you desire, wild one?

The voice—and Clove is certain it is a voice now—is as sharp as a woodcutter's knife yet is still layered with the echo of a hiss. Bile rises in her throat. Suddenly, her hands are so sweaty that it dampens the leather-bound tome. "Basilisks can't talk," she whimpers.

Sure they can, says the voice. *You just haven't been properly listening. But I've been listening to* you, *Clove.*

She can't stop shaking. "Stop this," she says limply. "Stop playing tricks, whoever you are."

I've been watching you, and I know exactly what you yearn for.

Clove closes her eyes. "No, you don't."

Someone who understands you, the voice says. It's so close now that Clove swears she can feel the beast's breath on her cheek. She opens her eyes.

A northern basilisk as white as winter sits before her, its head lifted so its pale pink eyes are in line with hers. Clove's lip trembles. "No. No, this isn't real."

But the snake ignores her. It sways before her, almost as if it's trying to hypnotize her. *You long to be truly known, to be protected, just as you do for your lesser beasts. It's true, isn't it, Clove?*

At this, Clove chokes out a sob. It *is* true—no matter how much she has tried to convince herself otherwise, the ache of loneliness has never left her. But this beast, how could it possibly know that? How could it be *telling* her this?

I can make that happen for you, you know, the snake continues, slithering closer. *We could make a bargain.*

A bargain. The word sears through her, cutting through the panic. A bargain. Clove and her brothers had learned long ago that nature never bargains—it bends and flows with fate and continues on with fortitude and grace. This is no ordinary basilisk plucked from the snow. This is dark magic.

Clove swallows. "No," she says calmly. And then she slams the book into the snake's pretty opalescent head with every ounce of her strength.

The beast goes flying. The hissing swells to a high-pitched scream that makes Clove's ears ring. She jumps to her feet and flings the book in the snake's direction, hoping to stun it long enough for her to escape.

Clove runs for her life.

You will die alone! the snake screeches. The beast nips at her dress. She gives the tulle a violent shake without daring to look back, praying that it's enough. The scream pierces through her like a barbed arrow, leaving her gasping for breath. When the stairs come into view, Clove almost cries in relief. She races up them, toward the safety of the crowded castle.

Almost there. She's going to make it. Tears stream down her face, hot and fast, and she doesn't bother to wipe them away. The cloying aromas of sweat and perfume waft in, along with candlelight, and Clove has never been so happy to see other humans.

She reaches the top step and trips once again.

This time, the object she runs into does not budge. Clove tumbles over the large mass and skids across the floor, the tulle of her dress now properly torn to shreds. She slowly pulls herself upright, panting, and looks back.

A man dressed in a crisp emerald Avendellian uniform lies limp on the floor, his eyes staring at nothing. A gold pin in the shape of an owl winks from his chest. His skin has already begun to gray.

NINE HOURS TO DAWN

25

OAK

Oak has never wanted to flee the castle more than he does right now.

He paces the length of the servants' wing, his steps methodical and measured. Something about the predictable tempo of boots on the ground has always been a balm, ever since he began training for Costis' kingsguard when he was eleven. Marching reminds him of citrus-colored mornings and weaponry and *order*. There is something soothing about knowing the exact next step to take, even when the world is crumbling around you.

And the world is definitely crumbling around him.

Oak pulls at the collar of his uniform. First, he couldn't get warm, now he can't stop sweating. He pauses his pacing and tries to catch his breath.

The crown prince—no, the future *king*—of Avendell just professed his love to him.

And all Oak could say was *I think I need some air?*

He slaps his palm to his forehead. The heat burning in his chest spreads to his cheeks. The heir to a nation told him he loved him. That he would burn down cities for him. That he had been willing to *kill his own father* for him. And Oak had run away.

He restarts his pacing, trying to tame the thoughts swirling through his head. Well, there's the issue of Kellam admitting he hired a mercenary to murder the next in line to the throne. That's the bigger problem here. Kellam could be tried for treason if anyone finds out, but Oak already knows they won't. He will never breathe a word of it.

Kellam loves me.

Of course it's flattering that a prince finds him—an orphan with no proper lineage—desirable. But it's more than that. Kellam is his *friend*. His confidant. The closest thing he's ever had to a brother.

Right?

In his mind, he sees the two of them—one with summer-blond hair and the other with midnight black—practicing with wooden swords in the garden. They couldn't have been more than twelve, maybe thirteen, both wiry and not yet muscular enough to fill out their frames. Kellam had always been a better swordsman, but Oak had strength. He pinned Kellam to the dew-drenched grass, again and again, and yet the young prince always came back for more the next morning.

The prince had no reason to train that hard. Neither of them said anything about that, though. Oak had looked forward to every single one of those predawn mornings, just the two of them, their breath fogging in the cold. The way Kellam always licked his lips when Oak pinned him to the ground.

Oak's breath catches. *No.* Costis warned him. He couldn't want Kellam like that. It would only end in ruin.

But that had been before. When Oak had been certain the prince did not reciprocate his feelings.

He had been wrong.

"How?" he mumbles, turning on his heel to retrace his path down the hall. "How did I not know?" Surely, there had been signs. Had Oak been so oblivious that he had missed every last one?

A series of memories parade through Oak's mind in quick succession. Kellam as a boy, his hair too long and curled around his ears, his gaze searching for Oak from across the sitting room. Kellam's hand grazing Oak's at the dinner table, even though he needn't be that close to reach the rolls. Kellam curled into his chaise, pretending to read while Oak trained, though his eyes strayed from the page quite often.

No. Some part of Oak had to have known, or at least hoped. He just hadn't allowed himself to believe it could be real.

A door creaks open to his left, causing him to startle. A young boy with stark blond hair pokes his head out. "Oak?"

"Mason." Oak attempts a smile at the young attendant-in-training. "You should be in bed, should you not?"

The boy rubs his eyes, his gray night tunic hanging well below his knees. "I was, but I heard a sound."

"I'm sorry for that. I'll quiet my steps."

"No, it's not that," Mason says. He takes an exaggerated yawn. "It was before. And it was louder. And farther away. Like someone fell."

Oak's whole body goes very still. He tries to quell the dread climbing up his throat. "And which direction do you think the sound came from?"

The boy shrugs. He points over Oak's shoulder. "Dunno. Couldn't be that far away. Maybe by the kitchen? Or the dungeons?"

The dungeons. Oak's pulse stammers. The beast tamer is down there.

The basilisk is down there.

"Thank you, Mason," he says, drawing his mouth into a tight smile. "Now go to bed." The boy grumbles under his breath, but Oak is already racing down the hall.

Kellam is still safe in the library. He's still safe, Oak chants in his mind as he dodges the forgotten statue of the Gardener and picks up speed. *Safe, safe, safe.*

Someone screams. Oak yelps and stumbles, just in time to see that he's about to crash straight into a large mass on the floor a few paces ahead. He angles his body at the last second to avoid the collision, instead landing on his shoulder with the full crush of his weight.

Oak groans as he forces himself upright and scans the hall. That scream. Where did it come from?

Slowly, his eyes land on the mass he almost crashed into.

The magistrate of Avendell lies wide-eyed and lifeless before him.

"*No.*" This can't be happening. Oak stumbles to his feet and rushes toward the dead man. "No, no, no. Please. *No.*" He knows the magistrate is dead and gone, but he nudges the corpse with his boot anyway. Oak is going to be sick.

"Oak."

His head snaps up. And then he sees her.

The beast tamer sits only a few paces from the body, her legs curled up to her chin and her willowy arms wrapped tightly around the pomp of her dress. Tears run in rivulets down her flushed cheeks.

Instinctively, Oak reaches for his knife. Clove's eyes widen. "Wait, no! It's not me! I didn't do this." She unwinds her arms and lifts them in surrender.

Something in Oak's chest hitches. He has no reason to feel sorry for this girl—especially as he's just found her sidled up to a dead Avendellian nobleman. A nobleman who he desperately needs right now.

And yet he does. She hasn't stopped shaking since she called his name. Oak's hand drops to his side. "What happened?"

Clove bursts into heaving sobs. "I was in the dungeons and I found a basilisk down there." She slides her palms across her cheeks to wipe her tears. "But it was . . . it was different. Like it was possessed or something. It *talked to me*, and then I ran up the stairs and found the magistrate dead."

She gags, and for a moment, Oak is certain she's about to vomit all over the floor. But Clove presses her lips together and swallows before releasing a shaky breath. "Look at his chest."

Oak does not want to look at Samson Crowley's chest. He fills his lungs to steady himself, then allows his gaze to drift downward. As soon as he sees it, dread crashes through him.

A white winter lily lies atop the magistrate's corpse.

With it, a note. An echo of the one before, written in Gaspar's cramped, angry hand.

Bring out the king or more will die.

Now Oak is the one who gags, and unlike Clove, he cannot hold it in. He stumbles to a corner and retches. When his stomach is empty, he wipes his mouth and presses his forehead to the cool stone wall.

"It's Gaspar's handwriting. We matched it to the writing we

found in his office," Oak groans. "Oh gods, I knew he was dangerous, but Crowley was his colleague. I never imagined . . ."

Clove appears beside him and, to his surprise, gently places her hand on his arm. "We have to tell the others. He might hurt them next."

Oak nods. He steadies himself, then turns to face her. "Yes. But first, help me hide this body."

26

MELARIE

As the clock nears nine, Melarie's nerves begin to buzz. Antoine has not returned; Gaspar is nowhere to be seen. She cannot shake the chill that Ellion's meltdown left in her, and as the night wears on, the ballroom only makes her feel more exposed.

The others will return to the library soon. Melarie is no longer helpful here. Either she bought Oak and Kellam the time they needed or she failed.

A thought creeps into her mind. Ellion was meant to guard Vesryn's body. But he wouldn't possibly leave it unattended—right?

It takes everything in Melarie not to leave the ballroom at a sprint. As she hurries toward the library, a hand catches her elbow.

"Princess?"

Melarie turns, heart in her throat, but it is only Pierre and Kaylie, her favorite of her guards. Pierre frowns at her, his pale brows knitted together. Kaylie tilts her head to the side, pretty face creased in concern. They're a welcome sight; a splash of familiar red against all this swirling, gods-cursed green.

"Princess," Kaylie says softly. "You're sweating."

Melarie's throat bobs. "It is, ah, terribly warm in here. You would think such a cold country would be more accommodating." She forces a smile. "I am going to get some air."

"I'll go with you."

"No," Melarie says. "I would like to be alone. Kaylie, if you see Antoine, please tell him I am looking for him. Pierre, I need you to keep an eye on the grand chamberlain—the one with the lily pin. Do not let him out of your sight. That's an order. Do you understand?"

They both nod. Neither is convinced; like Antoine, they have served her just long enough to read her agitation. Pierre nods, but Kaylie can't hide her frown. She doesn't buy Melarie's lie. But she steps aside.

Melarie leaves them behind before they can see the guilt on her face. When she sees the library door, her knees nearly buckle. She knocks twice and, when no one answers, pushes her way in.

Kellam kneels in the middle of the room, looking for all the world like a man who just gambled everything he had and lost. Impatience flares in her. They don't have room on their schedule for any additional emotional breakdowns.

"Prince Kellam," Melarie says. "What's wrong?"

The prince blinks owlishly. "I don't . . . I don't know . . . what I just . . . I can't believe . . . I . . ."

"Kellam." Melarie snaps her fingers in front of his face. "*Kellam*. What happened? Did you find the evidence you needed about Weatherington?"

Kellam blinks up at her, his expression lost. "What evidence?"

Divine Twelve, grant her patience. Melarie doesn't have time for this.

Melarie hauls her arm back and slaps the crown prince of Avendell across the face.

The crack echoes through the air. Kellam falls backward, and when he looks at Melarie, a perfect pink print of her hand is already forming on his cheek.

"Okay," he says. *"Ow."* He looks at her for the first time properly, and his gaze sharpens. "What's wrong?"

Quickly, Melarie tells Kellam of the scene Ellion caused. The prince's brow furrows. "What's his name?"

Maybe she hit him a little too hard. "Ellion?"

"I know who *Ellion* is! The man. Gabriel. What's his full name?"

"His name is Gabriel . . . well, it is . . . Gabriel . . ." Melarie's voice trails away. She hesitates. "Um."

Kellam's eyebrows shoot to his hairline. "You don't know?"

"Of course I know," Melarie snaps. But even as the words leave her lips, uncertainty blooms. How many times had Monseigneur Gabriel come to her father's palace and she'd never once called him anything else? It never seemed important. She didn't even know Antoine's last name until a year ago. There are so many people at court, their roles and significance changing like the seasons; it seemed like no sooner had Gabriel started to fill in the hollow places of Melarie's life than he was gone.

But surely she has to *know*?

"I know all the Istellian guests," says Kellam. "What? I always memorize the list. I'm not all beauty, princess."

Quickly, he rattles off the names of all the Istellians invited. *Antoine, Benoit, Beatrice, Kaylie, Pierre.* One by one, he goes through her attendants. With each name, Melarie's dread rises.

None of them could be confused for Monseigneur Gabriel.

"Perhaps he was a late addition or he traveled under a different nationality. I'm not entirely certain if he's even Istellian, if I am being honest. He would not be the first foreigner to serve in my father's court. He claimed he's been serving an Arbiter temple here in Avendell ever since my father dismissed him. Maybe your father invited him?" Kellam doesn't look convinced. She remembers her earlier mission and inches back toward the door. "We should find Antoine. He would know. And I promised to reconvene with him about Weatherington."

They stare at each other, their mutual unease swirling in the air. The back of Melarie's neck prickles. She feels trapped, and the dead girl on the table isn't helping. Melarie gestures at her. "What are we going to do with her?"

"I don't know," Kellam says miserably. "Someone ought to hide her, I guess."

This night has unraveled so terribly, it's almost comical. Melarie thinks, of all things, of the day her father died. She and her sisters stood in a ring around the corpse. No one moved. No one spoke. At some point, Melarie had realized they were waiting for an adult to show up and fix everything. She'd been quite horrified to realize they *were* the adults.

There was no one coming to save the Atilelet sisters then; and there's no one coming to save Melarie now. Not until Antoine returns with his plan.

"Grab her ankles," Melarie says grimly. "We can't risk dragging her down the hall. The stacks will have to do."

Kellam turns a bit green, but he doesn't protest.

Melarie tries not to look at Vesryn as she wraps her fingers around the dead girl's frigid ankles. Together, they heave Vesryn off the table. Despite her tiny frame, she's heavy. The next few minutes pass in an awful blur as she and Kellam wrangle Vesryn's corpse into the theology section and tuck her as far as they can into the corner.

"I don't remember this lesson in my etiquette classes," Kellam mutters. *"How to hide a body with the princess your dead father tried to force you to marry: a beginner's introduction."*

Melarie isn't sure if the noise that comes out of her is a laugh or a sob. "Antoine did always preach that the core of a good marriage was the ability to problem solve. Given the circumstances, I believe we are off to a great start."

"Well," Kellam deadpans, "if we make it through the night alive, you have a bright future ahead of you as a serial killer."

And though Melarie doesn't want to like Avendell's heir, she can't help herself. She smiles. Despite Gaspar's ominous warning, Kellam doesn't seem so terrible. He reminds Melarie, in a way, of Delphine—a royal hiding behind a mask. The court may have known Delphine as the most frightening of the Atilelet sisters, but Melarie knows better. It's the performers who conceal the deepest wounds.

As they linger in the stacks, Melarie searches for another conversation topic, eager to stretch this strange moment of allyship longer if she can. "What was Oak so upset about? Did you not find what you needed?"

"We found it," Kellam says. "Gaspar's handwriting matches Vesryn's note. He definitely killed her."

Melarie startles. "What? That's wonderful! Well, not wonderful, but you know what I mean. We might see the night through yet!" Dread pricks at her. "Why do you look so miserable? Did something else happen?"

Kellam's face turns a very interesting shade of pink. "That's private."

"I just helped you hide a corpse. And we are attempting to accuse your regent of murder. I think we've moved past privacy concerns." Melarie rises, fingering a chain on one of the books. They're a clever design; delicate to the touch, but the twice-smithed, enchanted links are so strong they'll break any normal blade. When Melarie's father redid the library, it took the metalsmiths three months to work through the protection charms her ancestors had put in place.

Kellam stares at the floor, visibly grinding his teeth.

"Prince Kellam," Melarie says gently. "We are allies tonight, bound by the Weaver's threads of fate whether we like it or not. What happened between you and the guard? Is he working with Weatherington? If he is extorting you, there are ways to protect yourself—"

"Oak would *never*." He looks horrified. "That's not what I—"

"Do you not feel safe in his presence?"

"There's no one I feel safer with!"

"Then what?" Melarie presses. "If you would just be honest, I could help you find a solution—"

"I love him," Kellam says miserably. "And I told him."

Melarie blinks. Kellam stares at the books like a man gazing upon the gallows.

Melarie doesn't know what to say other than, "Oh."

"I may have overdone it," Kellam admits. "He, ah, asked if I killed my father, and I told him I didn't, but I would have if it meant keeping him safe. I may have told him I would burn cities to the ground for him? And then he ran away. So that's lovely."

Melarie blinks rapidly as these new pieces of information click together. She believes Kellam when he says he didn't kill Costis—and he's too earnest and embarrassed for this to be a lie. But the prince is still hiding something. Melarie drifts down the shelves, skimming her fingers over a section about Avendell's practices for worshipping the Twelve.

"I think anyone would be overwhelmed by that," she says finally, her voice carefully light. She thinks of Antoine, who still complains about the dashing Avendellian man who broke his heart decades back. "But at least there is good news?"

"Is there?"

"I mean, the feelings are clearly mutual."

Kellam sputters violently. Melarie looks sideways at him. The polished prince of Avendell is choking on air.

"Forgive me," Melarie says. "I am unfamiliar with the customs here, but in Istellia it is perfectly normal for two men to—"

The library door slams open.

She and Kellam whirl at the same time. It's Ellion. His face is wan, but his eyes are the most lucid Melarie has seen them all night. Anger pricks at her.

"Where have you been?" Melarie demands. "We gave you a single task, and you left Vesryn's body here alone—"

"Shut up," says Ellion. He takes three long steps into the room and jabs a finger violently in Kellam's direction. His hand shakes. "You. Start talking. *Now.*"

Kellam draws back. "What's the matter with you? What are you on about?"

"I saw it," Ellion says. "I should have known something was up when Vesryn thought I killed her. I blew her off before, when she said something weird was happening here. But it's all you."

The library door opens a third time.

Clove and Oak burst in right as Ellion jabs his finger in Kellam's face and says, "I knew you were tied to those fucking flowers. No more hiding, Kellam. What's going on?"

27

CLOVE

CLOVE rushes into the library with Oak on her heels. They stand frozen at the entrance, the adrenaline of finding the magistrate's body dampened by the tension in the room. Clove wasn't certain she'd heard correctly at first, but she must have. The others seem just as disturbed as she is.

"Hold on," Kellam says slowly. Melarie's eyes dart frantically from him to Ellion and back. "Did you just say Vesryn thought you *killed* her?"

Ellion flinches. His mouth opens and closes, but no sound emerges, like a fish left gasping on land. His gaze darkens. "It's not what it sounds like."

Kellam crosses his arms over his chest. "This should be good."

The necromancer pinches the bridge of his nose. He shakes his head slowly. "It wasn't—look, you *know* I couldn't have killed her. We already went through this." When they keep staring, Ellion throws up his hands. "Fine. When I went to Vesryn in the Veil, she said she saw me. But ghosts get things wrong all the time. I assumed she was confused."

"And you didn't think to tell us this sooner?" Melarie asks.

"Would you have?" Ellion shoots back. "No offense, princess, but I'm still trying to figure out if you killed my king."

Clove casts a nervous look at Oak. They need to tell the others about the magistrate, but Ellion and Kellam are arguing too viciously for them to cut in.

Kellam interjects. "Who's to say you didn't talk to my father in the Veil, too, and he also accused you of murder because *you are the one who executed it*."

"Okay." Melarie steps between them. She places one hand on Kellam's chest and the other on Ellion's, holding the boys apart. "Let's table this for later. We know Ellion didn't kill Vesryn. But we also know Weatherington did."

The color drains from Ellion's face. "What?"

"We matched his handwriting," Kellam says quietly. "It was him, Ellion. I'm sorry."

Beside her, Oak shifts from foot to foot. Clove isn't sure if the guard's unease is rubbing off on her or if she's still recovering from the shock of tripping over a corpse, but her whole body is a jangle of nerves. She curls her hands into fists to stop them from shaking.

"There's something else," Clove says. Might as well lay it all out, she supposes. She clears her throat. "Oak and I found the magistrate."

Kellam's eyes light up. "Thank the goddess."

Oak's face crumples. "He's dead."

The guard pulls the note from his pocket as Clove continues. "Weatherington got to him before we could."

Ellion sways on his feet. His eyes scan the room. "Where . . . did you put her?"

"The stacks," Melarie says gently. "The theology section."

Ellion swallows and nods. He won't look any of them in the eye. "I'll . . . I'll get the other note."

The library falls silent. Clove watches as the pieces click together on each of their faces.

Kellam wilts. "Gaspar must know my father is dead. And if he can prove it before the treaty is signed, we're doomed."

Melarie is the first to come to the same horrible realization that Clove had in the alcove. Her shoulders visibly slump as she says, "There's no one to help us now—"

"There's another thing," Oak interrupts, his voice cautious. From his pocket, he withdraws the pale winter lily. "Another flower. The same we found on Vesryn."

"What the fuck?" comes Ellion's voice from the stacks.

"I know," says Clove. "It seems particularly cruel."

"No, not that. Forget the flowers." Ellion surges from the stacks. In his left hand flutters the note they found on Vesryn. But in his right, a cream-colored envelope gleams.

Clove glances at the prince out of the corner of her eye. His body has gone rigid, his face unnaturally pale. "What . . . where did you find that?"

"Find what, Kellam?" Ellion says, arching his brow. "Do you want to tell them, or should I?"

Melarie spins to face the prince. "Tell us *what?*"

Kellam's mouth works, but no words come out. Ellion doesn't bother to wait; he opens the envelope and slips out a very fancy, very familiar invitation. He clears his throat. "*Dear Ms. LaRue, I hope this message finds you well. I request the honor of your presence at my father's royal ball to celebrate peace between our nations.*" Ellion's eyes lift to meet Kellam's. "*I require the use of your services.*"

Time grinds to a halt. One by one, they each turn to Kellam. The prince pulls in a shaky breath. "That's not what you think it is."

"It's exactly what I think it is," says Ellion. "It's a request for Vesryn to kill your father."

"You lied to us," Melarie whispers. As if on instinct, she takes a step away from Kellam. "You planned to have him killed from the beginning."

"Not just his father," Ellion snarls. "Vesryn said something to me in the Veil that I didn't get at first. But now that I know what a traitorous heathen you are, it all makes sense. You asked her to kill Gaspar, too. With Costis and Gaspar dead, your path to the throne would be clear as day. Come on, Kellam—am I getting warmer?"

Clove closes her eyes to stop the room from spinning. In the blackness of her mind she tries to fit the pieces together. Kellam, framing Gaspar Weatherington as the true villain. Kellam, pretending to want to figure this all out for justice . . . when, really, he was just good at putting on a show.

But there was also the Kellam who had squeezed her shoulders and told her to relax—a prince who believed she was just as deserving of magic as anyone else. It isn't quite right. It wouldn't make sense for Kellam to encourage her to use magic and track down the basilisk if there was a chance Clove could uncover his plot to get rid of Gaspar. The prince may be pompous, but he isn't stupid.

Oak releases her arm. Clove opens her eyes. A muscle in the guard's jaw twitches as his eyes bounce among them. Slowly, his hand slips into his pocket.

His dagger. Oak is reaching for his dagger. He's going to use it to protect Kellam.

Panic thrums through Clove's veins. There will be more blood spilled tonight if she doesn't stop this. She opens her mouth to protest, but Ellion cuts her off. "You killed my best friend," he growls, rounding on Kellam.

"No! It's not . . . it's not like that!" Kellam's hands shake by his sides. "Yes, I'll admit, I wrote that letter to Vesryn after I'd seen . . . after I'd seen my father threaten someone. But you must believe me—I *never sent it.* I . . . I threw it in the bin. I don't know how it got to Vesryn. She confronted me, and said she believed me to be innocent. That is the truth, I swear."

Melarie's face hardens. "And why would we have any reason to believe this isn't another lie?"

Ellion is so close to Kellam now that he could easily grab the prince's throat. "How convenient that the one person in the king's chambers who knew your plan wound up dead. And I bet you thought that if your magistrate was dead, you'd get away with it. You didn't count on there being a necromancer here to sort through your lies."

"Stop!" Clove yells. Ellion's spine goes rigid. Slowly, he turns to face her. Clove's cheeks burn. She has no plan, and no idea if Kellam is actually innocent. All she knows is one more dead body is going to do them all in, if the other three already haven't. "We don't know for sure that Kellam did it. Gaspar is still a more likely suspect."

Ellion snorts. He lets out a sharp little laugh that makes Clove's cheeks blaze even hotter. "So they're working together. Kellam kills his dad and throws us off his scent by directing us toward Gaspar. We take the fall. It's obvious. Who else could have killed the king?"

Clove's mind works. She considers the evidence, the circumstances, and suddenly the answer dawns on her, as clear as a dinner bell. She opens her mouth to speak. "It's—"

"It was me."

The room freezes. Outside, the storm beats against the windows. The mage-lights flicker. Slowly, they each turn toward the voice.

He slips his hand from his pocket and opens his palm. King Costis' signet ring glints in the dying light.

"I did it," Oak says. "I killed the king."

EIGHT HOURS
TO DAWN

28

OAK

OAK has never told a lie.

He is not telling one now.

He hopes his honor will save him.

The room is as silent as a tomb. The windows let in no errant moonlight; only the dismal gray of heavy snowfall patterns the glass. The turrets groan beneath the weight of it. Mage-lights flicker. In the gasp of darkness, Oak hears a sharp, shaky inhale. But no one dares to move. All eyes are on him.

Oak feels . . . nothing. Maybe it's because his heart has been thrashing around his rib cage for hours, and now that the truth is out, it can finally settle. Or maybe it's his years of training; his ability to shut everything off when the world is a dangerous beast. *A defense strategy*, his trainer and the king's former guard, Bernard, had said as he'd shoved a mace into Oak's hands. *Protects the body from trauma.*

But as Oak stands here, a self-confessed murderer, feeling as empty as the castle's wine casket, he realizes that Bernard had been wrong. This instinct has nothing to do with protecting his body; it has to do with saving his heart. Oak knows, without a doubt, that if he could properly process the way Kellam is looking at him right now, he would shatter right on the spot.

At last, Kellam speaks. His question slices through the silence like a well-honed sword. An echo of the one Oak asked him earlier. "Why?"

Oak lifts his eyes to meet Kellam's, and without warning, the wall he has built around his fragile heart crumbles to dust.

"I didn't want to do it," he begins. "I loved your father more than anyone."

Well, almost anyone.

Something grazes his hand. Clove unfurls his empty palm and pushes a clean cloth into it. The gesture is a small grace that Oak does not deserve, and it makes him want to hug her and crawl out of his skin at the same time. He nods his thanks and blows his nose, trying to collect his thoughts. Where to even begin?

Eventually, Oak lands on the only way to tell this story—with the truth.

"Two weeks ago, King Costis called me to his chambers in the middle of the night." He stares at the cloth in his hands. "That wasn't uncommon; I'd been summoned to his chambers almost every night, sometimes multiple times before the breakfast bell, since . . . well, since he became unwell. You know how he was. Every year, there were more demons around every corner. Every festival, another traitor to be caught."

The others shift their weight. Oak has said the quiet part out loud; the part that the people in Avendell only dared to whisper at the dinner table or while working the fields.

He works the cloth into tiny, tightly folded squares. "But that night, he seemed different. Sharper, calm, *sane*. I was stupid enough to feel hopeful he was improving. Then he sat me down in front of the fire and told me that he had been plagued by a curse. He owed a terrible debt." He closes his eyes and forces himself to breathe. "It could only be repaid with his life."

He says the next part quickly, because he's certain that if he stops now, the tears will resurge with a vengeance. "King Costis told me that he only trusted me to carry out the job."

Kellam's voice is flat, distant, and bitter. "Father thinking the least of me, yet again."

"No." Oak's eyes meet Kellam's, and his stomach drops. "He asked me so your hands would remain clean. He knew his death would cast suspicion on you; that Gaspar, though he loved your father, has always loathed you. Your hands needed to be free of blood, your innocence unquestionable. And I, as Costis' sworn guard, had a duty to follow his command. He ensured that I would not be charged, that the magistrate would protect me. He . . . he held a knife to my side and insisted on showing me his weak spot so I would not miss."

Something flashes behind Kellam's eyes. "I thought he was going to hurt you."

Oak's face burns as the prince's confession flits through his mind. There are no words, at least not any that he can speak aloud without inflicting unnecessary pain on the prince. Oak doesn't add that as Costis held the knife to his gut, he whispered, *It has been the honor of a lifetime having you as a son.*

"So let me get this straight." Ellion rubs his temples. "Costis was cursed. He had ten years to escape it. He couldn't. And his solution to all that was to *die?* Tonight, of all nights, with us in attendance?" The necromancer looks grim. "Who makes that kind of deal?"

"Someone desperate," Kellam rasps. Now it's his turn to look haunted. "Someone with everything to lose."

"I pleaded with him," says Oak. "I begged. He wouldn't listen. And when I offered to help him find a different way to break the curse, he told me it was hopeless." Memory picks at him, strange and distant. "It was like . . . like his fate had already been sealed. He made me swear—on my life, on Kellam's, on my honor—that I would see it through."

"That's why he sent Kellam's letter to Vesryn," Clove says softly. "In case Oak couldn't do it. He needed a backup plan that wouldn't fail."

Oak pauses to breathe, surprised to find that as the truth seeps out, his pulse steadies. He hadn't realized the toll it had taken to carry this weight alone.

Kellam unwinds his arms and shoves his hands into his pockets. His brows knit together. "So why not kill him right then? Why tonight, of all nights?"

Just when Oak had thought the threat of tears had passed, his throat clenches. He bites the inside of his mouth, but it's too late—the tears come hot and fast down his cheeks. "I think knowing he had to die and being ready for it are two different things. Your father always told me so little. He didn't tell me when, where, or even how to get the task done. He told me only one thing." Oak raises his eyes. "*When you see the white winter lily, it's time for my reign to end.*"

Ellion lets out a low whistle. Melarie gasps, her head snapping to look at Kellam. But the prince isn't looking anywhere except straight into Oak's soul—if he still has one of those. The prince says softly, "He put the lily in Melarie's hair."

"King Costis had been erratic in his final years," Oak says.

"But tonight, he was . . . lucid. Bright-eyed, determined, and hopeful. He told me that he had invited the Evercraft boy to rectify the damage done to his family's reputation. That the Beaufortes had been summoned so he could restore their assets. And then, of course, the treaty. It was to be a night of healing; of moving forward." Oak blinks furiously. "I don't think Costis believed he would die tonight. His intention was never to leave Kellam with a mess. And then I saw the flower."

"But how did you do it so quickly?" Clove asks.

"My knife," Melarie pipes up. "How did you find and retrieve it in the few moments the lights were out?"

"Oh, I took that from you moments after you entered the room. It was clear you had never carried one by the way you fidgeted with your skirts, and as the kingsguard, it's my duty to dismantle any danger," Oak says with a half-hearted shrug.

"He's been trained to look for threats," Kellam answers. His face gives nothing away. "He knows exactly how to look for weapons on a person by sight alone."

Oak nods solemnly. "I guessed at who had what, and where, while you were all talking. I already had Melarie's knife and the basilisk venom on my person. I wanted it to be as painless for King Costis as I could make it, so I laced the blade and attempted to hide the venom when I left to check the locks. I did not want any one person to take the fall."

"The storm took care of that part for you," Ellion says, his gaze straying to the snow-covered windows.

Oak looks at each of them, one by one, his pulse sputtering when his eyes land on Kellam. He does not know what will become of them after this; he doesn't know how the prince could possibly forgive him. But at least Oak knows that when the snow thaws, and he is sent out into the cold with only his satchel and his shame, he will at least have told the truth. So he will take in Kellam, all of him, one last time.

"The opportunity presented itself," Oak says softly, his eyes drifting to the prince's lips. "And I did not refuse it. But I did not hurt Vesryn. I did not kill the magistrate. On my life, on my honor, I swear it."

Kellam stares at the floor, the crease between his brows deepening. "That's why you panicked when we found Vesryn dead. Because you realized there was another killer."

Oak nods.

Silence envelops them. It's strange, the relief that fills Oak. At least now they have the truth between them. Beyond the window, the storm gives a low, mournful howl. The roof groans, straining under the weight of the snow. And Oak cannot help but feel like . . . like there's something they are missing.

"So Costis dies," Clove says quietly. Oak can see the pieces connecting behind her eyes. "We panic and try to hide it. Weatherington gets suspicious. Vesryn tails him, learns something she shouldn't, and gets picked off. He gets rid of her. Oak, realizing there's a second killer, goes for the magistrate. Gaspar catches wind and picks him off, too. But why? It seems . . . sloppy. All he had to do was wait until dawn. We can't hide a corpse forever." She frowns. "We're missing something. Something important."

They all look at each other, tense in the cold, in the dark, in the shadow of the storm beyond the window and the one brewing within this castle's haunted halls. Oak's skin prickles. His hair stands on end.

He doesn't feel like someone relieved of a burden. He feels like a boy still on duty, preparing to face a terrible threat looming around yet another corner.

"The missing piece," Kellam says slowly, "is Gaspar himself. I don't know why he's chosen this path, but as far as I'm concerned, it doesn't matter. He's guilty. We'll get our answers once he's imprisoned."

"Why wait?" a new voice asks. "You can have them now."

Oak turns, hand flying to his sword, but there's no need. The man before them does not need weapons to be a threat. He watches them all with a dully pleased expression, head inclined to the side. There's no telling how long the grand chamberlain has been there. It doesn't matter.

He's heard everything.

"And here I thought," Gaspar says, "I was going to have to do this the hard way."

29

KELLAM

KELLAM no longer cares about power or the throne. As he stands there, breath fogging in the chill of the library, Oak's confession laid at his feet and their greatest threat lingering in the doorway, Kellam knows one painful truth.

He has already lost everything that matters.

Time slows as Gaspar Weatherington steps calmly into the library, pulls the door shut, and locks it behind him. The library burns with cold, but it has nothing on the ice currently creeping through Kellam's veins.

"Make one move toward me," Gaspar warns, "and I'll shout. There are guards just beyond the hall—and, I think, given you've confessed to killing the king, we don't want that, do we? Tell me, Ducasse—how *would* Captain Laurent respond to knowing you drove a knife through Costis' heart? I know he's fond of you. But I have to imagine that fondness ends at regicide."

"You're too late, Weatherington," Ellion says. In his hands, he still clutches the letter Kellam wrote to Vesryn, and the note they found on her body. "We have proof that you killed Vesryn. We matched your handwriting, you bastard."

Gaspar looks genuinely puzzled. "To what?"

"The notes on the bodies," Ellion says, uncertain now. "Of the people you killed?"

A look flashes across Gaspar's face. Panic, maybe? Or confusion? His demeanor shifts from confident to perplexed. "May I?"

He holds out his palm. Ellion hesitates and hands him the notes. Silence stretches through the air.

Gaspar holds their evidence to the light, squinting, and reads.

"Oh," Gaspar says dryly. "*These* notes."

And then, in one fluid motion, he rips them in two.

It's the worst sound Kellam has heard all night. There is nothing they can do as Gaspar shreds what little proof they had into smaller and smaller pieces. He flicks the remains away, watching as they flutter to the floor and form a pale ring at his feet.

The grand chamberlain raises his eyebrow. "Anything else?"

No one moves. No one even speaks. What can they say? Oak just confessed to the murder of the king. Gaspar heard everything and now stands before them with the air of a man who has been handed an unexpected gift. And hasn't he? They had only one angle tying him to the murders. It now lies shredded before them.

They're trapped.

All their planning and plotting. All their secrets and losses.

It will all be for nothing now.

Gaspar is acting regent. And in this moment, the full powers of the throne are his—as are the guards sworn to serve it. They are at his mercy, and for all his strengths, mercy has never been in Weatherington's vocabulary.

Kellam's eyes cut to the window.

His mind scrambles. A way out. Surely there's something

missing. Surely there's something they can *use*.

Gaspar looks at them each in turn, his cold eyes revealing nothing.

"Here is what is going to happen," says Gaspar. "First, the traitor Oak Ducasse will be tried and executed for the murder of King Costis. Prince Kellam will be tried alongside him and banished, but I think we both know, Kellam, you're not making it beyond the castle walls. You are a tumor that has been allowed to grow for far too long. For the good of the kingdom, I will see to it that you're permanently removed." His attention flicks to Clove and Ellion. "Then, of course, there's the matter of you two. I suppose I could have you killed. I've already seized the Beauforte assets, but the Evercrafts' wealth would be a lovely addition to the Crown's coffers." He tilts his head. "Or—you can confess."

Clove and Ellion stiffen. Kellam's heart pounds.

He knows what Gaspar is going to say before the grand chamberlain even breathes the words.

"You will testify to the prince's conniving plot," Gaspar says calmly. "You will tell the council how Kellam pressured his guard. You will explain that he is a power-hungry, cruel boy unfit to rule. You will cry when you recount the story of how he strangled that poor little assassin. You will tremble when you tell the courts of the way he lured loyal, stupid Crowley into an empty hall and murdered him. Your reward will be your lives and lives of your families—oh, yes. Their fates are tied to yours, too." He lifts a brow. "Families are a funny thing. Even when all they've done is cause pain, blood always pulls us back. I assume if I cannot motivate you to protect your own lives, I can inspire you to protect theirs."

Ellion is grayer than the corpses he works with. Clove is so rigid she doesn't breathe. No one speaks. The only sound is the ball in the distance and the whistle of the wind beyond the window. Low, long, and mournful. Or maybe it's just the air leaving Kellam's lungs as his last shreds of hope evaporate into air.

Kellam's mind spins. He has always known Gaspar hated him.

But this? This defies petty hatred. This is a loathing that poisons.

Kellam thinks. He backtracks, combing through everything that has happened, everything they know. There has to be something they missed. It's close, swirling before him, just out of reach.

A terrible idea pricks at Kellam. One that requires him to put his complete and utter faith in the others.

Melarie lifts her chin. Her voice wobbles, but Twelve bless her, the princess actually manages to meet Gaspar's eyes. "And me? I cannot simply go missing, Monsieur Weatherington. And your reach does not extend beyond Avendell's borders."

Gaspar gives Melarie a bored look. "You think I won't just push you out a window? There are many ways for a girl to die in a castle. And so many places to take a bad fall."

Melarie startles. "My sister would—"

"What? Declare war? Refuse to sign the treaty?" Gaspar lifts his hands in mock terror and rolls his eyes. "I will answer Elodie Atilelet's rage with fire of my own. And I will begin with Magnivelle."

Kellam has never been devout. The Twelve have never answered him, and it's clear the Gardener has no interest in him. But still, as Kellam looks at Gaspar—as he accepts what he's about to risk—Kellam can't help himself.

He prays.

"So that's what this is about," Kellam says. "This was never about Avendell. This is some pathetic grasp for revenge. You don't care about our country. You just want blood for blood."

Gaspar's lip curls. "You know nothing of what you speak, boy."

"Don't I?" Kellam taunts. "For someone who made their entire career about being a loyal servant to our country and its people, this is looking conveniently self-serving to me."

"Kellam," Oak hisses.

Kellam ignores him. He takes a step forward. "I think this was never about my ability to rule. I think you've been waiting for your chance, Gaspar, because you're a petty, cowardly man drawn to shiny things, desperate for a kind reflection of yourself." He looks down his nose at Gaspar; a feat, considering the grand chamberlain is taller than him. "My father always said you were pathetic, but I'll admit, he at least thought you had some moral spine."

Red creeps up Gaspar's neck. "You insolent little wretch. I will have your *tongue*—"

"You may," Kellam says, with a flat, mean laugh. "But it doesn't change the truth. Nor would it quell the whispers about you. That you're a leech; that you were little more than the king's dog. My father didn't make you regent because he thought you would be good for the job. He felt sorry for you. It was a consolation prize, one you were never meant to receive. But still, you were his friend, and you had nothing. He had to give you *something*. And how did you reward him for his faith? By plotting against him from the beginning."

"I loved that man," Gaspar says. A muscle in his jaw feathers, and his next words come out small and hateful. "We were boys together, and I loved him, and the king I thought he would become. But he grew into a coward. And then *you* were born, with a rot he could not bear to prune. He defied the law; he defied the gods. And after all that, despite my warnings, he let Magnivelle burn."

"Did he? Or did you?" Ellion jumps in now. Oak and Melarie look at him, horrified, but the necromancer stands tall. Kellam could kiss him. "Admit it. You wanted Magnivelle to burn. You wanted war, and what a small price to pay if the cost is merely a lost estate and some blood spilled."

"They burned *children*," Gaspar snaps. A slip in his composure. "They could have let the women go. The little ones. They burned them *all*. And still, Costis hesitated. I saw Avendell's destruction painted in the weary lines of his face, unable to face consequences, unwilling to accept the will of the Twelve, ignorant to the truth that Istellia was now ruled by a madman. I resigned in disgrace; Costis begged me to stay. And I was going to deny him, until the Builder's voice came to me. I was *chosen* for this. Everything I do, I have done for this country, because I have loved it and suffered for it more than Costis or his wretched son ever could."

"So, what?" Ellion goads. He wiggles his fingers at Gaspar. "This is some holy war? It wasn't me! It was the will of the gods! Why is it always tyrants who are chosen by the gods? It's never a healer or a farmer. It's always someone with a penchant for death."

"It *was* the will of the gods," Gaspar retorts. "I am a devout man, a holy man, something you would know *nothing* about. When the Builder calls upon me, I do not deny his will—I carried out the girl's and Crowley's murders with honor, and He gave me the tools to do so. Do you even know what honor is, you lowly little—"

"Just tell us one thing," interrupts Clove. "Why the flowers?"

Gaspar blinks. "What?"

All eyes turn to Clove.

Quiet, thoughtful Clove, who always watches first and speaks last. Clove, who, more than anyone, Kellam prayed would put the pieces together and know when to step in.

The beast tamer folds her arms. She cocks her head to the side, the genuine picture of puzzlement, and lays the cards Kellam has handed her out flat.

"Why tie yourself to the murders?" Clove asks. "Why leave flowers on corpses when you were already so certain you'd get what you wanted? You seem like a smart man. Why risk it all to gloat?"

"I didn't leave flowers on the bodies," Gaspar says, irritated.

"Well, someone did," Clove retorts. "I'm not devout, but even I know winter lilies have nothing to do with the Builder."

Gaspar goes still. "What did you say?"

"The Builder is associated with tools and laurels—"

"Not that," Gaspar says. "The other thing. The flower."

Clove points to where Vesryn was found dead. "You've been leaving winter lilies on the corpses. Your family crest is a lily, isn't it? Even a dullard could put two and two together."

The grand chamberlain frowns. His hand drifts, as if in slow motion, to the lily gleaming on his lapel.

"My family crest," Gaspar says slowly, "is a *tiger* lily."

The hair on Kellam's arms stands on end.

Gaspar looks at the five of them, and then, like oil, his gaze slides away. To the lily rotting on the library table, the petals long browned. He drifts toward it and lifts it to the light, a mirror image of Kellam's father only hours ago.

And all the color leaves Gaspar's face.

He takes a step backward, flinging the flower away. His hands rise, warding off some invisible terror.

Kellam recalls the books in his office; the obsession with which he researched every aspect of mythology tied to their lands. Kellam had thought it was only related to him, and maybe it was in the beginning, but surely even a man as prideful as Gaspar Weatherington would wonder about what whispered to him from the dark?

"Twelve forgive me," breathes Gaspar. "What have I done?"

His eyes fly to Kellam, wild and desperate.

"*You*," he accuses. "You were never meant to live. I knew I should have acted sooner. Oh, Twelve protect us. If the flowers are here, that means—"

Gaspar's words are cut short by a strange gurgle. He coughs, hand flying to his throat, and staggers backward. The grand chamberlain turns pink, then red, then purple, choking on his own words. Gaspar falls to his knees, a low, mournful noise leaving him.

And vomits winter lilies all over the floor.

There are dozens of them; impossible in size, freshness, and fragrance. They spill across the carpet, petals wet with blood. Melarie screams. Kellam's vision blackens, briefly, as Oak steps in front of him to protect him. But there's no need. As quickly as the event started, it's over. A sickly sweet fragrance fills the air. The lily petals twitch, as if stirred by an invisible breeze, and still.

Lying among them, eyes wide in terror, is the corpse of Gaspar Weatherington.

30

MELARIE

MELARIE has never seen a man die before. It's nothing like the stories Gabriel used to bring her. There is no dramatic pause or whispered curse from Gaspar Weatherington. There are no declarations of some final decree or vendetta left unavenged.

One moment Gaspar is alive, a threat to Melarie and everything she's ever loved, and the next he's gone. Just like that.

So why doesn't it feel like a victory?

"Uh," says Ellion. "That can't be good."

Already the lilies' edges are browning. Ellion steps over them and places his hands on the grand chamberlain's neck. Melarie holds her breath. A second ticks by, and then a third. But Ellion's eyes don't roll back; no color leaves his skin.

For the first time tonight, Melarie is devastated to see him healthy.

Ellion rocks back on his heels and blows out a frustrated breath. "The connection is broken."

"He moved on?" Kellam demanded. "So soon? What happened to spirits having unfinished business?"

Ellion shakes his head. "I'm not sure. It feels like the tie was... cut. Like someone pushed him on." He looks at all of them, his posture agitated. "This is bad. Really bad. Do any of you understand what this means? People don't just vomit flowers on their own. And entities don't mess with the dead unless they were connected to the person while they were alive. Something else is pulling the strings." He draws in a shaky breath. "We're on the same side now, right? Truly?"

"Why do I feel like you're about to say something ridiculous?" Kellam asks slowly.

Ellion presses his knuckles into his eyes and then he looks up. "Vesryn thought something strange was happening. I blew her off, but when she died, and she thought *I* killed her, I knew something was wrong. When you were off on your little missions, I went . . . uh, wandering . . . and I was led to an apparition—I'll explain later, it's ghost stuff—Kellam was a baby and his parents were leaning over his crib and talking about a curse—"

"I'm sorry," cuts in Melarie. "You are going to have to slow down. How did you find this . . . this apparition?"

Ellion looks like he's in physical pain. "A ghost cat led me to it."

"I saw it, too," Clove says quietly.

"Oh," Melarie says miserably. "Great."

"Perhaps," Oak says, holding up his hands to slow Ellion's panicked onslaught of words, "we ought to work from what we know? Costis tasked me with killing him because he believed he was cursed. That was the beginning of all this, wasn't it? Surely that's where it ends?"

His words snag on something in Melarie's memories.

She blinks, and though she stands in Avendell, her heart is back in Istellia.

"I just don't understand," Kellam says with a frustrated shake of his head. "Put aside Gaspar. My father was obsessed with staying alive. Every door locked; every servant searched for weapons. He was convinced he was cursed. And even if what Oak is saying is true . . ." He throws his hands up. Hurt bleeds into his voice. "He left me here, *alone*, after my mother died, to travel for three weeks to some gods-cursed temple and try to remove some imaginary curse!"

Every part of Melarie goes cold. What was it Gaspar said?

It's hard to imagine this was worth the three-week journey.

Oh, Twelve help her. What a terrible trap the Weaver has made for them.

"Kellam," Melarie breathes. "How long ago did your father try to break his curse?"

The prince frowns. "Several years. He was upset when he returned. Whoever it was refused to help him. And then the war started, and he had other problems."

"How long ago?" Melarie repeats. "Try to remember."

"A decade," Oak says. When they look at him, he glances away. "Laurent told me the prince was inconsolable. Actually, given that tonight is the anniversary, I'd say it was—"

"A decade exactly?" Melarie whispers.

Oak stiffens. He nods.

"I know who Costis met with. And I know what their meeting was about." Melarie's heart pounds. "I know, because I was there. Costis met with my father."

How had Melarie forgotten? How could she not have known?

Melarie looks at Kellam, but her mind is a decade away.

"I was just a child then," Melarie whispers. "But I recall my father's strangeness before Costis' arrival. Typically, when we had an esteemed guest, the palace would be upturned in a frenzy of cleaning and preparations. But on that day, he sent everyone away. Even the maids."

She can see it like it was yesterday. The sky had been clear the day Costis arrived. In those days, King Raphaël was already a shell of the man Melarie's older sisters recalled. His foul moods were longer, his paranoias broader, his cruelties more personal. Fewer and fewer guests were permitted through the palace gates, and Melarie was growing from a lonely child into a desperate one.

"My mother had just fled," Melarie whispers faintly. "When he shut the palace down, I thought perhaps she'd been . . . forcibly returned. He promised me that if he ever found her again he'd kill her."

One day Melarie's mother had been there, the fourth and final queen, and the next she was gone. Melarie might have thought her dead had her mother's favorite cape not gone missing with her. It had been her most prized possession: a knee-length cape made from pale pink basilisk scales. Of course her mother had remembered to take it with her.

She'd just forgotten to take her daughter, too.

Melarie paces the room, caught between the horror of the present moment and the terror of one ten years passed. "I hoped to see my mother again—but there was a man there instead."

What a sight she must have been—a child, slipping from her window, clinging to the flagstones of the palace's wall hundreds of feet above the cobblestones below. Melarie's hands had been too soft for the castle walls; they had bled as she crawled, inch by inch by painful inch.

"I stretched my foot out to the balcony," Melarie whispers. "And I fell."

For a terrible moment, she'd hung in the air, hundreds of feet above the cobblestones below. And this is where she feels pitiful, because she had thought not of her sisters, of her country, or even of her mother. Her only thought had been that she was going to die, and she did not want to. It wasn't fair.

Melarie fell.

And then a pair of hands caught her waist.

It was impossible. One moment Melarie was falling and the next she was standing on the balcony, heart hammering, tears springing to her eyes as it hit her just how close to death she'd come. And she was alone. No guard had emerged from the room below to catch her. It was as if the breeze itself had formed hands to snatch her from the jaws of death and set her safely on her feet. She recalls, even now, the warmth of those hands through her dress; the strength of them as they plucked her from midair and set her on the balcony floor.

In that terrible, strange moment, she had felt . . . protected.

A voice came from the other side of the curtain.

"You tricked me," someone accused. "You told me I could make a bargain. You did not tell me what it would cost."

When Melarie peered through the curtain, it had not been her mother in her father's private room, but a man. One she'd never seen before—beautiful, young, and golden. The stag signet ring on his index finger had shined like a star as he jabbed it accusingly in the face of King Raphaël.

Melarie raises her eyes to Kellam's pale face.

"They spoke of a curse and a bargain made," Melarie whispers.

"My father . . . my father was not in his right mind then. They argued. They spoke of debts—of a life for a life." She worries her lip between her teeth. "When Costis left, my father broke every vase in the western wing. Three days later, our troops attacked Magnivelle and the war began."

"The curse Gaspar spoke of," Clove breathes. "The bargain Costis struck. It was the same one your father made. And whatever was toying with both kings—it's here tonight, isn't it?"

Melarie opens her mouth to agree—and something knocks on the library wall.

She jumps.

Another knock comes to their left, and then to their right. The banging sound leaps through the room, the sound frenetic, urgent, and angry. Beyond the windows, the wind rises to a scream. The mage-lights flicker once, twice, and go out, plunging them into blackness. Tense quiet blankets the library. In the dark, Melarie can just see the outlines of five other people. They all hold their breath. A hand brushes Melarie's waist.

And the lights come back on.

Ellion, who very much looks like he's going to be ill, gives them an uneasy smile. "At least no one got stabbed this time?"

No one laughs. Melarie's stomach is still in knots. "Who touched me? That wasn't funny."

They all look at her uneasily and shake their heads. Every part of Melarie goes cold. Someone touched her waist. She's certain. The weight of that hand was as real as the fear that now sets her heart to hammering.

Something isn't right. Melarie counts her company and counts them again. Her skin crawls.

Unless she was imagining it, wasn't there—

"Did anyone else see," Oak whispers, "an extra person?"

Melarie opens her mouth to answer—and the door flies open.

It's two of the Avendellian guards, their faces red from running, their hands on their swords. Melarie tenses for an accusation, but the guards look to Kellam and Oak.

"Your Grace," one of the guards pants. "We must get you to safety. *Now.*"

Kellam pales. "Reed, what's happened?"

"There's no time—" The older guard stops short. His attention slides to Gaspar. The color leaves his face. "Is that . . . ?"

"Henry," Oak barks, his voice strengthened by authority. "What do you have to report?"

The guard's attention snaps up. But this time, he looks straight at Melarie.

"It's one of your guards," he says, his face drawn and pale. "The little blond one was on the ballroom floor and he was agitated, demanding to speak to you, shouting for us to turn the music down and end the ball entirely."

Melarie reels. "That's Pierre. What happened? Is he all right?"

The last bit of color leaves Henry's face. "We thought he'd simply fallen and spilled wine at first, there was so much red—"

"Pierre is dead, princess," Reed finishes grimly. "Your guard was murdered."

31

KELLAM

KELLAM cannot get out of this one. All their planning. All their careful maneuvers and silver-tongued lies. Midnight closes in, when surely most of the guests would have tired and made the last sprint toward dawn an easy one. Even Gaspar's betrayal and death could have been dealt with. Kellam can always find another magistrate. He can explain the disappearance of the grand chamberlain.

But a corpse in the middle of a *ballroom*?

There's no hiding it now.

"Prince Kellam." Reed's voice snaps him back to reality. The guard's eyes search Kellam's face. His voice is tentative. Unsure. "Where is King Costis?"

Ellion mutters an expletive behind him.

Dread sloshes in Kellam's stomach. He doesn't know what to say to that. His mouth opens and closes. Panic wraps icy claws around his heart.

A hand touches his shoulder. Light, and eternally steady.

"Prince Kellam bears the stag now," Oak says softly, holding Reed's gaze.

The junior guard's expression flashes between a dozen emotions at once—horror, grief, fear, and finally, resignation. Kellam knows Reed has never particularly liked him. But the boy loves Costis, and he respects Oak. After what feels like an eternity, Reed inclines his head.

"Very well," he says, his voice throaty and low. "Your orders?"

It takes Kellam a moment to realize, with utter horror, that Reed is talking to *him*. Panic bubbles up. He wants to shrink back and retreat; to hide in the library until this terrible nightmare of a night is over. His father is dead, potentially due to some strange, cryptic curse, and now he's expected to think up *orders*?

"The body," Oak prompts gently.

"Right." Heat leaps to Kellam's cheeks. He tries to wrangle back whatever shreds of focus still exist. "You said it's in the ballroom?"

"We have men blocking the view," Reed says, his voice low. "But that solution won't hold for long. Eventually, one of the more sober guests is going to wonder why a bunch of nervous-looking guards are standing in a very tight ring."

One problem at a time. "Take me there."

"Me too," says Ellion. He still looks unwell, but his eyes are bright. "I can help."

Kellam shakes his head. "You should stay with the girls—"

"No," says Clove. "I—I have to go back to the dungeons. Take Ellion. Figure out what you can. I think our answer to what's happening here lies down there, but we have to leave. Now."

Melarie's eyes cut to Clove and Kellam and back. Her hands shake, but she curls them into fists and says, "I'll go with Clove. We'll be safer together. Go, the three of you. *Hurry.*"

Kellam's skin crawls, but he nods. As much as he's loath to

admit it, the night has fallen to pieces. He'll take all the help he can get.

They leave the library at a sprint.

When the ballroom draws into view, Kellam dons his mask, suddenly grateful for the switch. Guests twirl and dance in the low lights of the ballroom; the scent of wine fills the air, but beneath it, growing stronger, is the familiar sting of copper.

How has everything gone so terribly awry?

A wall of satin and silk looms ahead. He tries to press his way through, but none of the guests move. A hand squeezes his shoulder.

"Allow me," Oak says softly. "My prince."

Kellam's heart constricts. They've not had a moment alone since—well, since Kellam had to go and make an utter wreck out of whatever friendship he and Oak had. If Oak is thinking of Kellam's confession, he does nothing to reveal it. He looks ahead, a glint of determination in those steady hazel eyes, and though the timing is wildly inconvenient and the circumstances horrifyingly inappropriate, Kellam can't help it—he falls a little bit in love all over again.

"*Move*," Oak booms, his voice pitched low. The authority in it parts the crowd like a knife through butter.

Suddenly, Kellam no longer sees the sweet, gentle boy he spent years getting into trouble with; he sees the man Oak will become.

Gods help him. Five people are dead, and he's *pining*.

Oak takes Kellam by the wrist. "Stay close to me," he orders, his voice low, and then he plunges into the crowd.

It doesn't take long to find the guards.

They stand in a ring of deep green, shoulder to shoulder,

their faces careful, blank masks. Guests dance around them, oblivious, their faces aglow with alcohol and the thrill of an evening spent overindulging. To their credit, Kellam's guards barely react when they see Oak, Reed, and the prince plunging toward them. Only the sweat beading on their brows betrays just how panicked they are.

At the guard's feet, seeping under their shoes and onto the dance floor around them, is a rapidly spreading pool of red.

Kellam freezes.

It's one thing to see his murdered father's body and the dead girl in the library. But here, in a roomful of guests and blood seeping across the floor, Kellam is finally, truly, at a loss.

He doesn't know what to do.

Something tugs at his arm. Kellam jerks. Oak is pulling off his overcoat—the hideous, pea-green monstrosity his father demanded he wear. In all his fantasies about Oak undressing him, Kellam can't say this was ever in the picture. Before Kellam can ask what Oak is doing, the boy wrenches the overcoat free and hurls it at the closest guard's feet. The guard reacts immediately, stepping on it and dragging it backward over the pool of blood.

Oak whirls and locks eyes with Reed.

"Find a drink cart or something else big enough to move the body. We have to get him out of here as quickly and discreetly as possible. Bring a sheet to cover him and towels for the mess." His eyes dart around the ballroom. "After that, find Captain Laurent. Tell him what's happened and prepare the wine cellars in case we need to shelter in place. *Go.*"

Kellam has never been so grateful to have Oak at his side.

The guards part to let Kellam and Oak through, and close back around them.

Pierre lies on his back, his face a mask of frozen shock. Blood spreads in a gory halo around his head, seeping from the open slit on his throat. It's a clean cut—precise, straight, and deep. The practiced cut of someone who has killed before.

"What . . . did anyone see what happened?" Kellam rasps.

A guard whose name escapes him answers. "The Istellian burst into the ballroom yelling for the princess. He insisted that she was in danger and they needed to leave at once. I . . . didn't see what happened after that. The room was too crowded."

"What's wrong with his mouth?" Oak whispers.

Kellam leans closer. The Istellian guard's mouth looks swollen, as if he took a great mouthful of water. The slightest sliver of something white is visible between his already graying lips. Foreboding rises in Kellam in a great, dark tide. He moves forward as if in a trance.

"Your Grace," Oak protests. "Kellam, don't—"

Kellam pries the Istellian's lips open.

The lily petals unfurl instantly. Even half-crushed, Kellam would have known the winter lily wilting behind the Istellian's teeth from scent alone. Revulsion rises in him. First Gaspar, now Pierre. The killer is taunting them. What kind of sick game is this?

"I'm starting to really hate those flowers," Ellion whispers.

Kellam is inclined to agree.

Horror squeezes him like a vise. Five bodies, five appearances of flowers.

Ellion drifts toward the body, fear and determination sharing equal spaces on his face. He kneels, and like a coward, Kellam does not stop him.

Kellam knows it's dangerous for Ellion to mess with the dead. But he's already done it twice tonight, hasn't he? What's once more? And if the Istellian can give them answers—wouldn't it be worth it?

Memory surfaces of Kellam's father, gray-faced in a war meeting, listening as a general proposed sending a decoy platoon to draw Istellian fire while a second platoon prepared a surprise attack. He'll never forget what Costis said when Kellam protested.

Sometimes we must weigh the odds.

Kellam had vowed to never be the kind of king who played with lives as though they were gambling dice. It seems he's already reneged on one promise.

He shoves his guilt away. He watches with bated breath as Ellion places his hands on the Istellian's flesh.

And Ellion frowns.

Kellam's heart drops.

Ellion looks up at him, an apology already forming on his lips, his head shaking slowly. "There's nothing here. No one to call back."

"But he was murdered," Oak protests. "He was murdered in service to his future queen."

"We can't all be as devoted as you," Ellion says. He looks grim. "It's the same as Gaspar. The connection is cut. One dead body is strange, but two?"

Panic prickles up Kellam's spine.

"Two means you're right," Kellam rasps. "Someone or something knows we have a necromancer on our side. And they don't want us to find whatever answers might lurk in the Veil."

The sounds of the ball roar around them; laughter and music, swelling with every passing moment. Kellam's eyes dart to the clock. Seven and a half hours to figure this out.

Seven and a half hours before everything Kellam holds dear is brought to ruin.

He wants to hide. To curl in a ball and let the night fall to ruin. But he's come too far to crumble now.

He's a Vernevau, isn't he?

It's time to start acting like one.

"We need to stop reacting," Kellam says. He forces a sureness he doesn't feel into his voice. "This entire night we've been chasing ghosts. There has to be some advantage we can find. Some way we can go on the attack."

Oak shakes his head helplessly. The backs of their guards form a silent wall around them, but Kellam knows they're listening to see what he does next. So much for an impressive beginning to his stint as Avendell's king. A cold sweat breaks out across Kellam's body.

They're going to lose everything.

And then Ellion looks up. "I have a really bad idea."

32

ELLION

THIS entire night Ellion has been running—from Vesryn, from his past, from the consequences of what happened in Costis' chamber. But Ellion can't outrun this.

The castle groans around them, and before Ellion, a dead man cools. His spirit is gone, just like Gaspar's. Whatever is lurking within these castle walls does not want to be caught. Behind Ellion, the prince and his king killer stand with pale faces and empty eyes. The guards form a silent wall around them, blocking out the drunken partygoers for now, but it can't last. Ellion shifts; a sticky, cloying feeling pulls at his knees. The Istellian's blood has soaked through his pants.

They're stuck. With no soul to call back, there's nothing Ellion can do, no information he can find, no door to the Veil he can sneak through.

Unless.

A flash of black catches his eye. The cat sits on the other side of the corpse, violet eye winking.

"He was murdered," Ellion says slowly. "That kind of violence leaves a mark. Extreme emotions always do. And unlike Gaspar, he might feel inclined to help us. I might not be able to bring him back." Ellion licks his lips. "But I could go to him."

He thinks of Costis and Greer standing over Kellam's crib. Whatever happened that day had been so visceral the memory had lingered after their souls had passed. Even if something has forced Pierre on—surely his soul is still somewhere in the Veil, at least for the next few minutes?

"There might be something on the other side of the Veil that could help us," Ellion says. "Even with the soul gone, the body can be of use."

Kellam frowns. "How?"

"Brains take time to die after a heart stops, even if it was stopped violently." Ellion chews his lip. "There was a woman, once, who was brought to the Academy. She had died hours before—but I saw her last moments when I touched her. It was a murky image and it didn't tell me much, but . . ."

"He might have seen the killer's face," Oak says. "And with Gaspar dead, it would be the real killer. The one who's been hunting us all along."

"I don't have to find Pierre to get the hint we need. Just a fragment of him." Ellion's heart begins to accelerate. "Kellam, you're a greenmage, right? Like your father?"

His hands move quickly. He needs to be fast about this, efficient and precise.

"Of course," the prince says stiffly. "Why?"

"Because we're about to find out if there's another way to cross the Veil," Ellion says grimly. "I usually rely on the spirits to slip into death's realm, but who's to say I can't use my own body, too?"

It takes a moment for his words to hit Oak and Kellam. Then their eyes widen, and Kellam flinches, as if Ellion has struck him.

"You mean to poison yourself," Kellam says, horror lining his face. "Ellion, you *cannot*."

He'd prefer another intense sedative. But they don't have time. Ellion doesn't want to hear about forbidden practices or risks or sacred laws. Five people are dead. One of them is Vesryn.

And Ellion is tired of running.

Before Kellam can protest, Ellion brings the lily to his mouth, chews, and swallows.

Kellam's eyes widen in horror. "Oh, Courier help us. Ellion, what have you *done*?"

Beside him, Oak looks like he's going be ill.

"I'll be fine," Ellion says quickly. "I think. All I need you to do is grow a new bud and jam it between my teeth. Fully bloomed winter lilies are fatal, but an unbloomed bud will slow the poison long enough to get me proper help."

"I can't," Kellam says.

"You can," Ellion says impatiently. "We learned it back in the Academy."

"You don't understand."

"Would you listen to me?" Ellion snaps. "I *watched* a greenmage do it himself—"

"I'm not a greenmage," Kellam whispers.

The world threatens to grind to a halt. A burning cold is already sweeping through Ellion. The room blurs. Everything around him is fading—well, almost everything.

The fucking cat is getting brighter.

"I have no magic," Kellam says hoarsely. "I've never had any magic at all."

"Oh," Ellion says faintly. "Well, that's not good."

Ellion wants to ask him about Costis and Greer; wants to tell Kellam about the strange scene he saw. But there's a heavy cold rushing through him. The world blurs; the dead of Castle Avendell lean in, but unlike before, when they clawed for his attention and demanded to be heard, they feel . . . welcoming. As if Ellion is a long-lost friend, returning at last.

Ellion lies on the floor and presses his cheek to the tile. The floor is cold and lovely. It's a nice floor. Maybe he'll stay here forever. Above him, Kellam and Oak are in a full-blown panic. There was something else Ellion wanted to tell him. Something he doesn't remember. Something important.

Everything fades. All Ellion can see are Rue's eyes, gleaming violet and amber, two stars blazing in a dark sea.

"Ellion," Kellam says. "What other antidote is there? What else can we do?"

"Can't talk," Ellion says blearily. "Too sleepy. Good night."

Someone grabs his shoulders. They shake him, shouting his name, but Ellion is slipping away. Instead of crashing through the Veil, he practically floats through. The world grows dark and cold.

Something winds around his ankles.

"Cat," Ellion mutters. "Hate you."

He turns, but this time, two violet eyes shine back at him instead.

"Ellion," says Vesryn, panicked. "We need to talk."

SEVEN HOURS
TO DAWN

33

CLOVE

For the second time tonight, Clove descends into the dungeons. Her instinct tells her it will be her last.

Neither girl speaks as they tiptoe down the sprawling stone steps. Clove can't tell if the stones are damp beneath her heels or if it's grown so cold since she was last down here that everything has that slightly wet feeling to it.

In and out, she chants to herself. *Grab the book and get out.*

Although she has to admit: She's morbidly intrigued by this supernatural basilisk. It's always been Clove's fatal flaw, this incessant urge to poke and prod at nature's unsavory bits. It's resulted in a lot of scars over the years, both inside and out.

But she won't put Melarie in danger. Clove never plays games when it comes to someone else's life.

"Do you remember where this book landed?" Melarie whispers as their shoes crest the bottom step.

Clove nods before she realizes it's far too dark for the princess to see her. "Follow me."

More accurately, she has a general idea of the direction she threw the book. Where it landed . . . that's a different story. But, still, she has a starting point.

In and out.

She doesn't realize she reached for Melarie's hand in the dark until she feels the princess' fingers wind through hers. Clove gives her gloved hand a quick squeeze, as if to say *We're going to be fine*, before heading toward the cells.

Clove's heartbeat is so loud that she's certain whatever beast or demon lives here can hear the echo of it. She clutches Melarie's hand a little tighter.

The single mage-light glows a venomous green, and there, just at the periphery of its pool of light, lies a tattered tome with gilded letters. Clove's pulse leaps into her throat. That's it. That's the book.

They're two steps away when the princess jerks to a stop. Clove stumbles, breaking her grip.

"Did you hear that?" Melarie whispers.

Clove grows still. After a moment, she whispers, "No. Let's grab the book and get out of here."

That's when the hissing begins.

It's slow and languid at first—more like a bubbling stream than a snake. Someone who doesn't know beasts like Clove might even confuse it for trickling water.

But Clove knows better.

The hair on her arms stands on end.

She lunges for the book.

Her fingers find purchase on the slick leather cover before it's knocked from her hand. Clove yelps as it skids across the stone and disappears into the shadows.

The hissing grows to a fever pitch.

"Melarie!" Clove yells. "Go! Get out of here!"

But the princess does not move. Her silhouette stands stock-still as she says, as calm as a summer morning, "What are you doing here?"

The hissing is so potent, so omnipresent, that it makes Clove's teeth ache. A ropelike shadow slithers into the pool of light, and Clove finally gets a clearer look at the one beast she regrets taking in.

It looks . . . different, somehow. It's bigger, its opalescent scales more defined, even beneath this murky mage-light. A silver tongue flickers. The snake rises until its pale pink eyes are even with Clove's.

It's going to strike.

"Melarie, run!" Clove chokes. *"Please!"*

Again, the princess doesn't budge. Clove spins back to shove her, but Melarie's calm demeanor knocks her off guard. What is going on right now? Is she drugged? "Do you not see that snake?" Clove screams.

"Snake?" Melarie says slowly. "Clove, what are you talking about?"

"*Melarie, please!* You have to get out of here." Frustration pierces Clove's temples. This stubborn, incorrigible, entitled—

"It's okay, Clove. I know him." Melarie steps past her, toward the hissing, frothing basilisk, without an ounce of hesitation.

Clove whimpers. "*Him?*"

Melarie slowly turns to look back at her, and for the first time, there's uncertainty behind her eyes as she says, "Do you not see the man standing right in front of me?"

34

MELARIE

MELARIE would recognize the man before her anywhere.

Monseigneur Gabriel's smile is sharper than usual—predatory, almost. Goose bumps prickle her arms. This is not the gentle, patient man who snuck her books throughout her childhood; and this is not the charming, well-dressed acolyte who spun her across the ballroom floor. This is a hunter in his element, one who believes his prey is already caught.

She's spent ages longing to know who Gabriel is unmasked. Melarie has a feeling she's about to get her answer.

Behind her, Clove trembles. "Melarie. There's no man there."

Melarie's mind spins. She wants so badly to reach for Clove. If they are going to be afraid, they can at least let their terror keep company. But whatever Clove sees cannot possibly be what Melarie does. And Melarie cannot afford to give herself away.

Melarie forces herself to think. To breathe. The air is so cold it bites her lungs.

Something strange is happening here.

She's reminded, of all things, of the dark, bleak days after her mother left. Every word spoken to King Raphaël carried risk. Every time Melarie was in the presence of her father, she had the sense of walking along a tightrope above a sea of broken glass.

One wrong word, one misplaced glance, and he would surely send her plunging toward ruin.

Is it any wonder that Melarie has spent a lifetime dreaming of running away?

That's the feeling Melarie has now. The man before her is Monseigneur Gabriel—and isn't. He regards them with the cocky smile of a fox that has cornered a particularly fat hen. He seems more vibrant, more alive—and for the first time in her life, Melarie is a little bit afraid of him.

Melarie drops her eyes to her toes. "What are we meant to see?"

"The most damning of desires," purrs Gabriel. "Longing, of the deadliest kind. I am the mirror to your heart's most dangerous, painful need. I am your most desperate want."

Melarie licks her lips. Can she deny it? Even as fear runs through her, there's a heat-fueled thrill, too. How long did she dream of him? How many years did she spend wondering and wanting?

Though he's several feet away from them, Melarie swears she feels hands on her waist and breath against the back of her neck. Gabriel's voice is a low rumble in her ear as he whispers, "You need only to reach, Melarie."

Melarie freezes.

Suspicion burns through her. For years, Gabriel refused to call Melarie by her name. At first she'd thought it some act of formality. He was a young man when Melarie met him, but still older than appropriate. She'd never really noticed the way he failed to age; had not thought twice about the formality he offered her like olives on a plate. It made the strangeness of their relationship feel safer. She understood, even then, that his presence in her life was a blessing she could not look too closely at, lest it unravel like fairy gifts crumbling at dawn's light.

Melarie's heart rattles in her chest.

She's not meant to see Gabriel.

Whatever trick this creature is playing—somehow, Melarie is already one step ahead.

She forces herself to speak carefully. "You know my name?"

"Of course." She can hear the smile in his voice, but Melarie refuses to look. "And I know what you long for. I know what you see, and what you seek."

"I don't think you do."

"Because you refuse to look," the monseigneur says, irritation creeping into his voice. "Look at me and tell me I am not what you desire."

She could be wrong. And if Melarie is wrong, this could *all* go south very quickly. But Melarie has made far more desperate gambles before.

She lifts her head and meets his eyes directly. "You already know my desires. You know them better than anyone."

He blinks. The action is so quick, so brief, that had she not spent years studying that face—those long, pale lashes, those cheekbones cut like glass—she might have missed it. For all his ethereal arrogance, it's painfully human.

Melarie casts a prayer to the Weaver's threads of fate and throws caution to the wind.

"Who are you, really?" Melarie asks. "Gabriel."

35

ELLION

ELLION blinks, but the image doesn't clear.

"Ves," he croaks. "What are you doing here?"

"What are *you* doing here?" Her eyes sweep over him and she pales.

Ellion looks down. His body grows more solid by the second. If he concentrates, he can just barely feel the cold press of the tiles beneath him and the heat of the ballroom. But it's fainter than it ought to be, and growing more distant by the second.

That's probably not good.

"Someone else is dead," Ellion says, and then, remembering, "Five someone elses, actually. We keep finding these flowers. And we thought the killer was that creepy grand chamberlain, Gaspar, but when we accused him he started vomiting lilies, which is just as upsetting as it sounds, and Melarie's guard was just *murdered*—"

"Melarie?" Her nose wrinkles. "What, are you on a first-name basis with the princess now? You don't really seem like her type."

Unease washes through Ellion. "I mean, I don't see why that really matters, but I'll admit trying to catch a serial killer and stop a coup is a quick way to become attached to someone." He shakes his head. "Have you seen anything in here? Do you remember anything else from when you were looking into Gaspar?"

Vesryn shakes her head, her expression helpless. Instead of answering, she moves toward Ellion and wraps her arms around him.

"I don't care about any of that," Vesryn murmurs. "I'm just glad you're here. I wish I had done this when I was alive, but . . . there's something I need to tell you."

Ellion stiffens in her hold. "Now? Ves, are you listening to me?"

Vesryn hugs him tighter. Ellion tries, again, to feel anything from his body back in the material world, but he comes up short. It's almost as if someone is blocking him.

Ellion's skin prickles. "What do you want to tell me?"

Vesryn tilts her head back, taking in his face. When she speaks her voice is low and soft. "What do you think? What have you always wanted me to say, Ellion? What is your deepest desire?"

Again, Ellion tries to feel his real body.

Again, he hits a wall.

"I don't know," Ellion says carefully. "Refresh my memory."

Vesryn's eyes glitter. She keeps one arm twined around him and with her other, she cups his cheek and guides his face down to hers. The whole world goes still.

"Luma never deserved you," Vesryn whispers. "And I was always too scared to tell you how I felt. I'll always be sorry I missed my chance. But—well, I know it's not the same, but maybe we can make up for it now."

She's so close Ellion can feel her breath on his lips. It's the scene of his younger self's dreams: Vesryn, looking at him with melted eyes, twined through his arms like a snake. Vesryn, *his* Vesryn, holding him, touching him, wanting him back.

Ellion recalls the despair he felt as a boy when he realized Vesryn could never love him the way he wanted. What a fool he'd been. He should have been better about paying attention to the ways people loved him—not just his parents, but Vesryn, too. So what if she never desired him? Lust was fickle, often faded, and led many a fool astray.

Vesryn was his best friend. She'd been his other half, the better half. She had loved him in every way she could. She had been there for him in every way that truly mattered.

And he'd lost her.

"I know you've always loved me," Vesryn says. "I loved you, too. I was just too afraid. I distracted myself, but it was you I wanted, Ellion. It was always you."

And that's how Ellion knows.

Dread curdles low in his stomach. What was relief only moments ago sours to fear. Fear—and anger.

"You're not Vesryn," Ellion whispers.

Her eyes narrow—and she laughs.

"You," Not-Vesryn sneers, "are all so *stupid*."

Ellion tries to jerk back, but the thing wearing Vesryn's face keeps an iron grip on him. With half-lidded eyes, it sinks its fingernails into Ellion's cheek.

"You know, I expected better of you. Didn't I tell you I was playing a game? All you had to do was stay out of my way."

"What is this?" Ellion whispers.

It pouts, voice taking on a dramatic whine. "You don't remember me? After all these years. I'm hurt! I thought we had something special." The nails sink deeper. "After all, you set me free—and your little friend ensured I made you what you are. And now you're telling me you forgot?"

I Killed the King

Horror crawls through Ellion. The voice in the gorge. That cold, terrible day, when his magic warped.

"It's you," Ellion realizes. "The thing from the gorge. Vesryn, the magistrate, Gaspar, the Istellian. You killed them all and now you're here. *Why?*"

Not-Vesryn rolls its eyes. "The little assassin was going to ruin things. I owed her a favor for waking me up. Crowley was on his way to sign off on the treaty well before I'd had my fun. Weatherington was the perfect puppet to carry out my will—well, until he started to annoy me. And the Istellian noticed Weatherington skulking around, watching the princess, and decided to make a scene about it. We can't have that, now can we? *I'm* the only one who gets to start trouble."

Vesryn had thought it was some kind of ghoul or spirit that they'd woken in the gorge that day. But any lesser being would have been trapped to its binding site within a radius of a few miles. Castle Avendell was hundreds of miles away from the gorge, and here the thing was, ten times stronger than it had been a decade and a half ago. It shouldn't have been possible.

Memories flash behind Ellion's eyes: of the day in the gorge and the cascade of terrible events that followed. Of every village burned, every temple smashed. His peers at the Academy, suddenly orphaned, their parents lost to senseless violence. The villages they visited, stripped clean of life, leaving only skeletons behind. Unlike past conflicts, it seemed like the more things went wrong, the worse the next event was. As if something was . . . feeding off it.

Only one type of being was powerful enough to wreak that much havoc.

And only one creature got stronger the more people believed in it—even if they didn't realize what lurked in the dark they were praying to.

"The gods are supposed to be dead," Ellion protests hoarsely. He licks his lips. "Dead or sleeping. Gone, either way."

"But it's not the same, is it?" Not-Vesryn's eyes twinkle. "Everything sleeping must wake. And even the dead can rise again. You ought to know that better than anyone, Ellion."

Ellion's skin crawls. He has to get out of here. He has to warn them. Whatever this godling is—whatever it wants—it's keeping him here on purpose. Panic slices through him.

He can't feel his body anymore.

"Let me go," Ellion gasps. He tries to jerk away, but he can't move. The god's laughter rings around him, bright and mocking, and dread spirals through Ellion.

He needs to get out of here. Now.

"Let me out," Ellion demands. "Please."

"Oh, Ellion," the god sighs. "You know I can't do that."

Ellion's heart thunders. The words wrap around him. "Why kill me now? You could have done it sooner. You could have hurt me instead of her."

"Don't flatter yourself. You're not my target. But you do pose a problem, considering you could bring that target *back*," the god drawls. "I knew you wouldn't be able to resist getting your hands on another corpse."

How could he have been so stupid? Pierre was a trick, a ploy to remove Ellion from the board. This thing had killed Pierre, knowing Ellion would be desperate for answers, *knowing* he would swallow the poison and enter the Veil.

After years of feeling like his necromancy was little more than a parasite, this isn't the way Ellion had wanted to gain a sense of purpose.

He's going to die.

In the early days at the Academy, he worked with one of his professors on a peculiar case—a woman who'd had her heart broken leaped from a cliff, but she misjudged the distance and instead of ending her life broke every bone in her body.

"It's funny," she said. "The moment I jumped, I realized I'd made a mistake. Every loss, every heartbreak, every humiliation suddenly seemed so, so small. So fixable. And, suddenly, I didn't want to die at all. But it was too late. I was already falling."

That's how Ellion feels now. Like he's in free fall. He's not ready.

"Let me *go*," Ellion roars, twisting and fighting, but fighting a god is like fighting a mountain. The thing that holds him is eternal in its strength, and immovable in its indifference.

Something howls in the distance.

"You might as well stop fighting me," the god drawls.

Anger courses through Ellion. Real, true fury, the first he's felt in years. It's not fair. It's not fair that he and Vesryn woke some god years ago and the world has paid the price. It's not fair that his friend is dead and he's soon behind her. Ellion would give his life for Vesryn's in a second, but she's gone. She's not coming back.

And Ellion isn't ready to follow just yet.

He fights harder. The god doesn't budge. Ellion thinks of Vesryn, of his parents, of Luma, of everyone who has suffered since that day in the gorge.

They were just kids. How was Vesryn to know what she was bargaining with? How could she have suspected what the cost would be?

"I said stop fighting," the god repeats, irritated. "Your body is already shutting down and I plan to—*ow!*"

Suddenly, the arm releases Ellion. The godling stumbles back, face contorted in confusion and pain. Bright, ocher blood spills down its calf.

Behind it, back arched, teeth glittering gold, is Rue.

"Creepy fucking ghost cat," Ellion gasps. "I love you."

The god howls, staggering backward, and Rue leaps at it again.

Ellion lurches away. He needs to find the others. He needs to put a stop to what he and Vesryn started all those years ago once and for all.

He needs to go back. But he doesn't know how.

The Veil tilts around him, pitched sideways on its axis, churning with the weight of his anger and his fear. It's an endless stretch of nothing—of cold, eternal black. Ellion has the sense that he could spend a lifetime running in a dozen directions and never find his way home. He's lost all sense of his body. Without a life to anchor him, he's as good as doomed.

Unless.

Memory stirs of the girl he's always loved, of her little rituals of prayer and worship that she insisted tethered her to the divine even as she knelt beside a greasy stove. The thought of begging for help now is so repulsive that Ellion's stomach turn. A part of him wants to refuse. He'll find his own way out. He'll tear through the Veil with bloodied nails before it comes to that.

What will it be? Vesryn had asked. *Your pride—or their lives?*

Maybe, if Ellion had been brave sooner, he could have found Vesryn. He could have reached out so many times; the day she'd been sent away, the morning she tried to return, and of course, later, when whispers of an assassin who killed their victims painlessly with poisons and healing tonics brewed too strong floated through the kingdom. He should have hunted Vesryn down the moment he heard whispers about her. He should have dropped to his knees and begged for her forgiveness.

But he didn't. Instead, he sent gifts from afar. He tracked news of her the way one follows warnings of a coming storm, feeding his guilt and letting it fester like a favorite sore. He put off reconciliation and turned his back on vulnerability.

Next year, he vowed. *Next year, I'll know what to say.*

But he never did. The words never came; no letter was ever sent. He must have written a dozen of them, all repeating the same tired pleas wearing new coats—*I'm sorry, I love you, forgive me, come home.* None of them was ever enough. No matter. He had an entire miserable life to find the right words. He'd told himself that if the Weaver brought them back together, he'd know exactly what to do and say.

And then when he least expected it, Vesryn came crashing back into his life. Ellion had looked at her and choked on his apology. He failed; he floundered. He did not forgive.

And Vesryn died.

So as the Veil pitches around him and the god shrieks, Ellion does the one thing he swore he'd never do again.

Ellion prays.

"I'll be better," he whispers. "If you—if you help me save them, I'll be better. Please. I have asked for so many things, but this is the only one I mean. Let me make a difference. Let me heal."

His breath hitches.

"Let me help them," he croaks. "The way I should have helped her."

The Veil shifts; something rushes toward him. In the distance, the god is still fighting with Rue. Ellion closes his eyes, bracing himself, swallowing the revulsion and horror that rises in him. Whatever god answers his new call will demand his patronage—and to save them, Ellion will give it. Humiliation burns in him.

It's come to this, then. Ellion Evercraft brought to his knees in all his shame, prostrating before the ethereal in the dark, swearing his loyalty and love because they're the last things he has left.

"Send me back," Ellion whispers. "And I'll spend my entire life worshipping you."

He waits for the crush of the divine. For the will of the gods to press down on him like a thumb squashing an insect.

Instead, the presence that wraps around him is gentle, warm, and familiar.

He'd know the imprint of that soul anywhere.

"Ves?" His eyes burn. "You shouldn't still be here. What—"

Familiar hands grip his shoulders.

They give a brief, reassuring squeeze, and then *shove*.

And Ellion stumbles back into life.

36

CLOVE

CLOVE is hallucinating.

She examines her arms, her hands. She slides her fingers down the length of her neck. Is it possible the basilisk had somehow bitten her and she hadn't registered the pain? Surely there must be poison leaching into her veins.

Because the snake, once as crisp and clear as temple bells, has started to take on a different shape.

I must be losing it. Again, she squints at her hands in the dim light. No bruise. No bite. No blood.

The basilisk melts into an iridescent pool on the floor. Clove blinks, and the amorphous blob slowly rises like bread in the oven. Its lines become cleaner, sharper, taller. Two broad hands form, then a head atop boxy shoulders. Even before the wide eyes and thick brows take shape, Clove knows. The god-thing is transforming into Oak.

Or something Oak-like. The form is right, but the color is blanched and muted, as if the guard is covered in a layer of snow. Clove blinks, and the thing shudders, shedding one skin and slipping into another.

"Kellam?" Clove whispers. The pearly prince gazes down the slope of his nose at her. Beside her, Clove feels Melarie's eyes studying her.

And, suddenly, the princess stands before her, Kellam's livery unfurling into a satin gown. A warm hand grazes Clove's shoulder and she startles. "What do you see?" the real Melarie whispers into her ear.

Clove's lungs constrict. She can't seem to remember how to breathe. Before she can answer, the false princess disappears.

Ellion stands in her place.

"Oh." Clove lets out a puff of air. The healer stares at her with soulless eyes. His lips part, and the thing inhabiting his form finally speaks to her.

That book won't do much for you, the figure says. Or at least, Clove thinks it says. She can feel the voice reverberating through her bones rather than hear it.

There's nothing in there you don't already know, Clove Beauforte.

"Who are you?" she gasps. "*What* are you?"

Clove's entire body begins to tremble. It starts in her fingertips and charges up her forearms and into her torso, where ice pools in her stomach. Perhaps it's the frigid air in the dungeons. Or perhaps this thing is about to send her to her grave. Clove swallows down the urge to cry.

A hand settles between her shoulder blades. Melarie. Her touch is warm. *She's taken off her gloves.* Clove doesn't know why that matters when she's on the brink of ruin, but it does, and a deep sorrow sweeps through her. This is the last she'll see of Melarie.

I'm your greatest yearning. I'm all that you long for, the voice echoes in Clove's head.

"I know what you are," Melarie says.

A pause. *Do you now?* the voice says with a hint of delight. *Then why don't you lay it all out for your friend?*

37

MELARIE

MELARIE has never felt more like a fool.

How had she not seen it? How could she not have known? Her sisters had never even mentioned Monseigneur Gabriel. No servants took note of him; no ambassadors came in escort. He always came and went as he pleased, and before Antoine came to work in the palace, Melarie was so starved for company, she never questioned it. Certainly, she had wondered; but it had been so easy to wave away the monseigneur's boundaryless movements as that of a confident man who knew how to slip through the halls of that big, lonely palace.

In all the time Melarie has known him, Monseigneur Gabriel has never aged a day. He looks exactly as he did when he strolled into her life all those years ago—a handsome young man who had only just turned twenty, bright-eyed and coy with eyes that promised some faraway, forbidden delight. There should be new lines on his face; streaks of silver in his hair. Scars, blemishes, *something*.

But he is perfect, as always. *Too* perfect.

Gabriel was not on Kellam's guest list. And no one else in the ballroom reacted to him at all.

I Killed the King

Melarie has spent a lifetime dancing with a ghost.

No, not a ghost.

A god.

"That day on the balcony," Melarie says faintly. "I fell and I could have sworn someone caught me. When I turned, no one was there. It was you. It's always been you."

As soon as she says it, Melarie knows it's the truth.

And the god winks.

Memory after memory, oddity after oddity. The fall from the window was the most dramatic time Melarie had felt the invisible hand of the divine, but it certainly wasn't the first or the last.

How many times had she reached for a burning stove when a maid suddenly appeared? In how many instances had a disgruntled noble been exposed for poisoning food the moment before it reached her lips?

Melarie had begun to think herself peculiarly cursed; terrible things kept happening, but she always escaped. Even tonight, when she'd been forced into marriage and then the king had dropped dead, she'd chalked it up to the odd humor of cruel fates—always putting her feet to the fire, but never quite letting her burn.

And then, of course, there was her father. Melarie had known he was dead the moment her eyes snapped open. When she'd turned to gather her sisters, something had fluttered.

Later, she told herself she'd imagined it. The windows had been sealed, and even if they hadn't been, there was no wind that morning. Only a stillness, like even the Shifter held his breath in waiting.

Melarie's head had whipped toward the sound. She'd spotted the letter in the fireplace immediately.

It had been crumpled into a ball, half-charred, and damp with wine, as though Raphaël had lit the fire and then immediately tried to put it out. Melarie unfolded the letter. Only then did her hands begin to shake.

My son is of age, King Costis had written. *And I believe it time to secure peace, before we must both pay back what we owe. No matter our differences, I think you agree, Raphaël. We cannot leave this world to chaos. It's time to repair what we set in motion all those years ago.*

When Avendell replied favorably to their marriage proposal and Melarie wept with her sisters in relief, it had been easy to forget the oddity of it all—the voice that roused her from sleep, the wine-snuffed coals, and the way the letter had crinkled, as if nudged by an invisible hand.

Her whole life, Melarie has managed to find an escape. It has become a part of her identity, her core. No matter how dire a situation, Melarie always finds her exit.

But it wasn't her at all.

It was the meddling hand of a god.

"It's not possible," Melarie breathes. "The gods are supposed to be dead. Dead, or sleeping."

"And who told you that?" Gabriel—or whoever he is—asks. "Your father? The texts? It's all a story, princess. And I've never been one to play along."

Melarie shakes her head. "It doesn't make *sense*. My entire life, you've followed me. You've helped me. How are you here now? Why spend all that time helping me and sneaking me stories if you were only ever going to bring me ruin?"

Beside her, Clove shoots Melarie a startled glance. If they survive this, she's going to have a lot of explaining to do.

The god's face twitches. "You were never meant to be here tonight. It was supposed to be your sister."

What did Monseigneur Gabriel say to her earlier?

You're not supposed to be here.

Cold creeps through Melarie. "Costis made a bargain with you. And my father. Who are you, really? What do you want?"

Why have you been following me my entire life?

Why, even now, do I not loathe you?

"I want what I am owed. I want the last debt settled." He hesitates. "You were not supposed to meet me like this."

Melarie doesn't have time to unpack whatever *that* means. She fights to keep her voice even. "And what are you owed? What did my father trade that was worth his own ruin?"

"Four lives, for four miracles." The god's eyes glint. "Beauty, power, wealth, and health. Raphaël received all four, but he only paid for three."

Horror grips Melarie.

Three lives. Three queens. Her mother was meant to be the fourth, and when she fled, the god had no choice but to collect a life from the very one who had made the bargain.

The tunnels close in around them as the god continues, his face twisting with resentment.

"Your father was a sickly prince. No one remembers—he made certain of that—but I do. Weak, cowardly, impotent. No one even questioned how the fourth son of a fourth son who had no power, no wealth, and no respect suddenly acquired all three. No one wondered how his brothers, uncle, and father, who had always had perfect health, lost it so suddenly." Its eyes glint. "I gave Raphaël all he could dream of. But he tried to cheat me."

Her father's paranoia. His hatred for Melarie and her sisters, his resentment toward the wives he'd lost. Suddenly, it's all rendered in terrible, blistering clarity. Melarie cannot breathe.

"So what?" she accuses. "You could not take my mother's life, so you killed my father instead?"

The god regards her with a neutral expression. "I collected a debt."

"So what are you owed now?" Clove asks. "There's another bargain, right? How do we pay it back?"

"Costis bartered for something precious. I agreed to let his son live ten more years. I could not fix him, but I could pause what was killing him. At midnight, Costis' decade is up."

"Midnight?" Melarie cries. "But we had until dawn!"

The god snorts. "Who said anything about dawn?"

"That's when we sign the treaty. When Costis tried to marry me and Kellam, he said he needed it done before . . ." Her voice trails away.

Before the bargain comes due.

But the treaty wasn't the bargain he meant.

Cold blisters through her. "We had it all wrong," Melarie says hollowly. "Costis wasn't worried about securing peace. He was running from a debt to a god."

Fear creeps into Clove's voice. "But midnight is in less than an hour."

"Perhaps you understand why I've run out of patience," the god says. "Bring out the king. Let this be done."

Clove shoots Melarie a panicked look.

"You don't know," Melarie realizes, her heart pounding so hard her body shakes. "This whole night—all the deaths, the notes. You didn't *know*."

Oh, Weaver help them. Melarie has spent her entire life looking for exits—but she has no idea how they're going to get out of this one.

The god shoots her an annoyed look. "Know what?"

Clove looks at her, her cheeks pale, but her eyes determined.

In the murky light of the dungeons, Melarie reaches for Clove's hand. She twines her fingers through the beast tamer's and squeezes. It's the same way Solene held her hand after Melarie's mother disappeared. The grip Delphine had the night her father hit Melarie so hard he fractured her nose. The same caress Elodie gave her when she realized Melarie would be sent to Avendell in her place. The squeeze Antoine gave her this very night, when she told him of her fears, and he promised he would do his best to see her through this.

It makes no promises of safety, of success, of happiness. It carries one vow—the only one Melarie has ever been able to keep.

I'm here, her touch says. *Whatever happens, we face it together.*

Clove squeezes Melarie's hand back.

And then the beast tamer looks at the god and says, "You're too late. Costis is dead."

38

CLOVE

CLOVE watches in horror as the god goes rigid. When it speaks, she hears the words echo throughout the dungeon instead of inside her head. "That's impossible."

"It's true," Melarie whispers beside her.

A pause. The figure stands stock-still just outside the reach of the mage-light. Clove squints. From this angle, the thing seems to have taken on yet another form—this one neither friend nor beast. It's slightly shorter than Oak or Kellam, but taller than Ellion.

"He had his guard kill him," Clove says quietly. "Whatever he owed you, he was willing to die rather than pay it."

The god hisses, but this time it sounds more human than snake. Clove blinks, and the lines of its frame sharpen, as if someone had wiped clean the lens of a looking glass. It shifts, and the left side of its body comes into view. The sharp angle of a jaw. A slender neck. A fine wool overcoat. Cold floods the air. Clove's breath fogs in front of her, and beside her, Melarie has begun to shiver.

The air grows so cold it's hard for Clove to breathe. Around them, the castle groans. The god backtracks, shaking his head, his movements frenetic.

"It was all I needed," the god says. "The last loose end—he can't *cheat* me like this."

Melarie squeezes Clove's hand and tugs her backward. The princess' eyes are wide with fear. She doesn't need to speak for Clove to know what she's thinking.

They need to find the others. And they need to get out of here.

"Can't you just leave the bargain as is?" Clove demands. "Or let someone else pay you back?"

"It's not that simple," the god snaps. "It's not how it works."

Every hair on the back of Clove's neck stands on end. Her eyes cut to the stairwell. She could do it. If she took off right now she might be able to make it far enough up the stairs to scream for help.

But Melarie. She could never leave her here. And without the book, they won't have a chance of figuring out how to satisfy whoever this god is.

A bone-deep chill ripples from the deity. Ice climbs up the walls as its chest rises and falls. Clove catches a glimpse of sleek, blond hair, the flash of a stormy gray eye. Just when she starts to piece together an image in her mind, the figure blurs. Gray eyes flicker to become snake eyes with a dagger-sharp slit down the middle. Full lips flash to a narrow jaw that belongs to the healer. The silhouette fills out to emulate the shape of the guard.

"You humans," the god seethes. "All your meddling—so many of you getting in my way tonight, and I got my hands dirty for *nothing*. All those years I wasted with that insufferable grand chamberlain, whispering and wheedling and muddling his dreams, guiding his hand when the little assassin stuck her nose in too early, and even *he* couldn't just do as he was told in the end. All of it for nothing."

Cold blisters through Clove. Whatever little sense of control she'd had over her emotions has shattered, and she wants to scream and laugh and sob all at once. She has to hold it together for just a bit longer. She has to keep him talking.

"You killed Vesryn and the magistrate," Clove spits. "You tricked Gaspar into thinking the Builder spoke to him and killed him, too, when he got in your way. Why? For fun? For power?"

"I've never been worshipped," the god says quietly. "Do you know what that's like? To be ignored, reviled, and cast aside? The Beaufortes have really held tight to their blasphemy all these years, but even you must understand how this works, surely." Its voice grows thick with longing. "All those flowers and fruits and sacrifices you humans make. The prayers, the festivals, the temple pilgrimages? All that feeds us. It's all a means to an end. The more energy and attention humans put into us, the more they believe, and the more powerful we become. I never got any of it. I wanted it." Its eyes glint. "I woke up. And suddenly, for the first time, I was alone."

Clove and Melarie inch backward. The air grows colder.

"Of course I made a bargain. I'd waited an eternity for it. You humans and your yearning—your delicious, foolish wants. It was so *easy*." The god seems to be talking more to itself now than anything. "I never expected to start a war. You know what happens during a war? People start *praying*." Its expression sours. "But it wasn't me they prayed to."

Out of the corner of her eye, Clove sees the princess nod. They need to make a run for it.

"I'm out of time," says the god. "And so are you. I want what I've come for. I want—*ow*."

It stumbles backward. Golden blood trickles down its thigh, and the god winces, batting frantically at the corner. Clove sees it—the shape of a cat, flickering in and out. It turns to her, amber and violet eyes winking.

Now's their chance.

Clove's eyes slide to the book.

"Clove," Melarie breathes. "We've got to go find the others. Now."

Clove nods.

And then she dives.

Before Melarie can stop her, she lunges for and scoops up the tattered tome. It snaps open at her touch. The pages flap wildly, and careful script appears where there had only been blank space.

Madness feeds what lurks beneath.
What is not pinned beneath stone or sea will wake.

"Oh, no you don't," the god says. The book trembles and bursts into a flurry of pages. "I've come too far to let—you little mongrel, get *away* from me!"

It staggers backward. The ghost cat leaps at it again, yowling, and when Melarie locks her fingers around Clove's wrist, she doesn't fight her. She lets the princess drag her away.

They race up the stairs, hand in hand, torn pages fluttering behind them like falling snow.

39

ELLION

ELLION wakes with a gasp.

Bitterness fills his mouth, cutting off his air, and the panicked faces of Kellam and Oak loom over him.

"Oh, thank the Courier and all his acolytes," says Kellam. "You're alive."

Ellion coughs. Something flies out and lands in a puddle of Pierre's blood with a sad, wet *plop*. It's a flower bud, pale green and bleeding sap from being chewed.

Ellion blinks. "I thought you didn't have magic. Nice work, princeling."

Kellam and Oak cut each other a panicked glance.

"Actually," Kellam says shakily. "About that—"

"No time." Ellion lurches upright. "Kellam, we have to evacuate. We're in danger. The second killer—"

"Is a god," a new voice says.

Ellion looks up. Clove and Melarie elbow their way through the guards, panic lining their faces. They try to fight their way through and Kellam barks at his men to let the girls in. They part, and Ellion realizes a beat too late what's about to happen.

"Melarie," Ellion blurts. "Don't—"

He's too late. Melarie's foot lands in Pierre's blood with a *squelch*. Her eyes drop. "Gods," she gasps. "*Pierre*."

Melarie gags and staggers back, colliding with one of the guards. The man goes sprawling.

And, suddenly, their wall is broken.

Ellion watches as the first of the guests turns to look. The woman is beautiful, red-haired and wild, but when she sees Pierre's corpse her smile dims. She screams and drops her wineglass. It shatters at her feet; the liquid spreads in a dark stain. The guards react, closing the loop once more, but the damage is done.

"Someone is dead," a guest on the dance floor whimpers. "I saw—look, the guard's feet! They're covered in blood!"

"Where is the king?" someone demands. "What is the meaning of this?"

The world blinks in and out of focus. Melarie is still trembling, staring at Pierre with a haunted expression. She's no use to them right now. Ellion lurches and hands catch his forearm. It's Clove—her eyes are bright with fear, but they're clear and alert.

"Ellion," Clove gasps. "It's a god. There's one here, awake, and it's been causing problems all night. That's what you felt in the Veil. It's been here all along, and everything we've done has only made it stronger. We don't know where it came from but—"

"Where is King Costis?" one of the guests shouts. The music grinds to a halt; panicked chatter fills the air. Beyond the castle windows, the storm rises to a furious howl. The snow is so thick they can't even see the world beyond.

They're going to be buried alive.

"We were wrong about the timing," Melarie is telling Kellam, her hand still shaking over her mouth. "We don't have until dawn. We have until midnight."

Oak goes rigid. "That's in thirty minutes."

"What does it want?" Kellam demands.

At the same time, Oak says, "Do we know which god it is?"

The girls exchange panicked glances before shaking their heads. An uncertain silence stretches between them. Silence they can't afford.

They're out of time.

"I can't believe I'm saying this," Kellam mutters. "But I kind of wish Gaspar was here. It would have been helpful for him to tell us his theories before he vomited up flowers and died. Or . . . was murdered, I guess?"

"Why kill him?" Melarie asks, burying her face in her hands. "Why kill any of them? When we told it Costis was dead, it didn't even *know*. It was more worried about the stupid book."

Ellion's head snaps up. At the same time, he and Kellam demand, "What book?"

"I didn't see the title," Clove says. "The pages inside were blank, except for two lines: *Madness feeds what lurks beneath. What is not pinned beneath stone or sea will wake.*"

Kellam looks uneasily between them. "There was a book in Gaspar's library. When I opened it, every page was blank. It disappeared when I turned back to show it to Oak." He licks his lips. "It had a title, though. It was called *The Thirteen*."

Ellion can't breathe. It's not possible.

Not here, not after all this time.

Kellam's brow knits. "I swear, I'd heard that name before. . . ."

"From Vesryn," Ellion croaks. "That damn book of myths she

loved so dearly about the original pantheon. It was called *The Thirteen*. Her favorite story was about the Weaver and her forsaken, slain child. That was the book I read to you, princeling. The one you took home."

Vesryn always insisted that gods drew power from belief. One didn't have to worship the Builder to borrow his strength; one only needed to be a good steward of the land. He had thought it nonsense, but it had brought his friend comfort, to believe that her tiny acts of setting things to right fed the Arbiter even in sleep.

And, suddenly, he knows.

That day in the gorge. The war started, and after that, it seemed like every conflict was worse than the last. Like something was feeding off things being thrown out of balance. And then, of course, there's tonight. Every step they took, it felt like something was toying with them. Every action they chose resulted in the worst possible outcome. Ellion had thought it foul luck.

But what if it was something else growing stronger?

That voice. The one deep in the Veil that had flung Ellion away from Vesryn and snarled that single, strange line.

My game has just begun.

Because to a god, that's all they could be. Some twisted, terrible game. And it had been willing to play—until they'd gotten too close to figuring out the truth with Gaspar and had ruined its fun.

The pieces swirl before him.

And, finally, they click.

The despair the king had felt over his death—and his anchor moment, that strange, haunting image of young Kellam, sickly and unmoving in his arms. Of course. When Ellion brought Costis back, his only concern had been for his son. He'd left him with the clearest warning he could.

They just hadn't known how to make the puzzle fit together yet.

"*Chaos comes for you*," Ellion breathes. "Kellam, your father's last words. He was being literal. The thirteenth god—the thing the other Twelve refused to let live in the world—it's the god of chaos."

And everything stops.

The snowflakes freeze against the pane; the ball goers pause mid-twirl. Dropped wineglasses hang in the air. Even the blood pooling beneath Pierre freezes.

Horror washes through Ellion, and when he looks up, his own terror is mirrored on the faces of Kellam, Melarie, Clove, and Oak. They are the only ones left moving.

"What is this?" Kellam whispers.

The guard behind him seizes. His eyes roll back in his head.

And everyone collapses.

Nobles and merchants wilt to the ground; servants fall where they are, their trays of drinks smashing down, bending like flowers mowed flat by a runaway carriage. Everyone collapses, plunged into sleep. Only the five of them remain standing.

From the entrance to the ballroom, someone claps.

A single man leans against the doorframe, gray eyes glinting, black wool suit drinking in all the light.

"Well," the god Chaos drawls. "It's about *time* someone figured that out."

~~FIVE AND A HALF
HOURS TO DAWN~~

THIRTY MINUTES
TO MIDNIGHT

40

KELLAM

KELLAM has no idea what's happening. As the ballroom hangs in suspension, the man Ellion just referred to as a god gives them all an amused smile.

"Ellion," the god says, with the familiarity of an old friend commenting on the weather. "Nice to see you again."

"You just tried to kill me," Ellion says flatly.

"Don't hold on to the past. It's not polite." The god spreads his hands. "Why the long faces, everyone? This is a historic night! Avendell and Istellia reunited at last, despite my best efforts. And I finally get to collect my debt."

Kellam's heart threatens to beat out of his chest. "Who are you? What is this?"

The god lifts a brow. "Would you like to do the honors, Ellion? No? Oh, fine, then. I suppose I'm not too proud to introduce myself. And I do love making an entrance." With a mocking flourish, the god sinks into a deep bow. "Chaos, at your service—well, technically your father's. You have him to thank for this whole mess."

Kellam's blood runs cold. "My father?"

"I hadn't been awake for long when Costis came begging."

I Killed the King

The god steps delicately over a woman who collapsed mid-twirl. He kneels, plucks her half-empty wineglass from her fingers, and drinks deep. Red runs down his chin. "I was so weak. I'd made my first few bargains, but they weren't really worth much—no offense, Ellion."

"What does he mean?" Oak says quietly. "What is he saying?"

Ellion is whiter than death.

"Cat got your tongue? I suppose I can tell the story."

In a blink, Chaos shifts.

Another Ellion stands before them, wineglass balanced on the tip of his finger, swaying like a drunken fool. When he speaks, it's in Ellion's voice, pitched into a mocking timbre.

"When we were children, Vesryn and I took a little tumble into Godmaker's Gorge," Chaos says, contorting Ellion's face into a mask of overdramatic shock. "I hit my head, quite conveniently, on the very stone Chaos was imprisoned in—no thanks to *your* lineage, princess. All that trouble poor Chaos went to in stealing his mother's spindle and putting the rest of the pantheon to sleep to protect his lover, and how did she repay him? By pulling a nasty little trick and locking him away. And Chaos would have slept forever, had it not been for two very clumsy, very stupid children."

Chaos pushes Ellion's face into a pout. "I was slipping away. So much blood. Ellion, am I getting it right? I'm going to take the fact that you look like you're about to faint as a yes." Chaos cocks his head to the side. "I was dying. And then I heard a voice that promised to save me."

"But I said no," Ellion rasps, the very picture of a boy haunted. "I said *no*."

"You did." Chaos shifts. Now Vesryn stands before them,

throat bruising under the strain of an invisible vise. "But someone else was in a bartering mood that day."

Ellion's knees buckle. Kellam's eyes dart around. Their guests are still unconscious. Outside, the storm itself is still paused. Somehow, that's much worse than the howl of the wind.

Kellam senses a subtle shift. There's a frenzy to Chaos. In the corner of his eye, a lone moth flutters toward the mage-lights, frosted over with supernatural cold.

"It was easy after that," Chaos continues. "You humans—you're so *hungry*. Imagine my delight when I realized I was the only one of the pantheon awake. After the way they treated me, it seemed fitting. Finally, here was my chance to play." He spreads his hands. "I started small, of course. Rain for farmers that turned to floods; gold for poor men that could never stay in their grasp. With every bargain gone bad, I grew, until finally it was no longer children and peasants who heard my whispers." His eyes glint. "It was kings."

"You spoke of a debt needing to be repaid," Melarie cuts in. Instead of fear, fury lines her face. "You struck a bargain with King Costis in exchange for his life, same as you did with my father. But Costis is dead. Terrorizing us will not bring him back."

"You've got one thing wrong, princess," Chaos says. "Costis didn't make that bargain to protect *his* life. He bartered his magic to protect another. I never received my payment—which means that the only way out of this bargain for me is to cut a certain life short."

He changes forms once more.

And this time, it's Kellam's own face staring back at him.

"No," whispers Oak.

"*Yes*," says Chaos. "I believe the original terms were that when I killed Costis and collected the last of his magic tonight, the curse within Kellam would finally reanimate. Costis tried to cheat me—he realized that if he died by someone else's hand, the hold on Kellam's terminal magic would keep." His eyes glint. "But he forgot one thing. The bargain requires the life of a *king* to fulfill, and would you look at that—we have one right here! Once Kellam is dead, I'll be free. Given that Oak has dutifully returned himself to the status of everyone's favorite orphan, one of you will have to do the honors instead. Now, who's feeling murderous?"

"You're insane," Clove stammers. "You monster, we're not—we're not *killing* Kellam."

Chaos looks at her and his smile vanishes. He returns to the form he entered in, the pale-haired man dressed in all black. His eyes are distant, ancient, and cold.

When Kellam was a boy, he attended a royal hunt with Costis. It had barely begun when a mountain lion slipped from the bushes and tore out the throats of the dogs. It didn't even bother to eat them. It killed them because it could—because it was bored.

That is how Chaos looks at them now. A predator cornering pathetic, palace-raised prey, ready to slaughter them simply because he has nothing better to fill the hour.

"This isn't a negotiation." The god's voice flattens, all humor drained away until only ice remains. "The prince should have died ten years ago when his father brought him to that gorge. Count yourselves lucky I gave him the time I did."

Knives appear in Melarie's, Ellion's, Oak's, and Clove's hands, the handles carved into the shape of a stag mid-leap. Frost forms along the blades. Melarie drops hers with a gasp; Ellion flings his away, and Oak sets his carefully on the floor. Clove clutches the hilt, her face a hard mask, then tucks the knife into the folds of her dress. "I won't do it," she spits, "but I won't let you have all the weapons, either."

Together, as if in silent agreement, they form a ring around him.

Kellam does not deserve them.

He wonders, faintly, if anyone remembers just how sick he was. His parents worked relentlessly to keep it contained, but truth is like water: relentless, patient, and always ready to slip through the smallest of cracks. Whispers followed their family everywhere—of the foreign queen and her cursed womb.

And of course, the Vernevau curse itself, all those heirs who disappeared over the years, snipped from the family tree like rosebuds turned to rot. Kellam had not been the first Vernevau born blue-faced and silent.

Some thought that they'd angered the Historian by reviving Kellam; that the misfortune of the years that followed was tied to altering the historical record overseen by Avendell's most patient god. Every year Kellam lived on borrowed time, until ten years ago, when it seemed the Courier had finally come to shepherd him through the Veil. Kellam doesn't remember much. But if he thinks—if he *really* thinks—he can almost see it.

A half-frozen river, winding through endless cliffs.

His father's golden hair, face lined with grief.

And a voice, filling his world, asking one simple question:

What do you desire?

And Costis, it seemed, had answered.

Kellam looks at the god. At his friends.

He looks, mostly, at Oak.

I Killed the King

Kellam has no magic. He was meant to die at birth; every year beyond that was stolen, squandered on a boy destined for disappointment. He couldn't even be a halfway decent marriage candidate. He'd gone and doomed Avendell's future by falling in love with his *guard*.

Costis bartered his life for his son, and what did Kellam do with it? Drank, flirted, slept, and gambled it away. That had been Costis' mistake. Kellam was never someone worth bargaining for.

You will have a grand legacy, Kellam's mother once promised. *You will change the world and undo the fabric of the Weaver's tapestry of fate itself.*

And what could be grander than this? A god, defeated. A castle, saved.

This will be the first worthwhile thing Kellam ever does.

It will also be the last.

Kellam draws a breath to speak—but someone beats him to it.

"Take me," says Oak. "You want Costis' son? I was his, by every right but blood. Take my life instead."

41

OAK

OAK looks at his prince for the last time.

He gives Kellam a meaningful glance. *Let me do this.*

But as usual, the crown prince of Avendell does not listen. He reaches for Oak, clamping his hand around the guard's wrist. "Oak, you *cannot*."

Oak swallows the dread creeping up his throat. His gaze drifts to Kellam's long fingers encircling his wrist, a spark of warmth leaping between them. It takes everything in him not to break down at the thought that the match recently lit between them will never burn any brighter than it does right now.

"You're lucky you're pretty because perception is not your strong suit." Oak peels Kellam's fingers from his wrist, then cups the prince's face in his broad hands. He leans close enough that he can almost taste the prince's wine-stained breath. "I would start wars and grind cities to dust for you, you idiot. And besides, it's well within my duty to give my life for my king."

Kellam's eyes glisten. Oak caresses the prince's cheek with his thumb. "Do you really think this world has meaning to me if you're not in it?" Oak blinks, and an errant tear trickles down his face and into the hollow of his jaw. His prince. His *king*. He can't believe he ever thought of leaving Kellam to the chill of this dark and lonely castle. It was only to escape the agony of loving someone he could never have.

But now Oak knows the truth of it—no matter where Oak ended up in this country or the next, this prince with the bottle-green eyes would cling to him like forest nettle. It's Kellam who whispers to him in his dreams.

For as long as Kellam is in this mess, Oak will be, too.

No. He will fix it.

"This is all very touching," Chaos says. "But it's not your life I'm tied to."

Oak and Kellam turn to the god. In the flickering mage-lights, this thing that's been haunting them all night looks . . . unimpressive. Chaos is shorter than both the guard and prince, his frame slender and nimble. Though he wears a fine woolen coat, the rest of him—his narrow nose and stubbled jaw and curious eyes—are not features Oak thought he'd see on a god. He isn't sure what he expected a god to look like, actually, but it isn't this.

Chaos' eyes sweep over the still and silent ballroom.

The god is nervous, Oak thinks. *But what could a god possibly be afraid of?*

"Let's *go*," Chaos says, snapping his fingers. The mage-lights click off as if the god had snuffed them out by hand. In the dark, the princess whimpers and the beast tamer moves toward her. The healer mumbles to himself. The prince reaches for his hand.

The rest of the bodies in the room do not move. In the watery gray light from the snow-covered windows, Oak can just make out their unflinching silhouettes. Above them, the beams holding up the turrets groan in protest. There's a sharp *snap* from high above as one of them begins to splinter.

A voice cuts through the dark. "You started the storm." *Melarie.*

"Surprise," Chaos drawls. "I couldn't very well let you leave, could I?"

"Make it stop!" Clove yells. "The roof is going to cave in!"

As if in response, another beam groans. A symphony of pops and snaps reverberates through the ballroom.

Oak steps between the prince and the god. "Please, take me. Just take me and do what you must for this to be over."

Another snap, this one loud enough to make Oak's teeth rattle. Someone screams. He spins back just in time to watch as a massive hunk of wood drops from the ceiling and smashes into the dessert table, sending glass and éclairs flying.

"If I give you my life," Kellam says slowly. "What happens?"

Cold seeps into Oak's bones. He turns back to the prince, but Kellam isn't looking at him. His eyes are locked onto Chaos, his face wore that unreadable mask Oak has always abhorred.

"All this goes away," Chaos says, flashing him a feline grin. "I get the payment I was due. I leave. The storm stops, the castle remains standing, and you all get to have a pretty little funeral for a prince who should have died years ago."

"Don't," Melarie says. "Kellam, we will figure out another way."

Kellam releases a trembling breath, then nods. He takes a step toward the god.

"No!" Oak clamps his hand on to Kellam's arm and yanks him back. This time when the prince turns, anger flares in his eyes.

"Release me," Kellam says, his voice dangerously low. "That's an order."

"I love you, too," Oak whispers. He feels Kellam soften, just a bit, beneath his touch. "I want to find out what it's like to know that you love me back."

The prince's shoulders slump and for one breathless moment, hope floods Oak's heart. Kellam smiles sadly. "I always have."

He lifts his free hand and uncurls his palm.

Three winter lilies, plucked straight from the corpses, huddle in the center.

Oak reaches for them, but the prince is faster.

Kellam swallows the lilies whole and drops to the floor.

NINETEEN HOURS EARLIER

42

ELLION

THERE'S a ball tonight—*the* ball, the one everyone in this kingdom and the next have worked themselves into a tizzy over. Somehow, impossibly, Istellia and Avendell have agreed to peace.

The healers' dormitories are empty. The other newly hired healers likely rose well before dawn, making their daily pilgrimage first to Avendell's temple of the Courier. As if it'll do them any good. Ellion knows better than anyone that if the gods can hear them, they have no interest in answering. He gave up praying a long time ago.

Sunlight filters through the window. It's been a warm spring, hot enough that the Courier's robes are uncomfortably heavy. He smooths them over the length of his frame. The arms are short and cut too wide. Given the state of his life, he shouldn't care about looking like a mess. But old habits die hard.

"What the hell am I doing here?" Ellion whispers.

When the dour man in Avendellian dress adorned with a lily pin sought him out and offered him a cushy job as a royal healer, it seemed like an easy yes. But Ellion hadn't anticipated what it would be like to be around other healers again. And unlike the weighted necks of his teachers, many of these fresh-faced healers have never fixed anything more than a cold.

Being around them only reminds Ellion of his failures. Of her.

Ellion has lost track of Vesryn recently. She'd hate him even more if she found out he's been keeping an eye on her—but she has to know, right? The conveniently stuffed wallets, dangling from the pockets of drunks that stumble past her; the parcels of food, carefully bundled, left on the stoop of whatever shithole lodging she's found for her latest job. He can't face her. He can't apologize for what he's done. But at least he can help her from afar.

It's a nice lie—to convince himself that any amount of money or pastries bundled in cloth would make up for the myriad ways he's failed her.

Ellion swings his legs over the bed and reaches for a drink. But as his fingers stretch toward the bottle, Vesryn's face looming in his mind, he misses. It falls with a shatter and Ellion swears, sinking to his knees, frantically trying to pick up the broken bottle before everything spills out. Pain slices through his hand.

Ellion stares at the blood welling on his palm, dumbfounded. If the gods *are* real, they have a twisted sense of humor.

"Fine," he mutters. "You want me to heal? I'll heal."

Head pounding, limbs shaking, Ellion drags himself to the practice cabinet.

It doesn't take long to find what he needs—yarrow to stop the bleeding, eucalyptus to disinfect, moss to pack the wound. Despite his shaking hands, he makes short work of the paste and binds his palm with deft, confident fingers. Poultice work was always his favorite. He loves the rhythm of mixing herbs, the craft that goes into the perfect balm.

It was the one class he always excelled at. His teacher had no healing magic; she was an herbalist and though the Courier ignored her prayers for power, she'd performed miracles in her own right. Not through the blessing of the divine, but after years of study, practice, and craft.

There'd always been something hopeful in that to Ellion.

Ellion packs the cut.

He may not be able to heal. But he can still mend.

Ellion collapses back into bed, takes a swig from the broken pint, and flinches as it cuts his lip.

He thinks, of all things, of the day in the gorge.

Who fell first? Him or Vesryn? He can't remember. They had been scrambling over the dusty red rocks, palms smarting from the roughness of the mudstone, and suddenly they were sliding, slipping along a great slab of ice pulling them down.

He remembers pain; the snap of his left arm, the twist of his right ankle, and then a blast to his skull so violent, for a moment, he thought he'd been struck. Then only darkness.

Darkness—and a voice.

Little healer, a voice had whispered. *You're dying.*

He had been so young, and death was a distant, foreign thing. He couldn't *die*.

I can help you, whispered the voice. *I can save you, for a price. A life, for a life.*

Ellion had not understood. He was dying. How could he give up a life he wanted to save?

Not your life, the voice had purred. *Hers.*

Ellion froze. The voice grew sultry.

What is she to you? A peasant. An orphan. Something to replace, something to discard. You are a noble; the heir to a great house. No one will remember her. There will always be more girls, hungry for a hearth to lie beside and a rich man's bed to warm.

Terror had gripped Ellion, and anger, too. Because he'd heard other people speak of Vesryn in that way. And though he was still too young to understand the chasm that status would open between them, he'd already begun to love her with the fierceness of a child starved for something to care for.

So Ellion said: *No.*

You will die.

No, Ellion said again. *You can't have her.*

He felt the voice's wrath; he tasted its disgust. But Ellion could not picture a world without Vesryn Novelle. He'd promised to protect her.

So as Ellion died, he did the last thing he could—he prayed.

Healing would do him no good here. The Courier was clearly done with him.

But Ellion had heard his father's lectures about choosing an additional patron among the gods. Alistair had always prayed to the Sage, and Ellion's mother to the Lover, but Ellion thought of a story—one of Vesryn's favorites from her little book of myths—about the Weaver and that lost thirteenth child. The Weaver had been painted a selfish fool for creating a second, cursed child, but Ellion always liked the idea of loving someone to your detriment. Of caring beyond reason, consequences be damned.

The healer's vow was one of sacrifice. Alistair Evercraft would never put his child before the fate of others, and Olivia Evercraft would never do anything to jeopardize the affection of her husband. They loved Ellion, but with limits.

It was a nice dream, to believe others would.

So as Ellion died, he threw a prayer into the void.

Weaver, he prayed. *Protect Vesryn. Keep her here, at all costs. Please.*

The world went dark.

And then the light came back.

Vesryn stood over him, her eyes red and raw, and when Ellion coughed she threw herself on him and sobbed. Ellion had lain there, gripped by a strange cold, one that grew only stranger as his father carried his broken body past the fenced-off wood and toward the estate's private infirmary. He'd felt the press of something hungry, lonely, and distant. That night, Ellion had crawled into bed beside Vesryn and whispered, "Do you hear it? The voices from the wood? The ones that won't stop crying?"

"No?" Vesryn had gone deathly pale. "The graveyard is in the woods."

They never spoke of the gorge again.

Not when Ellion's parents thanked Vesryn for her bravery and finding their son in the gorge; or later, when the war with Istellia began, and Ellion's home began to fill with the injured and the sick. They made no mention of the day Ellion was banned from the infirmary because the soldiers were terrified of the blank-faced little Evercraft boy who always materialized by the bedside of a soldier minutes before they died—even when that soldier was the perfect picture of health. No one breathed a word the day Ellion showed Vesryn the dead bird stirring in his hands, proof of the way his healing ability had warped into something wicked.

The gorge lived between them, a secret unspoken, until it grew so distant, Ellion thought it a dream. He prayed to the gods to fix him. He begged them to save him. He ached for it to end.

No one ever answered.

Voices come from the other side of the door. The Courier acolytes are returning. Ellion scowls. Felix is going to scold him, and Agatha is going to look teary-eyed and worried, and now Ellion is going to have to come up with another lie for why he can't make the rounds to mend the sick. Why does the ball have to be *today*? Ellion rolls his eyes to the dull wood paneling of the dormitory ceiling and mutters a sarcastic prayer—the only kind he can manage anymore.

If the gods are real, he hopes they can save his evening by making it interesting.

Ellion wouldn't mind a little chaos for once.

43

VESRYN

VESRYN jerks from her sleep, her clothes slick with sweat.

For a moment, she's certain she's back in Lessarde, the sun just beginning to crest over the mud-stained knolls that have yet to see signs of green this early into spring. With her eyes still closed, she sticks her hand out from beneath the blanket and feels for her bedside table.

Her hand finds only air.

Vesryn's eyes snap open, and she remembers.

She is not in her cloying rented room above the town apothecary, the one that always reeks of clary sage and embalming oils. She is in an entirely different rented room at an inn tucked into Fons. There are no muddy knolls outside her window, only a solemn stone castle.

Despite all odds, Vesryn Novelle is going to a ball tonight.

She cups her face in her hands. Why in the Arbiter's name did she agree to this?

When she received the gilded invitation a fortnight prior, Vesryn's stomach plummeted. At the time she assumed it was because of Prince Kellam's haphazardly scrawled note, and the magnitude of his request. But now that she's done her preparation and studying and traveling, Vesryn realizes she was wrong.

The sick feeling in her stomach was a warning.

She should have rescinded her acceptance when the dreams started again. Honestly, she probably shouldn't have shown up at all. Packed her single knapsack and headed to a different village, with a different view, and pretended like this had never happened.

But no—that would have worked for only so long. Vesryn had earned herself a bit of a reputation for the efficacy of her "work," especially among the powerful and wealthy. And the heir to the throne certainly had the resources to find her.

Eventually, his request may have turned into a command.

Vesryn's hands slide down her face. She's suddenly hot. She kicks off the wool blanket and hops out of bed. The wooden floor paneling is icy beneath her bare feet, but the chill does nothing to cool her down.

I can help you. I can give you what you long for . . . if you're willing to bargain for it.

The voice. It's still as crisp as midnight air, even after all these years. For a long time, it left her alone, but it returned to haunt her dreams with concerning frequency over the past month. Nowadays, it shows up in her waking hours, too.

She pauses in front of the small, circular window. The forest-green flags atop the west turrets snap wildly against a muted sky. A storm's coming. Vesryn has not packed the right shoes.

A bargain of equal measure.

Vesryn groans. She cups her hands around the back of her neck and tips her head to look at the cobwebbed ceiling. "What do you want from me?" she whispers to no one. "I gave you what you asked for. The deal is done."

Then something very strange happens.

The mercenary blinks, and suddenly she's no longer in her

room at the inn. Vesryn is back in Godmaker's Gorge on a day too cold for summer, on a ledge too high for a child.

Two children, actually. The memory comes in hot and fast waves, blips in her history that she only allows to seep in while she's dreaming. A younger, brighter Ellion with a laugh that sounded like a promise. The mudstone silt on her fingers. The bite of rock along her spine as they play-wrestled too high aboveground. Too, too high.

Vesryn blinks again. The memory goes dark.

She remembers this part, too. One moment she was looking up into Ellion's summer-flushed face. The next she was staring down at his broken and bloodied body at the bottom of the gorge with nothing but the voice to keep her company.

Vesryn must have been in shock, because she can never remember what happened next. Surely she must have called for help? Or at the very least screamed? But the only remnant of the memory is her own voice echoing in her head.

What kind of bargain? Vesryn had said inside her mind.

The disembodied voice had answered. *A life for a life, perhaps? I am so very weak after all this time, and a tragic fate breathes heavily down your neck, little girl. Make an offering of your life to me before you are too far entangled in the Weaver's tapestry and I will wake him. Make your choice, and quickly—the Courier will not wait to claim him.*

Terror blistered through her, making her whole body go numb. This voice—it talked of the Courier as if he was an old friend. *Friend.*

Ellion still wasn't moving.

Ellion wasn't breathing.

Is my friend alive? she choked out.

Only just. The Courier caresses his cheek, coaxing him through the Veil.

Vesryn paused, but only long enough to form the words: *I will make a bargain with you.*

Excellent, the voice said. *This will only hurt for—*

Wait! Her heartbeat thundered in her ears. *Surely there's something else I can give you that's worth more than a peasant's life.* As soon as Vesryn had shaped the words, an idea cut across her mind like a knife through silk.

What if I give you something that can restore life?

The voice was quiet for so long that she'd thought that maybe she had imagined it. *Finally*, it said. *Now that is an intriguing proposition. Go on.*

Vesryn had no coin, no prospects or station. Even her home belonged to the Evercrafts. All she had was . . .

My healing ability, she told the voice. *My magic.*

The entity grew quiet, though Vesryn could sense that it still lingered somewhere in the blackness of her mind. After a long moment, it said, *If I take this gift from you—if you make an offering of your healing magic to feed me—there will be a chasm within you for the rest of this life and beyond.*

The voice continued, *Your offering will bind you to the boy for eternity. Ooh, that could be interesting. A healer with too much magic would make him a—*

Just do it, Vesryn thought. *Do it before I change my mind.*

She gasps, and suddenly the would-be healer is thrust back into the present moment. Her hand flutters to her chest and she forces herself to breathe.

Beneath the warmth of her palm, the hole that will never heal still aches.

FIFTEEN MINUTES TO MIDNIGHT

44

KELLAM

WHEN Kellam opens his eyes, the first thing he sees is Costis. His father kneels on a frozen river, ten years of grief and worry washed away. Though Kellam has never been here before, he knows precisely where they are. Canyon walls reach endlessly to the sky around them, an overwhelming stratum of ancient rock carrying a history older than Avendell itself in layers of red, gray, violet, and pink. Behind Costis, the sun sets; ahead of them, a trail of ice disappears into the gorge.

Come, a voice beckons.

And the young king does.

In his arms, Costis carries Kellam as a boy. It's startling to see himself like this. He looks near death—too pale, too thin, too still. He is a shadow against Costis' shining gold, a blight against the young king's glowing health.

A hand touches Costis' shoulder. Someone is with him.

"It will work," Queen Greer says softly. "It must. Gaspar was certain."

Kellam's throat constricts. He remembers so little of her. Most days, he forgets his mother existed. Kellam isn't certain what that says about him.

I Killed the King

Greer and Costis walk slowly, careful not to slip on the ice, shivering in their summer clothes. Greer is beautiful, long-haired and rosy-cheeked, but it's only now Kellam realizes the portraits got her wrong. All the painters captured his mother as someone with eyes of steel, a timeless, watchful figure who bore the judgment of the gods.

But here, like Costis, she just looks scared.

Come, the voice whispers.

As Costis and Greer creep into the canyon, the ice thickens. Snow gathers on the rock though the summer sun has been blazing all day. The crack in the cliff face has grown big enough for a man to slip through, and Costis does. When they reach the tiny, broken urn, the Istellian script is long faded by weather and time, but the carvings of roots and florals on the broken pieces are unmistakable. A single pale stone lies in the heart of the rubble, crusted with old blood.

Costis steps foot in the chamber—and the air shifts.

One by one, winter lilies bloom. They spring from nothing, racing over the rock, white petals stretching open.

Only the king, a voice whispers.

Costis casts a look at Greer, who blanches but nods. When she retreats, Costis approaches the tiny altar, kneels, and presses his forehead to the ground.

"Gardener," whispers Costis. "I have been a faithful servant. I have never asked you for anything—but I ask you now. Please, remove the blighted magic from my son. Spare him. Ensure Avendell has an heir, and I swear, I will build a thousand temples in your name. Give me this—bless him, as you have blessed me—and I will do anything."

Horror rises in Kellam. He wants to reach for his parents, to shout and warn them. For all his wisdom about the gods, for all his obsessions with divinity, Costis should have known better.

When you pray to monsters lurking in the dark, there's no guarantee which one will answer.

I can save him, a voice whispers. *For a price.*

Costis stiffens. But he keeps his forehead on the rock as he says, "Anything."

The cost is steep.

"I know what the Tissere oracle said at my birth," Costis says evenly. "I know my reign is destined to be short. You want my fame? My wealth? My life? Take it. Everything I've built, I've built for him. Without my son, it's all dust, anyway."

What is his father saying? Costis never made mention of any oracle. He never told Kellam any of this.

"Please," Costis says. "Whatever you want, I will pay it. Grant me this one miracle. Grant me an heir."

The god pretending to be the Gardener pauses. When Chaos speaks, his voice comes not from the urn but from the center of the flowers that stretch in unnatural bloom, sounding just distorted and warped enough that it could be mistaken for the feminine whisper of a goddess.

I don't want your life just yet, Chaos whispers. *I want the gift that gives it meaning.*

Costis stills.

Your magic, Chaos says. *For your son.*

Finally, Costis raises his head, his eyes narrowing. When he speaks, his voice is careful, still the deferential pitch of an acolyte before their god. "I cannot hold the throne without magic."

And I cannot fix what is broken within him, Chaos says. *But I can give him time. I can lock away what kills him while you search for a way to heal what rots within, if I'm tithed the power to do so.*

Costis' face is wan. This is not the bargain he came for. Warily, he says, "For how long?"

Ten years, Chaos whispers. *Every moon, you will open a wound over your heart. Every moon, the block on his magic will be renewed. In ten years, Costis, I will come for the last of your power. Your life will end—and if you have not found a cure, what rots the prince will be set free.*

Costis hesitates, and Kellam can see the odds being weighed behind his father's eyes. He wants to weep. It's a terrible price—everything that makes Costis king to buy only ten years of time.

But can Kellam blame him?

Costis had been young. Ten years must have felt like an eternity. Kellam thinks of the books in his father's library, of his obsession and paranoia over the years of fringe cults trying to revive dead gods, like the prairie folk who cull entire herds of deer to honor the Huntress, or that mad sect in Tissere, poisoning themselves and praying their deadly faith will tempt the Weaver to return. Kellam had thought it the product of a paranoid old king worrying about a claim on his power. But Costis had not been trying to quash a rising god.

He had been hunting for one, praying it would be the same one who'd been stealing, piecemeal, the magic he'd lost.

How many years had passed before Costis realized it was not the Gardener he'd bartered with that day?

Hope shines on Costis' face. Kellam could kill Chaos. The god must have known he was making Costis false promises, but he hadn't cared. It was one thing to claim the life of a king; but to claim magic given to them by another god? It was no wonder he'd been so hungry to feed on Costis' desperation.

Kellam wants to run to his father. To shake Costis and drag him out of the cursed chamber by his hair. But he is only a phantom, trapped in the swirl of another's memory as he slips from life to death.

So he can only watch as Costis bends his head and says, "I accept."

"No," Kellam cries. "Father, *no!*"

He can do nothing as Costis opens a cut on his palm. As he presses a kiss to Kellam's flushed, sweating temple and wishes, "For an heir, I give my blood, and the power in it. For Avendell's future, I give everything. Even my magic." His voice hitches. "May it bloom in him instead."

Blood hits the stone and the memory collapses into dust.

But Kellam is still there.

He twists, but the vision is gone. All he sees is endless darkness. All sense of his body is gone now. If he's not dead yet, he will be soon.

What is this? Why show him now, when it's too late for him to understand the meaning of what Costis lost?

"Chaos?" Kellam whispers. "Father?"

Nothing answers.

But of course Chaos is busy with the others, and though the Courier is surely coming to claim him and the Mystic will bless his soul before he crosses over, the gods aren't yet here for Kellam. Ellion had said his father had moved on.

So who else is holding Kellam here, in the liminal space between life and whatever lies beyond?

Who else wants him to know the truth?

Something twines around his ankle.

Kellam looks down.

A single, reaching vine, hair thin and weak, stretches into the empty black.

Kellam follows.

As he does, the world shifts. Grass appears beneath his feet. Sunlight blazes overhead, and as Kellam walks, the familiar topiaries of the palace gardens come into view. The royal wood looms beyond them, timeless and untouched, a remnant of the wild land that was Avendell's capital city in a time when the Builder and the Lover, and eventually their children, roamed free. Servants pass Kellam, their gazes going right through him, vibrating with the morning's gossip.

"The king," they whisper. "He left with the prince and the queen and no escort."

Kellam's blood chills. Costis is likely bargaining with Chaos at this very moment.

So why bring him here?

The vine leads him into the trees, until the gardens fade entirely, and it is only Kellam and the wood. The Gardener statue looms into view—the image of a woman, belly swollen with child, long hair flowing as one hand cups her stomach and the other lifts a handful of seeds to the sun. A thick layer of white mold grows over her, blurring her features as though she's trapped behind a veil, though the pail from whatever servant is assigned to scrub the statue each morning still sits at her feet. Unease sweeps through Kellam. He always took the unnatural mold as a sign that the gods had truly abandoned them.

Something is off about the statue. While the Gardener has always been depicted as a young woman, he doesn't remember this statue depicting the goddess pregnant.

Costis' voice rings around him.

For an heir, I give my blood.

The trees still.

For the future of Avendell, I give my magic.

The woods groans.

May it bloom in him instead.

And the statue's eyes open.

Impossible green light blazes in the dark, burning away the edges of the memory. Kellam sinks to his knees. Terror moves through him in waves. Until tonight, he has never known the touch of the divine. He thought he knew what it meant to face a god when he stared in Chaos' eyes.

He was wrong.

By the standards of gods, Chaos is just a child. A weakling, an accident, the last born and the first to wake by chance. But the goddess who has brought him to these memories—the goddess who keeps him anchored here, even now—is as old as the dirt beneath Kellam's feet and the water that feeds the woods she claims.

Look, orders the Gardener.

And he does.

At the edge of the wood, an oak tree trembles. Something curls at its roots—a bloody bundle of rags, concealing whatever moves within. The oak's branches curve down, cradling the abandoned, filthy thing. Its branches fold inward, leaves blooming, reddening, falling, and blossoming again. There is a crack, and a split, and Kellam understands. The Gardener was never going to be able to answer Costis in words, but she's been speaking in her own way. All the wild irises in constant bloom; the moss that grew stubbornly on the walls, even after the servants scrubbed it away.

As Kellam watches, the oak tree withers. In its place, trembling on the earth, hazel eyes bright with alarm, is a boy destined to carry the prince's whole heart inside him. He has no name yet, but it doesn't matter. Kellam remembers the day Oak wandered into Castle Avendell, barefoot and shaking. When the servants asked the child how he'd managed to sneak into the wood, he had no answer. When they asked about his parents, he had no memory. When they asked the child his name, he seemed alarmed. Finally, he reached into his hair, plucked free a jagged leaf, and whispered, "Oak?"

Kellam trembles. He stares at Oak, curled in the roots of the tree, watching as moss blooms on the wood where he lies. Of course. How had he not seen it? How had he not known? Oak was always stronger in the sun. Even the flowers planted near his rooms grew brighter, clearer, as if his very presence fed them.

Costis had begged for an heir. He had bargained everything to Chaos—and the Gardener, unable to stop him, unable to save Kellam, had given him a prince a different way.

"But where does that leave me?" Kellam whispers. As the memory fades, the presence of the goddess looms. Fear shivers within him. "If you didn't place that curse on our line and neither did Chaos . . . who did? What are you so afraid will escape?"

What, exactly, does Kellam carry in him that would convince Costis to bargain his power away? To end his own life, in an attempt to extend the bargain's timeline in perpetuity?

The goddess does not answer.

Kellam feels her slipping away, like vines sliding over rock. Her power is weak. He doesn't know if she's recently woken, or if she's always been here, working her influence through the world in such fragile, tendril threads even Chaos wouldn't notice.

It doesn't matter. Her message is clear.

These memories are not a kindness. They're not a sudden fit of empathy, a parting gift from a goddess to a boy slowly dying to grant him final peace. The Gardener sensed Kellam clinging to life as the clock ticks to the final hour on the bargain his father made. And so she came to him, armed with the one truth that could convince Kellam to let go of the ledge.

For the first time in his life, Kellam can finally give Costis everything he ever wanted.

His father's greatest dream, realized ten years too late.

Now all Kellam needs to do is lie down and die.

45

VESRYN

VESRYN watches the prince take his final breath from the other side of the Veil.

No. She cannot let this happen. She cannot let this maniacal god win. If Chaos bests them all, then her prayers have been for nothing.

Even in death—or whatever this liminal space is—Vesryn still believes the Arbiter can hear her. And Chaos has not yet met the consequences of the destruction he's caused.

But he will.

She'll make sure of it.

"Kellam," she says. She blinks, and suddenly she's sitting beside the stone-still prince. The others gather around him, around *her*, though none of them can perceive her. Except for maybe Ellion. Vesryn crosses to where Ellion stands with a haunted expression. She leans in closer and watches gooseflesh rise on the back of his neck. "Wake him up," she whispers into the healer's ear.

Ellion says nothing. Vesryn's heart sinks. But then, ever so slightly, the healer angles his head toward her and whispers, "You know I can't."

"Yes, you can!" she explodes, throwing her hands into the air. "I gave up my healing abilities for you! Chaos said we'd be . . ." The rest of the words are lost on her tongue when she realizes what she's done. Her arms drop to her sides.

That's why she's still stuck here, in the liminal.

Her life and Ellion's are tethered to each other because of the bargain she made with a god she couldn't see. Vesryn had always assumed the god had scooped out her healing abilities, leaving her hollow and yearning, and poured them into Ellion so that his own magic became strong enough to raise the dead. And that had been the end of it.

She had forgotten the most important part.

Your offering will bind you to the boy for eternity, Chaos' voice whispers.

Vesryn squeezes her eyes shut. How had she been so naive? All those years she'd tried to make amends, to pay for her mistakes by bringing death to the doors of bad men . . . and on the other side of the tether, Ellion brought life back into them as best he could.

Balance. A covenant bound in the gorge.

It's her fault Ellion failed so miserably as a healer.

Vesryn's eyes snap open. Rage sears through her. *I was only a girl. I just wanted to save my best friend.* She leaps to her feet and stalks toward Chaos. Surely whatever other gods are listening would give her the means for one last murder. As a treat.

If Chaos can see her coming, he doesn't give her any clue. Just as Vesryn lifts her fist to swing, she jerks to a stop. The god isn't looking in her direction at all. He rakes his long, slender fingers through his hair as his eyes dart around the ballroom.

Vesryn slowly lowers her fist. She leans in, but Chaos still doesn't notice her. He's looking for something—or *someone*—else. She trails his line of sight, searching for the thing powerful enough to haunt a living god.

She feels them first.

Several entities press in around the edges of the Veil, their presence crackling with power. Vesryn realizes, with a somber sense of certainty, that she's felt them lingering around her ever since she found herself trapped in the liminal.

Gods.

As soon as she thinks the word, a sense of horror sweeps through her.

Perhaps Ellion hadn't been able to fully raise the others from the dead because something much more powerful would not allow them back into their bodies. Something like a curse from a god. As soon as she pieces together the thought, the truth of it echoes through her.

But.

If Vesryn and Ellion are truly tethered, what would happen if she slew a god?

Or at least put one back in its place.

Something meows at her feet. Vesryn glances down and finds Rue winding around her ankles, the cat's sleek fur gleaming like polished onyx.

An idea begins to take shape.

"Rue, tell them I'm here," she says. "Tell them I'm coming to help."

The cat looks at her curiously—one amber eye, one violet. It gives a tepid little mew, as if to say, *if you insist*, before vanishing.

Vesryn watches as Rue snaps back into focus beside Clove.

She whispers, "I'm going to bring this god to his knees."

46

OAK

OAK falls to his knees.

He knows Kellam is dead, but he presses his fingers to the hollow of the prince's throat anyway. Just to see. Just to feel him one last time while his body is still warm.

"He's gone," Clove whispers.

"I *know*," Oak snaps. The girl flinches, and regret washes through him. He opens his mouth to apologize, but Clove's hand settles on his shoulder and squeezes.

The gesture is small, but it's infinitely kind, and it makes Oak's eyes burn.

The mage-lights snap off as the storm hits the castle with so much force, the floor vibrates beneath them. The princess cries out in the dark. Oak searches for Kellam's hand, only to realize the prince won't be reaching for his. Oak's breath catches in his throat.

The mage-lights snap back on.

Chaos is still there.

Everyone flinches. It seems like an extra bit of cruelty, for the god to linger in Kellam's wake. No one speaks, waiting for him to vanish. But the god remains, his eyes darting uncertainly from Kellam to the raging storm.

It's Clove who says what they're all thinking.

"Why are you still here?" she demands. Clove gestures at Kellam, the sleeping guests, and the storm beyond. "You said Kellam had to die. He's gone. So call off the storm. Leave us in peace."

The god hesitates. His gaze darts nervously from them to the storm to something else—something only he can see.

Ellion pales. "It didn't work."

"It did," Chaos snaps. He winces, visibly unsettled. "It *will*. My bargain with Costis was for ten years of Kellam's life. Ten years to drain Costis' magic. Ten years to protect Kellam from what lurks within. When he died, the last of my bargain was fulfilled." He hesitates. "There shouldn't be anything tying me here. I should be able to return to as I was before, liminal and eternal, unnoticed by the others, slipping across the Veil with ease . . ."

The word *shouldn't* seems to ripple between them. Horror washes through Oak as he struggles to understand. He can't possibly mean—

"But you're still here," Clove says. Her breath fogs before her. "And it's getting colder. Which means you were wrong. Kellam died for nothing."

A feral gust of wind pummels the castle, rattling the windows.

"Not for nothing." Chaos shakes his head, his expression stubborn. "That boy . . . I should have never spared his life. I did all of us a favor tonight. Kellam surviving past dawn wouldn't just unravel the Weaver's tapestry—it would rip it in two." He hesitates and flexes his hand in front of his face experimentally. "But I will admit, I'm a little puzzled as to why I'm . . . still here."

Oak could throttle him. Kellam lies at his feet, lips blue with poison, and all Chaos has to say is that he's *puzzled*?

"Then how," he says tensely, "do we fix it?"

The god hesitates again, and Oak must surely be dreaming, because the next words that leave Melarie's lips are the thing of pure nightmares.

"He doesn't know."

As soon as she says it, Oak knows it's true. Horror fills the faces of the others, and Chaos' silence only makes it worse, because instead of protesting, the god is stoic. Oak's heart pounds. Memory tugs at him—of the dark, bleak days when Kellam's illness seemed like it was rebounding. Oak had only been living with the Vernevaus for a few years then.

"Ves and I had a book as kids," Ellion says. "About the gods and how they retain power. Chaos never had worshippers. No temples, no acolytes. He could only feed on the disasters he sowed. But now . . ."

"You've caused too much damage," Melarie says quietly. "We believe in you too much for you to slip back into nothing."

Clove's face is ashen. "And now that we know *you're* real . . ."

With an earsplitting groan, the wall breaks open. A crack as wide as Oak's forearm races up the stone, and snow-colored dust blankets the once-pristine dance floor. It peppers the frozen guests' hair, dulls the gemstones of their masks, and clouds the untouched wine in their goblets. The support beams above their heads are one strong gust away from snapping down the middle and bringing them all to ruin.

Oak's eyes flicker to Kellam's too-still body. Every muscle in his body coils; every instinct begs him to throw himself atop the prince to protect his charge. But . . . there is no Vernevau left who needs his protection. He balls his hands into fists and glances toward

I Killed the King

the east wing, where his satchel waits for him beneath his cot. He could run now with no consequences to his station. But all Oak wants more than anything is to stay.

Oak, a voice echoes in his mind.

A chill pulses through him. In the corner of Oak's eye, Chaos goes stiff as a winter branch.

"Do you hear her?" Clove says. Oak turns to answer her, but the beast tamer isn't looking at him—her eyes are on Ellion. Her lower lip trembles as her gaze drifts to that same empty spot at her feet.

Ellion swallows. "Yes."

"Vesryn," they both whisper.

Oak frowns. That isn't right. The voice in his head—that wasn't Vesryn. He doesn't know what or who it was, but it felt . . . *bigger* than the girl somehow.

Oak, the voice says again. *Come.*

It's as if the entity speaking to him has placed a hook into his heart and is pulling him toward the edges of the ballroom. And although it's with the gentlest touch, he knows he can't resist, even if he tried.

So he goes.

The howling wind drops away first. Then the groaning, shuddering stone. Then the murmurs and whispers of the others, until it's only Oak, the voice, and his own stupid, relentless hope.

Oak is standing a hairsbreadth from Costis' verdant greenery. The wall of wintergreen and sweet pea, of maidenhair ferns and ivy and forget-me-nots still manages to bloom, despite the destruction surrounding them. Despite the king's demise.

Without warning, an image sears through his mind—or a memory, perhaps. The Gardener's unkempt statue, tucked into a dark alcove at the end of the hall. The one Oak has passed a thousand times over without a second glance. The one that remains covered in a lush blanket of moss, though it should not be possible.

My son, the goddess says.

My heir.

Images flicker through the darkness of his mind in quick succession. A sprawling, knotted oak tree with roots that cradled him like a mother's embrace. The curdle of his breath in air too cold to claim summer. The relentless yearning to step outside the castle, to feel the grass between his toes, to crawl back to the forest from which some part of him had come.

"Oak." This time, the voice comes from outside his head. His pulse climbs as he turns back to the others.

There's a stag behind him.

The creature is as solid as stone, its heavy-lidded eyes glittering with a secret. It huffs once, then slowly bows its antlered head. Panic sets Oak's heart pounding, but the only one who seems to have noticed is Clove. The stag holds its stare and flickers, like a candle going out.

Or a spirit trying to grow stronger.

"You see it, too," Clove whispers. She lifts her hand as if to touch the stag's muzzle but thinks better of it.

"I see her," Oak says. He can't bring himself to repeat what she told him, or why she's shown herself at last. He swallows. "I see the goddess, the Gardener, in her wild form."

Ahead of him, Melarie is an arm's distance from Chaos. She looks so frail compared to the god. "You did all this for nothing. Kellam died for nothing. Why?"

"It was supposed to work," Chaos snaps. "It *will* work. I

just . . . I just need a minute to think. Perhaps if I wipe your memories, or I suppose I could just kill all of you . . ."

From the corner of his eye, Oak sees movement: Ellion, moving in a low crouch, his attention locked on Kellam's body, every line of his face bright with intent.

Melarie seems to notice him, too. She gives herself a shake and steps forward, blocking the god's view.

"Monseigneur. Gabriel. Chaos." Melarie clasps her hands together, and only Oak, standing behind her, can see the way her shoulders tremble. "Tell us how to fix this. Let us help you, *please*. No one else needs to get hurt."

The god looks at Melarie with drowning eyes. He hesitates, and in that moment, he seems younger—more mortal. Instead of answering Melarie's query, he rasps, "I loved her, you know. The first of your queens. The stories try to say it was a trick, a ploy to escape the pantheon, but I loved her before any of that. I would have shattered reality for her. I would have ripped my mother's tapestry to shreds if she'd asked. And she repaid me with betrayal."

Melarie stiffens. "What?"

"You weren't supposed to be here tonight," Chaos says quietly. "You weren't supposed to make me weak again."

"What do you mean?" Melarie asks carefully. "What weakness could I give you?"

Chaos opens his mouth to speak—and from beside Oak comes a crunch.

Ellion freezes, pale as death, his eyes trained on the wineglass that's broken under his foot.

All the softness leaves Chaos' face as he stares at Ellion. In that moment, his vulnerability and fear are gone. Only the anger of a god remains: distant, eternal, and divine. Horror prickles through Oak. It doesn't matter to Chaos that the castle is crumbling; that Kellam lies dead at his feet and so many others have suffered. What is the life of a mortal to that of a god?

"Ellion," Melarie gasps. "*Go.*"

Chaos lunges.

And Ellion dives.

47

ELLION

ELLION dives for Kellam.

Chaos shouts as Ellion closes the distance between himself and Kellam. Ellion reaches for Kellam's face but misses, his frozen fingers moving too slowly, catching cloth instead. Lightning flashes outside; the castle groans. Kellam is paler than death, his lips blue from poison. Skin. Ellion only needs to touch skin—

"Wait."

Chaos stands with a blank expression, his gray eyes unreadable as he holds Clove in front of him, forearm braced against her windpipe. Clove remains carefully, painfully still, her eyes wide, her chest heaving. He's not strangling her, not yet. But every line in his body is filled with murderous intent.

"Touch him and the girl dies," Chaos warns. "Listen to me, necromancer. The prince cannot live. If you bring him back, you break something that cannot be unbroken. Step away from the body. Let's discuss this like civilized creatures."

Ellion licks his lips. "Why are you so afraid of Kellam coming back?"

"It's not just me," the god spits. "You think I'm the only god ousted from the pantheon? There are far older and more terrible deities than I. The prince's precious Gardener has spent eternity keeping the foul touch of what claims him at bay. But if you bring him back, it breaks free."

"What does that *mean*?" Ellion demands. "Stop speaking in riddles! What has been killing the Vernevaus? What's so terrible that even the god of Chaos quakes with fear?"

The god looks at him. In the silence, the world seems to freeze. Finally, he speaks.

"Ruin," he says quietly. "Beyond anything you could imagine."

"Really?" Ellion says flatly. "I don't know if you've noticed, but there's already plenty of that in the world." His eyes narrow. There's something Chaos isn't telling them.

"You're afraid of the others waking up," Ellion realizes. "You're terrified of what they'll do to you."

"I'd be a fool not to be," Chaos snaps. "They ordered me killed as an infant. I spent my godlinghood in hiding, begging for scraps, ducking from every shadow. They deserved to be trapped. To know what it's like to be locked beneath sea and stone." His voice creeps toward pleading. "Listen to me. However terrible you think tonight's damage has been, the pantheon returning will bring ruin down on this land tenfold. Do you really think the gods will come back kindly? Do you think they'll be *happy* with what you've done in their absence?"

Ellion hesitates.

"You've never successfully resurrected someone before." Chaos continues. "You couldn't save Luma. You didn't even bother to save Vesryn. If you open the Veil, Ellion, there's no telling what or who will slip through. Is it worth damning us all for yet another failure?"

Ellion's world spins. His eyes go not to Chaos—but to Clove.

She shivers where Chaos holds her captive. But when she meets Ellion's gaze, her eyes are clear.

Ellion's never been much of a lip-reader, but there's no mistaking the message Clove sends him.

Do it.

Maybe Chaos has a point. Ellion's failed so many times. He's always taken shortcuts, borrowing the power of a distant god or the boldness of a drink. But for what feels like the first time in his life, Ellion's head is clear, and though fear moves through him in bright, bitter waves, he's determined to set things right.

Maybe some things are better off broken.

These gods never cared for him. Even in the old stories, when deities still walked the earth, the underlying message was always clear: mortals were disposable.

And he's meant to listen to Chaos now? After all he's done, after the pain he's caused and the lives he's taken? For all he knows, Chaos himself sent him and Vesryn tumbling down the gorge. Or maybe it was foul luck, and he swooped in and saw them for what they were—convenient pawns, to be moved about the board as he pleased.

It doesn't matter. The result is the same.

Whether that day was the result of divine intervention or an opportunity for a god to take advantage of, it doesn't change the fact that a deity left two children bleeding in the cold.

It doesn't change the fact that to Chaos—to all of them—he'll never be anything but a pawn.

No more. Ellion is tired of being used.

"Wait," Chaos begs. "Please, I'm telling you, *don't*—"

Ellion, whispers Vesryn. *Do it.*

Ellion slams his hands to Kellam's chest.

And this time, when the Veil rises, he punches right through.

48

CLOVE

CLOVE is going to die.

Chaos' body is flush with hers, the sharp line of his jaw digging into her temple. His forearm wraps across her throat, crushing her windpipe. Clove claws at his arm, gasping for air, but her fingers can't find purchase on the wool of his coat. The god squeezes tighter.

Stars blink in front of Clove's eyes. She thinks of Vesryn. Of the ropelike bruises encircling her neck—the marks she'd thought had been made by a basilisk.

This is exactly how Vesryn felt before she died.

Clove can tell by the look on Ellion's face that the healer's soul is already far, far from the ballroom. Even as her vision fogs, she can still make out the whites of his eyes and his rapidly graying skin.

Clove's pulse thrums in her throat. The god's grip tightens and she gags. The edges of her vision begin to fade.

"Kill the necromancer," Chaos orders flatly. "Before he brings back the prince."

Oak and Melarie look at each other uneasily.

Neither of them moves.

I'm going to die. And they're going to let it happen.

The thought is as clear as a frozen lake. There's something about stringing the words together in her mind that ushers in a sense of calm, muffling her stuttering heartbeat like freshly fallen snow.

But Oak and Melarie are better than her. They've grown up at court. They've watched kings calculate the cost of a few lives to save the many.

They're calculating now, and the results are clear.

Clove is a loss they can bear.

"Monseigneur."

Melarie is so close that Clove can see the small divot in her jaw from a hidden scar, the tiny dimple in her chin. Clove's thoughts crystallize for one instant, and she realizes with horror that Melarie is within the god's reach, too.

"Gabriel," the princess whispers again.

She approaches Chaos with one hand aloft, her expression calm even as she shudders with cold. The air has grown so frigid it hurts to breathe.

Clove squirms, but Chaos' grip is too strong. Still, Melarie doesn't seem afraid at all. Her pretty face is as smooth as glass as she lifts her chin.

"It must have been terrible for you, trapped and alone all those years. Forgotten, unloved, and unwanted." She moves closer. "I know what that feels like, too."

Amid the embryonic pulse in Clove's head, she senses that there's something Melarie is doing here that's important. That there's something she needs to know. *Pay attention*, she tells herself.

Pay attention like your life depends on it.

But she doesn't have much time left. Already the lack of air to her brain is causing her to hallucinate. In the blink of an eye, the ghost cat has reappeared, looking alarmingly *real.* This time, he doesn't twine around Clove's ankles. The cat sits on his haunches, mismatched eyes as wide as moons.

Behind him, face drawn, is Vesryn. She's looking at something else—Ellion, across the Veil, maybe?

The cat mews again, and this time, Clove senses the words between the drawn-out syllables, and she remembers: Vesryn has already spoken to her through this tiny, sharp-toothed mouth once tonight.

She'd said, *You are the one who can call them in.*

A boom comes from overhead. Cracks spiderweb across the tallest window, snaking closer and closer to the center. Already, some of the snow has begun to seep through.

Melarie's eyes dart to her, so briefly Clove would have missed it, then return to Chaos.

"What did you mean?" Melarie asks softly. "That you loved me . . . before?"

"Not you," Chaos says. "Your ancestor. The first of the Atilelet queens. The stories got it wrong—saying she found a god's weakness and tricked him into giving her a throne. *She* was my weakness. And everything I gave, I gave willingly." His gaze grows distant, and in his lapse, the pressure on Clove's throat lessens. "We were going to marry and build a world together. I didn't need my godhood, the pantheon, or power. Only her. We loved each other. But soon after I made her queen, she took me to the gorge and struck me. When I woke, the world had changed."

"What woke you?" Melarie asks carefully.

"Pain," Chaos says quietly. "I was born from pain and longing. And I woke to it again."

"And what kept you here?"

Now the god is silent. He seems unwilling to speak the truth they both know.

Melarie is so close now that Clove could reach out and touch her. Her throat aches with the weight of Chaos' arm, but she can breathe again, and as she does, the world gets stranger.

The stag is back.

And behind it, writhing on the floor, is an eight-armed creature the color of sunbaked coral with dashes of scarlet pooling at the end of each tentacle. She'd heard of these kinds of sea creatures before—beasts that live at the bottom of the Starless Sea, shape-shifting according to the time and tides, never dying.

The creatures flicker in and out, solid one moment and translucent the next, visibly straining.

Ahead of them, tail flicking, is the ghost cat, whose eyes gleam.

The hair on Clove's arms stands on end. She looks at Melarie, and wills her to understand.

Melarie's eyes skip from her panicked face to Chaos again.

"Gabriel," Melarie says, her voice soft. She takes another step toward Chaos, her red-slippered foot gliding soundlessly on the marble floor, one hand lifted as though to cup his face. "You were my friend once. My ally. Let us be that again. Let us fix this together. What happens if we bring Kellam back? What are you so afraid of?"

"You weren't supposed to be here tonight," Chaos says miserably, and Clove knows now that she wasn't imagining it.

The longer he's here—the longer he looks at her—the more solid he grows.

"What happens?" Melarie prompts again, in the tone Clove

often uses with the wildest of beasts when they're teetering on the edge of violence. "What are you so afraid of?"

"If you bring him back, the Weaver's tapestry unravels," Chaos says quietly. "There's still a chance for this to end tonight. No one else is through the Veil yet. But if you save that boy, it all comes undone. Forget the pantheon. Forget my bargain. You will release a force that can never be put back to rest."

The wild forms of the gods looking at Clove flicker.

Behind them, bright-eyed and determined, is Vesryn.

"*Call them,*" she whispers.

Clove stiffens. *Her?* She's just a girl. She comes from nothing, has never felt the touch of the divine until tonight, knows nothing of the gods or the ones who worship them.

But maybe she doesn't need to.

When Clove closes her eyes, the only thing she sees are her beasts. Her rescued cubs, sidling up to the sanctuary fence, watching her with curious eyes. Her unicorn filly, learning to walk on wobbly legs. An unhatched dragon egg that shivers with excitement beneath her touch. Warmth blooms in her chest, and something else: pride.

Clove has never known love. She has never had a template to follow. And yet she has still managed to give her whole heart to the fearsome and wild.

She can do this.

With Chaos' arm still around her throat, Clove looks at Melarie and mouths, *Keep distracting him.*

The princess' eye twitches. But she doesn't question Clove. It's such a small thing—that instant trust, that act of blind faith—but it makes Clove's legs buckle all the same.

With the determination of an acolyte heading to a pedestal for sacrifice, Melarie closes the distance between her and the god, and cups his cheek in her palm.

"You've been so lonely," she whispers. "I've been lonely, too. I know you felt me praying. I know this isn't what you want, Chaos. I know you care for me—and I believe, despite it all, that there is good in you."

The god shudders violently, as though she's struck him, and leans into her touch.

Overhead, a topaz-blue heron flickers in and out of view, its great wings spread in predatory flight.

Clove, Vesryn whispers. *Get ready.*

Get ready to call them all.

Clove trembles. But she understands.

Melarie is so close Clove could kiss her. The princess' chest nearly touches Clove's as she reaches past her, still cradling Chaos' face.

With her free hand, her fingers find Clove's and squeeze.

I trust you, that touch says. *I'm ready.*

Trembling, Clove moves her hand to her waist, and shifts something into the princess' grip.

What a sight they must be—Clove, held flush against Chaos' chest, his arm around her throat, Melarie to Clove's front, cradling the face of a heartbroken god. With tender eyes, Melarie slides one hand up into Chaos' nest of pale hair, her other hand cradling Clove's gift.

"I can't fix it," Chaos says miserably. "I don't know how. They're waking up and—I'm sorry, but I can't let him live. I can't let any of you live, if I'm going to live, too."

"I know," says Melarie, her voice suddenly cold.

Chaos stiffens—and Clove lunges free.

Before the god can react, Melarie grabs a fistful of Chaos' hair in her hands, drags him toward her, and drives a knife, the leaping stag on its handle just barely visible, into his heart.

"You may be a god," Melarie snarls. "But I saw you in that dungeon. You bled like a man—and I'm hoping you'll die like one, too."

The god rears backward. Vesryn shouts for Ellion, and the ghost cat leaps. Clove stumbles away from Chaos, dragging Melarie with her, their fingers locked protectively again. Behind them the god roars, golden ichor pouring down his chest.

It's the distraction Clove needs.

She leans into the instinct that has guided her entire life—the oldest kind of power, the primal heartbeat of every beast and wild thing. Images flicker through her; heron, stag, and moth.

An entire pantheon, waiting to be woken.

Clove leans into the feeling.

And she calls for the wild.

49

ELLION

THE Veil is tearing.

The liminal space that separated mortals and everything beyond has always been a place of absence; an endless dark, a swirling nothing. But for the first time, it feels alive. There's a sense of things rushing past Ellion, slipping into the realm of the mortal and real and back again. There's a taste of fear, of opportunity, of something waking. In the distance, Ellion hears something familiar.

Vesryn.

Clove, she says. *Get ready. Get ready to call them all.*

Creatures move past Ellion; a stag, a moth, an octopus, and something else, something small, horrible, and furry. Ellion hurries past them.

He hopes Vesryn knows what she's doing.

Ellion finds Kellam almost immediately.

Standing over him, eternal and still, is the Courier.

Ellion can't quite look at the god. He changes shape with the smallest movement, a blur of black to gray to white and back again, looming over Kellam like a late morning fog. Ellion tenses, waiting for a challenge, but the god only watches him.

He steps forward—and the god shifts.

Little healer, the Courier says with his father's face. *He is fated to die.*

It shifts again. Now the god is Luma, her eyes wide and pleading.

Costis cheated me for ten years. The Weaver's tapestry cannot bear the strain any longer. Let him go before grimmer threads are needed to repair the gap in his life.

The Courier changes form again. Vesryn, his mother, the soldiers in the house, the herbalist professor, and the drunk he rescued from freezing in the street. Everyone he loves, everyone he's been afraid to lose, and strangers, too, the tapestry of their lives now woven with at least one of Ellion's midnight blue threads. It ought to hurt. It ought to terrify him. But Ellion's head is clear for the first time in years, and right now, the god's attempt to play on old wounds just feels like the most pathetic kind of party trick.

And it clicks.

The Courier can't stop him.

Whatever will happen next is not foretold. For all their power and pomp, the gods are as bound to this moment as Ellion is.

Ellion reaches down and touches Kellam's shoulder.

The prince's eyes fly open.

"Ellion," Kellam babbles. "I'm not supposed to be—you don't understand—"

Ellion puts his hand on Kellam's arm. "Listen. We're running out of time. I don't want to hear about destiny and curses and the Weaver's threads of fate." He crouches down to meet Kellam's eye. "Just tell me this, Kellam. Are you done?"

Kellam looks confused. "What?"

"Are you done with life?" Ellion asks. "Because if you are—if you're truly done—I'll leave you here. I won't bring you back. But I'm not letting some overpowered ghoul decide when and why Kellam Vernevau dies. So you look at me, you think of your life, and everyone you're leaving behind, and you tell me honestly: Are you *done*?"

Kellam stares at him. He seems to shrink before Ellion's eyes.

"Why me?" Kellam whispers weakly. "Why would I get to come back and not him?"

"Costis felt his business was finished," Ellion says gently. "He died to protect you. He was at peace with his death. Are you?"

Kellam shakes his head, unable to meet Ellion's eyes. "It shouldn't be me. I don't know how to lead. I am selfish, and petty, and weak. All I've ever done is fall short. I don't deserve a second chance. I don't deserve any of this. And if it's the Weaver's will that I die tonight . . ."

"We're not gods-damned toys, Kellam," Ellion snaps. "We're not things to be pulled out and played with for the entertainment of gods, discarded the moment we break. We're *people*. That has to matter. It has to count. I'm not asking what the gods want. I don't *care*."

Around them, the Veil groans. Something scaled shoots past them, followed by a feathered bird.

"Something is wrong with me," Kellam says, his voice shaking. "It's been wrong since I was born. That's why my father made the bargain. If you bring me back—Ellion, I don't know what will happen. I don't know that it's something we can fix."

Kellam looks at Ellion with drowning eyes. His entire life spirals around him: Costis, teaching him about predators and prey, his mother, dark haired and so distant she's barely a memory. An acorn failing to grow, an injured soldier resting in his father's bed, a fight in the Court over the emptying coffers.

All that havoc wreaked on his country, his family, to save one child who should have died in his crib.

And Oak.

Oak, with his hazel eyes and patient smile and loyalty so steady it's near sickening. Oak, training under the summer sun. Oak, the only person Kellam could be comfortably quiet around. The only person he ever loved so dearly Kellam was scared to lose him. The only person who could make Kellam cast his cowardice aside and be brave.

Always Oak.

Kellam's expression clears.

And though fear still shines in his eyes, for the first time since Ellion has met him, Kellam Vernevau seems to know exactly what he wants.

"I'm not done," Kellam whispers.

The Veil shakes. The Courier shifts. In the twisting, blue smoke of its form, Ellion thinks he sees the outline of a bird.

The god extends a robed hand to cradle Ellion's face. The god's touch is the mist of an early morning, the warmth of his mother's hand; it is the first breath of a newborn and the desperate grip of a soldier not ready to die.

"I prayed to you," Ellion whispers. If he's going to die here, slain by a god who's long forsaken him, he's going to say his piece. "I prayed, again and again, and you never answered. You let them die. All of them. And then you let them haunt me. You could have fixed me, but you didn't. You could have helped me escape the Veil when I called and you refused. You don't get to command me now because you made a mistake. It's too late. I don't want your help. I don't need it."

The Courier's robes writhe. Though it has no face, no features, Ellion can feel displeasure crackling off the deity in eternal cold.

Good. He wants it angry.

Even gods make mistakes.

"Now," Ellion whispers. "If you're not going to help me, get the fuck out of my way."

The Courier's fingers slide from Ellion's chin to the right side of his face. With an open palm, the god covers Ellion's eye.

Images flash through him, too fast to understand, too many to process. He tastes graveyard dirt and the blood of a birthing bed; the sting of poison and the relief of a cure. An infinity of lives, of deaths, blurring together, bound by the threads of fate but ferried by the god before him. A loop of life and death over and over, the beginning of the cycle always reliant on the end. Ellion's knees give out. He sags, held by the grip of a god, as the Courier drags him to one final image.

A spindle, bone white, gleaming beneath a shaking finger.

I do not make mistakes, the Courier whispers. *It is the only way.*

And then the god is gone. Ellion lurches backward, the right side of his face burning, reeling, lost in everything the god showed him. It takes a beat for him to come back to himself. To see Kellam kneeling there, staring at Ellion with a stricken expression.

Ellion crosses the distance between them and holds out his hand.

"But the gods," Kellam whispers, but it's a feeble protest, pleading to be ignored. "We don't know what will happen if you meddle with fate to save me."

Maybe Ellion would have worried about that once. But that was before he found Vesryn again. That was before tonight, when he stared a god in the face and shared a moment of quiet peace with a beast tamer in a blood-soaked library.

And that was before he dropped to his knees in the Veil and prayed to whatever would listen—only to find an answer and salvation in the soul of the one girl he'd ever truly loved.

He couldn't save Vesryn. He couldn't save Luma, or so many other lives that ended too soon.

But he could save this one.

"Fuck the gods," Ellion says. "We write our own fates."

Ellion seizes the prince's soul—and drags him back to life.

50

CLOVE

CLOVE has never met a beast she couldn't handle.

She doesn't intend for that to change now.

As Chaos bleeds, godly beasts blip in and out of sight all around them. Clove backs away, her fingers still locked protectively around Melarie's, watching with horror and hope as Chaos cradles the knife in his chest.

When he looks up at them, his eyes glitter with dark fury. Clove continues backpedaling, leaning into the feel of the gods. Her back collides with something solid.

The stag snorts, sending a blast of hot air down the back of her neck.

"Of course," Chaos says bitterly, his eyes narrowing with hate. He's never seemed more like an animal. "You would be the first to wake. Tell me, did you ever truly sleep?" He laughs, the noise sharp and bitter. "It doesn't matter. You won't be enough."

Clove's mind whirls.

The healer, a voice prompts. Vesryn or the ghost cat, she's not certain. Does it matter? Melarie jumps. She heard it, too.

Clove thinks of Ellion, and the world goes quiet. His hands form in her mind—his fingers long and delicate, his skin smooth and uncalloused. The way they encircled her wrist, how his thumb grazes his bottom lip when he's thinking, how his touch summons a nightmare or a dream—or maybe, always both. A squawk echoes through the room as a stunning topaz-blue heron swoops through the air. It doesn't even look in their direction; the bird dives straight toward the crumbling wall, its massive claws clasping a shattered mage-light sconce. It tucks in its wings and begins to peck.

She thinks of Vesryn. Clove barely knew her, yet this girl did everything in her power—from this life into the next—to save them all. She cannot say she would have done the same, if she were in Vesryn's shoes. But she hopes she can become the kind of person who would one day.

In the corner of her eye, a moth flutters.

Ahead of them, Chaos is backing away from the stag. Chaos stumbles under its weight, crashing against the wall behind him. Panic flares on his face.

"We can talk about this," he says, his hands held aloft, dripping golden blood. "We can both be here, can't we? Be reasonable. I'll even let your heir live. There's a way to make this work."

The Gardener does not answer. Instead, the stag lowers its head and rams its antlers into Chaos' stomach, driving him backward, pinning him against the wall. Chaos grunts, writhing, his coat catching on Costis' ferns and taking them down with him.

"Well," Chaos pants. "Now you're just being rude."

Above him, the cracked window groans.

A cloud of cream-colored moths fly past Clove, surrounding Chaos in a flurry, obscuring his view. Overhead, the bird has nearly broken through the window. The turrets groan.

And now, that voice whispers. *Yours*.

Me? Clove thinks.

But she doesn't hold the thought long.

A soft hiss fills the room.

The basilisk that slithers down the wall is unlike any Clove has ever seen—ever *heard* of. Its rose-pink scales glitter among the ravaged greenery as it winds through the laurel and lichen. It weaves its way across the ballroom floor, heading in a straight line toward the god who sent it to slumber.

"Oh," Chaos says, a bit miserably. His laugh is quick and nervous. "You too? Well, this was fun, but let's be reasonable. You're really going to do the bidding of a bunch of mortals?" His voice turns desperate and wheedling. "If I die now, you're not strong enough to remain. Why not help me kill them instead? Think of what we could do, with the others still asleep. Think of what we might rule."

The beasts do not answer.

Instead, the basilisk rears and strikes. But instead of leaping for Chaos, it sinks its fangs into the hairline fractures of the window and bites down.

And behind them—Kellam gasps.

Color floods his cheeks. He jolts upright, and Ellion falls back on his heels, his irises returning.

The storm itself seems to pause. The gods flicker in and out. Behind Kellam, a small, mangy animal with fur the color of cobwebs glares at them and skitters away. Ellion lurches away from them, hand to his heart, looking as pale as death, eyes darting wildly from Clove to the beasts to Chaos and back.

As Chaos looks at Kellam, his smile fades.

The fear in his eyes has never made him look more mortal.

"You have no idea," Chaos says hoarsely. "What you've done."

Though it could just be fear or a fanciful mind, Clove swears she can feel the moment the Weaver's threads snap.

And when they snap—so does Castle Avendell.

The windows shatter all at once with a massive *boom*. Glass shards as big as Clove's fist drop from the ceiling and burst into glitter when they hit the floor. Someone shouts Clove's name, but she can't see them—there's only a waterfall of glass and stone. They grab her by the waist and drag her, along with Melarie, backward. Snow pours into the room, and with it, stones twice the size of a man, all of them falling in a terrible avalanche. The snow keeps coming, pressing in on all sides. It clogs Clove's ears and makes her mouth sting with the cold. It slides down her throat and makes her chest seize. But it doesn't bury her. Even if it did, she knows the princess who holds her hand and the guard who holds her waist would dig her out. They stumble backward, watching in horror and awe as the ceiling caves in, as stone and snow and glass bury Chaos entirely.

As quickly as it begins, it's over.

The castle is eerily silent in the aftermath. Clove squints through the dust and snow to the place where Chaos stood. The only thing left is rubble. The head of the Builder's bear fountain sits atop the debris, its snout cracked down the center.

There is no sign of Chaos. No hint of the other gods.

Only a tomb remains.

As Clove surveys the rest of the room, a cacophony of groans and murmurs and coughs swells. Piles of snow shift and shudder as guests dig themselves out from the ruin. Limbs poke through the snow like saplings in spring and gasp for air.

Oak, Melarie, and Clove reach for each other. They crowd

around Kellam and Ellion. Clove isn't sure who begins to cry first, but once one of them starts, none of them can stop. As the guests wake, they cling to each other as if their lives depend upon it.

In the blackness of Clove's mind, from somewhere between worlds, Vesryn appears. Her fingertips graze the top of the ghost cat's head as it purrs beside her. Clove cries harder.

Outside, the world is silent. The last of the storm clouds part. And the night clears.

51

KELLAM

KELLAM is alive.

He should not be alive.

As the air returns to his lungs, memory rushes in with it—Chaos, the poison, his father, and *Ellion*, finding him from across the Veil. He can feel the others crowded around him, whispering anxiously; and beyond them, stirring and groaning, the guests wake. Relief turns his limbs to water.

They did it. Somehow, some way, they've made it through this night alive.

Panicked energy bubbles around him. And is that . . . a breeze he feels, despite being indoors?

Kellam wants nothing more than to curl into a ball and hide. But his guests are waking. And recently resurrected or not, he's still a prince. He can have a mental breakdown later. Kellam scrapes together the last dregs of his ability to perform and cracks an eye open.

"Do *not*," Kellam groans, "eat the winter lilies."

Four worried faces peer over him. Ellion, Melarie, Clove—and of course, Oak. Kellam forces himself to stare at the ceiling. He's afraid if he meets Oak's eye, he'll break. Clove helps him up, and Melarie squeezes his shoulder. Only Ellion hangs back. The most the necromancer can manage is a tight, worried smile. Dread curdles in Kellam's stomach.

"What happened," Kellam says slowly, his eyes going to the giant hole in the ceiling, "to my castle?"

"Clove summoned the wild forms of multiple gods and they attacked Ch—our friend," Melarie says. "Vesryn helped. And so did you, I believe, by dying, and being resurrected."

Kellam blinks, several times, staring at the eerie pile of debris, and all he manages is a faint, "Well, if that's all."

"We'll explain later," Clove says tightly, eyes darting around. "When we're alone."

Oak supports Kellam's weight. As he clambers to his feet, the ballroom door swings open. A swarm of guards bursts through, red-faced and panicked, swords drawn. From the confusion on the guards' faces, the last thing they remember is being knocked unconscious.

Oak presses a small, cold weight into his hand. Costis' signet ring. It's Kellam's now.

He's not worthy of it. But what does it matter? There is no one else.

"Oak," Kellam says softly. "Call together the courts. I believe the princess and I have a treaty to sign."

They sign the treaty before dawn.

The hours that follow become a blur—the guests waking up, the palace staff stumbling in, and, of course, Kellam privately breaking the news over and over that his father passed peacefully in the night. Kellam braces himself for an explosion of questions about what happened in the ballroom, but every time the subject draws near, a cloudy blankness fills the eyes of whoever he's speaking to. As Kellam and his party approach the cliffs, he tries not to notice the moss blooming up the palace walls.

From a distance, Melarie and her party of Istellians are a blur of red. As Kellam draws near, their voices float toward him.

". . . so strange. The harbor was frozen solid and, suddenly, the water melted and cleared!"

Melarie only gives them a demure, uninterested smile.

When they draw near, though, her eyes soften. It feels wrong for Melarie to be standing opposite them, flanked by her diplomats and military escorts, who survey Kellam with open dislike. They're too harsh against the soft lines of Melarie's hair, the openness of her face. Kellam wants to seize her by the wrist and drag her away from them, back in the protective ring he woke to on the ballroom floor. But Ellion and Clove aren't even here. It's only him and Oak, followed by a sea of courtly Avendell green.

Besides, Kellam is pretty certain Melarie wouldn't take kindly to him making a scene. Still, when he looks at her, he sees a mirror of himself: an heir, trapped, with nowhere to flee.

Right before they reach the Istellians, Kellam hesitates. There's no threat here. He's entirely safe. But he can't make himself move.

A hand finds his shoulder. Oak, always Oak, knowing him better than Kellam knows himself.

"He would be proud," Oak says softly.

Pain spears through Kellam. But the words are what he needs. They propel him forward, and once they're closer, it's easier not to think about the fact that it should be Costis signing the cream paper unfurled between them. Someone begins to read off a bunch of poetic nonsense about the marriage of two countries in unity and a long-awaited peace. Kellam forces himself to breathe.

His father is dead. After all these years, after so many disappointments, Costis died to protect him.

And Kellam can't help but wonder if his father made a mistake.

"And now," Antoine says. "The signatures."

Melarie nods. She moves forward, and her guards start to move with her. The princess casts them a withering glance and steps forward alone. Kellam follows suit. Behind them, the first threads of pale orange wind through the clouds.

Melarie signs first. When she hands Kellam the quill, her fingers shake.

"Wait. One last thing." Kellam tries to ignore the swell of murmurs as he adds the twenty-seventh and final decree to the bottom of the parchment. He may not be king for long, but he will keep his promises while he can—starting with Clove and the Beauforte land.

He lifts the quill to allow for courtiers from each country to read his addition. When they nod their approval, Kellam scrawls his name.

"There," he whispers, raising his eyes to Melarie. His next words are only for her. "It's done."

Just like that—with two names, a sunrise, and a bit of ink, ten bloody years of war between Istellia and Avendell have come to an end.

Behind them, the sky bleeds coral, and dawn finally breaks.

52

VESRYN

VESRYN watches her own funeral from the liminal. It doesn't make her sad.

In truth, she'd never thought she would even have one. Once the Evercrafts disowned her, she'd realized that no one would ever notice if she died, let alone miss her enough to give her a proper burial.

But then she found herself on the doorstep of Castle Avendell, and everything changed.

With the ink still drying on the treaty, the five wrapped her body in fine cloth and brought her here by horse. Now they stand around her, facing an open cliff. Their faces are drawn and cheeks pink from the rapidly warming breeze. At the bottom of this cliff lies a murky mountain lake. At the bottom of that is where her body will dwell until it decays into nothing more than silt and bone, until it will be as if she never existed at all.

But she *does* still exist. Maybe not to anyone else, but to these five, she does.

Maybe that's all that matters.

"Does anyone want to say a few words?" Melarie says, her long hair catching on her lips.

There's a pause. Dread fills Vesryn with the thought that none of them can think of a single kind word to say about her. But then the beast tamer steps forward.

Clove tucks her hair behind her ears as she leans over the body. Her fingers work deftly to tie the stone to Vesryn's exposed wrist. "Thank you for everything," she whispers. "Thank you for helping me save them."

Oak steps forward next. He finishes the work of tying a second stone to her other wrist before speaking. When he does, his voice rasps. "I misjudged you. I assumed you were an enemy when you proved yourself the most loyal friend." He clears his throat. "It is one of my greatest regrets."

Heat floods Vesryn's face, catching her off guard. She didn't think she could feel things beyond death, but apparently she'd been wrong. Maybe she just hadn't let herself.

Though exhaustion defines his every movement, Kellam takes his time to make a careful knot in the rope binding Vesryn's ankle with another stone. When he stands, he gazes out beyond the cliffs and says, "I never should have invited you here. I was a fool."

"What wouldn't each of us do for love?" Melarie presses her hand between his shoulder blades. "If anyone can give you that mercy, I think it's Vesryn."

If Vesryn could cry on this side of the Veil, she would. Her eyes burn as the truth of Melarie's words echoes through her. *What wouldn't she do for love? What hadn't she done for it?*

Vesryn never yearned for romantic love—only the kind that soothed instead of seared. A balm she could come back to, again and again, without fear that it would dry up. She'd done everything for that love.

She'd followed a boy to the Academy of Healing Arts to prove her worth.

She'd bargained with a trickster god to save his life.

She'd even let down her guard when she'd thought she had a shot at Ellion's forgiveness, and it had cost her life.

The four grow silent as the healer steps forward. He sits on his haunches as he ties the final stone to her ankle. When he's finished, he remains crouched beside her body, his hand still lingering on her graying ankle. A new black bead gleams on the chain around his neck. Ellion's fingers shake when he touches it. "I didn't deserve you, but you gave me your friendship anyway. I can't say I'm sorry about it." His lip trembles. "I love you, Ves."

Love you back, Ellion. Vesryn squeezes her eyes shut when she thinks it, praying to whichever god or goddess may be listening to her in the liminal that the message gets to him.

The five surround her body. They lift and they heave. And then she's gone.

Well, that part of her is gone. Her body hits the water with a splash and disappears beneath the wind-whipped water. The others turn to each other and embrace before heading back to their horses, back to whatever destiny awaits them at the castle and beyond.

She knows she should have passed on by now. She should be scared that she's stuck here, that she has no way to escape. But she's not.

Vesryn doesn't know why she's still here, but she's glad she is.

53

MELARIE

THOUGH Kellam made it clear Melarie is welcome in Castle Avendell, she has a feeling if he knew where she was right now, he'd lock her away until her ship arrives.

Ahead of her looms the rubble of Chaos' tomb.

Light filters through the hole in the castle roof, letting in birdsong and the hum of insects thrilled to return to spring's warmth. Goblets, cracked and long dried, glitter across the ballroom floor. Dead moths drape over tables of rotting food and crunch underfoot as Melarie picks her way through the debris.

No one has been permitted to enter the ballroom since Chaos' defeat.

Melarie approaches the rubble. Her gaze lifts to the cracked and crumbling bear head. Something about its vacant, jeweled eyes makes her shiver. She draws her shawl tighter around her shoulders.

"I'm returning to Istellia," Melarie says. "My ship arrives in a few hours. Elodie wrote to me and asked me to come back. Thanks to your antics, I missed my chance to escape. I hope it brings you comfort, knowing I'll be returning to imprisonment, too. For all your talk of looking for a window, you certainly ensured I missed mine." Her lips thin. "Clove and Ellion are leaving as well. It's for the best, I suppose, if we never see each other again."

What is she doing, complaining to the tomb of a dead god? Why is she even *here*? Even if Chaos could hear her, it's not like he'd care. She ought to leave. Her ship will be here soon; Melarie is going to be late.

And yet she lingers.

Melarie stares at the rubble and thinks of Chaos. Of his smiles and private jokes, and last night at the ball, the way he held her flush against him as they spun on the dance floor and the world disappeared. It's ridiculous, really. At that point, he'd already driven Gaspar to kill two people. He was a monster made flesh, preparing to bring an entire castle full of innocents down on their heads. All that war; all that pain. It had been because of him, in the end.

And yet, when she thinks of that evening, of that dance, Melarie is unable to lie.

It was one of the happier moments of her life.

"You weren't supposed to leave me this time," Melarie accuses him softly. "Remember?"

Nothing answers.

It's a relief.

At first, there'd been some deliberation over what to do with the fact that a god was now trapped in Castle Avendell—and in its signature ballroom, no less. It was Ellion who suggested they leave it alone. Cast sealing spells over the pile of rubble, fill the room with earth, and lock the ballroom doors for good measure. They'd all learned the hard way how the smallest crack could let a god escape. They could not risk someone freeing Chaos again.

Today, the ballroom will be sealed. Kellam plans to use the

fanfare of Melarie's, Clove's, and Ellion's departures to conceal why so many masons and charm-workers are being brought into the castle. It's a good idea. For all his pomp, he might just make a decent king.

Melarie understands why it must be done. But first, she needs to say goodbye.

In the light of day, the god's tomb seems more pathetic than imposing.

Melarie casts a furtive glance around and kneels before the pile of fallen rock.

For a breath, she remains there, head bent, hair forming a dark curtain around her, trying to find the words. Memories flash through her; of the evenings she spent hiding from her father, the books Chaos had snuck her acting as the one thing she could cling to in the sea of her despair. Chaos had lied to her, tested her, tormented her—but he had saved her, too.

She doesn't know where that leaves her.

"You murdered people," Melarie whispers finally. "And yet you protected me. You tormented my family, and snuck me books. And though I hate to admit it, the day you killed my father, you set us free. You even killed him in a way that would never cast a shadow of doubt over my sisters' heads." Melarie curls her fingers into fists. Her voice breaks. "I am so angry at you. I had so many questions, but you've only left me with more. I don't know how to reconcile any of this. I don't know where the man who taught me to look for a window and spun me around that ballroom floor ends—and where the wicked deity begins."

Her fingers skim the stone.

"You can tell yourself I was only ever a pawn, but I know better.

You cared for me. You tried to set me free." Her voice catches. "I think you loved me, a little."

Melarie glances around. She's still alone. She leans down and presses her lips to the rubble, her lips scratching stone. "May you find peace, Chaos. And may it be long after I am returned to dust."

Voices sound in the distance. Melarie scrambles upright, her heart thumping, but it's only people passing through the halls, chattering about the day's work. She glances around, cheeks heating. What a foolish, needless risk this was. What would the others think if they saw her here, kneeling over Chaos' tomb, mourning like a village girl watching her lover head off to sea? She turns to leave when something catches her eye.

A single winter lily blooms in the heart of the rubble.

Melarie shivers. Suddenly she is glad for Kellam's plan. It was a mistake to come here. Her ship will be here soon, and if she's wise, Melarie will spend her last moments in Castle Avendell with the ones who helped her save it. Not mooning over a god who never cared if she lived or died.

Melarie casts one last glance back at the tomb.

"Goodbye, Chaos," she whispers.

Melarie hurries from the ballroom, back toward light and life, and does not look back.

54

OAK

OAK will need a bigger bag.

The satchel tucked beneath his old cot is much too small to hold the tome he retrieved from the library, or the vial of venom gifted to him by Clove, or the signet ring he isn't sure he should be harboring at all.

Kellam hasn't spoken to him about what had happened in the ballroom. Oak just entered his old room to find the prince's signet atop his pillow with a note.

You will always have a home here, it read. *If you want it.*

He spent the better part of the day pacing the perimeter of his room, throwing a glance at the ring and the vial and the book every so often. Each of the items asks something of him he isn't sure he can give.

The *History of the Gardener and Her Acolytes* book asks him to honor his true lineage.

The basilisk venom asks him to accept that he may need something stronger and stealthier than a knife to defend himself from now on.

And the ring . . .

He cannot think about the ring.

Oak jerks to a stop. He lets out a frustrated little laugh as he turns to look back at the ring. How did he get here? Only twelve hours prior he was an orphaned guard with a hidden burden that made him want to grab his bag and never look back. Now he is . . .

Who?

He's not the son of a dead king, yet Oak bears his magic.

He's not the new king's lover, yet he desperately wishes he was.

He doesn't belong in this room anymore, but he doesn't belong in the king's chambers, either. There is no room meant for who he has become, no in-between space for him to occupy while he figures it out. Even if there were, he doesn't have the right-sized bag to carry the things he now needs to keep close.

"Oak?"

He turns, and a boy's face appears in the doorway. Oak does his best to maneuver his mouth into a smile. "Mason! Can I help you with something?"

The skin beneath the boy's eyes looks hollow and bruised. *The staff has been working too much,* Oak thinks. *I'll tell Kellam they need a break from all the cleanup.*

His chest constricts. *Or am I the one whose duty that is now?*

"The princess is leaving," Mason says, his voice rasping with exhaustion. Before Oak can reply, he disappears into the hall. "The beast tamer, too."

"Thank you," he murmurs to an empty room.

Oak steals a quick glance at himself in the small mirror above his wardrobe. His eyes, too, look hollow and bruised. His usually perfectly cropped hair looks wild and overgrown, though it's been only hours since his last trim. Stumbling upon the dead and speaking to the gods will do that to you, apparently.

When he reaches the entryway, he finds Kellam and Ellion already present. Two broad men dressed in red stand on either side of wooden doors like cardinals in a winter wood. Melarie hovers between them, wearing a soft sage-green smock that one of the attendants found for her. It surprises Oak at how much gentler she looks without glitter and gems, bare-faced and hair combed straight to her hips.

The princess turns to him, and something about the way she looks at him makes Oak want to scream at her *don't go*, that she's still needed here. That they all still need her. Before he opens his mouth, she rushes to him and wraps him in a lung-crushing hug. "Oh, *promise* you will come visit me, won't you?"

When she pulls away, there are tears in her eyes. She quickly blinks them away and turns back to her escorts. "To the carriage, then." Her eyes drift to Clove. "Are you ready? I believe your carriage is here, too."

Clove nods, but no one moves. The five of them hover in the entry hall, unsure of what to do. The castle falls achingly silent. They have no reason to remain together. It's best this way.

Still, they hesitate.

"What about one last parting drink?" Kellam says. "The carriages can wait."

Oak nods. He's not usually one to indulge, but something—*anything*—to dampen the emotions swirling through him seems necessary at the moment. He looks to Clove, who also nods her assent.

The healer remains quiet. His hands twitch at his sides, and his slender throat bobs as he considers.

Clove speaks first. "Ellion, do you mind grabbing my rucksack from my room for me?" She lifts a brow. "If you're so inclined?"

The healer's eyes grow wide with relief. "Of course. Be right back, garlic girl."

"Don't ever call me that again," Clove says sweetly.

Again, the room falls silent. Melarie's eyes dart between Kellam and Oak, and before anyone can speak, the princess winds her arm through Clove's. "Come," she says brightly. "Let's find Kellam's most expensive bottle. We have a long journey ahead of us." She gives Kellam and Oak a meaningful look. "Join us when you're ready. Or don't. Clove and I can entertain ourselves."

Before Oak can protest, the princess is pulling the beast tamer away, her head tipped toward her as she whispers something that makes Clove snort.

And then it's just the two of them.

"Can I speak to you alone?" Kellam whispers. His eyes skip around the room, searching for something or someone that Oak cannot see.

"We are alone," Oak says slowly.

The prince does not seem well. It's the first time Oak has been alone with him since his resurrection, and the first chance he's gotten to really look at him. Kellam's usually olive skin has grown sallow, and the bags under his eyes are a relentless purple. And there's something about him that seems . . . hollow. Deflated. As if everything on the inside has been scooped out.

"Right," Kellam says, his voice clipped. Then he turns on his heel and marches straight toward the staircase.

Oak watches him for a moment as he climbs the steps and turns. His stomach drops when he realizes where Kellam is headed. He mumbles a quiet curse and follows.

Costis' chambers are exactly as they left them. The chamber

door is still open from when the guards removed the king's corpse. The air in the room is stuffy and stale. The scent of spilled wine and astringent makes Oak's stomach turn.

Kellam spins to face him. Oak startles. The prince looks positively unhinged. "Something's not right," the prince says, his voice shaking. "I . . . I am not right."

Oak's pulse begins to race. "What is it? What's wrong?"

"It's just . . ." Kellam drags his hands down his face. "I don't know how I can be king when I am . . . who I am."

Oak's heart seizes at the sight of the shattered prince before him. Already Kellam has faced the kind of trial most rulers pray they never see, and he has done so with the kind of grace that makes Oak want to profess his love for the prince to every listening ear.

"Who you are," Oak says, an edge of fierceness in his voice, "is exactly what this country needs right now. Whatever you're worried about, we will figure it out—together."

Kellam relaxes. He looks at Oak, some of the tension easing, and extends a hand toward him. Oak stiffens. They have not had time to discuss what Kellam confessed. They have hardly had a moment to breathe.

But as Kellam reaches for him, Oak closes his eyes and leans in.

Kellam's fingers brush Oak's jaw.

It burns. It *really* burns.

Oak jerks. Kellam lurches back with a strangled sound, his face blank with terror.

The sensation in Oak's jaw has flared into something unbearable—a pain like he's never experienced.

"What happened?" Oak gasps.

Kellam stares at him, wordless with horror.

Oak's pulse begins to steady. He forces his breath to slow, to calm, so he can think. He touches his jaw.

And finds a hole there.

Instead of answering Oak, Kellam holds up a mirror.

A black spot of rot has left a hole on Oak's skin. It could almost be a burn mark, except it's as black as coal and . . . mushy? Oak angles his head toward the light. A whisper-thin tree root pokes out from the hole.

He's . . . *rotting*.

Oak's eyes lift to Kellam; the prince knows it, too. They stare at each other for a long moment. In the silence, Chaos' words whirl between them.

Ruin, he'd warned.

Kellam staggers around the room, poking and palming every object in his path—chaises and carafes, vases and lanterns. Nothing changes. Nothing else shows signs of rot.

The prince's hand slips into his pocket to retrieve something. He opens his palm. A small acorn sits in the center.

Already it has begun to blacken.

THREE WEEKS LATER

55

KELLAM

KELLAM stands on the turret of Castle Avendell and watches as his heart leaves through the gates.

Early-morning light cuts through the recently repaired windowpanes of his father's study. *His* study now, he supposes. It's been three weeks since King Costis died; three weeks since the treaty was signed and Kellam ascended the throne. Three weeks since his touch turned Oak to rot and presented Kellam with an impossible choice.

"I wish to stay," Oak had said. "I don't want to abandon you. I love you."

"I know," said Kellam. "It will fade."

From the balcony, Oak cuts a small, lonely figure on the castle road.

The memory replays on a terrible, painful loop. The stricken pain in Oak's eyes, a mirror of the ache that threatened to split Kellam in two. It was a cruel thing to do—to lie. To pretend that that confession in the library had been an act of desperation.

But Kellam knows Oak too well. He knows that Oak would never leave unless he believed Kellam wanted him sent away.

And Kellam loves Oak Ducasse too much to let him remain.

So he stands there, a king, his father's antlered crown too heavy on his brow, and watches as the only boy he's ever loved walks alone down the castle road. He remains long after Oak is gone. Until the familiar line of his back has faded into the crowd. Kellam thinks he might stand there forever. It would be better, he thinks, than going back inside and walking the halls Oak once occupied.

"You did the right thing."

Ellion stands in the doors leading out to the balcony. The necromancer looks well; the best Kellam has seen him yet. But the misery that lines his face is a mirror of Kellam's own.

Kellam knows how that feels. On paper, Ellion has been restored; granted a title and the king's favor. None of it matters. Not with Vesryn's bead gleaming on his neck.

Funny, to get everything you ever wanted, and realize it wasn't what you needed.

"If it was the right thing," Kellam rasps, "why do I feel like I'm dying?"

Ellion tilts his head to the side. "Gone for now doesn't mean gone forever. And once we fix this—and we *will* fix this—what are a few years, Kellam? Truly?"

Kellam forces a smile. It's a kind sentiment, but the words are hollow.

If Ellion couldn't save Vesryn, what hope is there for Kellam?

"Are you sure you don't want me to stay?" asks Ellion.

"Do you wish to stay?"

"No." Ellion's head tilts. "But I will, if you need me to."

Kellam swallows. He refuses to break. He's not going to cry in front of *Ellion*, of all people. He wishes, foolishly and desperately, that Melarie were here. But last he heard, she was settled back in Istellia. They're all scattered now. Clove returned to her mountains,

Ellion to the Academy, bearing Kellam's seal and a royal decree allowing him to investigate his sickness in secret, and Oak . . .

Oak did not tell Kellam where he's headed. It's for the best.

Kellam knows himself; he knows Oak better. They are two planets in orbit, perpetually drawn together. The mark Kellam's touch left on Oak hasn't grown, but it hasn't healed, either. And so Kellam found himself facing his first terrible lesson as king.

Country over heart, his father had always said. *Duty before desire.*

Kellam had always thought this to be callous advice; the judgment of a cold, sick king past his prime. He understands now. Costis had not been trying to tell his son he could not love.

He had been trying to warn him of what it would cost.

"Kellam," Ellion says gently. "We'll figure it out."

Pain wracks Kellam. He turns back to the balcony, eyes searching the distance, as though any moment Oak might reappear. In the end, all he can manage is, "Perhaps. Maybe the next god who wakes will be a little kinder."

It's meant to be a jest. But even as he says it, panic lances through him. There have been whispers sweeping through the kingdom. Signs they cannot ignore. Visions of gods walking the streets; of statues moving in the night and animals with too-human eyes. Fields have begun to turn to blight; birds drop from the sky, stricken by strange plague. Already, the devout have claimed victory. Already, the skeptics have pointed an accusing finger. No one seems entirely able to agree on what, exactly, is happening to their world.

But they can agree on *one* thing.

Whatever is happening in their country—blessing or curse—began the day Kellam Vernevau became king.

Kellam can only hope Elodie Atilelet is having a better time than he is.

"Well," Ellion says. "Remember what I said. I'm only a fortnight's ride away. I'll be back at the summer solstice. But if I find anything..."

Kellam nods.

They both know Ellion isn't going to find anything.

"For what it's worth," Ellion says quietly, "I think you'll be good at the job. You have a gentle heart, Kellam. And chosen by the Gardener or not—you were born for this."

He leaves then. It's a gift. Kellam doesn't want Ellion to see the tears that slide down his cheeks. He watches the road a moment longer, and finally, Kellam turns and heads back into Costis' chambers.

He can't sleep here. It's too eerie. But he visits every day. Maybe it's Ellion rubbing off on him, but Kellam likes to believe that sometimes, in the quiet moments, he can feel Costis nearby.

"I miss you," Kellam tells the empty air. He stands in the very room his father died in three weeks ago. "I wish you had told me more. I wish you'd let me help. I wish there had been more time for all of it."

He looks around the room. Eventually, he'll have to have it redone. He can't keep sleeping in his old quarters forever.

But not now.

Not yet.

Kellam turns and walks out of Costis' chambers. He feels the urge to glance behind him, but suppresses it. He can only look forward now.

Had he looked back, he would have seen it.

Unfurling from the cracks of his father's favorite chair, white petals emitting an impossible fragrance, blooms a single winter lily.

ACKNOWLEDGMENTS

We always knew we wanted to write together. It wasn't until the barest thread of an idea presented itself during a delirious 5:00 a.m. text conversation that we knew we *had* to. Right now.

It was the kind of idea that started as a gripe: Why can't magic exist inside a murder mystery? Why can't gods and beasts coincide with red herrings? From there, the question became: Why can't we be the ones to write it?

Once we decided to give it a shot, we couldn't stop thinking about it.

That text turned into a phone call. A phone call turned into emails, hours of voice memos, Google docs, spreadsheets, color-coded infographics, and weeks of obsessive brainstorming, plotting, and laughter. Even when we were living off McDonald's hash browns and a prayer trying to turn an idea into a story, it was still (mostly) fun. This book is the result!

There are so many people to thank, but we have to start with the obvious: our wonderful editor Kristin Rens, who bought and believed in this book and gave us the funniest edit note of our careers after we turned in a murder mystery with no actual murder mystery plot by opening her edit letter with, "I can tell you guys had a *lot* of fun." We sure did! But bonus: now it also has a plot. Thank you for your guidance, wisdom, and patience through the many messy rounds of edits.

We are so grateful to the team at Storytide—editorial assistant Christian Vega, Michael D'Angelo in marketing, Taylan Salvati in publicity, Patty Rosati and team in school and library marketing, Annabelle Sinoff in production, and everyone in sales—who helped shepherd *King* through various stages. Corinna Lupp designed the cover of our dreams, and Matt Griffin brought it to life in a way we didn't know was possible. Special thanks to Jessica Berg in copyediting for noticing we had no sense of time or what dawn was.

Thank you to Victoria Marini, who loved this story from the beginning and has fought for it every step of the way, and Heather Baror Shapiro for helping these characters find new readers overseas. Thank you also to Jim McCarthy for being an early champion of *King* and for helping it find the very best home! And thank you to Stuti Telidevara and Pete Knapp for jumping in with enthusiasm to advocate for this book.

We owe a giant "thank you, what would we have done without you" debt of gratitude to our early readers—Cristina, Abby Foster-Mills, Keri Grieve, Austin Light, Kaylie Smith, and Iz—for responding to our cry by helping us wade through those early drafts. So much of the good stuff in here is because of you! (Becca would like to thank Austin, specifically, for sending a voice memo that exclaimed, "I loved it. But also, um, what the fuck is wrong with Kellam?" Stay tuned!)

Erin A. Craig, Ayana Gray, Margaret Rogerson, Sydney J. Shields, Kaylie Smith, Laura Steven, and Amélie Wen Zhao provided such kind blurbs for this book and we are very grateful. Knowing some of your favorite authors liked the thing you wrote is a weird and wonderful part of this job! Thank you also to Meriam Metoui, Kristin Lord, Aimée Carter, Aly Eatherly, and Brooke Light for your kindness, perspective, and friendship. This industry is wild; you make it worth it.

Our local indie bookstore, Sidetrack Bookshop, has been the most wonderful champion for this book and all the rest. Thank you to Jen, Jenny, Megan, Alyssa, and the whole Sidetrack team for hand-selling our books and hosting all our chaotic launch parties. If you're ever in Michigan, check them out!

Thank you to the readers, teachers, librarians, booksellers, and book bloggers who have been early champions of this story and all our books prior. There's a special kind of magic that happens when someone gets a book so perfectly they feel compelled to shove it into the hands of every reader and student they encounter. We hope we have given you a lot of things to shout about with this one!

A fun thing about being a writer is that after a few books, your families get numb to that phase where you lie on the floor, cry, and insist it's all hopeless, but they still have to be supportive anyway. We're both lucky to have great people around us. Thank you, Matt, Violet, Sam, David, Hannah, Mom, Dad, Grandpa, and the Lorias for believing in (and on the worst days, at least tolerating) this very weird job we do. Thank you also to Kristin Remenar, Natalie Fisher, Judi Noland, Melissa O'Keefe, Mara Bouvier-Schatz, Meagan Cotter, and Katie, Jackie, and Sarah for all your friendship and love.

Special thanks to Diane and Dusty Wilson, who are featured in Becca's dedication in this book. Long before Becca was published, they read those first, early, terrible books, and her aunt Diane has always been her biggest supporter. Thank you, Aunt Diane, for loving and remembering characters and arcs Becca's now a bit mortified by; and thank you, Uncle Dusty, for saying about her debut, "I read it and was like, wow, she's actually getting pretty good at this now." She'd like to think so, too. Your votes of faith in an unconfident teenage writer gave her the audacity to keep going. (I love you guys. I hope this was your favorite yet.)

Becca has a tradition of thanking a bunch of nonsense factors in her acknowledgments that sustained her during the hard parts of writing, and she's certainly not stopping now, so in no particular order, thank you to:

Salted caramel iced lattes, gluten-free sprinkle donuts, John Green's beef with tuberculosis, native wildflower gardens, *Fields of Mistria*, and rain. Yes, rain. I love rain. Special thanks specifically to the olive vendor at that farmer's market in Nice, France, who grew increasingly concerned as Becca showed up every day to buy more olives, and who, after about six days in a row of this, politely inquired, "You're not eating these by yourself, right?" The look of horror on your face when Becca said she was, in fact, eating like a pound of olives every day was very funny. Those olives were *so* good.

I guess Andrea is doing this now too, so here we go: Thank you to Tropical Smoothie Cafe, Spindrift sparkling water (but only Island Punch and Grapefruit, the rest of you are mid), Glossier perfume, animal crackers, and birds.

Finally, writing a book with someone means you'll either be bonded forever or never speak again. We're very lucky we landed on the former.

Becca, I have never laughed so hard in my life than when you crawled out of your gremlin basement room in Paris, or when you wrote a special scene for me in our book and we belly laughed on the phone for ten straight minutes while you were in a CVS. Every time something has gone awry with this book, I've always thought, "Thank god I'm doing this with Becca." This has been one of the most joyful experiences of my career, and I'm so grateful.

Andrea, if I had a nickel for every time I accidentally led us on a hike down a French mountain, I'd have two nickels, which isn't a lot, but it's weird that it happened twice. This book was pure joy, even when it threatened to break my brain. I can't imagine doing this with anyone else. Thank you for creating this wild, weird story with me, which mostly turned into me seeing how many jokes I could fit in here to make you laugh. Les poissons, les poissons . . .

(Also, for anyone reading this who is considering visiting Èze, do *not* listen to the people on Reddit who will tell you to hike *up* the mountain. They are lying to you and they want you to suffer. Take the bus and hike down. And bring some water.)

See you in Istellia!